BAHAMAS
BLUE

Novels by D. C. Poyer

Hatteras Blue
Stepfather Bank
The Shiloh Project

By David Poyer

The Gulf
The Med
The Dead of Winter
The Return of Philo T. McGiffin
White Continent

BAHAMAS
BLUE

························

D. C. POYER

A Tiller Galloway Thriller

ST. MARTIN'S PRESS
NEW YORK

ACKNOWLEDGMENTS

Ex nihilo nihil fit. For this book I owe much to James Allen, Judy Beck, Jim Ciotti, John Cook, Joseph Cosentino, Jack and Joan Ford, Frank and Amy Green, Dave and Melanie Hare, Lenore Hart, Alan Poyer, Carlos Sousa, Danny Sweat, Mark Ullmann, George Witte, J. Michael Zias, and many others who gave generously of their time to contribute or criticize.

Thanks also to Carlton Robinson, Nassau, for permission to quote from "Kiki," contained in his book *Cocaine Use: The Accident of My Life.*

All errors and deficiencies, I claim unreservedly for my own.

BAHAMAS BLUE: A TILLER GALLOWAY THRILLER. Copyright © 1991 by D. C. Poyer. All rights reserved. Printed in the United States of America. No part of this book may be used or reproduced in any manner whatsoever without written permission except in the case of brief quotations embodied in critical articles or reviews. For information, address St. Martin's Press, 175 Fifth Avenue, New York, N.Y. 10010.

Library of Congress Cataloging-in-Publication data

Poyer, David
    Bahamas blue / D.C. Poyer.
      p.   cm.
    ISBN 0-312-04858-0
    I. Title.
PS3566.O978B34   1991
813'.54-dc20   90-27075
                                            CIP

First Edition: July 1991

10 9 8 7 6 5 4 3 2 1

In times of war
Every body and thing is dispensible . . .
You have hurt me, enemy
From under your feet I will destroy you
Though we are among you
You are dead.
We have come back.

—From "Kiki"
by Carlton Robinson,
Nassau, Bahamas

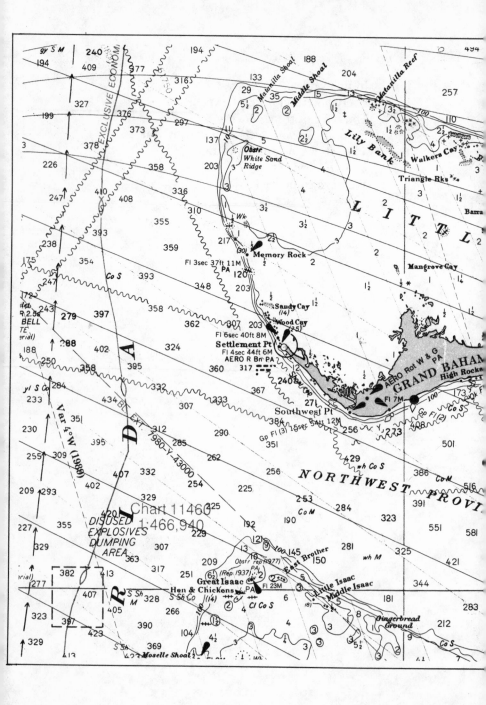

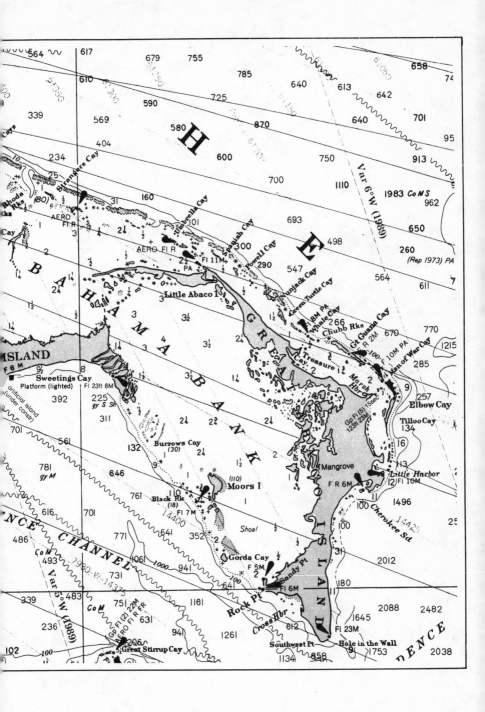

BAHAMAS
BLUE

1

The swell came in from seaward on a hot, calm day in early summer. Born in distant storm, it passed silent and massive beneath the surface's lazy glitter. It heaved up the butterfly sails of windsurfers. It lifted laughing children, considered for a moment, and set them down again. It crested as the bottom shoaled, and broke at last with a hissing ripple at the foot of the white and black spiral-striped tower of Hatteras Light.

Beyond a quivering ribbon of foam, the barrier shore rose from tide-washed flats, dotted with timbers from long-buried wrecks. Beyond them were rolling dunes stubbled with sea oats, cordgrass, and wax myrtle. A low forest of live oak and red bay crouched in their shelter. Through it wound a narrow road lined with motels and seasonal businesses.

Beyond it were higher dunes and more trees. Then the land dropped, first to marsh, then to water again. To the brackish, shallow darkness, like hammered lead, of Pamlico Sound.

The boat was headed east. Sunlight flashed occasionally off its fresh white and buff paint. A wisp of smoke drifted up behind it. The open cabin windows framed a woman's face, bent not on the shoreline but over a book. Above her two men stood on the flying bridge. The white man, deep-chested and stocky, wore a fishing cap, no shirt, stained khaki trousers, and boat shoes. The black man, who was frowning, held a spear in his hands.

Suddenly, it flashed silver and yellow across eight feet of space, and thudded quivering two feet above the paint splash it was aimed at.

"No points," said Tiller Galloway, glancing back from the wheel at his partner. "The longer you practice with that thing, Shad, the worse you get."

Shad Aydlett's face gleamed as he squinted toward shore, then

back along their wake. From the green depths, smoke-stuffed bubbles broke the surface and died. Then he bent. Huge arms swelled
under a cutoff T-shirt as the steel spikes tore out of chewed-up
plywood.

He said, "Shee-it."

"You scar up that handrail, Bernie'll scale you alive."

"You do better, Galloway?"

"Those are for underwater, anyway. Practicing up here ain't going to help you with that sheepshead you missed last week."

They fell back into a well-worn silence. The shore grew nearer,
shimmering, a green barrier between them and the sea. A blue
heron stood knee-deep on a mud bar directly ahead. Galloway
stared at it, pulling sweat off his forehead with a bronze-haired
arm, thinking about tide and draft.

At last, leaning into it, he spun the wheel hard right. Forty-two
feet of 1954 Chris-Craft pivoted beneath him. A staggered line of
sticks slid by. The heron pulled itself into the air and flew off,
rising and dropping with each beat of its wings. Beneath it, a
channel opened in the marsh ahead, a silver road into the heart
of the land. The sun burned down from zenith, heating the varnished oak of the wheel under his palms as he spun it left and
then right again.

Tiller Galloway thought, Binkey did a good job on those engines. They'd taken *Miss Anna* out yesterday for the first time.
They'd run the rebuilt Chrysler 318s for twenty hours straight,
idling all night southeast of Diamond Shoals, then finished that
morning with a full-power run between Cape Point and Ocracoke
Inlet.

Behind him, he heard steel bite wood again. Then a woman's
voice. "That paint smell's giving me a headache. What are you
doing? Let me try."

He glanced back to see her, tanned dark in a bikini bottom and
Blitz Brothers T-shirt. Her black hair was hidden by Aydlett's Red
Drum cap, pulled down, and her eyes were invisible behind sun-
glasses. Her nose and cheeks were shiny with sun block.

Bernice Hirsch tucked the novel into a binocular box and took
the spear. Aydlett showed her how to cock the rubber thong
against her thumb. Galloway squinted into the glare, toward
where a plank dock grew out of the live oak and scrub.

Rubber twanged and he heard a gasp. He stiffened, glancing down. The steel prongs quivered in varnished pine a foot from his ribs.

"That's enough. Practice that ashore, you two."

Aydlett said slowly, "This ain't purely your boat, Tiller. Remember?"

"Every minute, Shad. Bernie, get the bow line, will you?"

Her bare feet slapped. She disappeared for a moment, then came into view below, kicking over fenders. The engines changed from a hum to a burble. The dock and shed drifted closer. Tiller saw the old Texaco pump, the motionless dappled shadow of the overhanging dogwoods, the ghostlike lope and vanish of a yellow cat. He glanced aft. Aydlett stood motionless and somber, his arms crossed, watching the strip of water narrow. The smells of dead fish and marsh and gasoline, of land, came across it to them.

He'd given himself maneuvering room in case the reverse balked, but it shifted smoothly. Peat clumps and scum whirled forward, driven by the props. Bernice's hair streamed out behind her as she jumped for the pier and took two turns around a cleat.

He closed the throttle and pulled out the choke, and suddenly Buxton Landing was filled with silence and heat and the darting of dragonflies. Blue smoke walked slowly off into the trees. His fingers rubbed a surgical scar on his lower back as he watched bare brown legs flash and disappear up the path. When she was out of sight, he sighed, bent, and flipped open a cooler.

"Got another of those?" asked Aydlett, squinting up from the deck. Without comment, Galloway dropped him a can, then popped his. It was so cold it hurt his throat.

He busied himself below for a few minutes, shutting sea cocks and switching off circuits. He lifted a trap and glanced into the bilge.

Galloway paused for a moment on the dock. The half-eaten remains of a gull lay scattered across the worn silvery planks. He started to kick them into the water, then thought better of it. The cat would be back.

Two empty cans clanked into a waist-high pile in the weeds. Together the two men went up the path, toward the whine of tires on Route 12.

• • •

Blitz Brothers' Diving and Water Sports was a weathered frame house fronting on the main road. The path up from the dock ended at the back porch. As Galloway scraped sand from his shoes and unlocked the chain-link door he looked through it at the air bank, the water bath, the stacks of scuba tanks ready for rental.

He and Shad had beefed up the foundation with concrete blocks to take the weight of the hulking Ingersoll-Rand compressor. It was fifteen years old; they'd bought it surplus from a power plant on the mainland. It was running as he let himself in, vibrating the building with a deep hum and the clack of valves as it charged the steel cylinders of the high-pressure bank.

Annabel Rodgers looked up from cleaning the fish tank as he went past the gear room and office. She was a tall, bony, anxious-looking blonde with long feet. He glanced around. Two customers were trying on fins. Otherwise, the showroom was empty. "Hi, Tiller. How'd the test cruise go?" she said.

"Okay, Sticky. Engines ran good and the hull repair's solid. How's business?"

"So-so. Sold some mask-fin-snorkel sets this morning. Some people stopped to ask how to get to Portsmouth Island. I sold them a guidebook."

"Didn't Bernie just come in here? Where'd she go?"

"She went over to Gee Gee's."

The gate grated again as Aydlett came in. He looked at the girl, then at Tiller. "Got it covered?"

"I guess. Where you headed?"

"Latricia wants to go to Nags Head. Do some shoppin'."

"Say hey for me. See you tomorrow. Five sharp, help me fill tanks, okay?"

"Right." Shad nodded to the couple, who were staring at him over their fins, and sauntered past. A moment later, gravel clattered and Tiller saw his partner's pickup pull away.

"Do you need me this afternoon, Mr. Galloway? I thought I'd maybe go to the beach, things are so slow—"

"Sure, go ahead. See you tomorrow."

He hitched himself up behind the counter, staring out the window past the displays of regulators and wet suits. Cars and pickups poured slowly by, a tide-run of glittering glass and chrome. Twelve was the backbone of the Banks, two lanes from Nags Head to Ocracoke Island. In the summer, it was solid with tourists, mainly Northerners—Canada, Ohio, Pennsylvania. The Outer Banks were a major dive destination, too, with scores of offshore wrecks. He'd figured it would be a good place for a shop. Halfway through his first season, he wasn't so sure.

Anyway, they had a boat now. And they'd needed one. *Victory* lay on the bottom thirty miles off Hatteras Light, her guts torn out by hard ramming and several hundred machine-gun slugs. His fingers tightened as he remembered that his cousin was still out there with her. Jack had died on that job last year, diving on that sunken U-boat.

He pulled his mind away from that. He'd had his eye on the Chris-Craft since it had gone windshield-deep at Harry's Dock. The old 42 hadn't been down too long and the hull was still sound, except for a hole where the crane operator had skewered it on a piling pulling it out when Harry's had become Blackbeard's Harbour Condominium Marina. The owner wanted four thousand. They'd come up with two, but he'd agreed to take the rest at a hundred a month.

A metallic blue Le Sabre swung in from the road and parked a few yards up the berm. There were two men in it. He watched them for a while, but neither got out.

His momentary content began to bleed away as he considered how much money he owed.

When the shop opened, Dacor and SeaQuest had covered them for $25,000 (with Shad's name on the paper; a prison record didn't look good on credit applications). Even for a charter business, you had to have a storefront for the walk-in trade. Shad and Bernice had put together money for the building and dock, for *Miss Anna*'s overhaul, and for liability insurance, electricity, and the thousand other expenses of a small business. Shad had put in everything his father had left him after Captain Cliff Aydlett had died in the fire. Bernice had swallowed her pride and borrowed from her family in Queens.

Annabel came out of the back. She'd changed into a two-piece and thongs. "That toilet's backing up again, Tiller."

"I'll look at it. Have a good time at the beach, Sticky."

His eyes lifted from the Oceanic catalogue to follow her to the door. Then dropped again. She was attractive. But Bernie was about all he figured he could handle in the way of women.

The door jangled behind her and he stared absently out again. The Dacor dating order was due at the end of July. Based on retail sales, he wouldn't be able to meet it.

He'd advertised in *Skin Diver* and the *Insiders' Guide*, though, and the first charter booking, a dive club from D.C., was arriving tomorrow. All he and Shad had to do was charge tanks in the morning, herd twelve people around for seven hours, and they'd be—twelve times seventy, plus rentals, minus gas, drinks, and ice—between four and five hundred dollars to the good.

Chartering in the summer, commercial work in fall and winter, the odd job, light salvage or demolition—they could do most anything now that they had a boat again. It would be close, but they might make it. The next couple of months would tell.

He was thinking this when the door opened. He half-expected Rodgers again. But it wasn't.

The man was sunburned dark, with a broad coarse-skinned face and sloping shoulders. He had on jeans and new running shoes and a windbreaker. He looked around the store. At the chart of Hatteras Island on the wall, the display of Wenoka and JBL knives and spears, the skinsuits and dive flags colorful as tropical fish.

Their eyes met. Tiller said, "Help you?"

In return, he got a stare. Okay, great, some people preferred to look by themselves. He pulled the calculator toward him and began figuring how much fuel they'd use tomorrow.

The short man came out from behind the rack of wet-suit tops. He glanced out the door and raised a hand to someone outside.

Then he shot the dead bolt.

As he came down the aisle, Galloway, suddenly alert, studied him more closely. The swarthiness wasn't tan. The right pocket of the jeans was worn through, as if from a knot of keys. The squinted eyes looked straight through him. And he wore a windbreaker, despite the heat outside.

Behind the counter, Galloway's hand dropped, to rest on the worn butt of a sawed-off double-barrel.

"Ly-el Galloway?"

"Uh-huh. Who are you?"

"Hablas español?"

"Not a word," said Galloway. The windbreaker had come open a little and now he saw the automatic tucked into the jeans. His hand tightened on the shotgun. "Just English spoken here. What can I do for you?"

"You know Señor Nuñez, no?"

After a time, Galloway said, "I know Nuñez."

"He send me to find you. He wants you to work for him again."

Galloway blinked past him out the window. The other man had gotten out of the Le Sabre. He was taking a leak by the road, only partially screened from passing traffic by the hood.

"*Me oyes?*" said the man in the windbreaker. "You hear me?"

Galloway didn't answer. He was remembering the last time he'd done a job for the man they called the Baptist.

• • •

To San Rosario in the fall, the ganja came down from the mountains in two-hundred-pound bales. Even covered with ripe bananas in the backs of the trucks, it sweetened the dusty air with the autumnal aroma of marijuana.

He'd waited under four dead coconut palms that afternoon six years before. Their stiff, dry fronds had clashed to an ominous wind, and twice in the last hour the surface of the Golfo Triste had rippled with heavy drops like falling bullets. He'd stood by the forward line, watching the men who grunted in the blowing dust, slinging the bales into the deep, flared hull.

He'd looked at the sweating mulattoes and noted the sway of the palms. He'd examined the anvil-shaped thunderheads, gray as old lead. Last, he'd glanced at the stocky man in white linen who had stood a few yards down the pier, focusing a vintage Leica on the jut of land that screened the bay from the Caribbean.

Galloway knew he had only himself to blame. For deciding to go for the offer the slim, smiling man had made. The big score. Everything—or nothing. If he made it, this would be the last trip north.

Half a million: He'd figured that would be enough.

But it hadn't worked out that way. They'd gotten underway in the hurricane season, and the passage had been as terrifying a time as he'd ever had at sea. The Coast Guard knew his route and had assigned a cutter to bring him in. A rival combine had boats out, too, and no hesitation about piracy.

Aside from that, someone on board had been trying to kill him. It had to do with the Baptist's way of cutting costs. Juan Alberto Mendieta Nuñez-Sebastiano let the inexorable laws of economics work for him. He distributed the profits from a voyage by shares. Ostensibly, that made the crew partners. What it really did was make each the enemy of all the others, since the fewer left, the more each share was worth. And, of course, the Baptist's cut benefited most of all.

The result was a hell ship, an anarchic nightmare where each man guarded his back against criminals crazed with greed and uninhibited by conscience.

Galloway remembered Meshach Aydlett, Shad's older brother. He had played with Meshach as a boy, and worked with him on his father's boat growing up. But the fear and the greed had finally eaten through their friendship. Galloway had killed him in self-defense. That's what he'd told Captain Cliff years later, standing in front of the cocked barrels of the same shotgun his fingers touched now. And it was the truth.

Without Tiller Galloway leading the way, though, his boyhood friend wouldn't have been smuggling drugs at all.

"You hear me?" said the Colombian again. Past him, Tiller watched the other zip up his trousers and lean against the hood, turning his head to keep the shop in sight.

He remembered the lightning jolt of cocaine, the godlike breathless omnipotence he'd tried to duplicate with whiskey. But the liquor never scratched that coke itch. It had been years, but something in his brain had never forgotten how it felt. There was plenty of coke around Nuñez; plenty of money, too. Seventeen thousand he owed the hospital for his spine surgery last year. Twenty-five to Dacor and SeaQuest, hundred a month on *Miss Anna*, two thousand on the lease, and the septic field out back needed replacing. . . .

Then he remembered the downside. How, instead of half a million dollars, he'd ended up in prison. How the gray stone walls had cut five years out of his life.

"I never talked," Galloway said. His voice was hoarse. "Does he know that? Sure he does. Or I wouldn't have got out of Central alive. I did the time. I'm clean now. Why don't you tell him, forget about Tiller Galloway."

The man in the windbreaker squinted. At last, he said, "*Cómo?*"

"I said, I've got an honest business going. You go back. Tell him I said thanks, but no."

The squint darkened. "That isn't done. You know Señor Nuñez.

"*Mierda! Escuche!* Listen now. You will get orders from an American. His name is Señor Lax. Here is his card. He is here for only two days. So you call him now."

"I won't talk to him," said Galloway.

"*Cómo no?*"

"I won't talk to anybody if it has anything to do with Nuñez. The DEA, the cops, anybody. You understand? Just count me out."

The other man said nothing for a while. His hand wandered up slowly, as if to scratch his stomach.

Tiller let the butt of the double-barrel show above the counter.

The hand paused. He noticed several broken nails on it. Then it dropped again, away from the automatic, and scratched at the crotch.

"You say no?"

"That's what I said."

The other man unlocked his eyes. They moved over the gleaming spear gun tips, the racks of diving and fish identification books, the lenses and strobes and camera bodies in the Nikonos display. They lingered on the aquarium, the slow stir of gold and scarlet, cerise and iridescent sapphire.

"Tell me again," he said. "Why you do not want to work for Don Juan."

"Because I've got too much to lose."

The Colombian said nothing. He looked around once more and shrugged. Smiling apologetically, he closed the door so softly behind him that the bell made no sound at all.

2

"This all he give you?" grunted Aydlett, turning the card this way and that under the dome light. HAROLD C. LAX, JUNIOR, it read. ATTORNEY AT LAW. A Norfolk number was penciled on the back.

"That's all."

"Told you to call him?"

Galloway nodded. His partner sucked a tooth and looked out into the predawn darkness.

"And you don't want to?"

"Take my word for it, Shad, we're better off throwing this line back. These people will make it sound good. They'll dangle money in front of us. But at the end, there'll be just what your brother got. Or what I got the last time I danced with them. Nothing, if we're lucky. A bullet, if we aren't."

"This Nuñez—who's he?"

"He's a Colombian. A major trafficker. They call him the Baptist."

"Why?"

"Because anybody who gets involved with him, sooner or later they end up underwater."

Aydlett grunted. The truck leaned on its springs as he swung himself down. "If you say so. Making money—that sounds good. But like you said, about Mezey . . . well, we'll play it the way you call it. Thanks for tellin' me, though."

"We're partners, Shad. I owe you to level."

Aydlett nodded. He headed for the shop as Tiller got out, then suddenly went still.

"What is it?"

Shad waved him into silence. He pointed at the knob. Rotated his hand left and then right.

Shit, Galloway thought. He flattened himself paint-close against the wall opposite the black man. They stared at each other in the starlight.

Aydlett, in a whisper: "Did you lock it?"

"Hell yeah, I locked it."

Shad ran back to the truck on the balls of his feet. He ran lightly for a big man, and Tiller remembered watching him on the field for Hatteras High. When he came back, he hefted an ax handle. Galloway got a two-foot length of steel cable wrapped with electrical tape.

When they opened the door, he grabbed the bell. Instead of a jangle, it made a muffled clank. The interior was dark except for the bulb in the fish tank. Chrome and stainless sparkled faintly around it.

There was nothing alive in the front room except the guppies and neons. The still air breathed emptiness. They went quickly through to the back, clubs at the ready.

There was no one else in the store. Galloway came back flicking on lights, looking behind the doors: nothing.

"You sure you locked it?"

"Damn it, I said I did."

"Hello!"

It was Hirsch, looking unnaturally cheerful for 5:00 A.M., in a blue jogging suit and red and white boat shoes. She held up a thermos. "I hope it's warmer out at sea," she said, kissing Galloway on the lips and Aydlett on the cheek. "Hi, Shad. How's Latricia? Want some coffee? What's the matter? You boys look tense."

"It's nothing." He suddenly became conscious of the makeshift club and set it on the counter. "Well, let's get to work."

Aydlett's arms bulged as he plunged tank after tank into the water bath. Air hissed through lines from the high-pressure banks. The water smelled dank and moldy. Galloway sneezed as he kicked open the back door, his arms filled with wet-suit tops.

Miss Anna glowed in the center of the canal like a ghost ship on the black breast of the Styx. The stars glittered like shattered zircons in the burning arch of Hatteras sky. She bowed to him gracefully as he stepped aboard.

Suddenly, a swell of pride lifted his heart. Every dollar he'd earned in drugs had vanished like smoke, leaving a taste like a sales sample of death. He had nothing now. He'd worked like a dog getting the boat in shape. Borrowed himself deeper than anyone he'd ever known. Yet on the edge of bankruptcy, he felt free. It was like a rule of nature: That only what you worked for had value, that what you gained by evil means caused only evil in its turn.

You're getting to be quite a philosopher, he thought. But it can't bring your cousin back, or your father. Or Mezey. Or old Cliff. All those he'd hurt through his greed and foolishness.

Grinding his teeth, he threw his burden violently into an open locker.

• • •

They were supposed to meet the club at the Park Service dock at Oregon Inlet. The sky was paling over the low blackness of Buxton as they purred out of the landing, prowling from marker to marker. When Galloway's flashlight caught the last one, he waved it over his head. Aydlett's shadow lifted an arm in reply. A moment later, the engines rose to a drone. The deck slanted beneath their feet. The chuckle of spray built to a roar as *Miss Anna* lurched onto a plane.

Galloway leaned against the cabin windshield, rubbing his chin. He'd forgotten to shave. Well, they had time. It was a little over an hour, hour and a half to the inlet. That would make it—he examined the luminescent numerals of his dive watch—seven-thirty.

He glanced up again at the bridge. No problem leaving it to Shad. The Aydletts had been watermen on Hatteras for generations. Galloway had cut bait and scrubbed decks with him and his brothers Meshach and Abednego on the *Princess* when he was a boy. They'd grown up separate yet strangely close, as black and white had back then. And now they were partners.

He looked out once more. The lights of the new soundfront developments glittered to starboard. To the left, ahead, was only the empty void of the open sound. Stars floated on it, reflected by the calm black water.

Suddenly, from behind him, a cold white arrow shot out into the night. He'd grown up with it. But for some reason, it took him by surprise this time. The twenty-four-mile beam of Hatteras

Light. It swept soundlessly overhead, like the blade of an immense sword.

He turned from it, and went below.

• • •

He was scraping off shaving cream when the door of the little head clicked open. "Busy," he grunted.

Warm hands came around his chest and teased his nipples. "How busy?"

"Not that busy."

"I missed you last night."

"I asked you to stay."

"You know I can't do that too often." He felt her breath, the prickle of her hair move down his back.

"Uh-huh. Mister Mutton wouldn't approve."

"Mr. *Moulton*. And he's right. Parole officers shouldn't be seen to be"—she squeezed him—"*too* close to their clients. Will you be done pretty soon?"

"Done now." He tore a paper towel off the roll.

"Good." Her fingers hesitated. "Tiller. I know I asked already, but—is something wrong?"

"What could be wrong?"

"Well, usually when I do—*this*, something . . . different happens?"

"Nothing's wrong," he said.

Shrugging off blue cotton, she stepped into his arms, pulling the door closed behind her.

He buried his face in her hair. Sometimes he wondered whether she was too young for him. But she'd taken care of him after his back operation. Defended him at his cousin's inquest. Admitted at last that she loved him. This was where he wanted to be. He had all he wanted, right in his arms.

He hoped that what he had just told her was true.

• • •

Two vans were waiting when they slipped in out of the rosy detonation of a Pamlico dawn. Galloway stood at the stern, hands in his pockets, as Hirsch alternately gunned and backed, twisting the cruiser between the finger piers. The other slips were deserted.

Summer might be lemming season for tourists, but the fishermen disappeared as mysteriously as cicadas.

"Mr., uh—Kersten?" he called. One of the men raised a hand.

"Put 'em over," Hirsch called. Tiller swung and the watchers scattered, hands lifted for the settling coil. He swung up the gunwale gate, and then, favoring his back, slid the gangplank across. A moment later, he was shaking hands with the instructor.

"Mr. Galloway? Looks like a good day for diving."

"Sure does."

"Beautiful boat. You don't see many like this nowadays. They called this style Populuxe, didn't they?"

"Thanks. I think so, something like that. Got everybody? Have them take their gear inside. Don't use these stern lockers; the tanks and suits are in there."

Forty-two feet of cabin cruiser shrank drastically when packed with twelve divers and their equipment. They leaned over the stern rail, sat on the bow, chattering as Hirsch got under way again.

She pointed Miss Anna due east. Herring gulls fell like live manna out of the growing light, their cries imploring and at the same time ominous. A concrete rainbow grew before them, passed overhead, and subsided astern. The Bonner Bridge crossed from Bodie to Hatteras, linking the populous North Banks to the more remote South. The open sea spread like a blue arena ahead.

When they passed the last nervously tossing buoy, Galloway unrolled the chart. He gave Hirsch a course of one-zero-eight. A moment later, the engines went to full speed again.

Below them, Kersten came out of the cabin. "John," Tiller called down, "Can you get your people together for a minute? I need to give them a little predive talk."

While they were assembling, he swept his gaze around the horizon. He couldn't say why. From this height, he could survey sixty square miles of sea. The bridge was a dark bump astern. The only other craft in sight were two sailboats to the south, headed away. The bow pointed down a glittering road paved with gold by the rising sun. A good omen for his first charter? He hoped so. Wind buffeted his face. Beneath him, the deck rolled as green swells passed beneath. Already some of the divers looked queasy.

"Okay, please listen up. Welcome to the Outer Banks, Blitz Brothers' Diving, and *Miss Anna*. I'm Tiller Galloway, your dive master. This large gentleman is Shad Aydlett, my number two. At the wheel is Ms. Bernice Hirsch, who'll be in charge up here while we're below.

"As you know, the waters off Hatteras offer the finest wreck diving on the East Coast. We call this the Graveyard of the Atlantic, and you're about to see why. Today we'll do three sites. I'll brief you on each before we go down so the details are clear in your mind.

"This first dive is on a World War Two wreck called the *Marcon*. She was sunk in 1942, during the German offensive against American merchant traffic. She's in sixty feet of water, with the top of the wreck at thirty—so we're starting you off easy. The bow's pointing north, just as she was torpedoed.

"She went down in one piece and I think you'll find it a memorable dive. Lot of sea life, groupers, yellowtail, lots of growth on and in the wreck itself. Look for kingfish on the sand. We'll be in the Gulf Stream, so you may see barracuda and bonito."

The faces watched him. He searched his mind for anything else he ought to tell them. "I know you're all qualified, but let's review some precautions. Stay in sight of your buddy. Don't go into the wreck unless you have a reserve air supply, either a spare regulator or a pony bottle. My own rule is never to get into a situation where I can't make a quick and graceful exit. There's a big green moray lives down in one of the boilers. We call him Old Ned. He's not aggressive, but don't tease him.

"If you come up early, help yourselves to fruit juice and sodas in the galley. We'll break out the beer after the last dive.

"I guess that's about it. Any questions?"

A shout, faint against wind and engines: "Any current down there?"

"Plan on about a knot, setting north. Don't wander too far, it'll be hard swimming back against it."

"Tiller . . . we're almost there."

"Thanks, Bernie. Okay, y'all can start suiting up now if you want."

He checked their position on the loran and turned on the depth recorder he'd borrowed from Bill Foster. Right on time, the trace

jagged upward from a sloping bottom. Hirsch slowed and turned
south without being told. Aydlett was on the bow, running the
hook out with the hand winch. Its clatter came back to them.
Galloway dragged sweat off his forehead. There was less wind now
they were stopped. It would be another hot day.

A few minutes later, Shad shot his fist upward. Bernice centered
both throttles at idle and shaded her eyes. "Anchor's holding," she
called.

Galloway nodded, tossing a safety float over the stern. The deck
was packed with people zipping up wet suits, tightening backpacks
and buoyancy compensators, attaching regulators to air tanks. His
eyes snagged on firm bottoms and soft cleavages disappearing beneath Lycra and rubber. Almost half the club were women. A well-
heeled crew, too. Their designer gear bags held expensive diving
computers, camera equipment, camcorders in plastic housings.

His own gear was basic and rather old, but he liked it that way.
There was less to break and he didn't have to think too much.
There were times when that was an advantage underwater. He
pulled it on in the forward cabin, then clambered out on deck.
He strapped on his fins, sitting on the gunwale. Sweat was already
prickling his neck. Inside a quarter-inch of black neoprene, the
sun heated you up fast.

Aydlett's tank clanged against a coaming. He waddled out like
an uncomfortable bear. Tiller grinned up at him. His partner
hadn't been diving long. He had strength and courage, but skill
in the water came only with experience. Shad gave him back a
sour glance. "You ready to put 'em in?" he grunted.

"Let's go."

Sealing his mask and leaning forward, Tiller Galloway rolled
facefirst through the sparkling mirror of the sea.

• • •

His sudden descent startled several fish loitering under the hull.
They flashed away so quickly he couldn't see what they were. Cool
water flooded his suit. His weights were balanced for neutral buoyancy, and as the momentum of his fall dissipated, he came to a
dead stop six feet down.

He hung motionless, staring down in the wonder that always
took him when he entered the separate world of the sea.

He was surrounded by the moving melted turquoise of the Stream. The sunlight slid down through it in golden beams, flickering as the swell refracted them. They spread as they fell, melting into shifting gossamers of yellow-green and emerald as his eye followed them down.

Down to the wreck.

Thirty feet above the shattered junk of its superstructure, he couldn't make out much. In the dimness below his dangling fins, he could tell only that he was looking at something huge. Ahead of him the anchor line led down into a blue-green haze. Beside him, *Miss Anna*'s copper-painted bottom surged slowly, pulling down strings of silvery bubbles. He blew out to clear the regulator and sucked in air. It tasted dry, and a little nasty at the back of his tongue. Time to change the filter on the compressor. He was getting plenty to breathe, however, and his gauge read a standard 2800 psi.

He valved a shot of it into his vest and finned forward to the line. He held it for a moment, alert for the vibration that meant the anchor was dragging. It felt like it was bolted to Hell. He took a last look around, making sure there was nothing hostile in sight and that the current wasn't too strong. Okay. Fine.

He surfaced and spat out the mouthpiece. The faces turned toward him, and he called, "Water's great. C'mon in; she's right under our keel."

• • •

He went down to twenty feet and waited, holding the line with one hand as the others entered the water. Kersten had trained them well. They came in two by two, paused just under the surface to check each other's gear and adjust buoyancy, then continued down, clearing their ears as they descended.

Streaming on the line like a flag, he felt the slow, huge current move past him like a warm wind. Blowing north from the Caribbean, it warmed the whole Eastern Seaboard up to Newfoundland. While deep Atlantic currents flowed south, dark and cold, replacing it in the slow tao of nature. Not a bad arrangement, he thought. Better than I could have planned.

When he counted twelve divers, he waited another few seconds, his eyes on the surface. Right on schedule, Shad appeared in an inverted Christmas tree of bubbles. Watered-down sunlight glinted off his mask as he searched around.

Down, Galloway signaled him. His partner nodded, repeated the gesture, and surface dived. He was light and had to kick to get under. Tiller grinned again.

He pointed Shad toward the bow, where several pairs had congregated to read the vessel's name and gaze up at the anchor. He'd dived the *Marcon*, and the other wrecks they'd be touring today, many times. He had no desire to sightsee. He just had to be there, ready to step in if anyone got into trouble.

At the additional pressure of thirty feet, the air in his suit and BC compressed. As he neared the white sand bottom his descent accelerated. Finally, he stopped swimming and let his weight pull him the last few feet. He worked his jaw and his ears clicked. He adjusted his mask, tightened the straps on his backpack, and looked around.

He'd come down on the port side, and it towered above him like a rusty wall. A small group of jacks swam away along it, sticking close to the bottom. The plates were buckled where they'd slammed into the sand. A shattered area aft marked where the torpedo had hit. All in all, the wreck was in good shape—except when you raised your eyes. The Coast Guard had blown off her superstructure and the effect was like a headless corpse.

Two masks showed above him, looking down over the rail. Silver plumes of bubbles wobbled over them. He grinned around his mouthpiece. Lifting his hand, he waved a slow bon voyage.

Other plumes streamed upward beyond them. Most of the club seemed to be up forward. But the most interesting portion of the ship was aft. The hatches gaped there, square black wells no self-respecting diver could resist. Behind them, connecting via a corridor, were the engine and boiler rooms.

He decided to see what was going on back there. Valving air into the BC, he rose, then swam aft over the twisted junk that had been her bridge.

As he sank into the hold, darkness rose around him. His pupils opened as he dropped, and the blackness gave way to shadows and forms. One of the shapes uncoiled, moving away from him in sinuous twists: a shoal of five-inch schoolmasters, their silver-copper bodies packed so close they could have been sliced with a knife and fitted into cans. Another shape became a diver. She was investigating a corroded truck frame. As Galloway watched, she aimed a camera. The strobe glowed for an instant and then died, as if the pressure of the sea crushed light itself.

A headache nagged between his eyes. He reached up to ease his mask. That helped and he waggled his head from side to side as he reached the after bulkhead.

A tilted narrow passageway continued down and aft. Souvenir hunters had taken off the doors. He swam steadily down it, fending steel off with gloved fingertips, as the gloom grew deeper around him.

The engine room was the size of an indoor tennis court, but underwater it seemed larger. Narrow bright shafts slid through holes in the overhead and searched about in the sable blackness. Sparkling motes drifted through them, particles of rust settling as what had once been a ship, like everything gnawed by the all-devouring sea, returned slowly but inexorably to discreation. As his eyes adjusted, he made out the loom of machinery: gears, pipes, the rootlike clutch of cables, the rusted blossoms of valve handles.

His fingers found his flash. A moment later, light licked over the dead metal. The drab gloom burst abruptly into russet browns, chrome yellows, fungal algae red as arterial blood. Ted Turner, he thought, eat your colorizing heart out. He played it around, alert for the moray.

No Ned, but a lazy cyclone of kicked-up murk showed him where someone had gone ahead of him. Into the side tank. That was narrow and rather dangerous if you got hung up. Perhaps he should go in after the diver. He checked his depth, the time, and his air pressure. In the green. He clicked the light off, then winced, sucking rubber-tasting air with a hiss. The headache was back.

Sometimes when you breathed shallow, you got one from CO_2 buildup. He hadn't consciously been conserving air, but just on the off chance he drew in a deep lungful and blew out, did it again, and again.

The headache got worse.

He let himself rise, blinking as he peered over the hooded bulk of the engines. He couldn't see whoever was in there, but now and then he could see lights probing about through the rivet holes. But the pause had made him reconsider following. They didn't need a nanny. They were here for adventure, after all.

He looked back into the passageway. A strobe flickered again at the far end. A feeble gray-blue glow bled down from the surface. His sense of unease, the same apprehension that had made him search the horizon before they went down, grew stronger.

He decided that whatever was wrong, he'd feel better in the open. He exhaled and waved himself downward with his hands. He turned cautiously, keeping his tank clear of the overhead. Then, fixing his eyes on the light, he began swimming toward it.

It seemed to take forever. His legs felt like lead. The water dragged at his fins like cold honey as he emerged from the hold. Even forty feet down, beneath the silt a dozen divers were stirring up, the sunlight was so bright his eyelids crimped involuntarily. He didn't want to open them again. He wanted to sleep. He also felt sick to his stomach.

He jerked his eyes open by main force. Something was wrong with him. Perhaps he ought to surface. There were others to think of, though. He was responsible for them. He couldn't just leave.

He coasted to a stop above the wreck. Hovering there, wishing he could rub his burning eyeballs, he looked around impatiently for Shad. Then his gaze froze.

One of the divers was drifting downward, kicking and thrashing. He seemed to be trying to rise but unable to tell where the surface was. But even as Tiller stared, a groping hand found what it wanted. A black strip detached itself with a clack. The weight belt tumbled away. The diver began to rise, accompanying his ascent with feeble digging motions of his arms.

Galloway turned his head from side to side, blinking through increasing drowsiness. Other forms were rising from the deck and from the seabed—like a painting he'd seen once: the dead rising at the Last Day. As they ascended, whatever afflicted them seemed to intensify. Some stopped halfway to the surface, wrestling with invisible devils. Others went limp. Here and there, divers towed their buddies upward, their own distress and terror evident in the huge clouds of bubbles bursting from their regulators.

One diver in distress could be equipment failure: a split hose, a faulty valve. Or a physical problem—eardrums or vertigo.

But this was affecting all of them. Therefore—he suddenly remembered the off taste—it could only be one thing.

Their air.

His lethargy was shot with red pain now. His head felt as if it were being split for kindling. He stared upward at a tossing blue heaven. Up there was clear air. His whole body yearned for it. Wanted it more than it had ever wanted anything.

He folded himself at the waist, and swam downward, toward the figure on the deck.

Two yards away, he saw it was one of the women. Her eyes were fixed through the twin windows of her mask. She was blushing. Her hair waved like blond seaweed where she'd torn her hood off. Through the gathering murk, he saw hand beams glowing in the hold. How many were down there, trying to grope their way out in growing blindness?

His reaching fingers found her suit. He hit the valve on her BC. Air hissed and the vest bulged.

The limp body rose from the deck, and together they ascended at a steadily increasing rate. Halfway to the surface, he punched her in the stomach to make sure she wasn't holding her breath.

By the time his head broke the waves, he could barely see. A shadow loomed over them. He spat out rubber and croaked, "Bernie!"

"Here."

Wood knocked as *Miss Anna*'s hull slammed into them. Fingernails scrabbled at his head. He thrust the woman toward them. Her head lolled back. He couldn't tell whether she was breathing or not. "Take her. Got trouble below."

"I've got her. Tiller, what is it? What's going on?"

"Bad air. Listen. There's a half-full tank forward. From last week. Get—"

Then he stopped. By the time she found it, attached a regulator, and handed it down, people would drown.

"What do you want me to do?"

"Never mind. Try to get her breathing. Try mouth-to-mouth. Then CPR."

"Tiller! No! Come back!"

But the sea closed over his head, cutting off her scream.

Some of them were coming up. They rose as he struggled to descend. It was like fighting his way back into the grave. He couldn't tell whether it was in his head or in his eyes, but he could no longer see the wreck. Only a blue-black murk, and here and there writhing shapes.

A clatter burst abruptly all around him, the chatter of mad katy-dids on a summer night. The noisemakers divers carried to signal with. Only now, there was no communication. Only a staccato scream echoing in the sea.

A mouth opened under him. He sank toward it, unable to move his legs.

And through, into blackness.

A green glow deep in the hold. He struggled toward it. Slammed his head into something rusty. Coruscating jellyfish drifted across the blank screen of his brain, stinging as they pulsed. His ears beat with a hammering hum like spinning propellers. A band was tightening around his lungs, like a hose clamp of hot metal.

Another diver. The jade glow of a chemical light stick showed him curled like a fetus against the underside of the deck. He flinched under Galloway's hands, then, suddenly, lashed out.

The unexpected blow caught him on the cheek, knocking his mouthpiece from between his teeth. His throat locked as it filled with salt sea. His right hand searched in the darkness, hitting jagged steel, rubber, flesh, everything except the smooth chromed curve of a U.S. Divers Conshelf second-stage regulator.

The fist hit him again, colliding awkwardly with his mask. He felt his flesh tear as sharpness plowed his cheek. All right, you son of a bitch, he thought.

His fingers grasped something like a small turtle. They closed on it and yanked. Bubbles roared upward. An instant later, the regulator was clamped between his teeth, upside down, but that hardly mattered.

Now for the other man. His left hand found his weight belt. He wound his fingers into it blindly. Then he dropped his right, felt the double thickness of rubber at the crotch, and squeezed.

The other diver stopped struggling. He crimped around his hand like a stepped-on starfish. Tiller sucked air desperately.

The metal bands were turning red-hot. Flashes of light burst into dying sparks behind his eyes. He got his legs above his head, braced, and pushed off. Then he looked around, trying to find the way up.

He couldn't see a thing. Just seething red blindness, like a million cardinalfish schooling in the dark.

He backpedaled blindly to what he figured was the center of the hold. He was reaching for his weight belt when someone else's hand pushed his away.

He struck out, enraged, but his punch died in water. The hand jerked him around, dragged the two of them backward, and then let go. A moment later it came back, and air surged into his vest.

He felt himself lifting toward the surface. He turtled his head, anticipating the slam of steel, but the ascent continued. He breathed in and out raggedly. The metal bands were white-hot now, so tight that he shook with every squeeze of his heart, irregular and rapid, like the dying contractions of an octopus.

When his head emerged, to the slap of waves and a chorus of cries and moans, he had just enough presence of mind to spit out the mouthpiece before he passed out.

• • •

His moments of consciousness during the trip back were intermittent. He remembered a short conversation with Hirsch. She'd found the leftover tank, torn mask and fins off one of the women, and plunged over the side without bothering to suit up. She had dragged him back from the recesses of the hold and pointed him toward the surface. He whispered, through the lightning flashes of returning vision, "I'm glad I taught you to dive."

"You better be. You wouldn't have made it up the way you were going."

Later, he opened his eyes from where he lay in a slick of vomit and water to look into John Kersten's face. The club president's cheeks were livid, and not only with the cherry tint of carbon monoxide. "This . . . is . . . unforgivable," he said, coughing between each word. Spittle drooled from blue lips. "I can't believe this . . . incredible negligence."

Galloway stared at a light wand that dangled from the other's vest. It had been Kersten's balls he'd torqued. "How many did we lose?" he mumbled.

"They're all back up. They're all conscious now. Thank God. But supplying us bad air—this club will never dive with you again, Galloway. Nor will anybody else we ever talk to."

He closed his eyes on the angry stare. The dark descended again. This time, he welcomed it.

3

When he came back for good, he lay motionless for a long time, staring up into the sky. The engines throbbed through his skull. It was raining. Funny, he couldn't see any clouds. Then it moved away. It was Bernice, hosing down the deck. He rolled his head, and found himself looking into Shad Aydlett's red-rimmed eyes.

"You okay?"

His partner blinked. "Uh-huh," he said, as though he wasn't sure yet.

"Where were you? I didn't see you on the wreck."

"I was up forward. Helping them get topside. Then I come up and helped Bernie carry people into the cabin. Wasn't easy, neither."

"Why were you carrying them into the cabin?"

"To give them oxygen. Ain't that how you treat carbon monoxide?"

"Shad, oxygen's explosive. And that in the tank's industrial grade. For welding."

"I know that. I turned the power off up forward. And it was give them that or let 'em die." A spark lit in the reddened eyes. "Don't treat me like your goddamned nigger, Galloway. You know, sometimes you talk like I'm not too bright. And it's starting to piss me off."

They were cut off by a pailful of water. "Can it," Hirsch snapped. "If you two can argue, you can turn to. Get this mess cleaned up. We'll be pulling in in half an hour. And then we'll have a little talk."

They got up, eyeing each other. But once on their feet, there was no energy for reproaches. Galloway could barely stay vertical. His legs shook. Moving with slow decrepitude, he stripped off his wet suit and regarded his shorts. He took them off, too, tied them to a line, and tossed them over the side.

He inched below, sliding cautiously down the companionway to the head. He showered, toweled, then examined himself in the mirror. The hectic flush of monoxide poisoning was fading. He scrubbed clotted blood off his chin and dabbed bourbon over it. He filled his toothbrush glass and administered an internal dose, too. Then he handed the bottle out to Aydlett.

He found himself a fresh T-shirt and trousers in the skipper's cabin, stepping carefully around a hole in the deck.

When he went topside again, Aydlett and Hirsch were on the bridge, looking silently forward. He scowled at them, then looked in the same direction.

They stared for a long time at the pillar of dirty smoke.

Hirsch brought *Miss Anna* in to the pier too fast and scraped fresh paint off the starboard side. Galloway said nothing. When she shut down, they could hear trucks idling, the whine of sirens, the murmur of voices.

He had to stop twice to rest on the path to the shop.

The fire was out, but smoke still streamed upward. He pushed through the spectators and stepped over hoses through the front window.

The stench of alcohol and burnt plastic and rubber hit him all at once, making him gag. Sky came through the rafters. Glass crunched into the wet carpet with each step he took. White and gray smoke eddied up from masses of char and melt that had been wet suits, cameras, magazines, boogie boards. The walls were scorched and his charts and certifications were fragile tissues of carbon.

He waded toward the back. The counter was smashed and the fish tank was an empty cube outlined in metal. The castle and the mermaid and the little diver had melted together into a puddle of what looked like toasted cheese. Past that, the office was relatively undamaged, except that everything was sopping wet. Then he came to the rear. The distillery smell was strong here.

The whole back of the building was gone, blown apart into a scatter of metal shards and wood splinters. Rubbish hung in the trees. Apparently, the air bank had let go.

He was standing there when a yellow tabby came out of the

woods. It sidled up to him and rubbed against his leg. Buddy lived down the road. He had swallowed a fishhook once and nearly died. Another time, his owner had held a funeral for him, after a neighbor dropped off a headless yellow cat found on the road. But Buddy had turned up a week later.

He was a survivor. Patting him made Galloway feel better for a moment. Then he straightened as Bernie and Shad came out, and the fire chief behind them.

• • •

When the Buxton Volunteer Fire Department had rolled up its hoses and left, the three partners gathered in the office. Galloway worried a steel shard out of the desktop. The back wall, where the tanks had been, was a sieve.

Bernice had gone pale. She sat motionless except for a twisting of the hands.

"More?" said Shad, offering the bottle. It had started that morning full. Between them, it was half gone already. Galloway shook his head.

Hirsch said, "Who did it, Tiller? The—bad air, I mean. That wasn't your fault, was it?"

He told her briefly how he and Shad had found the door open. "After they carded the lock, they probably just drove their car around back. Ran a hose from the exhaust to the intake. Then ran the compressor for a few minutes. It wouldn't take long."

"And the fire?"

"Alcohol bomb." Galloway sat frowning through the wall for a few seconds, then shook himself. "A grenade, taped to a gallon of shellac thinner. Smells like two of them, one in front, one in back. But when the air bank went, it blew the flame out."

"What kind of people do things like this?"

Galloway said tonelessly, "Coke lords. It's one of their favorites. Easy, cheap, and effective—as you see. Though I never heard of Nuñez using it before."

Her face moved through shock to horror. She put her hand over his. "Tiller . . . ?"

He nodded. Once.

"But why? Why would *he* want to kill you? You never testified. At least that's what you told me."

"He doesn't. That's why it went off when we weren't here."

"But why bother you at all? I don't understand."

"He wants him back," said Aydlett. He slid open the drawer on his side, found a toothpick, and stuck it in the gap in his front teeth.

"Are you? Going back?"

"No."

"You sure about that?"

"Yes, Shad. I'm sure."

They sat there for a few more minutes. Water dripped from the ceiling. At last he got up. "I'm going across the road, make a call."

"Lax?" said Aydlett, cutting his eyes up at him.

"No." He took a deep breath, scared as he hadn't been scared sixty feet down, blind in the dark. "Not Lax. I'm doing what any good citizen would do, Shad. I'm calling the cops."

• • •

When he hung up, his face had set like concrete. He said a tight "Thanks" to Scott Busbey and walked down the steps of the Natural Art Surf Shop.

It was growing dark now, and the ebb tide of tourists was running north. They fought and honked to get back to their cottages and motels in Nags Head and Kitty Hawk and Kill Devil Hills before dark caught them on Hatteras.

Jamie Hooper, the sheriff's deputy south of the inlet, had let a moment pass in silence after Galloway said who he was. Then a snort came over the line. "Heard you suffered a little accident, Tiller," the reedy voice said.

"Not an accident, Jamie. It was a firebomb. Call Nate Green at the firehouse. He'll back that up."

"Oh, I'm not doubtin' that, Tiller. Not at all. I'm just kind of puzzling over why you're calling *me* about it."

"Because you're the law, Jamie. Remember that? What you're supposed to enforce in between campaigns?"

The high voice hardened. "I remember what the law is, Galloway. More than I can say for some people. What you want from me, anyway?"

He decided to make it simple. "Someone from off-island's trying to kill me. I want a guard till they leave."

"What? A guard?" Hooper chuckled. "Sure, I got three of 'em playing pinochle here right now. I been wondering what to do with all this extra manning the county give me.

"Now listen, boy. I don't know what you're trying to put over here. But you got to admit it's late in the game to come askin' us for help. You're the one's been running that shit into Dare County."

"I haven't—"

"Lemme talk, okay? I had my eye on you since you come back from Raleigh. Figured you'd be up to your old tricks sooner or later. I ain't caught you yet, you and that fancy boat, but I will.

"So now you got your ass in a crack? Tough titty. The law's like the power company, Galloway. You want to disconnect, fire up your own generator, that's fine with them. But when everything goes dark, you can't just pick up the phone and expect the lights to go on. See what I mean?"

"Yeah, but that ain't how it is, Jamie. I been trying to—listen. We been friends a long time. Remember how we used to row over to Great Island with Celie May?"

"Celie?" the reedy voice laughed. "Shit! You know she got four kids now. You seen her lately? I don't think we'd hardly get her in that little skiff anymore."

They both chuckled. But after a moment, the deputy went on. "Yeah, I remember. But that was a long time ago, Tiller. One thing I learned being deputy is, people change. Or maybe it is that you never knew them exactly how they really are, deep down. You know what I mean? Your brother Otie and I talked this over once. After the county commissioners' meeting. Otinus Galloway's done a lot for Hatteras. He's getting to be a big man in this county.

"Anyway, we got to talking about you. He said he didn't hold it against you, what your dad done after he found out about you being convicted. He and your stepmom, though, they just kind of gave up on you, boy. And so have I."

Tiller didn't have anything to say. So he just listened as the other man breathed on the line, chuckled, and then hung up.

• • •

The wind shifted at midnight. It brought the mosquitoes out
from the marsh. He sat in the darkened pilothouse, nursing a fist-
ful of whiskey and listening to the tiny sirens.

Finally he got up. He gulped the last inch of liquor, pushed
aside the netting, and emerged on the afterdeck.

The new moon was out. It ironed a decal of cool silver over
the calm black sound. A large shadow stood in the breeze, rubbing
its chin and looking out over the water. A mile away, the shore
glittered faintly. The only sounds were the mosquitoes, the sigh
of the wind, and the occasional distant bay of a hound.

"I'm turning in," said Galloway. The only answer he got was a
grunt.

"You staying up?"

"Not for long."

"About that oxygen cylinder. That was a good idea."

"I know," said Aydlett. "And now you figured that out, I'll tell
you another one. Maybe you ought not to be so goddamned hard-
headed, Tiller. Maybe you ought to call this Lax. See what he
wants, at least."

"I know what he wants. And I'm not going back into
trafficking."

The shadow was silent. Then it shrugged.

Galloway went below. Usually, he slept in the skipper's cabin,
in a double bed. But he still had the deck torn apart back there
to replace a rotten patch, and he'd moved into the crew's cabin,
all the way forward. It was eight feet wide, with two bunks stacked
to starboard. To port were a tiny sink and toilet. He pulled a curtain over the porthole, then turned on a light. As he sat down,
his eyes lingered on the short-barreled shotgun Aydlett had left
lying on his bunk. Then they rose, to a Polaroid, a copy of an
older photograph, taped to the bulkhead above a corroded, long-
stopped clock.

Admiral Lyle Galloway II, U.S. Coast Guard. A man of honor,
and a man of pride. He'd locked himself in his office the day the
verdict had come down condemning his son. And picked up a
gun.

And behind him in the photo, small, but there as Lyle Galloway III knew it was there, the engraving from the 1879 *Harper's*

Weekly of Otinus Randall Galloway at the oars of a pulling boat, putting out from Kinnekeet Station into the worst northeaster in memory. And in the offing, dwarfed by a fifty-foot surf, the canted, mastless wreck of the doomed *Floridian*.

His hand moved toward the bottle again, hesitated, then stopped. Pulled back again, crimped into a claw, it beat slowly on the wood.

• • •

When the bunk upturned and threw him to the deck, he thought in that first confused moment of wakefulness: Somebody hit us. Moored out, without lights, some early-rising trawler or workboat—

Then he heard the whine of high-speed props going away.

He scrambled up off the floorboards, slamming into Aydlett, and made for the doorway, slamming his leg on the bunk frame. He hesitated a foot away, then reached out.

The door opened on a white hell. It crisped his eyebrows and scorched his eyeballs dry in the half second before he got the door closed again. And it wasn't just fire. Already *Miss Anna* was listing to port and down by the stern. She groaned and lay over farther, making it hard to stand without sliding.

Something topside clattered across the deck and hit the water with a rattling roar. At the same moment, the half-fastened port-hole popped open. It was on the downside, and the Pamlico Sound bulged in, spurting over the sink and commode in a solid black column six inches in diameter.

Galloway jumped to it, slammed it shut, and spun down the wing nut. The water stopped, but he could see that the glass was underwater now. "We got to get out of here," he shouted at Aydlett over the growing roar.

Shad was pulling on his sweater. His head popped out. "How you plan to do that?"

"We've got to go aft. That's the only way." The forward berth was the only compartment aboard without a through-deck hatch. It hadn't been designed that way. There'd been a round scuttle once, but it had leaked when it rained.

"How? No, we got to go forward, Tiller. The chain locker. Get up through that access—"

"We fiberglassed that shut, Shad, remember?"

"Oh, shit, yeah. Whose bright idea was that?"

Galloway didn't answer. The boat rolled farther, almost to her beam ends. An explosion jarred her hull.

He could feel her sliding backward. Her engines were dragging her down. He remembered with sudden horror that he'd picked this spot because they had water under the keel. Not a lot, the sound wasn't deep. But it was deep enough to drown in. Tools—with an ax they could chop their way out. But the tools were aft, too.

The jamb of the door was outlined in yellow light now. He put his hand to the latch, then cursed as his reflexes snatched it back. The blisters were instantaneous.

"They caught us," shouted Aydlett. In the growing flicker that came through the upper porthole, he saw sweat shining on the waterman's face. "Another one them bombs, toss it into the cockpit—"

"They don't know the layout. They probably just meant to scare us."

"Yeah? They're scaring me, boy. We like to drown in here."

At that moment, something shifted aft, something big, and *Miss Anna* went over. He tumbled over the bunk frame again, hitting the corner so hard with the side of his head he saw stars.

Suddenly the firelight went out. The instant dark was loud with the gush of water and the snap and squeal of settling, breaking, compressing wood. In the second or two he lay stunned, he felt the fresh paint part beneath his fingers. The planks were weeping under his hands. The overhead he lay on gave a bump and something below them crunched.

At the same moment, his ears popped, and he understood. The bow still held a pocket of atmosphere. But the old hull was porous. It wouldn't hold air for long.

But by the same token, the sea, their executioner, had just murdered their jailer.

He heard a groan as his fingers found the battery-powered lantern. When the beam came on—more orange than yellow, an old battery, but he loved it then—it caught Aydlett's face, dripping blood.

"Fire's out, Shad. We're capsized on the bottom. We got to go, right now."

"I'll be behind you, case you get hung up."

Galloway slapped his shoulder wordlessly and spun to the door. The fading beam showed him water coming in all round the jamb. It was confusing to see everything upside down. Things floated on the black cool water at the level of his belt—a pencil, a cake of soap, a soaked pillow. He wrapped his other hand around the handle. "*Now,*" he said, and pushed.

The door didn't move. For a second, he thought it was the pressure holding it. Fifteen feet down, there'd be a thousand pounds a square foot holding it shut. Then he realized it couldn't be that. The water was trickling in, not spurting. No, it was jammed, some piece of beam or engines come down behind it.

They were trapped, and the Pamlico was still coming in. He could hear the air going, sizzling away through the garboard seams above his head.

The lantern flickered. He looked down; it was underwater. He lifted it, shook it, and it came on again, but even dimmer, ruddier. In its dying light, he looked across the rising water at Aydlett.

The black man said, "You figure any way to get out of here, Till?"

"Me?"

"Yeah, you. You figure any?"

He thought of all the openings from the cabin. The portholes: too small. The scuttle: fiberglassed shut. The door: jammed. They didn't have any tools to cut a hole, and even if they did, there wasn't time. The water was at his throat, and on tiptoe, he could reach up and kiss the deck.

"Not at the moment," he said.

Aydlett grinned through the blood. "Cover your ears," he said.

The shotgun came up dripping. Shad broke it, removed the cartridges, and tilted the barrels as water streamed out. Then the big ten-gauge duck shells snicked back in. He thumbed back both hammers, and Tiller, holding his hands over his ears, ducked under the surface as it went off with a yellow flash and a bellow like the day of doom.

If the air bubble had been larger, it might have blown them bodily through the hull. As it was, it tore the lantern out of his

hand. At the same moment Aydlett shoved him to port. His outstretched hand felt the splintered edge of a hole big enough to put
his fist through. So he did, grabbed, and pulled. The shot-riddled
wood crumbled reluctantly.

Crouched in the underwater dark, his heart slamming, he
clawed and dug, then shoved his arms and then his head through.
His chest pushed a strake loose. Nails harrowed his chest. He
shoved and wriggled into the gap, pulling off planks, and was suddenly free and then in a seemingly instantaneous transition splashing and coughing at the surface.

In the open air, under a dark sky, a mile out from shore. The
moon was a sliver of opal set in mist. The shore lights were just
as he'd left them, but lower. Life cushions, boards, debris jostled
about him in the dark, agitated by a hissing froth. A gasoline stink
bit into his lungs.

He gasped and hacked for a few seconds, then went suddenly
rigid.

Shad hadn't come up yet.

He sucked in four fast breaths, purging all the CO_2 he could,
and jackknifed into a surface dive, kicking back down into the
dark.

Six feet down, he ran into the hull. In the darkness, there was
no sign or way to guess where the bow lay. He could hear a rapid,
soft hammering that could have been fists. But he couldn't tell
which way to go. One led to his partner. The other, to the stern,
and by the time he got back—

He turned left and kicked along. Two strokes farther on, he ran
into Aydlett. Halfway through, and caught.

The only tool he had was his hands. He began tearing at the
planks. They'd been blown through at the center of the shot pattern, and weakened, gnawed by lead, at the edges. That was how
he'd gotten through. But they felt undamaged at the width of Shad
Aydlett's shoulders. His nails tore on sound mahogany. How long
had his partner been without air? It must be two, three minutes
by now. His own hasty rebreathing was running out.

He couldn't go back up. That would be leaving Shad to die.

Before he did that . . . one last try. He straddled Aydlett from
behind. Squatting, Galloway braced his legs against the hull
curve. As he bent, his spine gave a warning pang. The vertebra

that had fractured before, and put him in a full body cast for six months.

His arms locked around his partner, his teeth clamped on a soundless scream for air, and he pulled with all his strength.

A scraping, tearing noise came through the water. The man in his arms turned, twisted, and came free. Slid out into the cool sea like a second birth.

He shifted his grip to under Aydlett's chin, and one-armed them toward the surface like two devils paroled from Hell.

• • •

Half a mile from shore, they lay side by side on a mud bank. It stank of death and life, of fecundity and swift decay. Six inches of water covered a shoal bottom the consistency of quicksand. It was shallow enough to walk, but when they had tried, their legs had gone in trunk-deep. They'd crossed a hundred feet of it on their chests and bellies, crawling like creatures of a preliminary creation.

"Tiller," said a mutter from the moonlit dark, so close and low it was like another self speaking to him.

"Yeah."

"Thanks for coming back."

"Forget it."

"You know, you going to have to give in."

"I don't."

"I hate to say it, but you got to. Not a matter of choice."

He didn't say anything. Just looked toward the shore. So near he could make out individual porch lights now.

"Tiller, these people are not going to leave you alone. You can't just say no. You know? They making that clear. They done took all you own. All I own, too, but we don't have to go into that. Us Aydletts is used to not having nothing, why start now.

"But now it is all gone, and you keep on hanging back, they will start on your people. Your stepmom, and your brother. Your friends. Me. Sticky." He paused. "Ellie and Tad for sure, if they find out you use to be married. Latricia. Bernie."

Galloway didn't say anything. He looked toward the lights.

"You listening, boy? Listen to this, too. We see what they want. Okay? Maybe we can get some of our own back . . . for the shop, the boat. You say they got money. Do a good job for them, they might pay handsome."

"You think so, Shad? You think we'll come back rich from working for the Combine?"

"We don't have no choice, Tiller. We sure as shit aren't gonna do it this way."

Galloway whispered something in the dark. "What?" said Aydlett. "What's that?"

"I said . . . let's get swimming again."

4

Heads turned like compass needles as they navigated the lobby and bar, toward the smells of good food and drink, over the smooth, calm surface of a Persian carpet twenty-one floors above the Elizabeth River. Galloway didn't flatter himself that they were watching him. Not with Aydlett hulking behind him in faded work greens. Except for the servants, his partner was the only black in the Harbor Club.

When they'd gotten ashore at last, early that morning, he and Shad had parted. Aydlett had dropped him off at Bernie's, then gone back to his own home in South Hatteras, west of Frisco. Sometime thereafter, while Galloway showered and let Hirsch dress his cuts, he'd decided reluctantly that he had a phone call to make.

He hadn't wanted Shad at this meeting, but with no car of his own, he'd had to agree when Aydlett wanted to come to Norfolk too. They'd driven up two hours from Hatteras in the pickup, tools sliding back and forth behind the seat at each curve. But when Aydlett set the parking brake in front of the Sovran Building, he'd said, "Shad, hadn't you maybe better stay with the truck."

"No way, my man. Partners, remember? Whither thou goest, there goes Shad Aydlett, too. Been like that for a year. No difference now."

"It's for your protection. So far the Baptist knows you from Adam. Take it from me, that's the way you want to keep it."

Aydlett, his eyes going narrow as he squinted up at the granite obelisk of the Monument to the Confederate Dead had said, "'When you goes in halfs with a white man, make sure your X is on all the papers, boys.' That's what the Captain told us, Mezey and Abie and me. Nothing against you. You one of the square ones, Tiller. But I just—well, leave it at that: That it is my money involved, getting paid back for my boat and my business. So if there's a meeting, I am in the meeting, and if there's a deal, I'm in it, too. Equal shares."

And Galloway had grimaced, able to argue no further, for he knew what Aydlett meant. His great-grandfather had pulled an oar at the Pea Island Station, the only all-black crew in Lifesaving Service history, and just as much heroes as the Galloways. Only somehow, there'd been no medals for them. Shad's grandfather had inherited three miles of shorefront, and lost it in the Depression. Land that O. R. Galloway Realty and Construction was selling now at a quarter million an acre.

"Just a moment there. Where do you think you're going?"

He halted dead, staring down at a fat man in a tux.

"I'm sorry, but you can't enter the dining area without proper dress."

"What's he say?" said Shad. Several older women at a near table were staring at them. Their eyes, as they rested on Aydlett, were narrowed and their chins set, Tiller thought, like the narrow cruel mouths of blues.

He turned back to the fat man. "Look, buddy, we're meeting a man name of Lax. Is he here?"

"Mr. Lax is here."

"Well, show us where he is and knock off the—"

"I'm not letting you in, whoever you are, without these."

At first, he'd thought the man was joking. Till now, looking at what he held out: two soiled, limp, greasy-looking rags.

"We're not wearing those."

"Then you're not dining at the Harbor Club, sir."

He leaned forward, smiling in as friendly a way as he could manage, considering his growing rage. Losing everything, nearly drowning twice, and now this. "Listen. If you don't take me to Lax right now, you're going to be picking those shiny teeth off the floor. That clear, bubba?"

The maître d', mustache twitching, led them toward a window table. Past it, an eighth of a mile down, spread the gleaming silver tide of the Elizabeth River. To the left, the wind-wrinkled fingers of the South and East Branches groped back into the land. The old docks and warehouses were gone, torn down or converted into condos and marinas. Norfolk had changed. It wasn't the town he remembered. Sometimes he felt like a time traveler. Five years in prison had done that to him.

Years he owed to whoever had turned him in. Someday he'd find out who that was—and pay them back.

The fat man stood aside icily. Galloway looked past him, ignoring the murmurs behind them as Aydlett lumbered up. "You Lax?" he said. "Harold C. Lax, Jr.?"

The man who unfolded himself was taller than either of them. His gray suit and figured blue tie were subdued to the point of invisibility. His hair was silver, gleaming as if each individual strand had been polished and set in place with a template. It was styled longer than was fashionable in Buxton. Galloway hadn't intended to shake hands, but it happened before he could avoid it.

"I've looked forward to meeting you, Mr. Galloway. This is . . . ?"

"Shadrach Aydlett. My business partner."

"Mr. Aydlett. Pull up a chair, please. I haven't ordered yet, but I can recommend the smoked salmon as an appetizer."

"They got fried clams?" asked Aydlett. He fidgeted with his salad fork, giving it a close inspection, then laid it carefully alongside the others. He caught Galloway's glance, raised his eyebrows, and pointed at the spoons.

"What are you drinking, Mr. Galloway?"

"Bourbon."

"Mr. Aydlett?"

"Beer."

Lax ordered a tonic and orange juice, smiling faintly as he explained how he'd cut down after reading the studies. Galloway watched a tug maneuver a string of barges around Hospital Point. Through a haze from the Virginia Chemicals plant, he could see colliers lying to in Hampton Roads. The river was busier than he remembered it.

"Well, Mr. Galloway, I'm glad you were able to break away and see me. I understand you're doing well down in—where is it? Kitty Hawk?"

Galloway took a deep breath as his anger tided again. "Let's get something straight. I'm here because my business was ruined, my shop was blown up, and my boat was sunk. By the bastard you work for. So let's not pretend we're buddies."

Lax said softly, "Your objections are noted. Does that mean you don't plan to enjoy lunch with me?"

"That's exactly what it means. Now what does *your* remark mean—my 'objections are noted'?"

"Just that. I don't make up my mind after hearing one side of a story, Mr. Galloway. Do you?"

"You mean there's another side to threats and arson?"

"Only that to some extent your . . . difficulties apply to others as well. There's no point in making ad hominem accusations. That's not how our relationship should start."

"How should it start?"

"By trusting each other."

"Bullshit," he said. The linen tablecloth bunched under his fingers and a shrimp fork clattered softly on the carpet. "Nuñez wants me here. Okay, I'm here. You're his messenger boy. So give me the goddamn message and cram your bogus gentility up your ass."

The lawyer's face went rigid. "I caught a charter flight out of Starr Island to come here. I've been waiting for two days. I assure you, my time is valuable."

Galloway was opening his mouth when Aydlett kicked him under the table. He closed it, and took a sip of bourbon. It was the smoothest he'd tasted in years.

"And that reminds me. Before we discuss this, Mr. Galloway—this way."

Lax rose. Tiller hesitated, then got up, too. He glanced back once, to see Aydlett grinning at a flustered older woman at the next table.

In the wash room Lax pushed open the stall doors, then faced him. "Your shirt."

"What?"

"Take your shirt off, Galloway."

"One says put on a tie; the other says take off the shirt. You're awful concerned with clothing around here."

"You're wasting my time. And yours. Just take it off."

He unbuttoned it, lifted the tails. Lax's hands were raw oysters against his ribs and back and crotch. He winced as they patted down the bandages, where the hull nails had dug in.

"Very good; you may dress."

"Uh-huh. Now, your turn."

"Don't be ridiculous."

"I'm at risk here, too. As a lawyer, you should know that. From here on in, it's conspiracy to commit whatever you want me to commit. Give me credit for learning that at Central, anyway."

When they sat down again, Lax, flushed, was still trying to straighten his tie. Shad squinted at them suspiciously. Great, Tiller thought, he thinks we went off to make some secret "whites only" deal. "You want to pat him down, too?" he said, jerking his head toward Aydlett.

Lax shot him a virulent glance. He raised his finger for another tonic. Galloway refused a refill with a shake of his head.

"Very well. Here it is. My client wants to hire you, Galloway. He wants you to return to his employ. Why, I don't know, but there it is."

"Your client? Let's have a name. Just to make sure we're talking about the same bastard."

"Names are unnecessary at this point. As I was saying. He is extending an invitation to you to join him in a business venture. Obviously, you know something about that business. You have joined him in the past in similar or related ventures, from which I presume you profited. And are not entirely unwilling to join him again, as your presence proves.

"So to hell with your insults and pieties, Mr. Galloway. You're here, you're listening, and you and your partner are in fact eager to hear what I have to say. Isn't that right?" He smiled tightly.

"He wants me back. Doing what? Like the last time? Hauling pot and coke—"

"Keep your voice down. You're a diver of some sort, aren't you? He wants you for a salvage job."

"Salvage, huh?" said Aydlett. "What kind?"

"I don't know much about it."

"He asked you what kind," said Galloway.

Lax said grudgingly, "A small ship. It went down somewhere off the Bahamas. My client wants you to recover the cargo."

"What's the angle?"

"I don't know what you're insinuating. It's straightforward as far as I know."

"Then why would Nuñez be involved?"

"Don't be so suspicious, Tiller."

"Wise up, Shad. We just lost everything we owned. This guy toadies for the one who did it. That doesn't make you suspicious? It should." He bent forward. "Now, Lax. Nobody can hear us. There are no wires here. If this was a straightforward job, then Nuñez could hire a regular salvage company. Why doesn't he get Wijsmuller, or Watkins, or Selco? Or Comex, or Oceaneering International? Those are the boys he wants. Not Joe Blow from Manteo, got barely enough gear to scratch his butt."

"He wants you."

"He wants somebody he can control. Somebody who'll keep quiet. And somebody who'll be disposable if he decides that's what he wants. What, exactly, are we talking about salvaging?"

"Mr. Galloway, you bluster a great deal, but I don't hear anything but agreement. Do I?"

"Have I got a choice?"

"Everyone has a choice."

"Not with a gun at his head."

"If you're serious about that, I'd advise you to regard it as an opportunity."

"What are you talking about?"

"The law is quite clear: An act performed under duress is not a crime, or at the very least, not as culpable as an act performed voluntarily."

He stared at the lawyer's tailored smile. "How about two-syllable words, real slow?"

"I mean that if you can substantiate the fact that you were threatened, and there should ever be any legal problem over your activities for Don—for my client, we could raise that point in your defense."

"You slimy bastard," said Galloway, and his voice held a touch of wonder.

"Thanks. You might keep me in mind; I've represented some big names in the industry. My office is on Brickell Avenue, Miami.

"Back to the offer. In point of fact, you may be correct about the job being out of the ordinary. It may well be . . . something an established company might not be willing to undertake.

"The advantage to that, and it should figure in your calculations—"

Lax reached under the table. The briefcase snicked open. He laid an envelope beside the floral centerpiece.

"Five thousand dollars. For tickets and what gear you'll need to start. There's enough to cover your partner, too. Or will you need more?"

"We'll need more—"

"Pipe down, Shad."

"No; he's right." Lax reached down again. This time, the briefcase, balanced on its hinge, gaped for a moment. Galloway saw it. Stacks of it, green and new. He glanced at his partner. Aydlett's mouth had come open a little.

". . . There. Just to make it a little sweeter up front."

Aydlett said hoarsely, "Where?"

"Your destination is Green Turtle Cay, east of Great Abaco. Fly out there and link up with Mr. Christian. He'll take you to the location and arrange whatever assistance you need."

Galloway was about to say, Who? when he remembered. He said slowly, "Not *Troy* Christian."

"That's the name."

"What's wrong, Tiller? You know him?"

Galloway looked down at the river. He said slowly, "He's Nuñez's executioner."

"Your partner is addicted to overstatement," said Lax to Aydlett. "He's a businessman, closely associated with my principal."

"I can't work with him."

"Your previous assertion contradicts that."

"Say what?"

"Your statement that you're here under duress. If that's true—and I don't admit it—but hypothetically, if you were, then it would mean you couldn't choose who you worked with. You'd just have to go, and go now, and do what you were told. Am I right?"

He stared into the lawyer's polished smirk, his flat stamped-steel eyes. "Shad," he said, "take a look at what money does to a man."

"It is a sorry sight, Tiller."

"I'd advise against useless vilification, Galloway. You may need my help one day."

"Maybe I will," he said. "But first I'll tell you what you are. You're a remora, Lax. Know what that is? A little soft fish that sucks off the shark, lets it tow him around, and eats the leftovers when it kills something. You know what happens to them when the shark dies, Lax?"

"Haven't the faintest."

"They die, too. Let's go, Shad."

"Why don't we fix his face for him, Tiller?"

"Forget it. Let's go."

• • •

He didn't feel like talking on the way back. On the way up, he'd thought of dropping by Ellie's and seeing his son—it had been too long—but now he didn't feel like that, either. The industrial suburbs of Portsmouth and Chesapeake gave way to the flat green fields of coastal Carolina. At last, the Wright Bridge lifted them, held them above Currituck Sound for a time, and set them down in Kitty Hawk.

Shad said, "Is that right, what you was saying about that fish?"

"Sorry, I was thinking about something else."

"Said, is that right, what you said about them fish dyin' when their shark goes belly-up."

"I don't know," he said, looking out as the cottages and trailer parks slid by. "Probably they just find another one. Turn here, will you? Just drop me at Bernie's."

• • •

Hirsch wasn't home, and he couldn't get in; his key had gone down with *Miss Anna*, and he'd forgotten to ask for another before she left for work that morning. He thought about thumbing over to Manteo, to her office. Then he decided to wait. He sat on the sand-gritty deck, looking out at the rows of identical cottages. More were going up, their flimsiness naked to the sun before wooden shakes blended them into the mass. Till he fell asleep.

Bernice shook him awake a little after five and let him in. "You want dinner?" she asked him.

"Sure."

"I have some meat loaf I can heat, and we'll nuke a potato. That sound okay?"

It sounded great, and he said so, remembering his missed lunch. He followed her into the kitchen nook. Looking away from him, she began taking things out of cupboards and drawers. "So. How's your chest?"

"Better. How was work?"

"Tense. I was in a county meeting all day. They hired a consultant from Richmond. Nobody can tell what he's talking about, so all we do is argue." She paused, pushing her hair back, still not meeting his eyes. "Did you go to Norfolk? To see the lawyer?"

He cleared his throat. "Uh, yeah."

"I really wish you hadn't, Tiller. I told you that last night."

"Yeah, I remember."

She started chopping onions, quick sharp strokes like a rapid little guillotine. He watched the stalks lose their heads. "You can't afford to step outside the law again. Someone approaches you, you're supposed to notify me. Then the Dare County parole office can help you. And when they torch your business, and blow up your boat—God, Tiller! Doesn't that make you mad?"

"Sure it does. But I told you what Hooper said—"

"Hooper's not the law. Here, scrub these potatoes. He works for Billy Daniels, and Mr. Moulton knows Sheriff Daniels. We can get you protection."

"Yeah, but for how long? You don't know Nuñez."

"I know all I need to know about him. He's a crook."

Galloway didn't answer. The microwave door slammed open and closed. When she spoke again, her voice was softer. "I'm sorry. I don't mean to try to run your life, Tiller. I'm glad you and Shad made it out of *Miss Anna*. But we've lost everything, haven't we? You never insured her, or the shop, did you?"

"You know why. We couldn't afford to."

She sighed. "Can you take those plates to the table? What do you want to drink?"

"Water's fine, unless you got beer."

"You drink too much beer. So, you went to see Lax. What did he say?"

He told her over the meal. When he was done, they sat together for a while in silence.

"Well, I've had enough," she said, laying aside the napkin.

"Why do I always overeat when I quit smoking? You feel like a walk?"

"Sure."

They went down a little sandy lane, crossed the old coast road, and went between two houses over the dunes and down to the beach. Someone had built an immense black ceiling over them and painted it with radium stars. The sea haze smeared them into blurs, as if the sky had not been cleaned. They strolled south, holding hands, toward the glittering jut of Jennette's Pier.

"What worried me was, they could have made a mistake," he said.

"A mistake? What kind of mistake?"

"There are other stores in Buxton. There are other boats anchored off the landing. I don't like having people like that around Hatteras. Somebody innocent could get hurt."

"God! Not again! Tiller, *you're* innocent. *Shad's* innocent. And *I'm* innocent. They hurt *us*."

"That's not what I mean."

Her hand tightened on his as her voice rose. "I *know* what you mean. You have this attitude that since you've served time you're some kind of subhuman. That you've got dirt on you and can't get it off. But that's in your head, Tiller. Remember what you said you told that man when he came to the store? You paid your debt, and now you've gone straight. *That's* the self-image you want. You don't have to expiate some kind of guilt, some kind of inferiority, for the rest of your life."

He didn't know what to say to that. He didn't enjoy talking about his feelings. "Uh-huh," he said. "Yeah, well . . ."

She was still talking. "Now. You told me what Lax wanted. But you didn't tell me what we're going to do."

He took a deep breath. She wasn't going to like this. But there was no point in lying to her. "Bernie . . . I think it might be better for you, for all of us, if I just do what they want."

"Like hell!" His hand was suddenly flung away. Her voice blazed out in the dark. "Go back to—to what you used to be? For *me*? Like hell you will! Listen, Tiller. I told you, trust me, and trust the law. Or if you don't, run. Leave the Banks."

The night sea was a black emptiness behind them. A swell

tossed up hissing membranes of it that tangled their feet in foam. "Leave," he repeated. "And go where?"

"The West Coast. Or Louisiana. They need divers there, don't they? Couldn't you get a job somewhere else?" She paused, and he heard the sigh of her breath. "You wouldn't go alone."

"Thanks, Bernie. But I grew up here. My family's been here since that first Galloway came ashore in his whiskey barrel. Damn it, I got a right to live where I please."

"Then stay, damn it! I'm *telling* you to stay, and let me help you."

"Bernice, listen. It's not that I don't think you'd try. But these aren't the kind of people you see in your office.

"Listen. One of them, one of Nuñez's enforcers, he decided once that a distributor was holding out money on him. Down in Florida, in Winter Garden. The guy disappeared. So did his family. A couple months later, there was a thing in the paper about how a dog had brought in a human foot. They found the kid at Disney World, in Little Lake Bryant. They're still looking for her parents." After a moment he added, "They found the guy who pulled the trigger, though."

"They did. Good! See, the law—"

"They found him on an off-ramp from Ninety-five, hog-tied with duct tape and wrapped in garbage bags. Strangled and shot." Galloway sucked air. "I just don't think Jamie Hooper, or Billy Daniels, either, is up to facing down the Combine."

"Then we'll get the state police. Or the FBI."

"They got better things to do than guard me, Bernie."

"What you mean is, you don't think you're worth protecting."

The bitterness drenched her voice, and he felt his shoulders slump. How could he tell her what he knew so well? She knew crime from outside, from college courses, from seeing its perpetrators on their best behavior, dressed in suits in court. And even then, they were the losers, the ones who got caught. How could he tell her what he knew, about what it was like from within? About the men who were too smart, too powerful, and too rich to ever face a judge? And about what they could do to make a man do what they wanted.

Even as he thought it, he knew the answer. He couldn't.

But—damn it, couldn't she take it on faith, that he wouldn't leave her without a reason?

She interrupted his silence. "So what are you going to do?"

"Like I said, the only thing I can. See what he wants. Try to do it for him. And look for a way back to you."

"Tiller . . . tell me something. You're not still after the money, are you?"

"No," he said. "Money! No. I just want to get this settled."

But even as he said it he knew it was only what he wished was the truth. Something deep in him still dreamed that he'd make it one day. The big score. He only hoped that if the crunch came, the better part of him would come out on top.

"And you really think this doper will let you go? After he gets whatever, whatever he wants out of you?"

"Well . . . I hope so."

"After what they did to the shop? To *Miss Anna*?"

"It'll be all right. Trust me, Bernie. I love you." He reached out and pulled her to him. And he felt her push away, so hard he staggered back a step in the soft sand.

When she spoke again, her voice was different from any way he had ever heard it. Sharp, and slow, and inhumanly controlled. "I . . . love you, too. I loved you since you walked in the parole office a year ago. But according to Dare County, and the State of North Carolina, I'm responsible for you, too. So listen to me! You can stay here tonight. But don't even think about touching me."

"Bernie—"

"I'm talking! And one more thing. If you . . . leave me, for this—"

Her voice broke, and he waited in the darkness, in dread, for her to finish the sentence.

"If you go back to them, we're through. I don't want to see you again. If you go . . . don't worry about coming back."

"Don't say that. I need you. You don't have to agree. But if I don't have you here to come back to—"

"I said it, Tiller. And I mean it."

They faced each other for what felt like a long time. Finally, she said in a low voice that she was cold, and wanted to go back to the cottage.

He lay awake in the dark long after her breathing had turned to a soft familiar snore.

He wasn't listening to that, though. He was listening to the sea. Beyond the dunes it shouted endlessly, a sound that was no sound at all, an endless roar of negation. Its message that was no message but the absence of all message was carried by the sigh of the dark wind, the endless hiss of sand against walls, pillars, dunes, concrete, rock. The tiny flying grains ate day and night, eroding, blunting the edges, filing away, till what had once withstood them was worn to nothing.

She didn't understand. He was trying to protect her, and she thought he had a bad self-image. He'd asked for her trust, and she thought he was after money.

To hell with her, he thought. If she wanted out because of that—

He had a sense of falling. Out of control, too heavy for the medium that up to now had supported him.

He'd stepped into a hole once in Vietnam. The team was wading along a canal, coming down from a mission that even now he could not recall. That was when he'd been on loan to the green-faced frogmen, working with the PRUs in the Ben Tre. They went out wired, strung out, and sometimes the combination of Dexedrine and shock and terror erased memory into the soundless hiss of blank tape. Anyway, they'd been wading back, him on point, when suddenly there was no bottom under his feet. His bare feet bicycled helplessly as he dropped away into black water. He was overloaded with three AK47s and the slings got tangled in his fins. He couldn't get them on and he was too heavy to swim without them. No one had seen him, but he'd almost drowned.

When he thought of death, it was that moment he thought of rather than the firefights or even the time he'd tripped a mine. That moment when the stinking Mekong had closed over his open mouth.

He stared at the slowly changing numerals on the bedside clock, listening to the occasional drone of a light plane sliding in through the darkness to the field at Kill Devil Hills.

5

The flight from Norfolk went smoothly, but they were held on the ground for an hour in Jacksonville. He kept himself to two bourbons while Shad absorbed three beers, then another complimentary one as they let down into Fort Lauderdale. When they deplaned, it was five minutes past departure time for their Bahamas connection. At the Aerocoach counter, the attendant was taking down plastic letters. "Treasure Cay," Galloway shouted.

"She preflighting now, mister. Luggage coming? No? Hit that door running, you might get her 'fore she leave."

Outside, he broke into a jog, slinging the bag over his shoulder, blinking. The glare burned his eyes like a welding arc. He'd thought it was hot in Hatteras. Now he remembered what a tropical sun was like.

Their pilot was a Germanic-looking blonde. She was locking the baggage compartment when they panted up to the Piper. Only two seats left, and separated—one aft, one forward. The fuselage shook as Aydlett hauled himself up and wriggled forward, muttering "Sorry" and "'Scuse me" to the other passengers. Galloway took the after one, sinking back and clacking his belt shut with a sigh.

The pilot swung herself up and slammed her hatch. The right seat was empty. She shouted out the window; a baggage handler waved, and the engines burst into hoarse song, first the left, then the right. Hot exhaust battered into the swiftly heating passenger compartment. She gunned the throttle and they started rolling, wings rocking as the tires thudded over joints in the concrete. Tiller glanced forward at Shad. His partner's fingers were digging grooves into the plastic armrests.

He remembered then that Aydlett had never been in the air before today.

A shattering drone, a cramming of wind through a still-open window, and they were aloft, rising and dropping like a piece of popcorn in a hot-air popper. Aluminum parts buzzed in the seats. Fort Lauderdale, the glittering branches of canals, the rows of tract developments fell away. The horizon tilted and the world wheeled. The nose dropped, came up, dropped again viciously, tightening the belt against his bladder. For no good reason, he thought again of Vietnam. Then the engine drone dropped an octave and the silver disks settled into a steady flicker, and he relaxed, kicking his bag back under the seat.

His lips tightened as he looked down at the steel penetration of Port Everglades Inlet. What had he said to Nuñez's announcing angel? That he had too much to lose?

Now he had nothing to lose—except, of course, his life.

"*You coming from up north?*" someone shouted above the prop roar.

His seatmate was a graying man in glasses. A Star of David glittered in his chest hair. Casual slacks, white guayabera shirt, gold-rimmed aviator frames.

The pilot latched her window, and conversation became possible. "Sort of," Galloway said.

"You get so you can tell. Though you got a good tan. Working tan, by the looks of your hands. . . . Where you out of?"

"North Carolina. Hatteras Island."

"Know it well. Headed where?"

"Green Turtle Cay."

"I'm Al Zeno. A to Z, they call me. Going up to Grand for some fishing. You fish?"

"Used to when I was a kid. But it's work where I come from. What're you after?"

"Marlin, sail, whatever's on a run. I go after what's there. Know what I mean? What do you do?"

"I'm in diving. Scuba charters and such as that. Do salvage now and then, welding, underwater inspection. Whatever pays."

"That so? Doing some diving out here?"

"Could be." He looked at Zeno's glasses again. Dentist, he guessed. They always ran their mouths when you least wanted to talk. He said grudgingly, "How about you? What do you do?"

"I'm with the Drug Enforcement Agency."

The lenses glittered in the high blue light that slid down between the clouds. Fixed on him, but he still flinched. Eight seats, and he'd gotten this one. He swallowed carefully. "Oh yeah? Plan on catching some big ones?"

It was weak, but Zeno chuckled anyway. "One way or another. You know Manderell? The one we just got, you see him all over *USA Today*? I used to charter off his island—before he bought it. Then we started to notice strange things going on."

"Strange things?"

"Hell, he just took over the place; the runners just took it over. There was an archaeologist working there and he . . . disappeared. Then the locals hired on as *apuntados*. They didn't have much choice, I figure; join up, make six times what you make fishing, or feed the fish yourself. Not a tough call for your basic Bahamian. Then the air-traffic flow took this kink out over his backyard. We had airdrop photos, recovered coke, the works. But it still took two years to get the government off the dime. Finally, one of our CIs—informants—got himself shot. We held their nuts to the fire, and finally Sears, that's the Prime Minister, sent in the Mounties.

"Well, a mob gathered. They took sniper fire, had to pull out. That bad—civil war. We had to lay for him, get him separated from his entourage. It's Wild West down here. You know eighty percent of all the coke hits the States comes through the Bahamas?"

"I read that, in the papers."

"They cover a ten-thousandth of it. Reporters never see it. We never see it. We only hear about it after we get there to police up the bodies, you might say."

"Is that so," said Galloway. He was trying to keep the conversation light, but meanwhile his mind was going back over everything he'd said. So far, he'd admitted he was a diver, did salvage, did anything that paid, and might have a job here. Nice, very nice. Zeno had sucked him in like a big grouper inhaling a lobster. If only they had drink service . . . He tried to catch Aydlett's eye, but Shad, two seats up, was hunched over, head down. "Why doesn't the government do something? Put on more raids?"

"Protection. Pure and simple. When we picked up Manderell, he had four hundred and fifty thousand bucks in his shaving kit.

Was he making a buy? Was he making a payoff? Nyet. That was walking-around money. He kept it as like a tip for the odd customs man he ran into. Or who ran into him."

"You have problems in the DEA? Guys taking money?"

"I wish I could tell you no, brother. But every man has his price, and the number of zeroes the *magicos* can float out here. . . . Figure it: Six hundred miles from Colombia by air—that's two hours. They air-drop someplace off one of these cays—seven hundred islands in the Bahamas, right, no way can we cover them. Then they break bulk into Miami, thirty minutes by air. High turnover, terrific margin, that's good business, no? We got sixteen tons of it last year. We figure that's, oh, twenty percent? Fifteen percent? Can't be much."

Why was Zeno *telling* him all this? Was he really DEA? Galloway felt a familiar unreality close over his head. When you entered the world of drugs, it was like crossing into the Twilight Zone, into a mirror universe where nothing was as it appeared. He snapped his attention back. "So most of it goes by air?"

"I think more goes by boat," said Zeno. He seemed to be interested in Galloway's forearm, resting beside him. Tiller looked at it, at the tiny flecks of copper red: bottom paint, from when he'd hauled *Miss Anna.*

The interior of the plane seemed to have no ventilation at all. He rubbed sweat off his eyelids. He pushed the tote farther back under his seat, wincing at a metal clank. Not much there. The clothes he'd had at Hirsch's, toothbrush, underwear, a new Scubapro regulator, fins, mask, and spear—the basics. Actually, it was all he owned. Everything else was at the bottom of Pamlico Sound.

Then he remembered the cash. Yes, Zeno would be interested in that. In four thousand dollars in hundred-dollar bills.

"Don't dive myself, had asthma when I was little, can't even stick my head under in the pool. But it's great, they tell me—the deep frontier, the silent world. Where are you diving?"

He not only didn't know, he couldn't even think of a place to tell him. "Uh, I'm just going to skin-dive off the beach," he said at last. "Do a little spearfishing. Relax. I don't like to overplan."

He waited, hands clamped on the armrests, but after another few questions—how deep you could go with scuba, whether you could get a kingfish with a spear—the agent closed his eyes and leaned back. Galloway let his breath escape slowly, looking out the window, down at the passing sea.

The sea. A mile below them it was as smooth and unmarked as another sky. Only the moving glitter of the sun picked up the parallel furrows of a swell beneath the calm.

• • •

The field on Treasure Cay was surrounded by forest. As they came in, dipping and swaying in the thin hot air like a dragonfly, smoke was streaming up from it. They hovered above the rushing asphalt, then touched down lightly. The pilot turned sharply as the end of the runway rolled toward them. She threaded the Piper between a DC-3 and a Learjet—both with broad strips of tape over windscreen and hatches, and yellow placards that read CONFIS-CATED PROPERTY—and parked by a shed. The prop blurs wound down to a ticking and then the blades quivered and stopped.

The heat smashed down on him as he jumped down. It was like sliding into boiling grease. His shirt was soaked instantly.

"Scorcher, eh?" said Zeno, behind him.

He stretched a grin over his teeth. "You bet."

Aydlett eased himself down, feeling for bottom with his toes. "You okay, Shad?" Galloway asked him.

"Don't feel too good."

"Walk around a little. Breathe deep."

"I don't think I like flying."

"Open the bag," said the bored, fat customs agent. Tiller un-zipped it. Zeno leaned over his shoulder, nodded wordlessly at the chromed glitter of the regulator, and went past, tossing the Baha-mian a Boy Scout salute. No one asked about the zippered side pocket. When he was done with the paperwork, he looked around for Aydlett.

"Hey, Till, you got you a couple bucks? They got cold beer."

He got one, too. Carrying the sweating cans, they strolled outside.

No cars. No buildings. No people. Just woods, the rising cur-tain of smoke, and a red dirt road, shimmering like a mundane mirage.

"Now what?"

"Green Turtle. According to Lax, there's a shuttle boat from a pier somewhere."

The woman at the snack counter told them that the boat docked a mile or two down the road, and that the taximen quit at five. He picked up his tote bag and went outside.

Zeno was sitting in an official Land Rover. A black man in uniform sat at the wheel, smoking. The agent leaned out as they went past. "Need a lift?"

"No thanks."

"Sure?"

He nodded and kept walking. When they were out of earshot, Aydlett said, "I figure you got a reason for telling him no. Isn't that the guy you were sitting with?"

"He's DEA, Shad."

"DEA?"

"A narcotics agent."

"Oh," said Aydlett thoughtfully. He turned to look back. "Oh."

They lengthened their strides, and fell into a contemplative silence. The road was new, baking out a choking odor of tar, and hot as a short-order grill.

After half an hour, Galloway cleared his throat. "Uh, Shad?"

"Yeah, Till?"

"When you told Latricia you were coming here . . . how did she take it?"

"Well, there was what you might call a good deal of screaming and throwing things."

"She was upset?"

"No, that was me doing the screaming. She wanted to drive my truck while I was gone." Aydlett grinned slowly. "Actually, I kind of forgot to tell her exactly where we was going. Like my pa used to say, no use tellin' a woman any more than she needs to know."

Galloway chuckled, but it died fast. It was too hot to chuckle, or talk, or breathe. He unbuttoned his shirt and slung his duffel over his shoulder.

They hiked along the berm, looking longingly into the shaded woods. The smoke came up steadily, a great screen of it between them and the setting sun, lighting the road and the land and their faces with a weird red dimming light, as if it was shining down through many fathoms of blood-tinted sea.

• • •

The water taxi was at the pier all right, tied up at a finger channel blasted out of solid coral. But there was no one around. They sat in it for an hour while the sun sank and, paradoxically, the heat increased. Galloway considered stealing it but decided not to. The windless air smelled of burning.

"Fellows going out to the Turtle?"

They turned. An old man in frayed dungarees had come out of the woods. "Uh, yeah," said Aydlett.

"That is my skiff. By the taxi, mon. You see her? I going to White Sound."

"How about New Plymouth? How far's that?"

"Right across there, across the water, where I am pointing. See the houses? That is New Plymouth. Get you in, coom on; I will take you there."

The boat was half full of water and stank of long-dead fish. They settled themselves on the thwarts as the old man muttered over the battered-looking outboard. But it started on the first pull and they clattered out of the canal, past outcrops of blasted rock, into open water. Galloway craned around, checking the lay of the islands. They ran northwest by southeast, two or three miles off the solid coastline of Great Abaco. The water beneath his leaning face was a clear light blue, ten, fifteen feet deep he judged, well sheltered from any blow. He could make out patches of sand and the shamrock shadow of grassy bottom.

Turtle Cay grew as the light faded. They passed several anchored boats, motor yachts and cruisers. Dusk was falling swiftly now, and he couldn't see beyond the anchor lights. But the old man ran calmly in among them, threaded them, and left them behind. They buzzed around a low point, between channel markers—the ancient explained it was shallow here, very shallow, they could jump out and walk—and at last made up to a white-painted pier under a single incandescent bulb. The town started at its foot, tiny white and pastel houses, a church, door open, from which came the sound of many voices joined in a hymn. The heat had ebbed at last and the air was warm and soft and heavy with bougainvillea.

He gave the old man five dollars and got a soft handshake in return. When he'd vanished back into the dark, Shad stretched and looked around.

"So, what now? How do we find this—this Christian?"

"This is all we got for directions. Come to New Plymouth, and they'll find us." He looked around, too. "It doesn't look like it'll be too hard."

"Yeah, but will it be tonight? I don't feel too great."

They strolled around for a time, and at last found a double at the New Plymouth Club and Inn. Aydlett said he was giving out. As soon as they were done with dinner, he went to bed.

Galloway had a bourbon in the bar. Two other men were silently drinking rum. A VHF was on in the back room, and between the crash of plates and the gay shouts of the help, he listened to the crackle of traffic on Channel 16. The locals used it like a telephone, letting people know when their boat would be in, telling their wives what they wanted for dinner. The dialect was British mated to African; between it and the static, he caught only a word here and there, or the name of a boat. He thought about putting out a call for Christian, then dismissed it. They wanted him here. They could damn well find him.

Next he thought about going to bed, like Aydlett. He was tired, too. It might be good to get a few hours ahead. The Combine didn't work union hours. And he had a vague feeling he needed to stop drinking so much. Stop drinking, and stop getting into so much trouble.

After considering the pros and cons of this for a while, he slid off the bar stool, hitched up his pants, and went out.

The air was cool now. The moon was a sliver of pearl between the nodding crowns of the palms. Their stiff fronds clashed as they swayed to the breeze. The sound made him vaguely uneasy. He pushed through the gate and walked up a cobbled, unlit lane toward the distant beat of a band.

New Plymouth was as small as it looked from the dock. Seven minutes' saunter between the miniature houses, each with its little fenced yard and concrete cistern, brought him to the foot of a hill. He'd heard the band ahead for the first few minutes, but now, standing at the rising road, he heard nothing but the steady roar of a diesel generator. Could he have confused that with rock music? If so, he was more tired than he thought. Maybe he belonged back with Shad, and not out cruising the Bahamian night.

He turned toward the docks instead. Almost at once, he found a bar. THE BLUE BEE, read the sign. A shack, blue walls, blue doors. Most of the faces were black, but aside from a glance, no one remarked him. He ordered a Courage and drank it slowly in a corner, staring around at the bikini bottoms, divorce decrees, law licenses, boat deeds, checks, and diaphragms that had been tacked, pasted, stapled, and glued to every flat surface but the floor.

Then the conversation lagged. And faintly, through wood and night, he heard again the distant rhythm of a goombay band.

When he stood again below the hill, it came clear and raucous over the steady whine of power. Distant lights glittered in the foliage. Yeah, he thought, I ought to go back, get some sleep. No telling what could happen tomorrow.

He bent to the slope.

The Rooster's Rest was a low double-wide. A patio deck was hammered out of what looked like planks from shipwrecks. He could see the filaments in the lights vibrating from the bass inside.

When he slid the door open it hit him. A beat loud enough to jell your brain, and a crowd long past letting jelled brains interfere with fun. White and black and every shade of brown, packed hip to sweaty hip in a rocking seethe of crazy drunk. Enough grass fumes in the packed air for a five-minute contact high.

He found a gap at the bar and ordered strong black island rum.

Standing there, the sweet liquor scorching his throat, he tried to think about what he was doing. The smoke and noise seemed to help. For just a moment, in the roar of fifty people enjoying themselves, his mind focused like a polished lens.

Was it possible that Nuñez had invited him here to kill him?

What Zeno had said . . . the DEA man talked of islands the drug lords held like fiefs. No law reached there, neither American nor Bahamian. This didn't seem like one of them. But Green Turtle was still close to civilization, as represented by the Treasure Cay airfield. The Out Islands would be different.

But why should the Baptist go to the trouble? The squat Colombian with the leather face could have killed him without warning any day in Buxton. Walked up behind him at Burrus's Red and White while he was buying bologna and beer. That had been Nuñez's style in the old days—a silenced .22 in the back of the head.

Or could it be something he knew? He couldn't think of anything he knew that Nuñez didn't. You don't know that much anyway, Galloway, he thought, staring himself down in the dirty mirror behind the liters and quarts and fifths. And less every year.

Maybe it was as simple as Lax had put it: The Baptist needed him.

He ordered another Myers's. Reasoning was becoming difficult, but he ventured a few more steps down its slippery slope.

The trouble with that was that the very actions presumably meant to force him into cooperation had damn near done for him and Aydlett both. Assume they'd checked the shop before bombing it, or watched from shore as *Miss Anna* pulled out. But the poisoned air—they could have died from that. He shuddered and drank off the glass as he remembered how he'd gone down again blind. If *Marcon* had been a hundred feet down instead of sixty, he wouldn't be here now, Bernie or no Bernie.

And thinking that, he suddenly remembered where the bomb had gone off. Aft of the crew bunkroom. Well aft. In fact, it had gone off either in or very close to his regular quarters.

The space that, if he hadn't torn up the deck the week before, he would have been sleeping in.

Suddenly he found that his hands were shaking. Confronting the idea that someone had meant you to die . . .

"You be trying one them Goombay Smashes, Cap'n?"

"Why not," he said. He turned to face the room, anchoring his elbows on the splintery rough plywood.

And he saw her, watching from the corner table.

As soon as he caught her eye, she looked away. His gaze dwelt slowly down the side of her turned-away head. Honey hair, sunbleached, tied back; a curve of rounded cheek, a neck disappearing into a cutoff polo that showed her shoulders and the little pale pucker of skin under her arms.

Leaning back, he mused about how sensual the fine coat of down on stocky blondes can be against the light. The fuzz of a peach is often used in comparisons. But when the woman in question has curves, not angles, has spent a lot of time in the sun and sea, has just been dancing hard, sometimes a glow ignites beneath her skin. Some invisible radiation of . . . *ripeness* . . . was as close as he could come to it. Like a fruit ready for eating, she invited hunger. His eyes slid down to cutoff jeans, to the tanned curve of thighs, to strong ankles laced into broken-backed Dock-sides, soft as gloves, that had taken on the shape of the feet within.

When he looked up, the men at her table were scowling at him. Two were black and one white. They seemed to be discussing him, but the noise was like two feet of solid glass.

"You like that rum. It go down smooth, don't it?" said a voice close to his ear.

"Yeah. Smooth."

"You better not have no more, Cap'n. Got to get back down that hill. Got to row back to your boat. Don't look at that girl there, Cap'n. Don't look at her, she with them seldom-seen wham-whams, sitting with them rowdy pandas. Don't want to lose you tonight, want to see you here tomorrow."

"Another," Galloway told him.

When he looked back at her table, she was looking his way again.

Wham-whams, he thought. Whip up your scuppers, I'm laying alongside. He shoved off from the bar, taking along the glass of dark fire topped with lime slice and sugar, and set a course eastward. The floor heaved up and down, but he forged on.

"You boys don't mind if I borrow your sister," he said. "No? That's good. Let's see if you can dance as good as you look, Heidi."

He caught the warning in her eye just as he turned. It was just a flicker, a glance to the side. But it was enough to duck on.

The bottle went by his ear so fast it whistled before it smashed on the table edge. The arm behind it was black, muscular, laced with pink scars like comet trails in the night sky. He had time to think all this as he came around, feeling clumsy but at the same time balanced, and caught the man who owned it across the throat with his knuckles.

Just then the others hit him, one at his waist, the other sliding in low, like stealing third in a dirty sandlot game. His knee stopped the slider. Teeth snapped against his patella. It hurt like hell and they both howled.

Suddenly there was a terrific commotion in the room. But the band didn't stop. It played louder and faster, to cover up the fight, or maybe to celebrate it. The bartenders yelled, the drummer yelled, and the dancers, some of them screaming encouragement.

Galloway wasn't paying any attention to them. He was circling backward, hands out at shoulder width in front of him. He no longer felt drunk. He didn't know what it did to blood-alcohol level, but a six-inch conch knife did wonders to concentrate the attention.

In a stateside bar, somebody would call the cops. Somebody would grab them both from behind, or at least shove them outside. No one here did any of these things. The band played louder, faster, accelerating the beat. The crowd had closed in till they had just room to circle. Someone was screaming at Filly, whoever that was, to "cut Squatty Body's nuts off." The man with the knife was grinning, showing missing front teeth as he cut little circles out of the smoke. Great, Galloway thought. I'm up against the local favorite.

The man he'd kneed came up off the floor in a blind howling rush and knocked Filly backward over the table. Glass and wood smashed and collapsed under their weight. Galloway lunged in, getting a poorly aimed but reasonably effective right and then a left and another right into Filly's face.

Two big scarred hands grabbed him from behind like a Ditch Witch grabbing a piece of sewer pipe. They tried to lift him, but his shirt tore off instead. He stamped back and down but missed the instep. The hands came down again and closed around his neck.

Galloway fed him two elbows to the ribs, but he couldn't put power behind them with his head in a vise. Things started to go dim. "Twist it off, Wuckie," someone screamed in his ear. Was he Wuckie? Think not. Other man Wuckie. Feed Wuckie another elbow. No good.

Think, Galloway. Other man getting off wrecked table now. Girl nowhere. Other man looking for knife. Things getting very dim. Who turning lights down?

Then they went out.

6

Ants were walking on his face. He grunted, rolled his head, brushed them off. But they kept coming back, no matter how many he crushed. And kept on stinging.

He cracked his eyelids, to find the sun aimed into them and the ground rocky under his back. The late-morning light blazed down through the close, thick leaves of the bush he rested under. The leaves were dark and glossy. The air was hot and still except for the steady hammer of the power plant not far away. He sat up and rubbed his arm across his face.

And gasped. The skin of his cheeks and forehead and jaw itched and flamed, and as he jerked his hand away he saw it, too, was covered with a reddish eruption. He started to scramble up, slammed his head into the previous night's rum specials, and sank back with a moan.

Some minutes later, he crawled slowly out of the underbush, onto the path.

Bahamian children shrieked and pointed but stayed out of his reach. He rested on all fours, head hanging, then forced himself to his feet. Swaying, his stomach making wolflike leaps at his throat, he shambled downhill.

Several older guests were basking on the patio. He caught their startled eyes, nodded stiffly, tasting bile, and went past them to his room.

"Christ! What happened to you? Your face—"

He grunted and shoved past Aydlett into the bathroom. Sucked cold water, as much as he could hold, then raised his head unwillingly. What he saw in the mirror was worse than he'd expected: caked blood, cuts, a bruise like a bad egg on one cheekbone—and worst of all, the rash.

Scrub it down, that was the first thing. He shuddered, turned on the shower, and went to work.

Some time later, the door edged open. "You got you a visitor, Till."

"A what?"

"A visitor. A woman."

"What?" But his partner was gone. Woman, he thought. What woman? He winced as he dabbed his face dry. The little blisters itched like poison ivy. What had they done to him? He wrapped a towel around himself and went out.

She'd seen eighty, and likely ninety, too. She barely reached to his waist, black and desiccated as a currant. She looked like a shrunken shadow in a red dress. Aydlett stood behind her, arms folded, looking amused. "Uh, yes?" Galloway said.

"Somebody on the street say there a white man here be needing some doctoring."

"Uh, could be."

"Bend you down here to me, sonny. Oh yes. It is the poison-wood tree, all right. How you get you face in it, boy?"

"I fell."

"Fell into the one up by the Rooster, didn't you? Seems lots of the rowdy boys, they fall into that one. You go finish you bathe, I will be back with what you need."

• • •

When the doctor woman left, he lay back, feeling blackness slide under his brain like a cold blade. Aydlett made noises as he moved around the room. Then he said, "I'm goin' out, Tiller. You need anything?"

"Scare up some aspirin."

"Them roots ain't working?"

"My face feels great. It's my head's giving me hell."

Aydlett left. Galloway lay in darkness, letting the gumalima paste do its work. It felt cool, like mint on the tongue. He thought about how foolish he'd been the night before. It came back only in flashes: the blonde . . . the honeyed fire of a Goombay Special . . . the last moment he recalled, held from behind by the one they called Wuckie while the other circled in, murder in his eyes. . . .

Got to quit drinking so much, he thought. Cut down a little, things like this wouldn't happen.

When Shad came back, he felt better, felt hungry. He peeled the poultice off, then smeared on a thinner layer, as the old woman had instructed. "You ready for lunch?" Aydlett asked him.

"Sure."

He was glad to get out of the sun again near the dock. The restaurant was tiny but scrupulously clean, with oilcloths on the tables and a choice of fried conch or fried grouper. They were the only customers. They ordered conch and colas, and were hip-deep when the door came open. He glanced up, then stopped chewing, his fork seized in midair.

"Is that you, Galloway?"

Troy Christian's hair was thinner but just as fiery as it had been six years before. Galloway stared at narrow hips in tight white Levi's, at new Reeboks, at a hooded sweatshirt over a polo shirt. The nose was pertly tilted, the eyes the transparent blue of shallow water. He looked thinner, grainier somehow, but he was still as handsome as the picture Galloway had carried in his head through a long cruise and years of prison. Small and fair, that handsomeness had something feminine about it. Tiller thought, they'd have bullied him as a boy, where I come from.

Until the others found out what happened to them, one by one, when they were away from the gang.

"It's me," he said. He put down his fork, very slowly. It was always a good idea to move deliberately around the Baptist's chief enforcer.

Christian looked around the interior. His eyes were expressionless and slightly glassy, like reflective tape. Two men stood in the doorway behind him, their hands in the pockets of their windbreakers. They were both dark, both large, with faces like Aztec idols. He smiled at the waitress; she giggled nervously and backed away, disappeared into the kitchen. "*Espere afuera,*" he said to the others.

When they left, he reversed a chair and sat. A lock of hair fell across his forehead. Up close, Tiller could see crow's-feet.

"It's been a while, Galloway."

"Six years."

"Heard you did time."

"Did it straight. On parole now." He lowered his voice. "Where's the *jefe?*"

"I'm the *jefe*. What happened to your face?"

"Lost an argument with a bush."

The pale eyes examined Aydlett. "Who's this?"

"Business partner from back home. Shad, meet Troy Christian. This is Shadrach Aydlett."

Christian's glance lingered on Aydlett's biceps. Then he sniffed. "What's he doing here?"

"Partnerin' with Galloway. Like he said." Aydlett resumed eating. Through a mouthful of conch, he said, "You work for this Nuñez fella Till used to know, that right?"

Christian didn't answer. The waitress ventured out again. He stared at her till she shrank back into the kitchen, then switched his attention back to Galloway.

"You ready to do some diving?"

"I don't know. I haven't been told much about this job yet."

"You won't like it."

"Then why'd you get me?"

"It wasn't I wanted you. I don't like you, Mr. Lyle Galloway the Third. Never have."

"That reassures me, somehow. In the larger scheme of things."

"Still a wisemouth, too, I see. I don't trust you, either. You take the money but you don't deliver the allegiance. You can't have it both ways."

"Let's talk about my business ethics some other time."

"All right. Let's talk the job. Was it Lax you talked to?"

"That's right."

"He's an honest lawyer. He stays bought. What did he tell you?"

He caught Christian's glance out the window. He looked out, too, to see the back of one of the bodyguards. He felt uneasy that Nuñez wasn't here. Did that mean Christian was in charge? "He said there's a trawler you want salvaged. I assume it's the usual type of cargo."

"That's right."

"And it's been underwater? Then it's worthless." He shrugged.

"I'll be glad to take a look, confirm that for you, but—"

"Don't take us for fools. It was packed in fifty-five-gallon drums. There may be leakage, but most of it should still be there. Still, you're right: The longer it's down, the more we lose. So we need to get to it fast."

"I've never heard of packing drugs that way."

"You're not very creative, Galloway. They were distributed among several hundred similar drums of industrial petrochemicals. With all those stinks aboard, even dogs couldn't have found it during a board-and-search."

"Smart," said Aydlett.

Impressed despite himself, Tiller said, "Yeah, that was a good idea. And in a sealed drum, it might still—but how deep is it? Lax didn't know."

"Three hundred feet," said Christian.

Beside him, Aydlett whistled. Galloway shook his head slowly. He pushed back from the table. "Forget it. Nobody goes there but the Navy and some oil-rig service people."

"What do you mean?"

"I mean it's just too goddamn deep. Compressed air's unsafe past a hundred eighty or so. To go to three hundred—you'd need special equipment. Mixed-gas gear, dry suits, a dedicated boat. And if you're talking working down there for any length of time, that'd be saturation diving. That means a work capsule, a habitat. How many drums are we talking about? Just the one?"

"Fifty-two," said Christian, watching him with his intent, dreamy, gleaming eyes.

He felt his fingers cramp on the edge of the table. "*Fifty-two* fifty-five-gallon drums of coke?" whispered Aydlett.

"That's right."

Somehow, Galloway wasn't as surprised as he thought he ought to be. Even through the shock, he saw how well it fitted. He muttered, "He always thought small shipments were a waste of time. He planned my trips like that. Load gunwale-deep. Distract the honest cops with ten or twelve mules with three ounces apiece. Bribe the dishonest ones, and the top people in the ports. Then ram that load through no matter what.

"But that much—that's got to be marijuana. Still, that would be—"

"You're right about the mules, and the bribes. But we've been out of marijuana for years . . . too bulky, no margin anymore. It's cocaine. All cocaine. One-eighth the annual production of Peru."

"Only you can't bribe the sea," said Aydlett.

"Well put." Christian smiled at him like Columbus at the New World. "They were running without radar—since the Navy's started tracking us by it. There was a fog. They ran into a barge. The crew panicked, and it sank."

There was silence in the restaurant.

Aydlett grunted, breaking it: "And you want us to bring it up?"

Christian looked at him blandly. "That's the idea, my friend. You'll be well paid. I'm sure Lax made that clear. You'll leave here rich. If you succeed, that is."

"Yeah, well, I been hearing a lot of dollar signs, but it's all still kind of vague. How much exactly are we talking, for our cut?"

Christian blinked but didn't reply. It was as if Aydlett hadn't asked a question. Instead, he sniffed again, looking surprised, and took out a handkerchief. He put it carefully to his mouth, and coughed.

Galloway shook himself awake, back from the idea of—three thousand gallons?—of cocaine. "Look. It sounds—challenging. But salvage isn't simple. It never is. Especially that deep. How does the wreck lie? Is the hull steel, fiberglass, wood? What's the bottom like? All I brought was shallow-water gear. Where's the nearest supplier, someplace I can get helium and oxygen? We'd need a diving boat. Cranes, pumps, slings, pontoons, cutting gear, cofferdams, concrete—"

"Look at it first," said Christian from behind the handkerchief. He coughed again, then inspected the result. Finally, he put it away.

"Look at it. *Look* at it?"

"Yes. Today."

"Today? Wait. I told you, we need special gear—"

"Get up," said Christian, getting to his feet. He smiled dreamily down at them. "We're leaving now."

Galloway shoved back his chair and stood. Aydlett said, reaching for his cola, "In a minute. Soon's I finish this."

"Now," said Christian. His little smile sweetened.

He seized the table and straightened, flipped it over. Dishes and silverware flew. A plate hit the window, smashing glass, and disappeared outside. A muffled shriek came from the kitchen, but no one appeared. Aydlett scrambled up, brushing french fries off his thighs, his face darkening. Galloway grabbed his wrist as he started forward.

"He's feisty," said Christian, smiling up at him like a Nazi doctor inspecting a promising specimen. "As well as . . . *very* well put together. Isn't he?"

"You little bastard!"

"Come on, Mister Big Black Man. Hit me. You'll beg me to let you die. Won't he, Tiller? You remember the soldier who hit me once, in the Guajira—"

"Take it easy, Shad!" said Galloway. For a moment, his partner hesitated, still about to charge over the table. He tightened his grip. Then, under his restraining hand, he felt Aydlett relax. He breathed out.

They'd live a little while longer, at least.

Jesus, he thought.

Outside in the street, the swarthy men fell in behind them. Christian led, a few paces ahead. The sun was so brilliant Galloway could hardly see. It gleamed off the red-gold hair.

When he saw the boat waiting, he walked faster, came up beside Christian. "We haven't checked out yet."

"Forget checking out."

"All our luggage is there. Our diving gear, too."

Christian nodded curtly, almost jerkily. He motioned to one of the guards, sent him running back with a few rapid words. He stepped down into the boat, a sparkling white twenty-five-foot Liberator, and said, blinking up at them, "Emilio will get your things. I want to get started, Galloway. We're behind schedule. You'll go down today. Before dark. Go down and look at it. Then we'll talk about how you're going to bring it up."

"Troy, it's not that simple—"

"You said you brought gear."

"We have *scuba* gear. We don't even have anything to breathe."

"Again, give me credit. There's a dive shop in Treasure Cay. I picked up half a dozen tanks for you."

"Yes, but that's *air*, Troy. At three hundred feet—"

"Galloway," said Christian.

Something in his tone made the two remaining bodyguards beside him, by the wheel, stand up under the awning. Their onyx eyes regarded Galloway and Aydlett with emotionless attentiveness. Their hands slid into their jackets. The angular outlines of guns showed under the fabric, pointed at them.

"*Los matamos ahora, Jefe?*" said one. "*O más tarde?*"

Christian said, the hint of a smile curving his lips, "Are you being uncooperative, Tiller?"

"No. No, Troy, I'm not."

"Air is air. No? It may not be what you prefer. It may not be up to OSHA standards. But I'm sure it will do. I got it for you. You'll breathe it."

"Tiller—"

His mouth dry, Galloway said, "Later, Shad. I understand, Troy."

Christian went on as if he hadn't heard either of them. "Don't hold back on me, Galloway. Do you need more warning than that? You've worked with me before. Don't raise these little problems. That's what you're being paid for. To solve them. And don't make me angry. Your friend doesn't know me. I gave him the benefit of one misunderstanding. I can't always guarantee control. Tell him who he's dealing with here."

He hesitated then, his mouth open, eyes blank, as if he'd forgotten what he was going to say next. The bodyguards glanced at each other. Galloway said, "I'll tell him, Troy. I'll straighten him out."

"Tiller, why—"

He hissed desperately, "Shut *up*, Shad! *Please!*"

Christian came back from wherever he'd been. His half smile disappeared. He jerked his head. The bodyguards moved aside as the sailor scrambled fore and aft, cast off, and came back to the wheel.

Beyond the point, riding like a palace amid the schooners and motor yachts, Galloway saw something long and white. He was conscious of Aydlett at his side, a thundercloud about to burst into storm.

What he feared most had come to pass. They were committed. And not under Nuñez's direction. Under Christian's. Under a man who could kill, had killed, women and children, just as a matter of business.

But—major salvage from three hundred feet? It was crazy even to think about it. Not without proper equipment. Not using air.

It was a death sentence.

Sweating, he looked again at the back of Christian's head, the fine golden hair whipping in the hot breeze. Close up, there was gray in it.

Yes, he remembered Troy Christian. But this wasn't the man he remembered. He looked the same physically. Older, finer, worn like a blade whetted too often, but the same.

But the old Christian, dangerous as he was, had never had doubts about controlling himself. This one talked as if he couldn't tell from moment to moment what he would do next. The old Christian would use you till you were useless to him, then kill you. But this one—the shaking hands, the jerky gestures, the thinness that now, up close, looked like emaciation—sounded as if he might kill from pure momentary rage.

But was there a choice?

There was no choice.

Shit, Galloway whispered to himself over the roar of a V-8 454. *Shit.*

Beneath the rash, ants crawled across his face as if he was already dead.

7

Following Christian, he pulled himself up the boarding ladder from where the Liberator rode, its engine rumbling and gargling as the exhaust port slid in and out of the sea.

M/V *Ceteris Paribus* was 140 feet long and so new her sides gleamed like a new car's. Hove to off the inlet, she rode like a rock. Still numb, he followed the Reeboks forward on the main deck. It was hand-rubbed teak, oil-finished so dark and smooth that he could see himself, cuts and all. His face was white, like a Kabuki dancer's. It startled him before he remembered the poultice.

"Captain Roach, Captain Galloway," came Christian's high ironic voice as they stepped over a coaming into the pilothouse.

"At y'service, sir." A round, fiftyish man with blue-veined, stubbled cheeks rolled out of a leather skipper's chair. The hollows in it remained, molded to his body like the pocket of a baseball glove. His hand was hard, a seaman's palm. "Galloway, y'say. You our diver? Been waiting for ye."

Galloway came to suddenly, looking back along the deck. "Where's Shad?"

Christian said, "Your man's below. Pat, the launch will be back shortly with their gear. Then get under way. Don't waste time; we're behind."

"Yes, sir," said Roach to his back, descending the companionway. Looking after Christian, Galloway caught a glimpse of a chestnut and rose carpet with a curious, intricate, almost hypnotic pattern before the door closed.

"Cap'n, your tanks are lashed down along the starboard side. I rigged canvas to keep the sun off them. Understand that's tricky if it overheats."

"That's right." Galloway eyed him. "Do I know you, Captain?"

"Don't think we've met. Where you out of?"

"Carolina."

"Eire, m'self. By way of the New Providence fishing fleet."

"This pays better, I imagine."

"Whiskey's better, too." Roach opened a chart drawer. "You indulge?"

He grimaced. "Thanks, I'll pass for now. You've got quite a . . . craft here."

"She's my beautiful darlin', she is," said Roach quietly. He glanced at a color radar, touched a membrane pad. The scale reached out, and suddenly Galloway saw the islands like a twisted ribbon.

"Where exactly are we going?"

The skipper crossed to a mahogany table. A chart of the Bahamas was taped down on it. Great Abaco swept across it like an arm bent to the left. He laid his finger midway up the forearm. "Green Turtle." Then he slid it northwest, out along a diminishing string of islands, cays, rocks, reefs, the Little Bahama Bank.

"This general area. General, I say; *he* has the coordinates, y'see," Roach grunted. "He punches them into the navigational system alone on the bridge. Kettery makes the last few miles on her own. Then he unplugs the loran. It forgets everything then, you see. So he's the only one who knows exactly what's what. It's somewhere out here, though—off Strangers and Grand."

Galloway bent closer. The chart showed a fingernail of blue off the green of reef, then a plunge to depths that made his flesh creep—250, 400 fathoms. "What was she doing in there?" he said.

"Couldn't tell you. Huggin' the land, looking for radar shadow?" Roach straightened. "There's your effects. We'll be clearin' now. Cabin for ye below, port aft, number twelve. See y'later, Captain."

He stepped out on deck and watched as the launch reapproached. It nuzzled the boarding ladder as the crew off-loaded Shad's and his duffels, then drifted aft, snorting officiously. After a time, winches hummed and it came up, dripping, and swayed down into a keel frame on the afterdeck.

Hoarse shouts in English, Spanish, and brogue floated on the heated air. The yacht gathered way among the other craft. Galloway gazed down on sixty-foot yawls, seventy-foot Bertrams. They looked like toys.

He leaned against varnished teak, looking out over the water.

No sound came from aft, no hammer of diesels, no growl of power, but the whole hull rose suddenly, poising itself like a dancer on the tips of the waves. With wonderful smoothness, the shoreline began scrolling astern. The water turned from lime to azure. The palm-fringed hyphens of the cays slid by on their right. To port, the higher, darker line of Great Abaco stretched ahead for mile on mile, absolutely the same for as far as he could see.

"Señor Galloway?" The accent was on the first syllable.

He turned his head. One of the small men had come up soundlessly behind him. White slacks, canvas boat shoes, kelly Halston top striped with black. He was thin, like Christian, but without the twisted spring that seemed to animate and torture him. His face was a narrow, birdlike structure, and a focused wariness gleamed from eyes dark as frozen tar.

"Good morning. I am Fabio Martín Gonzalo y Moncado."

"Oh, yeah? What do you do aboard, Fabio?"

"Call me Señor Gonzalo. I take care of things for Señor Christian."

Galloway straightened. Feel your way, he thought. He had no idea who this was, but there was no point in making enemies. "That's good. What can I do for you?"

"We will reach Guapi in about five hours. Señor Christian has told me you will be diving then. Is there anything you will need?"

"Uh, the launch. I'll want that in the water as a safety boat."

"I will arrange that with Captain Roach."

"I may have some other requests later. Need to do some figuring. . . . You mentioned a name. Is that the wreck?"

"Guapi. Yes. It's named after a Colombian seacoast town. Very pretty."

"Have you been aboard it? Before it sank?"

"I advise you to ask Señor Christian about that, Señor Galloway."

Who was this? His English was formal, almost too perfect. He "took care of things" for Christian? Galloway saw nothing human, nothing accessible, behind the black avian stare. Those eyes were closed and formal as the granite lid of a tomb.

"See you later, then." He looked around for the hatchway, and
added casually, "Where do you call home, Señor Gonzalo?"

"Coconut Grove."

Cuban, then, not Colombian or Panamanian. Galloway nodded. They eyed each other.

The birdlike eyes blinked first. "Call me if you need anything,
Señor."

"Yeah. Thanks."

His duffel was lying on the bunk in number twelve. It was a
luxurious cabin, but he spared it hardly a glance. He sat, unzipped
the canvas, and pulled out a plastic-bound three-ring binder. The
cover said U.S. Navy Diving Manual.

He studied it for fifteen minutes. He got up once, found a pencil, and did calculations on one of the pages. Then he stared at
the blank screen of the built-in TV, sucking at the eraser.

There was no point considering work at three hundred feet with
air. That was clear. It wasn't clear if they'd die first of the bends,
nitrogen narcosis, or oxygen toxicity, but die they would.

On the other hand, it was just possible to take a quick look. It
would be what the manual called, rather grimly, an "exceptional
exposure" dive. Footnotes warned that he risked paralysis, stroke,
or death, and advised him to have a recompression chamber
nearby. He smiled faintly. Somehow he couldn't see Troy Christian calling in a medevac chopper for him.

But it didn't say outright that you'd die.

His guts felt loose thinking about it.

His alternative was to go to Christian right now and tell him he
wouldn't do it.

It was just a matter of choosing the lesser risk.

He rechecked his calculations. At a descent rate of seventy-five
feet a minute, it would take four minutes to reach the wreck. The
tables allowed him fifteen minutes on the bottom. He'd pay the
penalty in decompression. On the way back up, he'd have to stop
for two minutes at fifty feet, three minutes at forty feet, six minutes at thirty feet, fifteen minutes at twenty feet, and twenty-six
minutes at ten feet. Total decomp time: almost an hour. His air
consumption looked like one set of twin eighties going down and
another at the forty-foot mark. Fortunately he'd brought crossovers
and bands. He could set a line, with markers, and leave the sec-

ond set tied off at the proper depth. He'd rig two singles for Shad. That used up all the tanks Christian had brought.

After he came up, he couldn't dive again for twenty-four hours. If he did, the tables guaranteed he'd regret it.

He thought about it for a while. Then reached for the telephone on the bulkhead.

Pushing buttons at random got him first a Spanish-speaking voice, which he didn't answer, and then Christian's, crackling and hostile. He hung up on that, too. His third try got him Roach. He asked for Gonzalo's number. The captain said he was there, in the pilothouse, and put him on.

Tiller briefed him on the dive plan. The assistant, or purser, or whatever he was, made notes. Galloway felt a little better. Gonzalo seemed to have his shit together. "What about your partner, Señor?" he asked when Galloway was done.

"He'll be safety, lingering at the first stop. Singles will be all right for him. I'll start making the gear up—"

"I will do that for you."

"I'd better, I know how. If you'd—"

"I dive, Señor Galloway."

"You?"

"Not with your experience. But I've been down a few times. In the Yucatán, between business trips. I will rig your tanks for you. Why don't you get some sleep? You don't look so good, if you don't mind my remarks."

"Well—thanks." He thought, but didn't say, that whoever rigged them, he'd still check everything himself.

"Consider it done. It will be four, five hours before we reach the *Guapi*. I will call you before then. I'll let your partner know this, too."

He said "Thanks" again and hung up. He was relaxing back into the bunk when he wondered, Why hadn't this Gonzalo been stuck with the diving?

The only reasons he could think of didn't make him feel very good. That Christian knew it was dangerous, and didn't want to risk his assistant. On the other hand, even a tyro diver would understand why he couldn't do certain things. Gonzalo might be a valuable back channel, a way to influence Christian without arousing what sounded like advanced paranoia.

His duffel lay open beside him. He reached out to it again.

The Polaroid, framed in drugstore plastic, showed Bernie crouched underneath *Miss Anna*'s stern, holding a power sander above her head. Her dirty face was turned toward the camera, piqued at being surprised. He half-smiled as he remembered taking it. Then the smile froze. He cocked it for throwing, glancing toward a trash can in the corner. And stopped.

He stared at her face. She looked young and vulnerable and at the same time tough, Queens tough.

Why had he bothered, last night in the bar? Just because it was over? Just because she'd told him if he went, he didn't have to worry about coming back?

But there was no getting around it, she could be an arrogant bitch. Trying to tell him—

The phone chimed. His hand tried once more for the waste can, then changed its mind and dropped the picture back into his duffel.

It was Aydlett, just off the line with Gonzalo, confirming that he'd be diving safety. He didn't like the idea, wanted to go down all the way. Galloway smoothed his feathers patiently. It took a while, and when he was done he hung up and was almost instantly asleep.

• • •

"Señor Elway."

He sat up instantly, pushing away the face over him, then relaxed. "Sorry," he said. "You startled me."

"You no answer *teléfono*."

"I'm sorry," he said again. He didn't recognize the man. Another crewman. How many did this luxury liner carry? Christian, Roach, Gonzalo, two bodyguards, at least four sailors and deckhands—had to be more in the engine room; he obviously hadn't seen them all.

"You need carry?" said the sailor, indicating his duffel. He shook his head.

When he came on deck, his shadow slanted toward the bow. The sun was dying behind him, maybe two hours of full light left, max. He twisted, looking for the land. They were headed away from it, between two white wastes on either side. Reefs.

The olive crayon smear of a cay away to starboard. As he examined it, the bow came left, paralleling it, but still headed generally east.

He strolled aft, rubbing his chin.

Aydlett was busy on the stern. Gear was scattered across the twenty-foot width of burled teak.

"Ready to go, Shad?"

"Gettin' there." The black man pinged a fingernail off one of the tanks. "Gauge shows thirty-six hundred. Whoever filled these meant business."

"I imagine they had directions." He remembered their last dive. "Did you taste it?"

"Yeah. It's good. You meet Fabio? He's been helping me lay this shit out."

"Yeah, I did. Have you got a line—yeah, good. I want tags tied in at ten, twenty, thirty, forty, fifty—"

They squatted together as the barrier cays fell astern and the sea widened around them. The air was cooler out here. *Ceteris* began to roll. Spray blew up over the bow occasionally. It felt good.

Roach came forward, strolling along with his legs set wide. He had a fisherman's cap on, pushed back, and a wood-tipped Tampa Nugget clamped in his teeth. He glanced over their equipment, raised his eyebrows silently, and perched himself on the capstan head. Glancing past him at the pilothouse, two decks up, Galloway caught a flash of red-gold hair.

Aydlett asked Roach, "We going to anchor?"

"Don't plan to." The Irishman talked around the cigar. His face glowed in the wind. "Just put the launch in, and loiter about while you're down."

Galloway asked him, "How about current? Is there a current out here?"

"None to speak of."

Tiller nodded, looking at Shad. "Uh, Pat—I need a descent line." He held up the end. "I've made one up. Got a hook for this?"

"Sure," said Roach. He got up and went aft.

Suddenly the breeze died, and the roll took on a different period. The yacht coasted forward for a few yards, then swung around slowly to face the declining sun.

"Guess we're here."

"Looks like it."

"Three hundred feet. Damn deep."

"It is." Their eyes met as Aydlett stepped into his suit bottoms. "Uh . . . you want me to safety you, that the idea?"

"Right."

"Where?"

"Fifty feet. No deeper. Hear me?"

"Uh-huh. What's the signal? For me to come down after you?"

"There isn't one." Galloway lowered his voice. "Understand? If anything goes wrong on the bottom, there's no point coming down."

"Screw that, you don't expect me to—"

"I mean it, Shad! If I'm not back in time, I'll be so far over the safe stay we won't have enough air to decompress us both." He examined his weight belt, thought a moment, then slid a two-pound chunk of lead off. "If that happens, it's your choice as to what to do. You haven't done much salvage. I don't think you could do the job alone—or with Gonzalo. But Christian might decide you could. So you might think about, if I don't come up, just heading on ashore."

He glanced landward. Seven miles? Eight? "You heard Roach; no current. Swimming ten feet down, you'll get two hours out of a twin-tank set. That'll get you out of sight. Then ditch everything but your vest and snorkel. The cays are close together; just head south till you hit a village."

Aydlett muttered, "We could do that together. Right now."

"They'd come after me. I don't think they'd come after you, Shad. No offense, but you're not worth it to them."

A three-foot triple hook of gleaming stainless clattered at their feet. "There you go," came Roach's cheery brogue. "We're over her, says the boss. Bend her on, and my boys will make her fast."

• • •

He stood on the boarding ladder, looking down. Two steps below him, and then the sea. Through it wavered the lower two treads, fine figured mahogany. The Atlantic sucked at it with clear lips.

And below them . . . nothing.

He patted himself down. BC and tank pack, checked, twin eighties and lead weights sagging his knees. He'd rigged an octopus, an extra regulator, in case the primary one should jam. That had happened to him last year inside a wreck. It hadn't been a good feeling. It would be cold at three hundred feet. A dry suit would be best, but he didn't have one. Instead, he was wearing cotton pants and shirt under the wet suit, two pair of socks under his booties, and a wool cap borrowed from one of the deckhands under his hood. He didn't have a light, either. That was something else he'd miss, that deep.

Panting under the weight and heat, he waddled down another step.

Mask: He pulled it down and adjusted it. The sea, the sky, the side of the ship contracted to a rubber-ringed oval.

Regulator: He tucked it into his mouth and sucked the first breath. Cool, dry, and sweet. He hit the low-pressure valve and air crackled into his vest.

He took another step down, and coolness seeped into his booties.

"Get a move on." The voice was high and impatient. "You hear me through all that crap? Get in there! We can't hang around all day waiting for you to get used to the water."

Laughter followed, and Galloway looked up. Blond and slim, Christian leaned over the life rail. Behind him, the bodyguards lounged against the bulkhead, their faces as alert and yet remote as ever. He'd not seen Christian yet without them. They didn't bother to conceal their weapons at sea.

His eyes went back to the boss. One hand had gone around one of the sailor's waists. A youth, little more than a boy. His face, turned away, was scared and shy.

As if hearing his thoughts, or seeing them in his upturned eyes, Christian leaned forward even more. He coughed delicately into his fist. Then he spat. It drifted down and landed a few feet forward of the boarding ladder, on the blue clean sea. Their eyes met. And Christian smiled.

Galloway took one more step, and fell into the deep.

• • •

He fell with arms flung wide, like a suicide—but only at first. He came to a stop ten feet down, and bobbed up again. His face burned with salt sting. But he kept his mask in the water as he swam forward, looking around for the descent line.

It came into view off the stern, stretching down, taut as a mast shroud. Good, as long as it didn't break. He finned toward it, trying to relax. God, he was tense. Shivering already as the sea filled his suit. Below him was only blue, a cheerful, luminous hue like the bottom of a suburban pool. How clear the sea was! Seventy feet away, he could see the launch's slowly spinning prop with perfect clarity.

He reached the line. The braided polypropylene was smooth under his glove. He clung to it for a moment, turning his mask from side to side.

Aydlett hit the water with a crash. He stabilized, windmilled back to the boarding ladder amid shoals of mercury-coated bubbles, and attached himself to it, holding to the lowest step.

Galloway's wrist came up and turned toward him. 6:10 P.M. He set the outer bezel to zero. He took a deep breath, blew it out, purging his lungs.

Time to go, he told himself. We know you don't want to do this. But you got to. Christian's right. No point putting it off.

He ducked his head, bowing to the sea, and went on over. His flippers pointed gracefully upward, exposed to those who watched, and the weight of his legs drove him under.

He was light, would be till he was deep, and so he kicked strongly down the line. It stretched down into a hazy blue. The air forced itself from his regulator into his lungs. That was normal when your head was lower than your body. It made him feel like a balloon being blown up by a child. He worked his jaws, and his ears equalized with a metallic snap.

Ten feet. He passed a flutter of cloth braided into the line. Twenty. The sea leaned again. This time he had to hold his nose through the mask and blow.

Forty feet. He didn't have to swim as hard now. He turned his head as he sank, and caught, over his shoulder, the incredible beautiful brightness of the surface. Already it looked distant. Against it, the black outline of a man was swimming toward the descent line. Then, as he stared yearningly upward, bubbles blotted him out.

Three hundred feet down, Galloway thought, turning his gaze downward again. He felt motionless, as if he was floating, but the yellow rope zipped steadily between his gloved fingers. Fifty fathoms, a hundred yards—no problem to hit a golf ball that far. You could run it in fifteen, twenty seconds. It wasn't far, on the surface.

But when it meant three hundred feet of water above you, that translated into ten atmospheres of pressure. . . . Something like 150 pounds per square inch. Or, for a man his size—he multiplied it out in his head—the equivalent of 108 pickup trucks pressing in on his body.

The only reason he wouldn't be crushed would be that the air in his lungs, sinuses, and ears would match that pressure as he sank, adjusted automatically by the regulator.

A scarlet flutter slid upward toward him, through his glove, and was gone. Fifty feet.

Pressure had other effects, too. The human body was mostly water. And like water, the higher the pressure of a gas in contact with it, the more would dissolve. Air was a mix of nitrogen and oxygen. Pressurized nitrogen was an intoxicant. And beyond a certain critical pressure, oxygen itself became a poison.

That critical pressure, with compressed air, was three hundred feet.

Falling, he was surrounded by green.

One hundred feet. A blue the color of an old Vicks bottle.

The bends were a separate problem. Once the nitrogen dissolved, he was locked at that pressure. If he came up too fast, his blood would fizz like an uncapped beer, and for the same reason: decreased pressure on a saturated solution. He'd have to come up slow, let the gas come out gradually and be exhaled.

But he couldn't stay down too long, or he'd run out of air to breathe.

The tied-on markers were long past now. He glanced at his depth gauge, strapped to his left wrist along with his watch. One hundred and fifty feet. Halfway there. The blue was fading into gray.

He remembered the last time he'd gone this deep. Diving on

the sunken U-boat the year before. With Shad, Bernie, his cousin Jack, and the Californian who'd called himself Richard Keyes. That had been at 180 feet. It had just been possible to work for short periods, with close attention to stay time and long periods of rest topside. There was an old saw called the "martini rule": Every thirty feet on air equaled one cocktail. At 180, inside the submarine, he'd barely been able to scrawl words on a slate.

But at three hundred . . . he had no idea what would be happening in his head a few minutes from now.

Two hundred feet. A twilight world. He checked his watch again: 6:13:15. A little slow on the descent, but he was going down faster now, dropping like a sky diver in free-fall, with the sea a cold wind in his face.

His breath squeezed in and out. Bubbles roared in his ears.

Two hundred and fifty.

Below, in the dark, he saw a shape.

Command to hand: close. His glove tightened. The line whined, slowing his descent. He was heavy, too heavy. His left hand found the inflator. He cut it off reluctantly. He wanted to bleed more in, till he started to rise. He'd made it down. Now he wanted to go back up.

You're too deep, every instinct he had been born with told him. Too deep, every lesson he'd learned in twenty years of diving told him. Too deep, Tiller. Way too deep.

His body told him, I'm afraid. He swallowed with a dry throat. Join the club, said his mind. I'm afraid, too.

He stared down, his eyes widening.

The ship lay on its side in near darkness on a rough sand bottom. Ropes reached upward from it, a weird reversal of gravity. He was sliding down a thread that ended at its stern. The water was so clear that he could see it all, though the bow was very dim, very shadowy; a mast forward, a shorter one aft on the little superstructure. Actually, it wasn't very large. It was no larger than the yacht he'd just left, though the swell of its hull was deeper, giving a capacious hold.

More air in his vest. He looked at his watch. So dark he could barely read it. If only he'd packed a dive light back in Buxton. But how could he have known?

He started to curse his stupidity. Then thought coldly: No.

You don't have long. This is very dangerous now. Don't curse.
Just do it.

Steel gleamed suddenly. The grapnel. Sharp points. Avoid.

He opened his hand. The line vibrated dully as he let go. The
air he breathed was dense, viscous, icy, and he had to labor to
pull it through the hose and regulator. Taking a deep lungful, he
swam slowly forward.

Time: 6:15:09.

Very dark, very cold. He knew any physical sensation of pressure
was an illusion, but his unconscious told him otherwise.

He felt as if he was buried already.

He passed the open door of the pilothouse. It opened like a
well. Black inside. Movement inside: fish. Immaterial. Go on.

Curve of rusty steel. Over it, and down. Down a near-
vertical wall. Rusty, rough. The forward deck, forward of the
pilothouse.

Hatch Cover, his mind said in slow, capitalized words. He
forced himself to slow his breathing. He was using air ten times
faster here than at the surface. Stop swimming. Coast. Very slow.
Push your glove into the cover—

Steel. Feels solid.

Should try to get inside somehow. Do internal survey. See
about these drums.

But got no light. Internal survey very dangerous. At three hundred feet? Don't want to do it.

Scared?

Super diver not supposed to be scared.

Go on, he told himself patiently, as if talking to a stupid but
obedient dog. Look at the rest of it.

He swam forward, dread like a lead core inside a fuzzy coating
of nitrogen gaiety.

Another hold. Hatch cover cracked. Busted during the descent,
the long tumble to the seafloor. Through the crack: implacable
blackness. Fear stirred in him again, then sank back. What was
he so afraid of?

Holding the edge of the coaming, he poked his head and upper
body down through the split, into the dark.

Gradually, he made out a jumbled mass. Drums. They lay in
a tumbled heap to starboard, on the down side. There was a

strange texture to the water around his inserted head, as if something heavier was mixed with it. At the same moment, a taste seeped around the edges of his mouthpiece. A faint, strange pungency he couldn't identify.

He withdrew slowly, like a hermit crab sensing something unpleasant. Considered for a moment, and then swam on.

Over the mast. It lay almost horizontal, still erect, braced by pipe work. He expected booms but didn't see any. Past that, still proceeding forward.

He found himself in a cave. Absolute black. He felt around slowly with outstretched hands. A sort of cuddy, formed by the high bow, partially decked over. He backed out clumsily, hesitated for a moment, and then swam over it and continued forward.

The ship ended. At the bow, atop the raised forecastle, were the remains of chicken wire and battens: a cage. Pigs, chickens, most likely. Dopers often sailed with fresh meat aboard. He swam over them, looking for a bow chock or bullnose. There: a heavy-duty set of bitts and closed fairleads. The gunwale bars and stringer plates looked solid.

At the bow itself, he slowed and let himself drop, following the curve of what was now the underside of the wreck.

Blacker gaps in the starboard bow, below the sheer strake. The shell plating was pierced in one, two, three places. He moved in, glancing at his watch. Big hand between three and four. Not sure exactly what time it was, but he couldn't stay much longer. He ran his glove lightly around the holes, then measured the largest one, using his forearm, elbow to fingertip. The biggest was one forearm and one hand width. Nineteen inches and four inches. That was . . . he couldn't remember how to add nineteen and four.

Other dimension . . . Who cared? Big helluva sumbitch. He gazed into it blankly.

Funny pattern on that carpet, back on the boat. Or had he dreamed that? How did he know this wasn't a dream, right now? Be funny to wake up and find himself someplace else. He smiled around his mouthpiece.

Funny hole, too. He'd seen them like that before. Wasn't no barge made that. This was from a shell, or rocket. Like the RPG-7s the VC had used. They opened up the plating on armored personnel carriers just like this.

He started to go inside, felt an edge dig into his arm, and hesitated. Wise? Not wise. He backed out. The metal cut him on the way, but it didn't hurt.

Invulnerable, he thought, and giggled.

Ought to go on aft, look at the screw. Screw? Odd name for a propeller. He kicked slowly along the keel. What color in light? No way to tell. Next time, bring flashlight. No, no way coming down here again.

Oh, why not. Not so bad down here. Kind of cold. Made you feel sleepy. Be nice to take a nap. Drift of silt under keel. Looked soft. Nap? Well, maybe just a short one.

He blinked drowsily, settling to the bottom. The silt swirled up, covering him with powdered blackness. He nestled against the curve of the hull like a cat, yawning around his mouthpiece. It bothered him and he pushed it around with his tongue. Need this? Might not need it. God, it was cold. A quick forty winks, then finish up.

He closed his eyes, and the sea drew its blanket over him.

• • •

He was lying in his bunk, and the bell was ringing.

The bell. Every morning at 6:30, it started echoing off the pale puce concrete of the interior of Block 5.

Then, somehow, he was out of his cell. He stared down at the carpet. It was brown, with a complex, enigmatic patterning. A labyrinth. Funny, he didn't remember a carpet here. Here, in the in-processing room of Central Prison, Raleigh, North Carolina.

"Galloway. We been looking for you to come back."

Always Benton, the one they called the Juice Man. The warden's sly smile and his rumpled, wrinkled suits, his brown shoes.

He looked slowly around. They were there with him, slumped against the wall, or leaning their chairs back against it. Danny. Oliver. Jim. Their eyes were empty. Danny was smoking, his heavy-lidded eyes almost closed as he winked at Galloway.

He said, "I'm dreaming."

"Thass right, Till," said Oliver. "You dreaming. Right, boys?"

"We-all felt that way, too, first couple days back," said Danny.

"'Cept those of us who was innocent," said someone else, a black man with a peanut-shaped head. What was his name? He should remember. He'd bunked with him once. There at Central.

He was back in that concrete hive of men, in that concrete tomb. Back in the close, low corridors, a whole sealed universe of shabby green tile and barf-green walls and too-often-breathed air pressurized by fear and boredom and rage. Benton's way of running a prison was divide and conquer. The blacks hated the whites, who hated the Italians, who hated them all. The guards versus the civilian staff, the cops versus the administration.

But it couldn't be true. "I'm dreaming," he said again, looking down at the impenetrable crazy pattern. Funny, he didn't remember a rug here.

"You're dreaming, all right," said the Juice Man. He came closer and closer, till his breath stank in his face. "Welcome back . . . Mr. Galloway. For a little while, at least."

"What do you mean, Benton?"

"You call me Warden in here, you two-bit druggie asswipe. I mean we're going to hang you this time, Galloway."

It was true. He could feel the noose tightening around his throat.

He would have screamed, but there was something in his mouth. He clawed for it blindly, trying to get it free so he could breathe.

"You're dreaming," said Benton.

And Danny said, "You better wake up."

• • •

He shuddered and opened his eyes, suddenly filled with an anesthetized panic, a cold, slow-motion, reptilian terror that was at the same time remote, muffled, wrapped in the nitrogen elation. His hand hesitated, then stopped tugging at the regulator. He thought about this, slowly, and then, slowly, took his hand away.

He smiled. Lying down on the seabed, he thought. Napping with the fish. Not a good idea, Till.

Anyway, it would be more comfortable in a bunk, topside. He yawned around the mouthpiece, adjusted it so that it bit more comfortably, and swam upward. He was lighter now; less air in the tanks. His body had a slight tendency to rise.

Ought just to take one more look. . . . He groped aft along the sheer strake. Freeing ports were square black absences. He tugged at each absently as he went by. Good places to attach lifts, if they were solid. He came over the pilothouse again. His eyes went to his watch, but he couldn't read it. He couldn't see the hands and he didn't remember how. Or why.

The door was open below him, and without thinking he swam in. A shadowy stir surrounded him. No flash of light this deep, only the noiseless nervous churn of fins and bodies. Grunts of some kind, but he couldn't make them out very well. Five, six inches long. They gave way slowly in front of him, making short darts as if to escape. But there was nowhere for them to go. He pressed on. Toward a darker clump ahead, a black, solid, wriggling mass. He put out his gloved hand slowly, giggling.

The fish parted slowly, their wavering fins like the curtains of a theater, and he saw what they had been eating.

The flesh of the face was almost gone, and pale bone glowed. The eyes were gone, gnawed to the depths of their sockets, and black hollows stared up at him. A small eel protruded from the open jaws, swayed back and forth in the black current, its mouth gaping, then darted inside again.

He stared down at the skull in creaking silence. Bubbles howled in his ears.

His right hand fumbled at his BC. The pocket unsnapped with a click. He groped with numb fingers.

He extended the spare regulator, jammed the mouthpiece between the open, faintly shining teeth, and mashed the purge button.

The blast of air burst the fragile bone apart, exploded it. The last memory he had was scraping the back of his hand across his face, wiping away something that clung, that was cold, that moved, but that was not alive.

Then the black black came up again, like a soundless murk rising from the abyssal depths, covering all light, blotting out all thought, till he fell in a thoughtless scream forever and ever and ever ten thousand miles deep into a midnight that had no end.

• • •

He suddenly came out of the blackout with his hand on the ascent line. He couldn't remember where he was or how he had gotten there. Or even who he was. He shook his head violently,

sucking air past a rigid, guarding tongue. His head throbbed as if
it had been blown apart and wired back together. Christ, he
thought. Have I been drinking? Have I been sick?

He remembered a little then. A hint, as if his brain was teasing
him. Troy Christian, it said. Bahamas.

Shit, he thought, furiously and fearfully. Shit!

He realized now why his chest hurt. He had to suck harder for
each breath. His regulator wheezed, and he dragged at it. Almost
dry . . . one more reluctant breath . . . dry.

He was out of air.

Meanwhile, he was finning hard upward along the yellow line.
He could tell it was yellow. Had to be above a hundred feet, then.
Sea-deep blue around him. A little more knowledge seeped back.
He swam harder, locking his teeth against his growing lust for air.
What time? Didn't matter. Without air, it didn't matter how
loaded he was with nitrogen.

A golden glow above him, and a human figure. With immense
relief, he recognized Shad Aydlett. And recognized, tied off beside
him, the silhouette of a fresh set of twin tanks.

He came up the line with a rush, ignoring Aydlett's extended
arm, straight to the dangling regulator. He spat out the dead one,
thrust the fresh one into his mouth, blew out, sucked in.

Air, fresh and sweet, copious, cool, charged like lightning into
his bloodstream. He closed his eyes in bliss, shuddering, drinking
it in like a baby at a teat. Gradually the fog in his head cleared.
It was like coming back to life.

After several minutes, he opened his eyes and swung his wrist
up. Blinked and focused on the minute hand.

His throat closed in disbelief and horror.

He'd overstayed. Had been down for half an hour, with a bottom time of twenty-two minutes. Seven minutes more than he'd
been allowed. Not that many minutes, but another 50 percent
exposure.

He hung in the blue sea, sucking air, invaded by a growing
fear. How far beyond the tables had he gone? What would happen
now? The rash and itch of bends? Sudden, crippling pain? Con-
vulsions? His skin prickled beneath the suit. Was that the first sign
of it now?

He had another hour to wait before he would know for sure.

8

The water blasted down into his face, cool, fresh, scented. He didn't know why, but from the instant the sailors had pulled him out of the sea, he'd lusted for a shower like a blind man for light.

Turning it to warm—he wanted to go scalding, but heat was a contributing factor to decompression sickness—he remembered that moment of provisional resurrection. He'd sat on the afterdeck, shuddering with cold and the bone-deep nitrogen fatigue, staring into the scarlet glow in the west as Aydlett and Gonzalo stripped off his gear, wet suit, and the soaked clothes underneath. When he was naked, he'd flexed his arms slowly, waiting for the stabbing agony of the bends.

Someone had leaned in then, a black shadow between him and clouds like cotton wool soaked in blood.

"Did you see it?" Christian had snapped. "Is it down there?"

His jaws hurt. They wanted to stay clamped. He mumbled, "That's it, all right."

And he'd seen the dawning want in the pale blue eyes, and known suddenly that at last he had, not the whip hand, but at least a little leverage.

So when Christian pushed past the handlers and began barking more questions, he'd said quietly, "In a few minutes. Okay? I'm going to hose down and find dry clothes. Then we'll talk."

And the *jefe* had stopped, his face going first blank and then flushing a little on the cheekbones. Then he'd smiled. "Sure. Fabito, get him whatever he wants. We'll get together in an hour, in the main salon. That sound all right, Tiller?"

Galloway had muttered, looking down at the pale, wet, deadlooking skin of his feet, "That sounds great . . . Troy."

He nudged the tap a tad warmer. No goddamn Coast Guard showers, thirty seconds warm and then ice-cold, aboard this floating palace. He could have done without the perfume, but it seemed to come with the water, or anyway he couldn't figure out how to shut it off. He felt clean now. Odd, how that taste lingered on his tongue.

He shut off the stream and blinked in the humid air. He sucked in his breath, then did a deep knee bend. No pain yet. No numbness, except a tingle in his toes.

Maybe he was lucky. This time.

He noticed what the stall was made of, and tapped it with his fingernail. Black marble. He ran his hands through his hair—it squeaked—and went out into the cabin. A new white terry robe lay on his bed. On his nightstand were a fifth of Rebel Yell, a glass, and an ice bucket.

He decided a little stimulant wouldn't be out of place.

When he opened the door, he looked into the barrel of an Uzi. One of the Indians had it slung over his shoulder, pointed at him. He halted, then went on, feeling less comfortable, in the direction of the jerked gun. At the end of the corridor, he tried a left. The guard hissed. He turned right, found a stairway, and shuffled up it.

He limped slowly down a grand foyer lined with mirrors and red-orange neon tubes and into the main salon.

"Hail, the intrepid hero," said Christian, glancing up as he was ushered in. He stopped, shivering in the chill of air conditioning, looking around.

He'd never seen a room like this before at sea, and damn few ashore. An E-shaped divan in pale lavender with a blue papyrus pattern extended from beam to beam. Burnished lacquer paneling veined with gold set off pale silk curtains. Sliding glass doors, closed now, led to the afterdeck and pool. Colored lights flickered under the water. Beyond that were the upper works of the hoisted-in launch, herself nearly as large as *Miss Anna*. A fully stocked bar stood against the far bulkhead. The remaining wall was covered by a huge mural of Neptune emerging from the waves in his chariot, accompanied by bare-breasted mermaids. No, not a mural, a mosaic, rather crudely done. The tiny hand-set cubes glittered in the accent lighting. A glass case held corroded-looking weapons, antique swords, a spear. The windows were black; it was full night at last.

"Like it? Make me an offer."

Christian and Gonzalo were sitting at a thick glass table set off centerline. Aydlett was hunched on the banquette. The enforcer went on: "Don't stand there like an orphan in the snow, Tiller. Sit down. We'll have some refreshments in a moment."

He sounded expansive and triumphant. Galloway felt danger like a sheet of cold air. He knotted the robe tighter. The carpet caught his glance again, a complex and seductive pattern. He jerked his eyes up and selected a low chair. The gunman moved to his left, where he'd have a clear shot at both him and Shad.

Christian leaned back and called something in Spanish. A voice replied from the galley, and a moment later sailors came in. They arranged silver and crystal, then stood rigid, watching the *jefe*. He flicked his fingertips impatiently and they left, stepping on each other's heels in their anxiety to be gone.

"Help yourself, Tiller; uh, Shadrach," he said, indicating the table.

Galloway ran his eyes over it. More Rebel Yell, as well as scotch, rum, and vodka. No bar brands here. Mangoes, guavas, husked coconut, sugar bananas, grapefruit, limes in crystal bowls. In another, a huge silver one, powdered sugar for the grapefruit—

No. His heart suddenly speeded up.

It wasn't powdered sugar.

"Wine?" said Christian, lifting a long bottle from a salver. "Lafite-Rothschild, the last of the forty-nine."

He swallowed. Suddenly, his palms were wet, and his mouth was filled with saliva. He made himself look away from the coke. "I'll stick with bourbon, thanks. Maybe try some of that coconut."

"You'll like it, it's fresh. Shadrach? Love that name, by the way."

Shad grunted and accepted a wineglass. It looked threatened in his huge hand. He sipped at it, made a face, and put it carefully back on the table.

When Galloway looked back at Christian, the slim man was loading a delicately curved glass pipe. He glanced to the side, and Gonzalo leaned forward, his hand coming out of his pocket.

A butane lighter clicked. The hiss filled the room. Christian relaxed his eyelids, and inhaled.

Flame touched whiteness, and a faint blue fire danced.

Christian's eyes suddenly bulged open, glaring in horror or ecstasy at nothing. His lips went white as ice, bit shut on the hot gas.

When the Cuban leaned back, the bowl was filled with a crisp black ash. His master sat with his mouth open, eyes protruding. A gleam of saliva drooled down. Then, suddenly and violently, he began coughing, doubling forward over the table.

Gonzalo stared expressionlessly at them across his boss's heaving back.

When he recovered his breath, Christian patted his lips with the handkerchief, then wiped his eyes. His face was bathed with sweat, like an ice sculpture melting in the sun. He nodded at the bowl. "As I recall, you didn't mind a line now and then, Galloway. That's ENACO, pharmaceutical quality. Feel free. You've earned it."

Galloway felt sweat slide down his back. How many nights had he lain awake in Raleigh fantasizing just this? Face-to-face with a kilo of cocaine hydrochloride. He'd have to be careful; this wouldn't be cut at all. Only a short line. He blotted his trembling hands against his thighs. That was all he wanted.

For now.

But then he'd need more.

He wanted it. Wanted what he remembered so well: the sudden blaze of elation and power, like the best ten orgasms of your life lap-wrapped with lightning and jammed from your chest up into some ready-made socket in your brain. So good your breath stopped, and your heart, and you didn't care whether they started again or not. He wanted it so desperately that his legs began to shake.

But he'd stopped *needing* it in prison. Danny had helped him. And he hadn't started again when he came out.

So he still had a choice. Yes or no.

But if he said yes, even once, there'd be no more choices after that. He knew himself well enough for that. It would be yes, and yes, and yes.

And he'd be dependent on Troy Christian, or someone like him, forever.

Through bruised, frozen lips he said, "Uh, I'll stay with the bourbon for now, Troy. But . . . thanks."

"Turning it down?"

"That's right."

For a moment, he read surprise in the blue eyes. Surprise and suspicion. But then the *jefe* was turning his head. "Mr. Aydlett? How about you?"

"I never had any of that," said Shad, looking into the bowl. He reached out tentatively, then caught Galloway's warning glance.

His hand hovered, almost touching the silver straw, then dropped. "No thanks," he said, a shade reluctantly.

Christian seemed to withdraw his attention. His eyes looked sleepy, perhaps a trifle sullen. He wiped his nose again and tossed the handkerchief to Gonzalo. Then he seized the wine and drank it off thirstily. "All right. Let's do business. What have we got, Galloway?"

"She's down there. Three hundred feet, sloping sand bottom, with a forty-degree list to starboard."

"What kind of shape?"

"Overall, the hull looks sound. There are solid lifting points at the bow, stern, and at least three points along each beam."

Christian nodded. He glanced at the pipe again, and tapped his thumbs together. "Were you able to get inside? Could you see the cargo?"

Tiller began describing it. He'd organized what was essentially his survey report in the shower. Except for the period of blackout, he could see it all clearly. It was a learned skill, like taking video-tapes with your memory. He told about the two hatch covers, one intact, the other cracked. He told how he'd been able to peer into the hold, and mentioned the taste he'd noticed.

"Those are the chemicals," said the Cuban. "In the drums. Ether, sulfuric acid, acetone, hydrochloric acid, ammonia. Some of them must have broken. That is no doubt what you tasted."

"Acid? If that's leaking, you'll have corroded drums, weakened containers."

Christian said, "Those are details. All you have to do is bring up the cocaine."

Galloway took a deep breath. He said levelly, "I'd rather raise the whole ship."

After a moment, Christian said, "Please explain."

"Could I have—do you have some paper, a pen? And a calculator? That would help."

Christian called into the other room. A sailor came running with a steno pad and a ballpoint. Gonzalo shoved a credit card-sized calculator across the table.

Galloway flipped the pad open and leafed past columned figures to a blank page. He poised the pen, then hesitated. "It might be good to have Captain Roach here, too."

Christian didn't answer, just reached under the table. There was no sound, but a few minutes later a side door came open and the Irishman rolled in.

"All right, Tiller, you have the floor."

He cleared his throat. "Okay! The trouble is all this loose cargo. It's dangerous working inside a wreck . . . time-consuming. And we'll be knocking these drums around getting them to the surface. If they've been rusted or corroded, we'll lose some. Plus, there's the drawback of working in an acid environment, and the whole business of getting in past those hatch covers. That's why I think raising her makes more sense."

He glanced at Christian, but the other only stared at him over his tented fingers. So he went on. "Assuming that's agreeable, the next question is how. There's only four ways to get a sunken hull to the surface. Pumping it, floating it up with bags or cans, raising it with internal air pockets, or lifting it by main strength—cables, cranes, and winches."

"D'ye really think you can pump it out? Even when it's already underwater?"

"In shallow water, it'd be the simplest way, Pat. Seal the hull, run a line down, and an air hose to replace the water you take out. But not this deep. It would crush the hull like a tube of toothpaste. It's got to be one of the others."

He hesitated, tapping the pen on the still-blank page. "Uh, Troy, Fabio, you don't have any figures at all? Length or anything?"

"No."

"And neither of you've been aboard it, or seen it before?"

They both hesitated, glancing at each other, then shook their heads.

He wondered about that briefly, then went on. "Well, a working estimate: I figure it at about a hundred feet by say twenty-two beam. And that looked like about an eight-foot waterline." He punched the calculator. "Assume a block coefficient of seven, thirty-five cubic feet to a ton of water, that's . . . three hundred and fifty tons." He looked at Roach.

"For a trawler? Sounds about right."

"That rules out a straight lift. We'd need shipyard cranes, a couple of them. That leaves external floats, pontoons, or else putting a bubble in her."

"Like we did with that Huckins," said Aydlett.

"Yeah, that's right, Shad." He explained to Christian and Gonzalo. "We did a job down in Morehead City not too long ago. Fishing boat broke a water hose and went down one night. She landed upside down in sixty feet. We went down, hammered plugs into the intakes, then got under her and vented a couple of tanks up into her. She came up like a porpoise. We towed it to shallow water at high tide, rolled it over, and let it sink again, right side up. Then put a pump aboard, dewatered it, and towed it in to the boat yard."

Roach said, "Can't do that here, surely?"

"No. First off, it's a lot deeper. And the hatches worry me. That, and the holes in the bow."

"Holes?" said Christian.

"There's three of them. About eighteen inches across, the largest." Something nagged at his mind, something about the holes, but it was lost in the fuzzy black glow that surrounded the latter part of the dive. "We'd have to patch those. Actually, we could lift it either way, keel up or keel down. Keel up—" He began sketching, shaping a tubby hull. "Let's say we want to bring her up capsized. First, we blow off the masts. Then make a cable fast to the port side and parbuckle her over."

"Parbuckle?" said Gonzalo. "Is this English?"

"Seagoing English. Means, roll her the rest of the way over. Do that either by towing, or else with beach gear, compounded with a tackle. I'll have to do some calculations on that. So now she's upside down." He sketched quickly. "We patch the holes. Then blow in compressed air . . ."

"What about the cargo? All them loose drums? Upside down, they'll fall, won't they? And smash all to hell."

"Damn. You're right, Shad. Thanks." Galloway stared at the paper, then ripped it out and crumpled it. It bounced on the carpet and came to rest at the feet of the Indian with the submachine gun.

"So, it's keel down. Let's start from where she lies. We patch the hull, find any fuel tanks or compartments that will hold air, and fill them. Then trim her up. No need to blow off the masts now. This time we parbuckle to port. Now she's upright.

"Now we attach pontoons or lift bags to the freeing ports, or anyplace else we find an attachment." He sketched it from the side. "Last, we drop lines or chains from barges, or boats, at low tide.

"Now it's lift day. As the tide rises, we fill the last bags with air. Finally, we blow air or play hoses under the keel, to break the suction of the mud. The cables from above add their pull. Bingo! She breaks free and comes up, but only about ten feet off the bottom."

"Why?" said Christian.

"Because we calculated it that way. Air expands as it rises. If we make it too buoyant, it'll shoot up like a goddamn Trident missile. It'll explode the lifts, slam into the boats topside, just raise holy Ned. Slow's better."

"Then what?"

"We move her toward shore. Slow and easy, a lift and move every twelve hours. When we're in shallow water, thirty feet or so, we ground her and start pulling the drums out. I can train your sailors for shallow work. It'll go fast with six, eight guys down there. The cargo—well, you'll have to have another ship here by then, or however you're going to take them north after that."

"Why not bring it all the way up?" said Gonzalo.

"I thought you wanted not to be seen. If the wreck stays underwater, it'll be pretty effectively hidden."

Christian slammed his hand down on the glass, shaking the bottles. The others jumped. "No! Ten feet every twelve hours, that's two weeks! It has to come up in one day. Understand? You're making this too complicated, Galloway. I'll tell you how to do it. Ping-Pong balls! Fill it with them. Then bring it all the way to the surface. We'll do it at night, unload before dawn, and when it's empty let it sink again. That'll hide it, all right."

Galloway sat silent, rolling the shot glass in his fingers. In a way, it was like every planning conference he'd ever been to. When you talked salvage, everybody was an instant expert.

At last he said, "Sure, Troy. You're right. Not about the Ping-Pong balls. They crush flat fifteen feet down. But two weeks, that's too long. I wasn't thinking.

"But not all the way in one blow, it's too goddamned easy to lose it that way."

He paused, taking a reading of Christian's face, then went on. "How about this: We combine internal flotation, tide hoist, and crane lift. First, we'll use the tide to break it free. Then, when it's clear of the bottom, hanging there, we'll go down again and add enough additional flotation so we can hoist it. That gives us control of how fast it rises. That'll get it to the surface in maybe a day, two days from the time we start hoisting, if all goes well. How's that sound to you, Captain? Señor Gonzalo, you're a diver, that sound practical?"

Roach and Gonzalo both nodded. He looked at Christian, waiting. After a moment, he nodded, too, and leaned forward to load the pipe again.

Galloway breathed out, feeling ants crawling down his ribs. It was worse than handling explosives. He wasn't cut out for this diplomatic shit.

"All right, that's plan A. Now let's discuss what we'll need. Number one, a lift vessel—"

"Gunwater has a barge, with a crane on it," said Roach.

"Who?"

"Gunwater Boat Yard, on Pass Cay. I know the owner. He uses it for draglining channels, but it'll give you a couple tons."

"It'll give us more than that with a set of threefold blocks. Okay, we'll break it out with the tide, then use the crane to—"

"No," said Christian around the glass stem.

They waited, listening to the hiss of flame, the tiny sucking sounds.

When he lowered the pipe again, his face was beaded with sweat. He blinked five or six times and licked his lips.

"No cranes," he said.

Galloway said patiently, "The cranes are necessary to get lift."

"I said, no *cranes!* They're too big, too *yellow*, they'll attract *attention!* Or is that the idea, Galloway? To get the DEA, the Coast Guard interested? Is *that* your plan?"

He paused, and his ragged breathing was the only sound that lived in the huge cold saloon. No one else said anything or moved. The man with the gun watched them all. Outside the windows, the night was dead black.

"You'll raise that cargo with the gear you have aboard now. Nothing else."

"That's impossible."

"All right, Galloway. You've just—"

"Wait. Wait, Troy." He tried to swallow but found it hard without spit. He had no doubt that the man whose slitted eyes glared into his was capable of ordering them taken out on the stern and shot. Was about to do it. And there was absolutely nothing to stop or even inhibit him.

All he could do was try to buy them a little more time.

"Okay, no crane." He cleared his throat, looked down at, and then away from, the carpet. "No crane. Just the barge. Can we use the barge?"

"What color is it?"

"Sort of a rust color," said Roach. "Think it was black once, but now it's a sort of a rusty brown."

"That's all right, then. The barge is all right."

Galloway nodded, not trusting himself to speak. Anger was growing beneath the fear. He looked across at Aydlett, and saw it in his eyes, too.

But aloud, he said only, "That's good. But we *do* need more equipment, Troy. Lifting a ship, heavy salvage, it's not like bringing up an outboard motor somebody dropped. You understand that."

"I have confidence in you, Tiller."

"Then trust me. There's no way anybody could get it up with what we've got aboard now. It's like asking me to jump to the moon, Troy. I'd love to do it for you, but it's just impossible." He went on quickly, before Christian could answer. "Pat, what's the size on this barge? You remember?"

"About thirty by fifty. Eight, ten feet deep."

The pen scratched. "Thirty by fifty, that's fifteen hundred cubic feet for one-foot immersion. Saltwater's sixty-four pounds a foot.

That's about fifty tons for each foot. What's the tide around here, Captain?"

"About three feet."

"That'll be a hundred and fifty tons." He looked up. "I'll have to do more figuring on internal lift, but that's a good start."

"You thinking to sling her underneath?" said Aydlett.

"That's the simplest way. Three or four loops of cable, and a single one fore and aft for balance. For the rest of the lift, I'll figure something out."

"You'll figure it out?" said Christian.

"That's right."

"But how will you do it?"

Keeping his voice very calm, he said, "Well, a crane would be best. But you're right, they're too conspicuous. So I'll have to figure on it for a while, talk it over with my partner. Maybe we can come up with something."

"You'd better. Now listen. Captain Roach, let's get under way. We've lingered here too long. Galloway, make me a list of what you need. Fabito will take care of the money. I want this lift day you're talking about, I want that next week."

No one answered him, or contradicted him. They sat around the table as rigid, Galloway thought, as if they'd been freeze-dried.

Christian picked up the pipe again and filled it. Instead of heating it, though, he shoved back his chair and called out. There was arguing, and he called again, louder, peremptory. At last, hesitantly, one of the sailors came out. The young one. His face was white as new paint. He cast a despairing glance around at them but said nothing at all.

Christian took his hand. It lay limply in his. "And now, if you'll excuse me, gentlemen."

When they were gone, the four men stared at each other. Finally, Shad reached for the pad. He drawled, "Well, that's settled. Now, what are we gonna need to do this job, Till? From what he said there, before he took off, sounds like it's shopping time."

"Right." Galloway swallowed, then reached out. Liquid chuckled as he added bourbon to his glass. "Okay. For the patch, we'll need reinforcing wire and hydraulic concrete—make it two, three hundred pounds of Speed-Crete. Chipping hammers, wire brushes, to clear the area. Put down some big sheets of copper, too. For the lifts—can we get fifty-five-gallon drums here? Are there empty ones around?"

"I think we can find some on Pass Cay," said Roach.

"How many? Thirty, forty?"

"Sure."

"And on this cay, can they keep quiet? About what we're buying from them?"

"I think you'll find everybody at Pass Cay very cooperative," said Gonzalo.

"Then we'll need chain and U-bolts." Aydlett was writing fast, his big hand folded around the pen. "Pat, how you fixed for wire and cable?"

"Got a deal of braided nylon, various sizes. No steel, though, if that's what you mean."

"Uh-huh. We'll need wire rope for the lift. Have to be"—he stared out at the pool—"at least inch and a half. Two inches'd be better, but it gets hard to work. Any of that on Pass Cay, Captain?"

"I don't think so."

"Then we'll have to buy it, and the hardware to fit. Shad, get all this down: cable clamps, a hundred of them, and C-clamps, big as we can buy, a dozen or so. Cable strops, double eye spliced. Thimbles and shackles. A wire-splicing kit. Saw wires, silicone sealer, plywood sheets. Tools, we'll want a handy billy, some big bolt cutters, wrenches, screwdrivers—big ones. Some of that plastic pipe, PVC pipe. Is there a compressor aboard, Pat?"

"Two, low pressure and high. The HP's rated at a hundred cubic feet a minute."

"How much hose?"

"A hundred feet."

"Get three hundred more. And we'll need a hydrogen torch and bottles and tips."

"Diving gear," rumbled Aydlett. "Can't use scuba down there. Right, Till?"

"Señor Gonzalo, you understand why we can't use air, right? It's got to be mixed gas if we're going to get any work done." The Cuban nodded. "So—two band-mask rigs, Kirby-Morgans or DM-5s, what the Navy calls Mark One lightweights. Oxygen and helium, premixed; I'll have to work out the percentages. Explosives—"

"No explosives. Señor Christian will not like it."

"You're probably right. Okay, we do without. More shit: We'll need battens, to avoid crushing the hull—"

At last they ran out of things to list. He sat motionless for a time, going over it all in his head. To be sure, he resketched the wreck and went through the calculations again.

It would take time, and hard work. It would be expensive, and dangerous. But it ought to be possible—with luck.

"Okay, when can we go back and get all this?"

"You aren't going anywhere," said a voice from the foyer.

He turned his head with a feeling of doom, to see a limp, swaying Christian leaning naked against the bulkhead. The mirrors multiplied him so that it seemed like a thousand Troy Christians faced them at the far end of the bar.

Something dropped from his hand, and shattered on the deck.

Galloway felt sweat start again under his robe. "What do you mean, Troy? I need to buy this gear. We can't do the lift without it."

"I mean that *you* are not going. *He*—"

He was interrupted by a cough. His doubled fist came up. Then, as the coughing went on, grew, his body doubled to meet it. The raw sound echoed in the huge saloon, harsh, agonizing, endless.

At last, Christian straightened. The neon light glowed red on his shining face. He took a slow, huge, tearing breath, as if air were some unfamiliar, poisonous gas.

"*He* can go. Your Cuban friend you're whispering with. Whispering about me. You're not going. You're staying here, where we can watch you."

"Troy—"

"Shut up. And there's someone on his way who wants to see you, too." He turned his head, fuzzily focusing on Gonzalo. "They found the boat, Fabito. Take them below; reward them. Then come back and see me. *He's* coming back. We have to get ready."

"Yes, *Jefe.*" Gonzalo jumped to his feet. "Señor Galloway, Señor Aydlett. Follow me, please."

The man with the Uzi fell in behind them as Gonzalo led them out through the foyer, then down. He stopped in front of another of the staterooms, number five, and tapped lightly. Someone shouted inside. Gonzalo said a few words in a tone of command. A moment later the door clicked open. One of the sailors brushed by them, his face flushed, hair awry.

"Please," said Gonzalo, motioning them in ahead of him.

A woman lay naked on the rumpled, dirty bunk. Bottles, syringes, and vials overflowed the nightstand and littered the floor. The pillow was over her face. Galloway froze, staring down at her spread thighs.

His horror deepened as she moved. An arm came up. The pillow came away, and he looked down at her face.

"This is Conchita," said Gonzalo, behind him. "Interesting, no? She was with a gang of Communist bandits in Peru. They thought to enrich themselves by robbing one of our paymasters. She was the only one Don Juan permitted to live. Now, as you see, she enjoys everything a woman could want. Señors, I leave you now. Enjoy yourself. Conchita will not object."

Behind them, the door clicked. He thought for a moment that Gonzalo had gone. But when he turned his head, he was still there. Only the bodyguard had been left outside.

The Cuban came closer. And closer. He put his arm up next to Tiller's head and his mouth next to his ear. Very softly, he said, "Do you approve of this sort of thing, Señor?"

Galloway's breath stopped as if it had become solid. Through numbed lips, he whispered, "What are you talking about?"

"Not so loud. I said, Do you approve of this? This kind of thing—whether of this woman, or of men. This cruelty. This . . . exploitation."

He saw Aydlett staring, his eyes wide. For an endless moment, he couldn't answer. Suspicions, emotions tumbled through his head. Then he muttered, "It doesn't concern me."

"I'm sorry?"

"I can't fix this woman. I can't fix Colombia or the drug trade. I can't take on Nuñez and the Combine. See? All Shad and I want is to do what we have to do—get that shit to the surface, turn it over to Christian, and go home."

"Is that really all?"

He nodded grimly.

"In that case, Señor, I beg your pardon. I must have misjudged you—very badly."

The door clicked again. This time when Galloway turned, there was no one there.

He looked toward the bed again, and found the woman staring up at them. Tiller Galloway swallowed, unable to move or speak. His back crawled with the same reptilian horror he had felt at fifty fathoms.

Her eyes would have been easier to meet if they had been dead.

9

Ceteris met the next dawn twenty miles away. Galloway was standing on the afterdeck as above him the wing beats of a small helicopter filled the sky.

He leaned into its wind, gripping the rail. The clatter and whine of its turbines and transmission filled his ears, and the smoky hot downblast tore at his clothes as the copter balanced delicately above him. He saw three men in the bubble canopy. One raised a hand; Galloway couldn't see his face. He raised his slightly, a gesture of recognition to another human being.

The helicopter decided to land. It slid forward along invisible wires, swaying in the blue morning air, and bumped to an uneasy halt a deck up from him.

"*El helicoptero ha aterrizado. Continue con el trabajo,*" crackled an announcing system. A moment later, it added, in Roach's broad English, "Mr. Galloway, please come to the main saloon."

When he emerged from the mirrored foyer, the room was empty. The glass doors at its far end were open. They framed the aircraft, which was squatted on an articulated metal grid that unrolled over the pool. The wind that stirred the silk curtains was dense with the stink of burned kerosene. The blades were still ticking round uneasily.

"What's this all about?" shouted Aydlett over the noise, coming up behind him.

"Hi, Shad. No idea."

They stood waiting. Galloway wiped his hands on his pants. His own khakis, freshly laundered and pressed in *Ceteris*'s laundry.

He was thinking not about the helicopter but about the ruined eyes he'd looked into the night before. Sometimes, when he saw things like that, he didn't know what to think. He knew what his stepmother had taught him, the lessons backed up by the Nags

Head Baptist Church every Sunday morning of his youth. That men were inherently evil.

His own observations were that he'd never met one who was all evil or all good. But when he saw certain things . . . he had to wonder whether Anna Galloway had been right.

"Good morning, Señor Galloway, Señor Aydlett."

It was Gonzalo, carrying a leather zipper bag. He looked tired, as if he'd been up all night. "Leaving?" said Shad.

"To Marsh Harbour. There'll be a plane there to Port Everglades. Our people there are already at work finding the materials, the equipment, the list you gave me last night. I will be back in a day or two."

He dropped the zipper bag by the bar and went out to the helicopter. Aydlett said he hadn't eaten yet, and went below. Galloway stayed.

He was still there, still staring blankly at the machine, when the shrill whine of its engines finally declined. The right-side hatch hinged down and became a stairway. A paunchy man in a white suit came down it, visibly relaxing as he gained the solid deck. A taller man in gray pinstripes unfolded after him, carrying a briefcase.

Galloway blinked, recognizing Lax. The briefcase was the one the attorney had carried in Norfolk. The two men shook hands with Gonzalo, who bowed. Then they stood in the sunlight under the now-motionless blades, shading their eyes, looking toward the island that glowed white and green off the yacht's slowly swinging bow.

Galloway stiffened. He knew the other, too.

He was Juan Alberto Mendieta Nuñez-Sebastiano.

The man they called the Baptist.

Screened by the glass doors, he took a step closer, examining him from cover. That was the face. Subtly aristocratic, with the faint smile of a Buddhist in samadhi. He still dressed the same way: white suit, white suede shoes, white tie—the Panama must still be in the aircraft. Even the rims of his sunglasses were white, though the lenses were opaque. Slung over his shoulder, gleaming in the tropic sun, was the classic Leica he affected like a piece of jewelry.

But time had changed the Baptist, too.

For one thing, he was heavier. The Nuñez he'd left on the shore of the Golfo Triste so many years before had been stocky but not heavy, and it seemed then they'd been of an equal height. Now he was rotund and looked much shorter. As he turned and started for the saloon, Galloway saw that his color was bad and his cheeks had sagged. The hands had grown pudgy. But they still wove delicate traceries through the air as he spoke, and the dark hair was still full, combed back from a high forehead in the style Robert MacNamara had favored.

Now they called him Don Juan. He looked more like a professor or a scholarly poet, some kind of studious intellectual, than ever. But since then, he'd lasted six years in the most competitive business in history, and to all appearances was now very near the top. That was no surprise. Despite his appearance, he could act swiftly and mercilessly. That could be said of hundreds of men in the drug trade, however. Nuñez-Sebastiano was also almost always right. He didn't just look smart. He was. And not just street-smart, but school-smart, too.

Galloway could almost hear what they were saying now. He took another step forward, and sucked air as something hard jammed into his kidney.

The guard marched him out into the sunlight with the gun barrel firmly in his back. "*El escucho, adentro,*" he said to Gonzalo.

"*Deje a el con nosotros,*" said Nuñez. Then, curving up the edges of his mouth, he reached out his hand.

"Why, hello, Tiller," said the Baptist softly. "Nice to have you back."

"Hello again," said Lax, smiling, too, beside his boss. He didn't offer to shake hands. Galloway didn't, either. He wanted to say he wasn't "back," or anyway not for long, but he didn't.

"It's good you decided to join us again," the Colombian went on. "I thought of you often, do you know that? But then, I felt someday you would return. I felt that deep down you belonged with us."

"There didn't seem to be much choice."

"What's that? What are you trying to tell me, Tiller?"

He explained about his customers, his store, and his boat. Nuñez nodded slowly, his shaded eyes on the horizon. When Tiller was done, he shook his head sadly. "That wasn't done at my orders. I don't operate that way."

Galloway didn't say anything. To Lax, Nuñez said, "I have to point out, Harold, that I am much maligned. Like most human beings entrusted with power, with responsibility for others, I have to bear the blame for the excesses of subordinates and competitors. In actuality, I play three roles. To those governments which oppress liberty, I am a criminal. To those who depend on me, I am a *patrono*, obligated to care for those he employs. To those who deal with me, I'm a businessman, supplying a commodity, satisfying a demand. It is this last role, I think, that comes closest to the truth."

"I can understand that," said Lax.

"And finally, of course, to those who choose to be my enemies, I must be an enemy, too." He paused; neither man answered or objected.

Nuñez pivoted, waving at *Ceteris*, the flight deck, the helicopter, the sailors at work below them. "All this—my entire corporation—is based ultimately not on force but on the supply of a good to willing consumers. Persuasion is involved only very occasionally. Its precipitant is not my will. What causes it, in the final analysis? Only the artificial restriction of demand by politicians too ignorant to understand the direction of social progress."

As Lax smoothly agreed, Galloway stared at Nuñez's slightly bulbous, peeling nose. He'd been in the sun recently.

He remembered now why he'd hated the Baptist so much. And why, since he'd turned his back and walked out of stateroom number five, turned his back on the naked woman with the mad eyes, he'd carried rage in his gut like an indigestible lump of fatty meat.

No matter how smoothly he lied, this was the man who was responsible for her; for dozens, scores, perhaps hundreds of murders, as he'd welded rival gangs into a sophisticated international organization; for the death of Mezey Aydlett and the Panamanian mate and all the others on *Victory* so many years before. And for his father, dead by his own hand because of his shame. For years of his life, gone forever.

Face-to-face with him again, he understood suddenly that only when he or Juan Nuñez was dead would he be free of the devil's bargain he'd made so long before.

Don't think about that now, he told himself. Free? No man is free. It doesn't matter who Gonzalo really is. What you told him last night is right. You have only one goal—to cooperate, and stay alive.

"This is your partner?" said Nuñez, looking past him.

He turned. "Shad, come on out. This is the man I told you about. The big boss. Señor Nuñez."

"This the one they call the Baptist, huh?" said Aydlett, shielding his eyes with one big hand, smiling into the sun.

The guard was fast. Before Galloway could speak or move, the butt of the gun made the hollow sound of an ax into dead wood. Shad grunted, hard, and fell to one knee in front of the man in the white suit.

"Let's go inside," said Nuñez. Lax nodded, and walked around Aydlett, who still knelt, waggling his head, probing the back of his skull with his fingers.

Tiller helped him up. "He doesn't like being called that to his face," he muttered.

"Damn, now you telling me. That son of a bitch . . . Okay, you convinced me. I got him marked down."

Gonzalo lingered, too. "Señor Aydlett. Are you hurt?"

"Get serious, my wife hits me harder than that. Little bastard just took me by surprise. Just let me rest here a minute."

"I will be going, then. See you in two or three days."

They shook hands hastily as the rotors began to whine around, then the turbines fired. They moved back as the Cuban climbed in. The guard folded the door closed as the ship's announcing system broke into staccato Spanish again.

It lifted in a great roar of wind. As it shrank to a speck, then winked out, Galloway stared after it.

Suddenly, he felt alone, and scared.

Lax and Nuñez were sitting in the main salon. The air conditioning was turned up full. Nuñez had leaned back and closed his eyes. He headed past them, hoping to get back to his room, but the lawyer said, "Mr. Galloway, we need to talk. Sit down."

He sat unwillingly, refusing a lifted glass with a shake of his head. He could still hear the sound of steel hitting bone.

"How's the job going?"

"All right."

"You got to the ship?"

"That's right."

"What's it like?"

He went over it again, glancing at Nuñez. The *jefe de jefes* reclined motionless, giving no sign he was listening, although he didn't seem to be asleep. This was a new trick. He finished: "As soon as we have the gear, we can start rigging. I can't say for sure how long, but I'd guess we'll be ready to lift in three, four days, if we aren't interrupted."

"By what?"

"By anything. Storms, or police."

"Don't worry about police," said Nuñez, still without opening his eyes. "Tiller. Where is Troy Christian?"

"Uh—I don't know."

"He should have met me when I landed. Fabio says he's ill. Is he? Or is something else wrong?"

Galloway chose his words carefully. "He seems tired and on edge. He may be using too much. He has a bad cough. But I don't see enough of him to give you a dependable opinion."

Nuñez hoisted himself out of the chair and crossed to the bulkhead. He touch-toned the phone, listened for a time, then interrupted with something short and angry in Spanish. He hung up and stood looking out the window at the cays. "We'll go over there this afternoon," he said, apparently to Tiller, though he didn't look around.

"All right."

"Now, if you don't mind, would you leave us? Señor Christian is on his way up. We have some things to discuss with him."

This time, he wasn't sorry to leave.

• • •

They went ashore that afternoon, after a long and copious lunch.

The sea seemed very empty as *Ceteris*'s launch left her, purred across a mile of open water, and threaded several rocks awash between narrow strips of shoal.

Gradually, the sea narrowed and the shoal rose into low islands. They made for a dark gap, like a knife cut. The sea glittered in it like beaten silver. As they neared, it became an inlet. To the right

scrub green slid past. No trace of other color varied its blank ver-
dure. The shore to the left was lower, set with a black line of
mangroves, like enamel decoration. A dark, deep water chuckled
past, and the foam hissed as it swirled away in their wake. A half-
sunken cabin cruiser appeared, swayed past, vanished in silence
back into green invisibility.

Galloway thought with sudden regret of *Miss Anna*. Then came
more islets, a thickness of them, and the launch turned again and
again, sniffing a meandering way through a maze of narrow channels nearly choked with the silent, trailing mangroves.

Past that, quite suddenly, they emerged into a sheltered harbor
a quarter mile across. Skiffs lay in attitudes of abandonment at
anchor. They rocked uneasily as the launch moved by. Two
wooden piers reached toward them from a low building, promi-
nently identified as Telly's Bar, Marina, Hotel, Restaurant, and
Store. There seemed to be a town beyond it, but Telly's blocked
the view. As they made up on the dock, the smells of gasoline
and conch reached out from the silent town.

As the launch drifted the last few feet, two pier-head idlers came
out of the shade to stand with their hands outstretched, apparently
for the lines. They were very thin and very black. One was bare-
chested, with a burn scar near his armpit, and a huge handlebar
mustache. The other was smaller, with a twisted leg, a double
row of bottom teeth, and continually blinking, reddened, painful-
looking eyes. "Hello gen'll'mun," he muttered. "Welcome, Pass
Cay. Where you want go? I take you there. Only two dollars."

The bodyguard pushed by them without comment or look and
they faded back into the shade.

He and Shad reached the pier behind Nuñez, Christian, Lax,
and Roach. As they paced down it flies swirled up like black smoke
from heaps of penetrated conchs, garbage, and dead dogs. On the
other side, a huge black Cigarette boat, brand new, crouched low
in the water.

The bar was hot and airless and dominated by a huge color
Panasonic with a Palm Beach station on. Six or seven islanders
were drinking bottled Kalik and arguing. Above them a fan turned
listlessly in a haze of marijuana and tobacco smoke. They fell
silent as the strangers filed through.

Outside again, he saw that they were in a kind of waterfront compound. They followed concrete walks across a lawn hissing with rotary sprinklers. Abruptly, the air was wet and cool, and he looked into the open, unscreened windows of a house. A Duvalieresque fantasy, two stories of white stucco, with cream planter chairs, pale eggshell sofas, an ivory grand piano on stark white carpet. No one was in sight, but somewhere children were screaming.

The luxury ended at a chain-link fence topped with concertina wire. A squat man with a revolver on his hip watched them through the gate.

Outside, concrete and grass petered into bare dust. Dust-colored dogs panted up as they followed Roach into the village. Five dogs per person seemed to be the rule.

The main path was unpaved and eight feet wide. Small concrete-block houses lined it, each with steel grates set into inadequate windows and heavy cylinder locks on the door. The roofs were galvanized steel. They were painted cheap bright colors, but the effect wasn't gay. Others were half-finished and abandoned, or burned out and deserted. Here and there, patches of bare ground were littered with cigarette butts, torn bits of foil and paper, and hundreds of paper matches. The smell of feces was strongest there. Occasionally, the path passed an open lot or tree. Knots of thin men in faded tank tops and jeans or bathing suits, their eyes stuporous and inflamed, sat motionless in the oval shade, like groupers under a coral head, staring back with incurious passivity. Obese women waddled by, wearing small blue or red hats with veils against the terrible heat. One stopped, babbling something about her babies; they hadn't eaten; her man had spent the money. She was pushed aside and fell silent, staring after them.

The path dipped toward the water. A small boat yard nestled amid the mangroves, a ramshackle pier whipstitched of crate wood and old hull planks, covered with cylinder heads, motor covers, drive shafts, bottles, and nets. The cay was covered with beer cans, kids, and dogs; and over it all, the silent Clorox glare of the sun, leaving a taste in the mouth like bleach.

He wondered if this was it, but Roach led them past without a glance. They passed a trash pile. Spindly-legged children sifted through it like herons on a mud bank.

"That's not the yard we want, is it?" he asked Roach.

"What? Oh, hardly. No, Gunwater Cay's just ahead."

Gunwater Shiplifts lay across a short bridge on pilings. Three charter fishermen were drawn up in front of a junkyard that went for acres back into the scrub. A marine railway thrust rusted rails into water as clear as tears. A boat lift on wheels had wrapped itself around a motor cruiser. It looked, he thought, like a spider crab that had just caught a meal. Two black men were crouched under it, manipulating long-handled scrapers. Heaps of barnacles, marine slime, and paint chips crunched under their boots as they toiled in the broiling sun. The smell hit him a hundred feet away.

The sun burned like a thin sheet of glowing metal hammered down over everything he saw.

Following Roach and Nuñez, he went up a little rise and into a low building painted in peeling turquoise.

A broad, bald white man in work blues was talking into a cellular telephone. He raised his eyebrows as they came in and swung his legs down. He pointed to a sideboard, glasses, a bottle.

"Don Juan, a drink?" asked Christian, going to it.

"Just water," said Nuñez.

When he hung up, the broad man introduced himself as Rolf Von Arx. "Call me Babe," he said. He lit a cigar and pointed to the box. "Help yourselves. What can I do for you, Don Juan? Captain Roach?"

"This here is Tiller Galloway," said Roach, pouring a second shot of rum. He tossed it back, stared at the ceiling for a moment, and sighed. "He's doing some work for us. Needs to look at your barge; might want to rent it. Also some of those old fuel drums you've got lying around out back." He winked. "This is all on the Q.T., now."

"Treasure hunting?"

"Something like that," Galloway said. He decided he could use a drink, too.

"Let's go out back," said Von Arx, pulling a Dolphins cap off the wall.

The barge was sitting in the shallows. It was a transport barge, decked over, raised slightly fore and aft, with steel samson posts every six feet. The crane, a tracked Dixie, sat atop it. Galloway had to admit, it *was* rather yellow. He waded out, kicking the plating as he went. It was scaly but solid. He turned to yell back. "Does it float?"

"Sure, once we pump it out and roll the crane off. It's low tide now, that's all."

As he waded back, his eye fell on two huge wooden spools under a shed roof. He turned and splashed toward them. Small white razorfish zagged away in panic ahead of him. He waded up the shore, skirted a row of rusting engines, and entered the shed.

The spools held steel cable, several hundred feet of it, shining amber with grease. He looked back and saw the others talking. He called, pitching his voice above the clatter of a chipping hammer, "Hey! Babe! What about this stuff?"

Von Arx picked his way over. "It's elevator cable. New. Got it in Freeport. Company started a resort casino, but they didn't pay the right people, lost their permit. That's prime goods."

"We'll take that, too." He looked around. "Look, you know what you got here better than I do. I need some pontoons, something to hold air at depth . . . something big. Have you got anything like that?"

Von Arx worked his cigar around for a moment, then said, "Follow me."

There were two of them, two painted iron cylinders. Lying on their sides, they were higher than a man, and three times as long. He circled them, then bent to inspect their bottoms as the owner said, "They're fuel tanks. From the marina at Dorros Cove. They put in fiberglass, but far as I know there's nothing wrong with these. That something like what you want?"

"You've got welding gear here. Think you could cut some holes in the bottom? Say eight, ten two-inch holes, in a row? And weld a couple padeyes?"

The cigar angled upward. "My welder's laying out drunk today. But I can do that for you first thing tomorrow."

"Got any pumps?"

"Two three-inchers. They'll cost you, though. I hate to let 'em both go at once, in case I get an emergency call."

"Load 'em up." He slapped one of the tanks. Its metal boomed hollow, burning hot.

Suddenly, he felt more optimistic. Maybe he could do it, after all. Lift the ship, get the coke, make Nuñez happy, get paid, go home. Maybe he was looking for disaster when it wasn't really there.

"What are you salvaging?" said Von Arx.

"Salvaging?"

"What else? Cable, a barge, pumps, pontoons . . ."

"Better ask the boss that."

"Any chance of my getting in on it?"

"You don't want in on this one, friend."

Von Arx gave him a close squint, but didn't ask any more questions on the walk back.

Galloway didn't see too much else he could use, but Roach asked about labor. Von Arx offered to recruit some locals, men who knew their way around boats and ground tackle, and deliver them with the barge. Roach looked at Christian; Christian strolled a few paces off with Nuñez. Then came back, looking unpleasant, and said to Von Arx, "Ten thousand."

"For what?"

"For everything."

"What a kidder. That's a joke, right? That cable alone's worth twice that."

They haggled for a time. Finally Von Arx agreed on $22,000 for the lot, in advance, including the barge and pumps for a week, with Christian to pay wages direct to the men. Barge, pumps, cable, and the welded-up tanks would be ready the morning of the day after tomorrow. As soon as Nuñez nodded, Lax reached into his jacket.

When the money was out of sight, Christian spoke to the bodyguard, who took out his walkie-talkie.

The launch came into sight a few minutes later, sliding along the blue line of inlet toward the Gunwater dock. They strolled around to it, shook hands with Von Arx, and stepped aboard.

On the way back, Nuñez stood beside Galloway at the stern. Leaning against the gunwale, he said, "What about it, Tiller? Is that what you needed?"

"They're close. Those tanks, especially. They'll be the pontoons, for the second-stage lift. And the pumps will give us more hoist from the barge."

"The second stage?"

"After we get it off the bottom. A tank that size, we'll get twenty tons out of it easy."

"I'm glad I thought of you, Tiller. You're the man for this job, all right."

He didn't answer, looking back at the island as they left it. From this distance, Pass Cay looked beautiful. A piece of Paradise, set down on a sea bluer than the sky. How different it was when you were walking through it.

"I have an invitation for this evening," Nuñez said.

"I'm sorry?"

"I said, I have an invitation for tonight . . . at a nearby cay. There are some people there you might enjoy meeting."

"I don't know. I need to do some calculations, get a plan together."

"He won't be delivering till day after tomorrow. You can take a few hours off. Take tomorrow off, too. You'll be working hard after that.

"Now. Tonight. You've heard of Tanner Cay?"

He had, though he couldn't remember where. Nuñez said, "You have, I can see that. It's Harleman's summer place."

"Harleman. . . . *President* Harleman?"

"The same. It should be an interesting gathering. Harold and I will be going. I'd like you to accompany us."

From the corner of his eye, Galloway saw that Christian had been eavesdropping. Now he moved closer. "I can make that," he said.

"You will stay aboard, Troy. And you will stay in proper condition—*comprende? Tu me esta agotando la paciencia.* I have no use for a man who cannot control himself."

The tone was not unpleasant, but he saw the redhead flush, saw his hands whiten on the rail. And saw his look, directed not at Nuñez but at him.

They passed the foaming line of reef. Ahead, the yacht shone white as a cloud in sunlight. Suddenly, he understood why Roach loved her. She was built of nightmare. Paid for by nightmare. But still she looked like a dream.

10

Again, again, the beacon marking the Tanner Cay entrance flashed a stubborn beam into the tropic darkness. A fine spray chilled Galloway's face as the stem of the launch shattered a wave at twenty knots.

He leaned back against the transom, tugging at his tie. It was the only thing he had on that fit. The trousers were Roach's, and though the waist was roomy, they were too short. The coat was Lax's, and tight in the shoulders. The shoes were Nuñez's, and they pinched.

He sighed and looked back. *Ceteris* rode to the warm wind like a floating island. Her portholes were rows of gold coins. That afternoon the sailors had dressed ship, rigging lights from the stem to the mast and back down. They glowed red and white and blue, the national colors of Panama.

"You haven't told me yet what you think of her," said Nuñez, beside him.

"She's a hell of a boat."

"Designed keel up for business cruising. Hull and engines, twenty-two million. Electronics and communications, four million. Art, two million two. Et cetera . . . Total, thirty-four million U.S."

After a moment, Galloway said, "You've done well for yourself."

A chuckle. "Thanks."

"Her name. What does that mean? Greek, isn't it?"

"Latin. *Ceteris paribus;* it's a common phrase in economics. It means, 'all else being equal.' That is, it isolates the effect of a single variable, so it can operate without perturbation from outside."

"I don't get it."

"Think about it . . . she was the right idea. A floating home, a floating office, secure communications. And at sea, you feel, well, free."

"I felt that way on *Miss Anna*."

"I'm sorry about what happened. Sometimes one has to . . . get a person's attention. But perhaps you can replace her with something better." Nuñez paused. "You know, we're not that different, you and I."

"How so?"

The calm, slightly pedantic voice spoke from a velvet dark. "Aristotle said that happiness is the exercise of the functions for which a creature was designed. Freud said it was the fulfillment of a childhood wish. To both of us, I think, that means freedom. *Real* freedom, beyond the rules and laws lesser men would like us to impose on ourselves."

"I guess it meant that to me once."

The Baptist didn't seem to hear the interruption. "And we're both fighters. We believe in the struggle, not the hog trough. That's how I judge a man, in the end.

"You see, my family hasn't always been *peces gordos*. My grandfather picked coffee on a plantation in the Aburrá Valley. My father founded the fortune in Antioquia, smuggling emeralds. A real *paisa*. An entrepreneur, as Americans say. I have simply continued the tradition. Coffee, jewels, marijuana, *ipadu* . . . whatever the North Americans wanted, we supplied."

"I don't understand what you're getting at, Don Juan."

"Well. Think about it."

Nuñez turned away, and began talking to Lax. Galloway leaned back. He puzzled over the exchange for a few minutes, then turned his attention once more to the approaching land.

Tanner was south of Pass Cay, another in the chain of islets that veiled this northeast face of the Abacos from the open Atlantic. It was higher than either Pass or Green Turtle. He could see lights climbing two hills.

Red and green, set close, appeared ahead. The launch slowed. Nuñez rapped rapid Spanish; it sped up again, and the horn blared out, echoing from the island. The lights hesitated, then the green one winked out. The red one moved off to the left.

They slid past it, slowing as they breasted the steady flash of the beacon, into the embracing arms of the quay.

The stone wall enclosed a circular basin. Galloway looked out over the glitter and sway of dozens of motor yachts and billfish charters. Music came from them; shrieks; laughter; the rattle of firecrackers. More than one party was in progress tonight. The launch slowed to a wakeless crawl as it passed a candy-colored shoal of Expresses, Magnums, Fountain offshore powerboats jostling uneasily at a floating pier.

The tender swung slowly to starboard, crept past the high sterns of Bertrams, Vikings, and Cheoy Lees. Pivoted again, and eased alongside a pier. Bow and stern lines floated in the warm thick air, then rattled down in front of a harbormaster's office. It was white and turquoise stucco under the dark palms, a 1950s seaside look.

"Ready?" said Lax.

Galloway followed them ashore and up the hill. Past houses and low carefully groomed shrubbery. He recognized pipe-organ cactus and rabbit-tail. He fingered a wide-leaved shrub, and Lax, looking back, said, "Pittisporum." He breathed the scents of bougainvillea, poinciana, and jasmine, but with them, too, a dozen more, dense and dizzying, like a psychotropic gas. The winding path upward was lit at ankle level.

The hotel had an outside pool and a patio bar. He half-expected to stop there, but they kept climbing. Past short, heavy, muscular men in billed caps. Looking at their jaws, he thought they'd take a hook well. Not mullet mouths. Tarpon, maybe. Their jaws were so hard and bony, you'd lose your tackle before the fish.

Beyond the hotel was a wide, level blackness. He caught a vertical wedge bitten from the stars—the tail of a light plane. And another building, hangar or terminal, the lawn and plantings illuminated in motionless waiting incandescence, yellow light and shadow blacker than the sky. A hidden radio played salsa. Two black men sat motionless at a picnic table, watching them pass.

Woods now. Black dark, but with fireflies. Something different about them. He blinked, losing sight of the others. Behind him, steady as a clock, echoed the Indian's heavy pace.

For a moment he thought, I could escape now. Duck into the brush, hide overnight, tomorrow talk his way onto one of the charter fishermen. Then he dismissed it. For the same reason he'd given Aydlett before. Nuñez would just send someone after him, or after those he loved.

And neither Troy Christian nor dozens of Nuñez's other purchased souls would have any compunction carrying those orders out.

The path rose again. Gradually the basin opened below him, the piers splayed fingers rammed so solid with gems they could no longer close. Beyond, floating in blackness so complete that there was no distinction between sea and space, lay *Ceteris*, a shimmering blaze of color, like a swarm of fireflies come to rest on the sea.

He followed Nuñez and Lax out of the woods onto the grounds of a high-peaked house. The stone was dark and didn't look native. It was buttressed, with high narrow dormers rammed into a roof that gleamed faintly in the starlight, like wet slate. It made him think of a monastery, or a fortress. The lawn was smooth as a golf course. Then he stumbled over a disk in the ground; it *was* a golf course.

"There it is," Lax tossed over his shoulder. "Bayou Serene."

He'd heard of it. Not for years now. But once it had been as common a name as Camp David, Plains, Georgia, or San Clemente.

They came round the west wing, and went down a short flight of steps to a sunken garden. Thirty or more people were already there, eddying against a red glow of three lighted fountains. Huge koi intertwined in the ruby light. A string quartet was tuning up.

"Where's Galloway—"

"Here," he said, moving up beside Nuñez.

Don Juan squeezed his shoulder. "Tiller, get yourself a drink. I have people to talk to. I'll introduce you to some of them later. Make yourself at home. Anybody asks, you're with me."

He nodded. He felt ill at ease, like Aydlett had at the Harbor Club. That seemed like months ago, but it hadn't been a week. Even the fireflies were different from home. In Carolina they glowed a reticent, homely yellow-green. Here, they flashed a cold and brilliant white.

The bar was set up by a Florida room that seemed to be the back entrance to the house. When he asked for bourbon, a black man with a British accent poured him Jack Daniels with ice. He held out a bill, but the barman gave him a fish eye. He put it back and sipped at the whiskey. "Nice party," he said, just to say something to somebody.

"They do those, yes."

"You work many of them?"

"Most of them," said the barman. He didn't seem interested in conversation. "'Ave you try the cuisine? Authen-tic Bahamian cuisine. Scorched conch, crab and rice, pigeon pies, turtle pie. Right over there."

As Galloway glanced toward the tables, his eye stopped on a tall, grizzled black man in a gray pinstripe. Whoever he was, he had a wonderful tailor. He was surrounded by whites. Next to him, they looked short, fat, and undistinguished.

"Who's that?" he asked.

"That is our chief of state." Galloway started at the tone in his voice. Beneath the lilt was open contempt. "That is the Right 'Onorable Sir Kinsman Sears, Prime Minister of the Bahamas."

Just then, Galloway recognized one of the men by Sears. He was wearing slacks and a sports jacket, not work blues, but it was him. "And that fella beside him? With the cigar?"

"That is Mister Von Arx. He owns most of this island . . . and others. He is one of the Prime Minister's 'consultants.'"

"You don't seem to have much use for these people," said Galloway. "Why's that?"

The barman shrugged, as if the question was stupid. He busied himself stacking glasses. Galloway tried again to get him to talk, but all he got was another mackerel glance.

He shoved off from the bar into the crowd. After a few yards the current caught him, twisting him here and there. The voices blended in a submarine murmur. American accents, British, and the British-derived but softer, more musical Bahamian. And here and there, the rapid inflections of Spanish.

He hovered at the edge of one or two conversations. "He's a wily beast," a sunburned man in a sarong and white golf shoes was saying. "Got to present the bait just right, or he's a memory, not even a memory, just not there. You hire Reggie, he'll get you bonefish, out there on those flats. That's an adventure you'll not soon forget, believe you me."

Another was about some kind of investment credit. This circle was more soberly dressed. The one talking was an aggressive, very ugly older woman he'd seen in the newspapers. There were others he almost recognized. Only one, though, was he sure of, a woman with short hair and a heart-shaped face he'd seen in a science fiction movie Bernie had made him take her to.

"How's the diving?"

He turned. Tall drink in hand, aviator glasses, a glint of gold at his throat. The guayabera was terracotta, embroidered with tiny violets.

When he didn't answer, Al Zeno patted his arm chidingly. "You don't remember? The flight from Lauderdale?"

"Sure, I remember you now. How's the fishing going?"

"I've got all the lines out." The DEA man seemed to be examining his clothing. "Nice jacket."

"Thanks."

"The parties up here are pretty exclusive. Don't take this wrong, but I wouldn't have expected . . . Who you with? Anybody I know?"

Hell, Galloway thought. "No—nobody. I saw the lights. And walked up."

"Is that right? That's great. Chutzpah, I admire." He smiled and raised the glass. "I don't know why—just something you develop, in my business—but when I saw you on that plane, my beeper from God said, 'Al, baby, that *hombre no es turista.*' So I got hold of the passenger list. Are you Aydlett? Or Galloway?"

"Galloway."

"Figured so. Funny, we got a former player by that name in our data bank."

He couldn't think of anything to say. So he started to sweat instead.

"Anyway." Zeno looked across the patio, past the fountain. "Anyway, it's nice to see you. Hey. Remember what we were talking about on the plane?"

"Yeah," he said, sweating.

"You see that short fat guy?"

"Which one?"

"In the ice-cream suit, playing with the camera?"

"Uh-huh."

"That's one of the heavies. Even bigger than Manderell. There're people who do more volume. Buying from the Indians, running the *pozos*, paste refineries. But he's vertical integration. Financial advice. Venture capital. Brokering. Weapons deals. Bottom line: one point two billion gross last year, our estimate. Net, who knows? Don Juan Alberto Mendieta Gomez."

He was just alert enough not to correct him. Zeno waited, then said, "I meant, *Nuñez*. But we're gonna fry him, too. The Financial Intelligence guys got letters rogatory out to Zurich, Nassau, and the Canaries. All we need is to flip somebody on the inside." He let another two beats go by, swirling ice. Then said casually, "You met him?"

He didn't know how long Zeno had been here, whether he'd seen them arrive together. He decided to hope he hadn't. "I was introduced. I didn't know who he was."

"Course not." Zeno took another sip and looked over his shoulder. ". . . Be right there, Doctor. . . . Like I was saying; something like that, helping out, that could make us overlook a lot of things. Like a convicted runner being out of the country, in violation of his parole. And his personal security could be guaranteed. . . . Am I coming in loud and clear? Good. My card."

He excused himself then and strolled away with an older man, talking excitedly about a white marlin he'd caught the day before from the *Happy Hooker*.

Galloway felt cold. It was all too obvious that Zeno suspected that his presence had something to do with Nuñez. He loosened the tie, letting the air cool the perspiration that covered his chest.

He got another drink, reminding himself that this ought to be his last one, and stood by the fountain, worrying. Guarantee his security. That was a joke. He'd known two people associated with the Combine who had cooperated, or been suspected of cooperating, with the law. One had died in her hot tub, without a mark on her. His FBI handlers had found the other one in his laundry room, with his wife, mother, three children, and their maid—all shot in the back of the head.

When no one seemed to be looking, he crumpled the card and let it fall from his hand. One of the koi circled it, rose; it disappeared in a gulp and a swirl.

Come to think of it, the laundry room had been one of Troy Christian's jobs, too.

• • •

Gradually, as time passed, his unease gave way to boredom. He started to think about the lift. You didn't really need padeyes on the pontoons. The vent holes would be enough. Thread the cable through them, then lead it down. And double it on the end, so it wouldn't slip.

Then, not ten feet away, he saw her.

The last time she'd been in cutoff jeans and polo shirt. The honey hair had been tied back, and she'd glowed with tan. Now her hair fell like a squall over bare shoulders, and her bronzed calves were veiled by shimmering silk the color of key limes. She was looking away from him, and her cheek still showed, against the fountain light behind her, the fine blond fuzz that made him want to bite into her like a ripe fruit.

Then the ugly woman began again about tax credits, and she glanced away. And saw him watching. She looked away instantly, but a pucker appeared on her forehead. He took a sip, waiting. Sure enough, she looked back, narrowed her eyes, and half-smiled.

He drifted in the last few feet and tossed over the line. "I never got to ask your name."

"Lynne Parkinson. I remember your face. But not where we met."

"I'm Tiller Galloway. We met at Green Turtle. Last week. Sunday, I think it was." He waited, but she still looked puzzled. So he said, "At the Rooster. How's Wuckie doing?"

"Oh, God. That was you? That drunken madman?"

"Guilty."

"You almost got yourself killed. Do you know how hard it was to keep them from seriously damaging you?"

"There was some damage the next day."

"I couldn't stop *that*. Parking a trouble-making foreigner under a manchineel, that's local custom. Believe me, that's the least of what could have happened."

"Who were those boys, anyway?"

Her voice dropped ten degrees. "Not 'boys,' Mr. Galloway.

They're Family Islands residents. Bahamian citizens."

He said quietly, "I meant nothing offensive. I call myself a boy, too. In my part of the world, that's the way we talk. They're your friends?"

"Yes."

"So you live here? Or are you a visitor?"

"I work here."

"And what do you do?"

"I'm an artist."

She said it with a hint of defensiveness. He took a sip of JD, letting whatever it was ebb and pass. After a moment, she added, "I paint. Came here from Chicago three years ago for a long week-end, and never went back."

"The weather's better."

"I need color like other people need vitamin C. The Midwest is muted, monochrome. Have you been snorkeling here? Have you seen how much those fish love color?"

He hadn't thought of it that way, but he saw what she meant. He nodded. "Yeah. I haven't had . . . much free time lately, but I'd like to."

"There's a beautiful reef on the other side of the cay. Two miles out. That's where I go."

"Maybe I could do that tomorrow," he said, thinking about Nuñez's offer of a day off. But she didn't seem to be listening. She went off into something technical about hue and saturation.

Meanwhile, he looked down the front of her dress. His hands kept wanting to crawl down there and see whether it was all real. She threw her hair back, still talking, and caught his lowered eyes; smiled slightly, the same way she had in a darkened bar.

Invitation and coldness, mixed, were a potent lure. He wondered who she was here with.

Then his mind asked, Why? Did he really want to move in on this woman? Just because she made his mouth water? He'd been drunk at the Rooster. That was an excuse, sort of. But he wasn't drunk now. Maybe it would be wiser just to clink glasses and move off.

He was still wrestling with it when she raised her arm, waving past his shoulder.

"Mr. Galloway, this is Telly Pepper, principal consultant to the Minister of Tourism."

He looked up. Pepper was bald, naturally or by design, he couldn't tell, and as big as one of the tanks at Gunwater. His skin was a medium ginger. The hand that crimped his knuckles felt like it could squeeze a lot harder. "Mr. Galloway," he rumbled. "Friend of Lynne's, friend of mine. You here on your own? Or with?"

"With."

"With whom? May I ask?"

He said, unwillingly, "Nuñez-Sebastiano."

"Oh, you're one of Don Juan's men?"

He caught her glance. Of surprise—and something darker. He shifted his attention back to Pepper. "Not exactly. I'm working for him temporarily. Not in—" He halted himself; they might not know Nuñez's line of business. "I'm doing some repairs. On his boat."

Pepper slid a huge forearm around Parkinson's waist. Beside him she looked willowy. Her arm went around him, too, or at least partway round.

Pepper said, "Repairs, eh? Come, let's get away from this crowd."

It was dark by the low wall that overlooked the harbor. The principal consultant pulled out something and laid it on the stone. The shadows bent. Parkinson laughed. The shadows swayed together.

"You there. D'ye care for some?"

"What have you got there?"

"Some of your boss's goods. Help yourself."

His fingers touched foil, the smooth fragility of a plastic straw. Before he had time to want it, he said quickly, "Thanks, I've got to cut back."

"Can do that when you're dead," rumbled Pepper.

Parkinson laughed again, a little high, disconnected. "When you're dead," she repeated. "I like your technique, Telly."

"Like yours, too, m'lady. You accompanying me tonight?"

"Maybe. Another hit?"

"Help yourself."

He had the sudden feeling he was intruding, and backed away. They didn't seem to miss him.

When he got back to the party, it had fissioned into smaller groups about the patio, the fountain, the bar, and the Florida room. The quartet was playing Mozart. He looked around, still wary of Zeno. Then he saw them: Nuñez, Lax, the ugly woman, and the Prime Minister. He got a fresh drink on the way over.

As he came up, Nuñez was saying, "It's a momentary fluctuation, nothing more. Prices went down; now they have gone up. Marginal producers will increase supply. The market will correct for it."

"But the government of Colombia's talking extradition now," said the woman. Galloway decided she looked like a batfish.

"Governments often talk. What else are they for? There will be no treaty and no extradition. Of that I can assure you."

"I'm glad we met, Mr. Nuñez. You have decided opinions, don't you? May I ask, what exactly do you do?"

"I'm a practicing economist."

"Is that right? May I interview you sometime?"

"Why not? You can reach me through Mr. Lax. Give her a card, Harold."

"What are your politics, Mr. Nuñez? You're a free marketeer, I'm sure."

"Absolutely. Even—a libertarian? At least on a micro scale."

"Hands off by the government, even when it's operating for the common good?"

"Complete nonintervention in the market process." Nuñez's voice had lost its dry tone. It vibrated with a passion it had lacked even when he talked about *Ceteris*. "I believe in freedom even when it operates to my detriment. For ultimately, it serves all. Any intervention for normative reasons deforms the market. Any deformation leads to inefficiency and further reasons for intervention.

"I say, let the market rule! The United States calls itself a capitalist system. But even that great country has never taken it uncut."

Sears said, from a cloudy distance, "Babe said you attended Harvard."

"Yes sir, I took my doctorate there," said Nuñez courteously, turning to the old man. "I'm a neo-Spencerian. It's a small school, but growing in influence. Are you familiar with Spencer? He followed Darwin. He's out of the mainstream now, but his economic theory was grounded in biology. Nothing since has invalidated it. In a way, we've papered over a rather harsh reality with the soothing fictions of liberal sociology."

"The Dam-ocrats have, you mean," drawled Von Arx, joining the group.

"In the United States, both parties have. Both deform the market, one for the benefit of lower-income groups, the other for people like ourselves. Oh, I understand why. A trade-off for votes. But with modern campaign techniques, is that necessary anymore?"

"Do you mean that, Doctor?" said the older woman.

"Oh, please, no titles," said Nuñez modestly. "But yes, I do. As a Spencerian, I believe in government not by the most popular but by the fittest. How can that be compatible with vote counting? Democracy and good leadership are fundamentally incompatible. This is widely recognized in Latin America, due to our aristocratic tradition."

A young woman's voice: the actress had joined them. "But isn't that kind of cruel? I've read Darwin. You don't want to—this struggle for existence, doesn't that mean you just let people starve if they can't make a living?"

"That's exactly why I'm a *neo*-Spencerian, Margaret. The more advanced the means of production and distribution, the more it eliminates the struggle for existence. The welfare state simply moves faster along the same road. It becomes less a struggle for existence than a struggle for enjoyment."

"A *struggle* for *enjoyment*," repeated Sears, looking blank.

"Or for pleasure. If you prefer. Have you ever heard of an economist named Simon Patten? He was a Darwinian, too, but he criticized Spencer for staticism. He taught that the essence of evolution is not success in competition but *escape* from competition. The favored organism leaves behind the arena of struggle for scarce resources, either by destroying all competitors or by moving to a new environment.

"But that's a side issue. Where Patten astounded me, when I discovered him back in the stacks at the Littauer, was when he predicted that evolution would operate differently as the means of production developed. He argued that as man achieved control of nature, he would pass out of a classical Ricardian economics—a 'pain' economy—to a 'pleasure' economy. Fear and want would disappear as motivating factors as basic needs were supplied to all.

"Yet the struggle for existence would not end, but alter its form. Patten said that in this new economy, the unfit, surplus population would be carried off by temptation, vice, and disease. The fit then would be not the strongest or most intelligent, but those with the self-control to resist dissipation and self-destruction."

The shadows around him murmured surprised half-agreement. Nuñez hardly paused; he plunged on, his rings flashing as he gestured.

"I immediately saw that Patten was right on both counts. First, the way to success for the individual is to transcend competition. Second, and on a much broader scale, without some mechanism of selective attrition, Western society cannot evolve. But if it doesn't, it will succumb to those who do—the Japanese, or a united Europe."

The actress said, her tone horrified and at the same time fascinated, "These murders, these gang wars—you're saying those are good?"

"You're confusing two distinct phenomena, my dear. The gang wars, as you call them, are merely territorial feuds among competing distributors. We economists recognize them as what we call 'rent mechanisms,' an effective means of allocating desirable markets. Over time, the most efficient will win and competition will decline. No, the attrition I was speaking of occurs mainly within the lower strata of the population. Nature no longer provides that mechanism. Therefore, those who presume to lead us must."

Galloway felt it coming. He tried to stop it but couldn't. "It sounds like updated Nazism to me," he said.

Someone muttered a protest. "No, I'll deal with that objection," said Nuñez, turning to face him. "This is Tiller Galloway, an associate of mine. One who sometimes speaks before he thinks things through.

"Here's my response. You will accuse me of genocide, no? That's the crux of it. But genocide labels a racial group and eliminates it by murder. While what I call Pattenian selection operates without prejudice. Victims nominate themselves. Those who don't indulge survive. Those who sample dangerous pleasures but are strong enough not to be mastered, they survive, too.

"And then there are the weak, those who cannot resist beginning and cannot stop once begun. They're unfit by any measure, biological, social, economic. It is a hard thing to say, but it is the truth: They should not survive, and certainly shouldn't propagate." He shrugged, glancing around at the circle of faces.

"And you should decide that?"

"Mr. Galloway, are you being deliberately obtuse? I just told you that was the essential matter, that no human agency would decide it; that it is a new form of natural selection."

"It sounds crazy to me. Like not filling in potholes so bad drivers will hit them and have accidents."

Nuñez smiled benignly. He patted Galloway's shoulder. "That's because you're still uneducated. But that can change."

Suddenly, he understood that Nuñez was courting him. It was subtle, but not so subtle that he couldn't recognize it, even be flattered by it for a moment. But it wasn't his agreement on some long-dead economist the Baptist wanted, or to win some theoretical argument. It wasn't even fifty drums of coke.

But that can change. . . .

Juan Nuñez wanted him back in the business. Not for one job. Full time.

He was offering him a share in the kingdom.

The realization confused and frightened him. They were all looking at him, the ugly woman with the hawklike eyes, the well-dressed old men, the girls who clung to them. He said, swallowing his words, "Well, maybe you're right." And he faded back, stepped back, blended again into the shadows.

● ● ●

He was so shaken, he had to have another drink. The barman didn't look at him. He clung there like a castaway who has found a resting place after a long swim but who has even farther to go. He watched the shadows move to and fro under the cave of the night sky. One was Parkinson, clinging to Von Arx's arm this time. He scowled but didn't move.

Finally he pushed himself away. Said, swaying slightly, "Say, friend, where's the can?"

"In the house. Back there, to your right, sor."

Inside Bayou Serene, he moved through dim light. Through a glass wall, he saw four men sitting together at a table, drinks at their elbows and cigars lifted. Smoke eddied upward. He couldn't see their faces, but one of them was tall. Sears? And was that Zeno?

He was bent over the sink when the door opened behind him. He reached for the towel, blinked into the mirror—and froze.

The visage he turned to meet was familiar. The bushy brows, the bloodhound jowls, the gloomy look. Older now, but utterly familiar from a thousand newspapers and television screens. Galloway stared, then sidestepped left at the same moment Harleman did.

He stammered out, "Ah . . . I voted for you, Mr. President. In Vietnam."

The ex-President grunted something that did not make a full word. His eyes went past Galloway. He turned sideways, and slid by.

He found himself beside the fountain again. The water chuckled beneath the song of the violins.

Looking down from the top of the hill, he had a sudden queer sense of being at a summit. At a shadowy apex where diplomacy, finance, crime, and espionage were all facets of the same bloody jewel: power.

And where one missed step could take him over the edge.

11

"No," said Christian the next morning. "There's too much to do. Gonzalo will be back this afternoon. And tomorrow you're starting work."

"Why not? What harm will it do? It was Don Juan suggested it." Galloway glanced around *Ceteris's* private dining room. "Where is he? He'll tell you."

"He flew off at dawn. Business." Christian chuckled unpleasantly. "So you can stop sucking up to him. You're working for me now. A morning off? Don't make me laugh."

He knew there was no point arguing with Troy Christian. Not unless you had a gun in your hand. So he didn't say anything more. Just finished his coffee and got up. As he did so, Aydlett glanced up from boiled fish and toast. He signaled him to follow with a movement of the head.

"What you think?" Shad said in the passageway. "No dice, huh?"

"Screw him. I'm going."

"That's what I say. But how?"

"We go to the man in charge."

"Nuñez? I heard he took off."

"No. Roach."

The captain was on the stern, watching two sailors hose down the launch in the cool, bright morning wind. He tipped back his cap as Galloway explained the situation. "Don't see how I can help you, friend," he said at last. "He could want the launch anytime. If you had it, after he . . . well, I value my job, y'know."

Galloway stared past the old man's stubbled face. To the outer reef, where lavender and azure gave way to jade, sapphire, and indigo. The Bahamas held blue holes that some said harbored giant squid; drop-offs that went down forever; tide runs, sea life that made the colder water of the north seem like a desert. And visibility like nothing he'd seen, at least not since the South Pacific.

He said slowly, "So you're saying, there's no way to get over there for a swim?"

Whisky sweetness tickled his nostrils as Roach laughed. "Now, that's not what I said, boyo. You wanted the Liberator, didn't you? Can't have *her*. But as to getting to the reef . . . come along with me."

• • •

Half an hour later, he and Shad shoved off from *Ceteris's* slowly heaving hull. From their point of view now, two feet above water, it loomed over them like a smooth white wall, still frosted with dew. The tributyl-blue bottom of the hoisted-in twenty-five-footer bulged out above them. They rotated for a moment in its shadow. He fended off with an arm to avoid the curving spatter of an overboard discharge. Then they were clear, dropping aft with the current, cramped together in the little inflatable dinghy like twins in the womb.

"Got the paddle?" grunted Aydlett.

"You're sitting on it."

"Screw this. Let's start the kicker. Won't nobody hear it."

Galloway rolled to his knees cautiously. The little outboard was thumbscrewed to a stern board. It had no gearshift and only a rudimentary throttle. He set it at START, squeezed the bulb to prime it, pulled out the choke, and yanked the starter. Nothing happened, other than that the raft rocked till water slopped in. "Watch it," grunted Aydlett, behind him. "You near to got me in the eye with your elbow."

"Sorry."

It started on the third try, clattering like popcorn in a tin pot. He settled back against an inflated thwart and aimed the bow at the right-hand cut of Tanner Cay.

"Watch the tip of that spear, Tiller."

He shifted his rump, trying to find a comfortable place amid gas can, anchor, masks, snorkels, fins, and spears. With two large men in it, six feet of rubber-coated air met the waves without enthusiasm. The sea spattered in over the pointed yellow prow.

But above them the sky was blue and bright, the wind was

scented, and the sea itself was warm and clear. Its salt was sweet to his lips.

"Damn. It's good to get away from there."

"My feelings, too, Shad."

"Understand there was some kind of fancy party last night."

"Uh-huh."

"Well? What was it like?" He sounded envious.

"It wasn't anything terrific. Just a lot of fat cats feeding their faces and getting drunk."

But now that Shad had brought it up, he thought about it some more as the wind blew spray over them, dried it, wet them down again. About the people he'd met, and what Nuñez had said.

After a minute or two, he added, "He wants me back in the organization."

"You figured that. Didn't you?"

"I was afraid of it."

"What are you gonna do?"

"Say no."

"You decided that awful fast. For a man who don't have a pot to piss in or a window to throw it out."

"I don't have to think about it very long."

"He don't make this offer to everybody, right? He's not gonna like it if you tell him to walk."

"You're probably right there, Shad."

"So then what happens?"

He didn't know, so he didn't answer. Instead, he tried to relax, to forget Nuñez and Christian, Von Arx, Parkinson, the woman in cabin number five, and, above all, the fear that grew with every hour. He didn't want to go back down there. Not to three hundred feet. No matter what kind of equipment they had.

But tomorrow he'd have to.

Forget it, he told himself, looking upward into the warm blue bowl of the sky. That is tomorrow, and tomorrow is tomorrow and today is today. The steady buzz of the motor tickled his arm. The sea burbled past the rounded rubber sides. Looking over, he could see individual stones on the bottom, ten feet down. They were leaving the harbor behind, angling toward the southeastern point. For just a moment, he caught a glimpse of the house, far above. Gray, brooding, like a fortress rising above the low scrub.

He twisted his head away and faced the sea.

As they rounded the breeze picked up. It blew from the northeast, from the open Atlantic. The water shoaled as he aimed between the tide line and a black islet offshore. Beyond it were scattered rocks, bare and tortured-looking, and far off on the hazy horizon the low storm cloud of Pass Cay. He wasn't sure they could get through, but the raft didn't draw much. If they could, they'd save a mile. The bottom drew closer, only a shoal of multicolored pebbles, but now in the clear light a treasury of sea-polished jewels sealed under the glassy tide. And closer.

"Jeez, maybe we better walk."

"It's deeper than it looks."

"Well, don't go so fast. I don't want to break a shear pin out here."

That was good advice and he throttled the toy motor back. They buzzed across a stretch of bottom covered with what looked like a heavy dew. Then, suddenly, it fell away. The water darkened from the clarity of a fine diamond to faint blue, aquamarine, turquoise.

Aydlett had his head down in the bow. Then he lifted it, and sneezed suddenly. "Over and clear," he shouted back gaily. "Lobsters, here we come."

"Like I said, they're not really lobsters, Shad. Watch those spines on them. They can't nip, but they'll tear your hands open."

"Funny lobsters with spines on you, here we come."

He grinned unwillingly. One of them sounded happy, at least.

• • •

Roach's chart showed the major reef system two miles off the cay, just as Parkinson had said. That was where the big ones would lurk, the tasty ones: grouper, hogfish, jewfish that grew so huge they tried to inhale divers. Blue-hearted waves rolled toward them from the white line of surf. He twisted the throttle and the little engine buzzed like a slapped wasp. The raft plunged and tossed, wrestling with each surge. Spray drummed on taut rubber. The cool saltwater felt good, the wind felt good, even the cramped pretzel of his legs didn't bother him. For a few hours, they could be free of the miasmic suspicion, violence, and threat that crammed the luxurious corridors of the white yacht that now was cut off from their sight by the hills of Tanner Cay.

A bottle-blue comber roared toward them. The inflatable dipped, then rose, rose, rose. "Yippee-yah-yo!" shouted Aydlett. He stood up, grabbing the painter like a pair of reins.

"Sit down, Shad!"

"Powder River, let 'er rip!"

"Damn it, you tip us over—"

"Unpucker yourself, Till! You getting too serious all the time. Worrying on everything like it was life or death. Yee-*howww*!" he shouted as the raft shot skyward.

He didn't answer, just squatted in the stern, trying to keep them right side up. Sometimes a partner tried a man's patience.

When he looked toward it again, the reef lay not far ahead, a white roaring cauldron between them and the open sea. The waves flung themselves in like attacking troops. Their blood blew salty on the sea wind.

Shad yelled aloud at the sky.

• • •

He was cautious about anchoring. Snag the lunch hook in a crack in the coral, and they might lose it. Set it fouled, and the raft would drag downwind and be gone when they were ready to come back. So he maneuvered about, staring into the water, avoiding the vibrating russets and velvet browns that meant shallow spots. Finally a patch of light blue opened ahead. "That sand?" he shouted.

Aydlett, sprawled on his belly, lifted his mask from the sea. "Coral to port," he shouted back. "Stay clear of that."

Finally, the black waterman lifted his arm. His hand hovered open, then crimped into a fist.

Galloway turned into the wind and throttled back. They slowed rapidly. Aydlett sat up. "Put 'er over," he gasped. "Right now, 'fore this wind blows us back."

The little anchor flashed in the sun. It lay on the air for a moment, spinning out line behind it, then plunged into the boiling sea in silence, lost in the sullen roar that came from all around them.

"Take another look, see if she's holding."

"You got a reverse on that motor? Hold on . . . yeah, it's diggin' in good. It's good, Tiller."

He pulled out the choke, and suddenly they were alone with the sea. The raft bobbed in the foamy wrack, turning its nose to and fro as if sniffing the breeze. A hundred yards ahead, the ocean was deep blue. We're right at the edge, Galloway thought. The chart showed a drop to nearly a mile, right out there. Didn't look like it got dived much, either. Should be grouper, langouste, something worth eating.

They busied themselves with their gear. Tiller had on trunks and a T-shirt. Now he slipped off his shoes and tied them by their laces to the oarlock. He untied the gear bag and pulled on his fins. He spat in his mask, rinsed it out, and put it on, though he didn't yet seal it. Finally, he took out three yellow fiberglass rods. He fitted them one to the other and slipped his hand through the spear's rubber loop.

He glanced at Aydlett. His partner had his fins on but not his mask. He had his head down again.

Galloway half-stood, looking over the broad bent back, to see what was going on.

The big hands cupped a plastic vial. White powder lay canted in its bottom.

Aydlett glanced back and up at him, his eyes going wide.

Before he could think, he slapped it over the side. The vial hit the curve of a wave and skipped once. Then the sea ate it. It overturned, released a bubble, and sank. The powder was a veil in the clear water, a mist, a shimmer, nothing.

"Damn you, Galloway!"

"Where'd you get that? Do you know what the hell you're doing?"

"You son of a bitch!"

"Shad, that shit—don't you understand what it does to you?"

"Oh, tell me about it. You used it. Then you quit."

"I didn't *quit*, Shad. I kicked it in prison. And I still want it. Every day. Every minute. Don't—"

He stopped. He'd been about to say, Don't start. But it looked like it was too late for that. "Where'd you get it?"

"Troy gave it to me. Where else?"

"Shad—"

"Last night, while you and the big boss was out partying, he took me around. Till, you wouldn't believe what they got on that yacht. Roomful of computers and radios—it's like some kind of space center. And another room so full of money, they got it baled like hay."

"That impress you, Shad?"

"Don't go high and mighty on me! It impressed the hell out of me."

So all he said was, "Aw, Shad."

"Get out of my face, Galloway. You got to get used to the fact that Shadrach Aydlett is his own man."

"Okay, *partner*. You do whatever you want. But if you want to use, I don't want you diving with me."

"Goddamn it, Tiller—"

He turned away. He didn't feel like talking anymore. Now the raft was too small for them both.

Sealing the mask to his face with his left hand, holding the spear clear with his right, Galloway, still seething, lifted his legs and rolled backward out of the tossing dink, through the undulant membrane of the sea.

As the silvery floor became his ceiling, some heavy internal carapace came free, dissolved or dropped away. He felt like a molting langouste fighting out of its old shell. Free, but at the same time naked to any predator till the new one hardened.

Behind him, he heard a splash as another shadow returned to the heaving womb. Aydlett fell four or five feet, clamped a hand over his mask, and steadied as bubbles streamed up.

Galloway checked his sling. Six feet long assembled, the fiberglass rod was tipped with three needle-sharp spring-steel spikes. A fish hit with a paralyzer tip went rigid, its vitals gripped by the converging points. He slipped the guard off and tucked it into his glove.

Then he sucked a deep breath and surface-dived, angling down.

He could see a hundred feet through water clearer than the finest crystal. They'd anchored in a canyon between two walls of reef. Semitransparent jellyfish drifted across his vision. A loose school of silvery black bar jack came toward him as he finned downward, clearing his ears with a swallow and pop. Yellowtail snapper, glowing luminescent marigold and white, moved slowly away. Around him the sea crackled steadily, like the rustling of cellophane in a theater. Conchs wove across a coarse bottom white as salt. They were motionless for seconds, then jerked ahead an inch or two, leaving random trails like snails in a garden.

Fifteen feet. To his left rose a rampart of agonized stone. The reef. He swerved slightly, finning along toward it. As the wall neared, the jacks wavered, then left him, moving off into the blue haze. Atop it, awash at low tide but four feet under now, elkhorn coral branched fuzzy brown as long-dead maple leaves. Brain coral made him imagine some future race, evolved till only cold intelligence was left. He thought of Nuñez, then shook his head angrily; he'd come out here to forget that. Beneath their tiny cruel faces flitted schools of blue tang and sailor's-choice.

Twenty feet. A large white fish, perhaps a porgy, eyed him, considered for a moment, then cruised slowly off into the turquoise haze.

Thirty feet, and bottom. He cleared his sinuses, streamlined his left arm along his side, and finned slowly forward. He remembered Aydlett then and glanced back. His partner was behind him, T-shirt fluttering, legs driving up and down like some tireless engine.

They slid over a furrowed, pitted moonscape. Chest brushing the sand, Galloway could see beneath the coral ledges now, into the mouths of caverns. Carpeted in soft white sand, current-rippled, they invited him back into blackness. Rippling light played and shimmered deep within, and in the shadow moved inchoate shapes.

Part of the reef breathed then, and suddenly a silhouette crystallized in his brain. A mustard-brown lemon shark, eight or nine feet long, lay beneath the ledge. Its eye followed them, but save for the slow flex of its gill slits, it moved no more than a shadow.

He moved on. Lemons generally didn't bother divers, though they'd bite if you teased them, or if wounded fish agitated the water.

The coral had formed itself into overhanging masses, warped and fissured. At first it looked brown. But as he closed, it gained color—blue and green and red, and then suddenly every color that light held, coruscating, livid hues, bright as warning signs. A squirrelfish froze, lurking like a saint in a grotto. Dozens of wrasses and chromis, hamlets, damselfish hovered, brilliant and scissile as the shattered windows of a bombed cathedral. A stoplight parrotfish, clown-striped with cornflower blue, violet, verdigris, and marigold, gnawed at the coral with a birdlike beak. It eyed him expressionlessly, defecating a mist of fine sand.

It was another world, a universe without man, where human guilt and regret had no place.

Then, without warning, he saw it suddenly in a different way, as his mind had suddenly grasped the pattern of the shark. Not as a garden, but a battlefield, a grim charnel of creatures that warred to eat and reproduce. This brilliant beauty grew from a billion-year war. But only to those outside that eternal tao of killer and victim, like himself, was it visible.

He heard again a calm voice in a garden, speaking in cold syllogisms of evolution, selection, the elimination of the unfit. For a chilling moment, he wondered whether it could be right.

But now he needed air. It was time to go up, and with something not far from sorrow, he lifted his face once more to the bright surface.

To the world where he had to survive, or die.

• • •

They moved along the reef face for perhaps an hour. Gradually his anger at Aydlett eased off. His partner was right. He'd make his own mistakes. God! He'd made enough himself.

He passed over a rope half-buried in the sand. It was old hemp, crusted with weed and sea growth. He dove, and ripped it up smoking from the seabed. Finally, it went taut. He followed it for a few yards, then saw why. A huge old iron anchor, rusted and crusty with coral. The reef had grown around it, incorporating it like a great amoeba that took centuries to move a yard.

He was getting ready to surface again when he saw yellow-brown filaments probing the sea. He swallowed to push back the air hunger, and altered course toward the gap in the coral. His mask was fogging and he eased it, let in half an inch of water, and rolled it across the glass.

When he looked again, he saw them clearly: two, three pairs of slender whiplashes, and below them, backed into the crevice, the clumsy insectile bodies. His mouth watered. Fresh langouste tails, boiled for two minutes, then soaked with liquid butter—there was nothing more delicious in the sea.

He was thinking this, edging through the coral, when out from the flickering liquid shadows darted black arms, a snaky writhe of hair, and a silver flash.

Galloway rolled, the fiberglass spear haft a yellow bar between him and the knife. The point retreated, then came in again, gleaming blue in the beautiful soundless light.

He parried it again, and this time got a knee against the other's chest. He shoved, crashing the other into the coral wall, then broke free and burst upward, heart hammering against his ribs.

He shot up, to see the buckled dinghy drop beneath the knife curve of a trawler's keel. As his mask broke the surface, a thin black form swiveled toward him, yelled, and pointed.

Three more men plunged in. They carried thin black lines in their hands: spears. Their masks turned here and there beneath a reversed fountain of bubbles.

Galloway sucked a last breath, pulling it all the way down into his balls, and dove again.

The little outboard hit sand with a grating clunk, trailing torn rubber.

They were trapped out here, miles from shore, alone on the reef with these men—whoever they were. There were at least four in the water now, and one in the boat. Not good odds. Not hand to hand, against people who looked like they knew what they were doing underwater.

All this streamed through his head as he sank, looking around for Aydlett. His heart, suddenly accelerated, was slamming in his ears.

At last he saw him. The waterman was locked nose-to-nose with another diver. Not the one he'd fought off. This one was white. Stocky, with red shorts. Aydlett was forcing his arm backward. As Tiller neared, a crack like a breaking branch came through the water. Shad let go. The other recoiled, then corkscrewed for the surface, one arm bent at an angle that meant he wouldn't be back.

A man emerged below him from behind a clump of fire-red anemones, preceded by a terrified parrotfish big as a small pig. It was Snaky Hair, the one he'd tangled with already. His back was bleeding from dozens of small cuts. Sliding his hand forward on the sling, Galloway lined him up. The Bahamian, aiming his goggles from side to side, still hadn't seen him. Galloway waited for him to come into range, swallowing to drive back the need for air.

He was about to shoot when an arm clamped his windpipe from behind. He saw from the corner of his mask the serrated saw blade of a homemade knife, already slicing inward, toward his throat.

The only thing he could do was duck his head, and bite, hard.

It didn't work very well. The point tore through his cheek. But he clamped down, his teeth grating on the rough steel.

The blade stopped. It had anticipated softness. The resistance of teeth and jaw took his assailant by surprise, puzzled him for a second—enough time for Galloway to pull his spear back, anyway. Too close to thrust with it. So he pulled it across, raking the prongs across the other's face.

The steel spikes tore furrows in flesh, caught in the goggles, tore them off, too.

The other diver forgot about cutting Galloway's throat and grabbed his own face. Galloway let go of the spear and went for the knife. They struggled briefly over it. He won. He stabbed clumsily and felt the point go in. He got it out and thrust again. This time the saw edge caught in something. The knife turned out of his grip as the Bahamian pulled away. The man swam a few feet, hands clamped to his stomach, then stopped kicking. Bubbles roared out of his open mouth. He flailed his arms, craned his face backward, looking up at brightness above.

When it was finished he drifted for a moment. Dead, he looked very young. Then the body rolled over slowly. Bent at the waist, like a man sitting down in an easy chair, it met the sand and settled back. It came to rest in the shadow of the reef.

Then, below him, that shadow lengthened, like an early coming of night. Galloway stared.

The lemon shark slipped out from beneath the ledge. It hesitated, then slid toward the body.

He became suddenly conscious that he had to have air or die. And his mouth was filling with warm liquid. He turned quickly, making sure there was no one behind him, and kicked upward.

Air. He coughed out blood and sucked it in. The strange boat was a hundred yards off now, rolling wildly as it came beam to the reef. He thought of boarding it, trying for the man in it, then dismissed the idea. If he and Shad got out of here alive, that would be more than they deserved.

For the first time, he found a second to wonder: Who were they? Islanders—Bahamians—that much was evident.

But why were they trying to kill them?

This was no casual mugging. This had been planned. The way the boat was patrolling between them and the shore, they weren't to be allowed to swim back. With the blood, there'd be more sharks on the scene soon. Not lemons, either. Sharpnoses or bulls.

Now that he had air, he realized that his hands were empty. He'd lost his spear in the last desperate hand-to-hand.

This all passed through his mind in the time it took to draw three deep whooping breaths. He drew another, and plunged his mask below the surface.

For a moment, he didn't see anyone. The reef doubled back here, coral heads and ramparts separated by the narrow cracks floored with white aragonite. He swam rapidly along the surface, looking down. There was the crevice where they saw the langouste. And there was his spear, the yellow shaft bright against the sand, the rubber loop waiting for his hand. No one around. Get it, right now. He pulled a last huge inhalation through the snorkel tube, rising as he did so to get as much into his lungs as he could, and surface-dived.

He was ten feet down when two men came around a projection of the reef, saw him, and began swimming as fast as they could.

Both were armed. He doubled his speed as his down angle steepened. The distance between them shrank rapidly. They came fast as barracuda, their arms streamlined back. They were divers, no damn doubt about that. So fast that when his desperately outstretched hand seized the slim shaft and lifted it, he realized he couldn't face them both. As they covered the last few feet, their fins kicking puffs of powder-fine white up from the bottom like smoke, he turned his mask this way and that.

To his left was a tunnel. One of the black caves under the coral. There might be a hole big enough to come up. There had better be, because he was going in. Only one at a time to fight then. And if they didn't come in after him, he might lose them in the labyrinth of the reef.

His chest brushed the sand as he slid under the ledge. He glanced around, alert for the odd moray, as jackknife fish darted away in terror. No telling what else lived back in these tunnels.

Eels for sure; they covered the reef at night, but in daylight they hid within it, filling the coral convolutions like maggots in rotten cheese.

The blackness deepened ahead. Strange shapes moved in it at the limits of his vision. The sand he flew over was fine and white as cocaine. Then everything was lost in blackness. He kept swimming, desperate now, his hand outstretched ahead. Was there a way out? He couldn't stay down much longer.

There, ahead, the dancing light, flickering in the midst of velvet dark. He drove toward it, his legs starting to numb. Above his head was a bottleneck gap, then a chimneylike ascent, like a backstairs to heaven. Light. Air, up there. He bent, slid snakelike through the neck, and started up, his throat closing as he swallowed.

A shadow moved between him and the sun. He grabbed a projecting coral knob to stop his body's rush.

The man was waiting for him. His goggles flashed as he looked in the direction from which Galloway had come. He raised his hand jauntily. The gesture was clear: I've got him at this end. All he has to do is come out.

He thought in despair and terror, They lived here. They knew every cranny and exit of these reefs the way he knew the *Marcon*'s sunken engine room.

The man above him was huge as a bear and looked twice as big underwater. His bare arms were laced with pink scars. One hand was wrapped around a five-foot length of reinforcing bar, with a barb brazed to the sharpened end. It was a crude but no doubt effective weapon, as effective as his own.

The scars triggered something in his mind. He stared at them as the man moved his fins gently, staring down.

It was the man from the Rooster, the one he'd fought on Green Turtle. What was his name?

Wuckie.

The black man hovered above him. Obviously, he couldn't see him. It was too bright up there, too dark down here, halfway up the tapering chimney of coral. He was safe as long as he didn't come out. But he had to breathe—

Galloway crouched in the shadow. He swallowed again, but it didn't help anymore. Through the need for air, the realization that he'd been set up penetrated him like a dull knife.

Wuckie had been with Parkinson. And she knew he was here, aboard *Ceteris*.

No time to think about that now. He stared up, concentrating his attention. It was harder and harder to wait, but he had to. His hands began to shake, wanting to release rock, to push himself toward the light. Above him the Bahamian turned, the smooth big body graceful underwater as a sea lion. Then, for the second time, Wuckie's goggles flashed as he looked toward the far end of the tunnel.

Galloway went up the chimney, kicking with all the power left in his legs. A school of sergeant majors hesitated, then broke in sudden terror as he lunged up through them.

The goggles flashed again. They turned downward, warned by some tremor in the sea. The big body doubled suddenly, and the iron point came around.

Galloway thrust his right arm out and up, too fast to really aim, and released the spear.

It went low. Five feet below, he looked into Wuckie's eyes as the paralyzer head slammed into the meat of his thigh. They widened, and the mouth opened. A huge gout of air came out. Galloway held the thong grimly. The big man kicked, struggling on the shaft like a game fish.

Then the Bahamian bent, and the scarred hands closed. The shaft crackled, then suddenly snapped away, leaving the spikes embedded. Blood formed a slowly whirling cloud, like octopus ink.

Slowly, glaring back at him, the big islander pulled himself upward and away. I didn't kill him, Galloway thought. But Wuckie was out of *this* fight.

Galloway reached the surface in time to see the other man, the snake-haired man, drown.

He was twenty feet down. One fin was gone and his goggles hung at his throat like a necklace. Other than that, he seemed unharmed.

Just above him, Shad Aydlett made for the surface. He was hurt. Tiller saw that right away—not only by the frog kick that his partner reverted to when he forgot himself but by the black mist that curled after him.

The man below him gave up trying to swim upward. He looked yearningly up, then, reluctantly, down again.

Then he bent, and began pulling at the rope that tied him to the seafloor. The inch-thick, weed-covered anchor rope, knotted around his waist. His fingers slipped and tore on the barnacled hemp. As he pulled at it in increasing fury, he drifted toward the bottom.

Galloway glanced away, and saw that Shad, trailing black blood, had made the surface. His legs kicked and dangled, kicked and dangled.

The whine of a propeller seeped into his ears, sounding like a huge outraged mosquito.

When he looked back, Snaky Hair was pulling himself down the rope. When he reached the bottom he braced his feet and yanked. As it had for Galloway, the rope ripped up. Clouds of powdery sand boiled up, turning the sea smoky. Galloway sculled with his hands, watching in horror.

The man came out of the smoke, yanking himself hand over hand along the cable, his face contorted. His eyes caught Galloway, then slid off. But no, Tiller thought; He couldn't see me, not without goggles. Without glass and air over your eyes, the sea was only a green blur.

He dove, half-intending to help, but slid to a stop five feet down. You couldn't get within reaching distance of a man in that situation. You'd just die with him.

The whine grew louder. It seemed to come from every direction. He knew that wasn't right. Sound traveled faster in water, so the human directional sense didn't work very well. The long-haired man heard it, too. He glanced upward again, toward the light, then bent again to his mad struggle.

The last fathom of cable ripped up, and he came face-to-face with the anchor, grown into the wall of living coral.

From somewhere distant, Galloway thought, The eels will feast tonight.

When the man below was done with drowning, swaying like a wilted blossom on a hempen stem, Galloway kicked himself back to the surface. He tilted his head to clear his snorkel, and broke the undulant mirror that gave him back in the last moment before he surfaced his own distorted, bloody face.

He was looking at the bow of an oncoming boat. At almost the same instant, he caught the snarl of the man in it, caught a lifted object that swung toward him—

The shot tore the water apart a yard away. The shock hurt his skin. He went under by reflex. But not quite deep enough. Directly ahead of his blown-open eyes was the keel, bow on. And below it, reaching down, was a silver cyclone that grew larger and larger, the whine drilling his skull like a high-speed trepanning.

The prop chewed past a foot over his drawn-in head. He tumbled helplessly in the wash, then straightened and dug himself another five feet deeper.

What could they do now?

They had to come up.

And when they did, they'd die.

Shad, he thought then. Shad!

He saw him ahead, on the sandy floor, next to the raft. Or the remains of the raft, dragged down by the little engine. He was lying motionless beside it. He was bleeding. For a moment, Galloway thought he was dead.

Then he saw that he was breathing.

He saw it as he angled down. One cell had been torn open, losing its buoyancy. But it still held a bubble of air. Compressed, too; pressurized by the sea. Aydlett rolled his eyes as he neared. He had one of the inflation valves in his mouth. Bubbles trickled from his mask and rocked toward the surface, expanding as they rose.

Shad closed his eyes, sucking in a breath. Then took the plastic tube from his mouth and held it out.

• • •

The air in the raft, each breath locked back till their lungs ached and their eyes grew dim, lasted for ten minutes. Then they came up together, ready to face a shotgun with sharp steel.

The sea around them was empty. As the swell lifted him, he glimpsed the trawler far away, between two of the black islets. He could see men in it, but he couldn't tell how many. Then he dropped to a trough. When he lifted again, it was gone.

He spat bright blood and called hoarsely, "Shad."

"Yo."

"How you doing? How's your side?"

"Bleedin', but I can swim."

"You see those bulls? That eight-footer?" The hole in his cheek made the words hiss.

"Yeah. They moving in, all right. What we ought to do?"

"Stay on the surface. Swim for the cay." A wave slapped his face casually and he swallowed some; the salt sea stung his wound. He coughed and finally got out, "Swim slow. Don't splash. Wind's with us, anyway."

"Got you." Aydlett's voice was faint, but it was there.

He took a deep shuddering breath. The air stank of salt and blood. His mouth was filling. This time he remembered to swallow it. The less blood in the water, the better.

Turning on his back, he began finning slowly toward the low green hills.

12

The next morning, his tongue probing the lumpy cable stitching of *Ceteris*'s semitrained medic, he steadied himself against the yacht's roll as he looked back along a hundred-yard droop of wire to the barge.

Today was sunny again, would be hot, but the wind was up and the Atlantic had built some bigger waves while they'd been inside. Though not, he was sorry to say, so much as to make it impossible to dive. The yacht, with her high freeboard, rode easily. But from time to time a sea larger than the rest broke over the barge in a shower of green and white, soaking the men who were laying out wires and cables about her unprotected deck.

The polished teak fantail looked serious today, too. The deck chairs and awnings were gone. Gonzalo had flown in to Marsh Harbour in a chartered cargo plane the afternoon before. He'd come aboard not long after they'd gotten back from the reef. The little helicopter had shuttled back and forth all night long, ferrying in the gear and supplies he'd bought in Fort Lauderdale and Port Everglades.

Now it was laid out on canvas ready for the first dive. And over it stood the Cuban, his large nose and bright eyes alternating between it and his clipboard.

Removing his tongue from the stitching with an act of will, Galloway strolled toward him. "Señor Gonzalo. We lose something overnight?"

"Hello, Señor Galloway. I'm checking double. I like to be sure."

"That makes triple. Shad and I went over it before breakfast. But it's a good attitude."

"When you are dealing with diving."

"That's right." He smiled tightly, and the small man smiled back. Galloway wondered, What exactly had he meant, that night in cabin number five? When he'd said . . . what was it . . . "Do you approve of this sort of thing."

He'd sidestepped the question. It sure as hell wasn't because he approved. It was because he didn't trust him. He didn't trust Gonzalo or anyone else aboard, with the possible exception of Pat Roach, to inform him of the state of day or night.

He remembered again, with sudden shortness of breath, how Parkinson had betrayed him. After that, as close to death as they'd come on the reef . . . no. He couldn't trust anyone at all.

"Nervous?" said Gonzalo, his eyes glittering like black coral beads. He even cocked his head like a parrot, Galloway thought.

"Some. Yeah."

Christian appeared above, aft of the turbine funnels. He looked down, then disappeared. A few seconds later, he came out on deck. He had on white shorts, a white terry shirt with blue piping, and a pale blue bandanna twisted around his neck. He looked rested and well. Galloway grunted, "Morning."

The *jefe* arched an eyebrow. "Did you hear that, Fabito? You realize that's the first time he's greeted me?"

Gonzalo smiled quickly but didn't answer in words. After a moment, Christian went on, looking toward the distant mascara line of the cays. "Oh, my. Rough this morning, isn't it? But Captain R. says it'll drop later in the day. You ready, Lloyd Bridges?"

"No. I need another day. My partner's never dove with this equipment, never breathed mixed gas before—"

"We're not here to train your employees. We start today." Christian leaned closer. "You look like you'd been dragged through a hedge backward, Galloway. Is that cheek okay? Does it bother you?"

It wasn't; it hurt steadily. It had hurt like the devil the night before, getting sewn up; he'd refused the proffered anesthetic, pure cocaine. But he knew how much weight anyone else's pain or inconvenience carried with Troy Christian. So he just said, "It'll do. At least with a band mask, I won't have to bite on a mouthpiece."

"Good. And it taught you a lesson. Not to disobey. Didn't it?"

Christian meant their excursion to the reef. He winced again as his tongue brushed the sutures. It hadn't taught him much that he could see, but to preserve the prevailing good humor, he nodded.

The *jefe* hadn't been in a good mood yesterday. Galloway and Aydlett had crawled ashore on Tanner Cay after two hours in the water. When they called Roach from the harbormaster's office, Christian had been in the pilothouse. Galloway had had to explain where they were and how they'd gotten there.

He could hear Christian's icy fury over the crackle of the VHF. There'd been no threats then, not over the air, for everyone to hear. But he'd felt a worm gnawing his intestines. There was going to be trouble.

When the launch brought them back, and they'd faced Christian alone in the saloon, he'd started with a dressing-down. At least it had started out as one. Then it had degenerated into threats, coughing, and shouting. Christian had started smoking, rock after rock, and then began screaming accusations of spying and conspiracy. Aydlett had made the mistake of trying to argue. Tiller tried to stop him but failed.

And then at last, even Christian had run out of words. He'd turned away, trembling, and ordered them out, smiling the cold smooth smile that promised all too clearly that once their work for Nuñez was done, then they would answer to him.

But then Galloway had explained how they were attacked, why they were both hurt. Instantly, rage at their disobedience had changed to anger at the idea of "natives" attacking "his" people. His ravings had been redirected, transferred, like electric current at the flip of a relay.

It made him shudder. The man they were working for had left reality behind. Something was loose in his brain.

Christian came out of the pilothouse again. He called down harshly in Spanish. Sailors shouted at the bow, and the anchor clattered down. He swept his eyes around the horizon. Then leaned down.

"We're alone—for now. But *they* will be out here sooner or later. I want to get done fast, Galloway, as fast as you can. We're not out here for safety records, and you're not being paid by the hour. Understand me? You, Aydlett, you understand?"

Shad nodded, glancing sideways at Galloway. "Who's 'they'?" he muttered.

"Stow it, Shad."

"Are you two listening?" Christian rose on tiptoe. His face had gone pale.

"Yes, Troy. I'm dressing out now."

"I don't see you dressing out. I see you talking! I see you lounging around! Get them into the water, Gonzalo!"

Beside him, expressionless as a police reconstruction, the two Indians stared down with slung Uzis.

The Cuban motioned Galloway to a makeshift seat on a gear locker. He sighed, pulled off his shirt, and picked up his wet suit bottoms.

The night before, he and Shad had looked through the gear Gonzalo had brought back. He'd asked for Mark One–style band masks, rigged for open-circuit mixed gas. The Cuban had found three of the commercial versions, made by Kirby-Morgan, heavy wet suits, a selection of umbilicals and fittings, and most important, eight big 244-cubic-foot tanks of helium/oxygen breathing mixture.

Gonzalo hadn't done badly; but still they were by no means properly equipped. A commercial outfit working this job would lower a surface-supplied diving chamber. The divers would live in it between work periods on the wreck. A specialized support ship would supply hot water for heated suits, electricity, breathing gas, even cabled-in entertainment. There'd be a decompression chamber on site; a diving medic on five minutes' call; and ten to thirteen more support personnel, including master divers, skilled tenders, timekeepers, gas kings, and console operators. There'd be backups suited and ready to go over the side at the first hint of a problem.

Here he had Roach and Gonzalo, for tender and rigger. And for safety man, Gonzalo again, wearing Galloway's scuba—Gonzalo, who'd confessed that the deepest he'd actually been at Cozumel was sixty feet.

The partners had put together the dive plan late last night in Galloway's cabin, Shad sucking a pencil, Tiller punching a calculator between bouts of staring at the bulkhead.

At first he'd thought, Saturation dive. That was how a commercial outfit would approach a job like this. He'd thought of using one of the fuel tanks as a habitat. Anchor it at depth, fill it with breathing mix, fix it up with makeshift bunks, and just stay down for however long it took—two days, three, a week; once your tissues were saturated with helium, everything stabilized, as long as you stayed at the increased pressure.

But when he started calculating, he hit a brick wall.

At three hundred feet, a diver breathed ten times as much gas as he did at sea level. He had eight 244s of heliox on hand. On the surface, that would last two men a full day. But at depth, they'd use it up in two and a half hours.

Gonzalo said there was more in Fort Lauderdale, and though it was expensive, he didn't have to worry about that. The problem was transport. Nuñez's organization could fly gas in to Marsh Harbour as easily as they flew cocaine out. The catch was that at three hundred feet he and Shad would breathe it faster than the helo could deliver it, even flying round the clock; the little Bell Agusta could only carry one cylinder at a time.

He opened the manual and reread the section titled "Saturation Diving Underwater Breathing Apparatus." Then he frowned.

The Kirby-Morgan band mask was supplied through an umbilical hose. In commercial operations, the breathing gas went from a gas bank on the support ship down to the personnel capsule, then through a shorter line to the diver. But the KMB had a valve and connector for an emergency breathing supply, too. This connector took a standard eighty-cubic-foot scuba tank. He wondered whether he could use these and swap them out. But when he did the math, that was impossible: working where *Guapi* lay, a diver would suck an eighty dry in minutes. They'd be so busy changing tanks, they'd never get to work.

He finally had to give up the whole idea of saturating. They just used gas too fast.

He didn't like the corner the figures were forcing him into. If they didn't saturate, they had to surface at the end of each work period. This meant decompressing, and every day. He flipped through the tables, followed them down with a finger, and grimaced.

"What you grinching up about? Bad news?"

"We got to come up at the end of every work period."

"That's not so bad."

And Galloway had said, last night, "You'll be singin' a different tune when you try it, Shad."

"How's this go on?" said Aydlett now, squatting in his wet suit opposite him. Galloway started, coming back to the present. Something else you'd never do in commercial work, send a man down without any training on the gear, the first time he used mixed gas. Should he protest again? Ask Gonzalo to back him up? One glance up at Christian put that idea to bed.

He took a deep breath, leaned forward, and clamped his hand on Aydlett's shoulder. They were face-to-face, and for the first time it occurred to Galloway how bad it would be if something happened to his partner. "Listen up now, Shad," he said. "This is important."

"I understand, Tiller. I'm listening," he said; and for that moment at least, they understood each other as perfectly as two men could.

"This is a band mask. It goes on like this," he said. "Covers the whole front of your face, and the straps hook around and snap—see? The window part's separate from the oral/nasal unit. This's the mike. This here's the earphone."

"What? We can talk?"

"Yeah, but it'll take some getting used to." He explained the rest—the defogger valve, nonreturn valve, frame exhaust and drain valve, regulator, emergency gas-supply valve to the single eighty on which they'd descend. Aydlett nodded. Galloway put it on him and had him manipulate each control. Then he took it off and explained the umbilical assembly, the gas-supply hose, phone cable, and lifeline.

Above them, Christian cleared his throat and spat. The sun was raising a heat shimmer off the sea. Sweat covered Aydlett's face. Galloway felt it dripping off his nose, slipping down the inside of his suit. He couldn't cut it short, though. There'd be no margin for error at three hundred feet. Finally, he said, "The rest of the gear's pretty much what you're used to. Think you got it?"

"We'll find out." Aydlett pulled the straps tight on his buoyancy compensator and stood up with a grunt. "Let's go. I feel like a baked ham at Easter."

Galloway fitted his own band mask as they penguin-waddled toward the stern. He made sure the steady flow valve was off and cracked the EGS valve. Then sucked in. Helium/oxygen came, but it took effort; he adjusted the dial-a-breath till it came easily.

Two sailors supported him as he descended the stairs. He lifted
one leg; Gonzalo snarled Spanish; someone slipped on his
fins—first one, then the other.

He stood at the edge, looking down into the water. He was
sweating like a pig. The cold, dry gas hissed into his throat, tasting
like metal shavings. He checked the tool belt, his BC, the bulky
coiled-up umbilical. Beside him Aydlett moved up, shaking his
head as if trying to get out from under the 110 pounds they each
wore and carried.

From the barge, across the heaving water, black men watched
them. A few raised their hands, in salute, warning, blessing, or
farewell. Or perhaps a mixture of all these things.

Without looking up, he stepped forward, into the cool blue sea.

• • •

The coolness laved his body like a refreshing drink. One hand
gripping the yacht's anchor line, the other holding a steel shackle
and a heavy line, he slid into the abyss feetfirst. He didn't have
much time, breathing off the eighty. No point using it up faster
by swimming. He looked up; Aydlett was a bulky shadow above.
The tapered silhouette of Nuñez's floating pleasure dome cut a
black wedge from the sunlit blue around them.

As he passed the fifty-foot mark, all his suspicions and misgiv-
ings, fears and theories of the past few days gave way now to one
goal: a fast salvage, without major damage to him and Shad.

If he could manage that with about eight strikes against them
before they even hit the water. Even in the best of conditions,
salvage diving was dangerous. Working at three hundred feet,
without backups or rest or the other safety measures he was used
to from oil-field work, it would be exhausting and almost suicidal.

He had a good idea of what this was going to be like. The
human body wasn't designed for fifty fathoms. The cold—it was
cold down there, even in the tropics—would penetrate a suit in
about half an hour. In an hour, their teeth would be chattering.
Later their arms and legs would go numb and they'd find it hard
to breathe. Still later, they'd get clumsy, drop tools, be barely able
to clip a messenger to a line.

All this, of course, assumed they didn't get the bends, embo-
lism, oxygen poisoning, high-pressure nervous syndrome—

Two hundred feet.

He slid down the cable spread-eagled, the weight in his right hand plummeting him downward. His left glove, tightening on the line, slowed him when the rate of descent got ahead of his ears. He stared downward through high-impact acrylic as below him a black length coalesced from the dim murk of depth.

The job was razor-edge from start to finish. It was bad diving. Bad planning, bad equipment, bad methods. But their only chance of surviving was to succeed.

Two fifty, and there it was: the canted, pointed bow of the sunken trawler. He left the anchor line, which angled off into the gloom, and swam for it as he dropped the last fifty feet. He shifted the tending line to his right hand. Glanced back, twisting his body. With the band mask it was harder to turn. There's Shad, he thought. He faced forward again, and crashed slowly into the rusting wire mesh of the animal cages.

He fought free, trying to keep sharp edges clear of his BC, and moved a few feet forward. A short search for the mooring points, and he shackled the line fast.

Trying to pitch his voice low, he said, "Tender, Galloway."

"Go ahead." Gonzalo, in his earphone.

"Can you understand me?"

"Your voice is high and garbled. Speak more slowly, please."

"Roger. Send . . . down . . . the . . . tanks."

"Si, sending down the tanks."

They appeared almost immediately out of the blue above, a huge lashed mass of the big 244s. They came sailing down the guideline, faster than they should, and crashed into the cages, raising a cloud of silt and rust. Not wasting a moment, he twisted a steel cap off and screwed the end of his umbilical to the fitting underneath. He beckoned Aydlett in and connected his, too. "Okay," he said. "Deep breath, now."

He closed his EGS valve. The hiss of gas stopped. Then, hoping this was going to work, he closed his eyes and cracked the valve to the umbilical.

Water spurted instantly into his mask, tore at his closed lips, and kept coming. God, how much was in the damn hose . . . he fought animal terror, knowing that if there wasn't air behind it, a free ascent from three hundred feet was like playing Russian roulette with a double-barreled shotgun.

The blast of water gave way suddenly to a hiss of gas. He gasped out, in, out. The tension in his shoulders ebbed. He was on the 244. They had half an hour to work before they needed to change again.

The first order of business was to get their safe space set up. The men on the barge had already flooded the former marina fuel tank. Now he told Gonzalo to lower it. He watched it come down, already-attached lengths of wire rope dangling. A command brought it to a stop a few feet above them. Moving with deliberate speed, he shackled it to the bow, tethering it like a balloon.

Once it hung properly attached, suspended in the water, he checked its moorings one last time. Then swam upward, trailing his umbilical, and slid through the open manhole.

There was still a little free space of air at the top. He waited till he heard Shad beside him, then unsnapped his mask and groped at his belt.

His hand light showed him Aydlett's eyes first; then, as he flicked it around, the rusty, echoing interior. It smelled of water and rust and, very faintly, of oil.

"Our little home away from home," he said, his voice a reedy squeak with the helium. "On and off, for the next couple days, anyway."

Aydlett, sounding like a rubber ducky: "Shee-it."

He'd asked Roach to send it down packed with wood pallets, blankets, canned meat, and water. That must be what was bumping into them as they floated about. He put his light on a Spam can. The pressure had crushed both ends. It wasn't luxurious, as work capsules went. But at least they had air, food, and water.

He'd been unable to think of any way to provide heat, though. And already he felt cold. So during their break, as their exhaled gas drove the sea downward, they huddled together suit-to-suit. After a while he turned the flashlight on again and searched around. Roach, bless his heart, had thought of everything. The pint of bourbon had come down not in glass but in a soft plastic squeeze bottle.

"Okay," he squeaked at last. "Here we go."

He'd decided to start the salvage proper by locating the wreck's fuel bunkers. They found two, port and starboard. Galloway began measuring the wreck with a tape reel while Shad rigged standpipes in the fill holes with underwater-setting concrete.

The 244s lasted for almost exactly thirty minutes. When they stopped getting gas, they turned the eighties on again, pulled themselves back to the bow by their umbilicals, and switched to the next.

He began calculating in his head as he finished his measurements. He had a pretty good idea now how he could raise her. He wouldn't bother to patch the holes in the bow, not if *Guapi* wouldn't be refloated. Christian wanted to lift it, get the drums out, and drop it again. That was fine with him. In some ways, it made things easier to have the ship be disposable.

At the end of the second hour, shaking, numb, dizzy, and tunnel-visioned, they disconnected their umbilicals from the last empty 244s and kicked them over the side of the wreck. They tumbled down slowly, almost weightless now that they were last empty. Galloway had asked about returning them, refilling them, but Gonzalo had just shaken his head. They pulled themselves slowly back through the manhole, into a nearly dry tank.

"Ready to call it a day?"

"I been ready for the last hour. J-J-Jesus! It's cold."

"This part's tricky now, Shad. Listen close."

Ten minutes later, breathing off fresh eighties, they emerged. Galloway looked around again at the silent, listing wreck, the gray light, the bottom stretching silently away.

Then he pressed a valve, and began to rise.

• • •

It took them four hours to reach the surface. They stopped six times, for longer and longer periods as the sea grew slowly brighter, and at that he was cutting the recommended number of stops in half. At 130 feet they switched to compressed air, to speed decompression. At the first breath, nitrogen narcosis hit him, softer than any drug, a weird high that made him want to gibber like a chimp.

They spent hours like monkeys, hanging on ropes like chimps on vines, only less comfortably; his whole body convulsed with shudders. He'd never seen the hand on a watch move so slowly.

He had time to think, though, to think over everything, hanging there in blue space, waiting for gas to bleed out of his tissues. To plan tomorrow's work; to calculate buoyancy and stability in his head; and last, to think about what was going to happen next—when *Guapi*, and her cargo, came to the surface.

Suspended like a fly in blue amber, he thought it out slowly, point by point.

Nuñez. At first, the Baptist had promised to let them go as soon as the cargo was retrieved. Now, it looked like, he wanted them—or at least, him—back with the Combine.

When he turned him down; when he said to the man in white, Send me home—what would he do then?

Christian. Once the coke was topside, he'd be trouble. His mood swings were getting more violent, and more paranoid. He wouldn't be surprised if the *jefe* intended to shoot them. Only if Nuñez was here was he safe. And he was safe with Nuñez only if he said he would join up.

Could he lie? Say he'd join, and then, at the first opportunity, slip away?

It would be short-term safety. He'd have to live the rest of his life expecting a knock at the door. Expecting another swarthy stranger in Buxton. Wondering whether every Latin who came into the store had been assigned to kill him.

Zeno? His offer of protection? Unfortunately, he didn't trust the DEA agent, either. If he was intimate with Sears and Von Arx, he might be capable of turning him back to Nuñez, or burning him in a dozen other ways. Even cops who started honest had a way of buckling when they saw everybody else playing the game.

He sucked compressed air doubtfully. None of his options sounded appealing.

The last stage: ninety-nine minutes at forty feet. He stretched and looked upward. The surface looked close enough to touch.

And there, yes, was the little Cuban, dropping toward them out of the light, trailing two sets of fresh tanks. . . .

Two hours later, he clicked the door of his cabin closed and collapsed on his bunk. He lay there for minutes, but the shuddering grew worse. At last, he forced himself up. He slid open a drawer; held the bottle to his mouth for a minute. Then he capped it, breathing hard, and put it away. He stared blankly out the porthole. Then he pulled his shorts off and padded barefoot into the head.

He stood under the shower for fifteen minutes, leaning against first one smooth marble wall and then the other as the yacht rolled—blazing hot water this time—till the frozen core inside him softened.

Wrung out, he toweled slowly while he looked over what little he had to wear. Finally, he put the robe on and sat with a grunt. After a moment he leaned back full length.

He was thinking of going down to eat when sleep took him as suddenly as a silenced bullet in the back of the head.

13

The next day, they spent three hours on the bottom. Six full 244s apiece. That was all the helicopter had managed to fly in.

Galloway took a hose from the compressor down with him. The concrete sealing *Guapi*'s fuel bunkers had set overnight. Working rapidly, exchanging an occasional terse remark, he and Aydlett manifolded the air hose to the standpipes. After fifteen minutes he told Roach, topside, to start the compressor.

When the first bubbles appeared, he twisted the connection tight and finned with his hands, backing away. Job number two, done. It would take time; at this depth, the compressor could deliver only a few cubic feet a minute, but soon the bunkers would be filled not with seawater and oil but with compressed air.

If both bunkers held, he calculated that would add thirty-eight tons of lift to the motionless hull.

He wished he could add some lift to himself. He'd woken groggy, still weary and sore. He'd had to force himself to eat. Well, he reassured himself now, glancing around for the paleness in the dim that would be Aydlett's bubbles, with luck it would be today, and tomorrow, and then they could lift.

And after that . . .

He decided not to think about that right now.

They passed the next two hours in a routine that quickly became so mind-numbing that he would have turned off his brain to save oxygen if he could have. The riggers on the barge bolted wire loops onto Von Arx's used fifty-five-gallon drums, filled them with water, and slid them down the tending line. The two divers picked them up on the bottom and wrestled them first into the forepeak, arranging them carefully with fill holes down, and then, when that was full, into the superstructure aft. When each drum was secured they filled it with gas. They wedged, chained, and wired for what seemed like an eternity, rolling drums up and down the deck with a slow rumble like submerged thunder.

Occasionally, he had to stop, go limp and float and just suck air, cough, suck air. Yesterday's lethargy was nothing to this. By the time the superstructure was full, he was reeling about blindly, jamming his thumbs and fingers, slamming his head into coamings till he saw stars. Or down here, he thought, are they starfish?

Funny, since that first visit he hadn't seen any fish at all.

Finally, they had all the drums aboard they could cram in. He'd counted forty-two. He blinked at his watch. He couldn't remember how long they'd been down. He looked around but didn't see Aydlett, or his bubbles. He wheezed into the microphone, "Shad."

"Yeah?" A voice in his ears, but no presence.

"Where are you?"

Aydlett swam out through the shattered window of the pilothouse. "You know there's a skeleton in there?"

"Yeah. I got to swap out. Let's talk."

"Huh?" Across the slanted deck, Aydlett stared at him. Bubbles roared out of his mask. Galloway watched them rise. Those were expensive bubbles. They were 84 percent helium.

He pointed toward their makeshift habitat, made two hands talky-talk to each other. Shad nodded.

When they came up inside, they were both shaking. They clutched each other chest-to-chest. But there was no warmth there, and reluctantly they let go.

Galloway found the canteen and drank thirstily. For some reason, being in the water made you piss four times as much. And the fluid had to be replaced. A dehydrated diver was asking to be bent.

When he was full, he looked around. Aydlett was squatting in the bottom of the cylinder, cramming chunks of wet chocolate into his mouth, staring at the iron wall.

"Shad."

When his partner turned his head, Galloway held up his band mask, extended the communication umbilical, and pulled the plug out. Aydlett started to speak; stopped; nodded, and pulled his out, too.

"What goes on?" he mumbled around a mouthful of candy.

"We got to do some planning." Galloway wished he didn't sound so much like Donald Duck. Helium was so thin, it changed the pitch in the vocal cords. "For when this job's done. What happens then?"

"We get paid. Then we go home."

"You still don't get it, do you?"

"Get what? I told you before, quit pat-ronizin' me."

He took a deep breath. "I don't mean to patronize you, Shad. I'm just saying I know these people better than you do."

"They don't seem that bad to me. Christian, he gets crazy, but other'n that, they not treating us too bad. Why you worrying so much?"

"Shad, let me ask you something. Are you still using?"

"Using what?"

"Don't give me that. The coke you had out on the reef. You said Christian gave it to you. Did he give you any more?"

Aydlett said unwillingly, "Yeah. He did. What about it?"

"Shad, I'm asking you as a friend. I saw this shit destroy your brother. *Are you using it?*"

"Maybe, maybe not. What's the big panic, Till? It ain't no major deal, havin' a little hit."

"Have you seen anybody else aboard doing coke?"

Aydlett shrugged.

"Roach? Gonzalo? Nuñez?"

"No. Just Christian."

"You just told me how crazy he was. Would you want him diving with you? Would you want to depend on him, in a jam? Do you see what I'm getting at?"

"Okay," said Aydlett unwillingly. "I haven't done any since the reef. I kept what he give me, but I ain't used it. And I won't. Okay? That what you wanted to hear?"

"That's good, Shad. Thanks."

"Now, why you worrying so much about what happens after we done?"

He reflected. He didn't think there was any way they could be overheard, not with the mikes disconnected. But he still lowered his voice. "Because there's something going on between Christian and Nuñez. What, I don't know, but when it breaks, we're going to be in the middle. Once this shit's topside, Shad, we got to disappear. Go over the side the first chance we get. If Nuñez gets the coke, I don't think he'll come after us. And if we're not around, Christian can't kill us, whatever's going on in his head."

Aydlett didn't answer right away. Then he said, "We don't wait to get paid?"

"No."

"Nothing for the shop, and the boat? No goodies for the little woman? Forget it. I ain't going back to Hatteras broke."

For a moment, Galloway found himself thinking unexpectedly of Bernice. One thing she'd never cared about was how much money he had. She wanted him to be a success, but it was never a condition. As long as he was straight, she'd been happy, no matter how poor he was.

Then he remembered again that it was over.

"Shad—"

"You heard me," said Aydlett, and there was no argument in his voice, only fact. He looked at his watch. "Man, it's cold as one of Moon Tillet's fish trucks down here. What we got to do next? Let's doot toot and get topside."

Galloway was filled suddenly with rage. He wanted to smash his face into the fist; no, that was backward, his fist into the face opposite him in the dim light. Shad wouldn't listen to somebody who'd been through the mill. Had to smart-ass it through himself. He let the anger burn for a few seconds, let it warm him.

Without answering, he pulled on the mask and plugged in. "Topside, Galloway."

"Here, Señor. Where have you been? I have been calling—"

"Must be a loose connection, Fabio. Send down the lifting cables, we'll get them around the shaft now."

Without another word, he dropped his legs into the manhole, lifted his arms, and slid again into the shadow world of the sea.

• • •

He wasn't sure whether decompression was worse than work, or vice versa. The trouble was, when he stopped moving, he felt like he was going to pass out. Finally he rigged a clamp out of a gear strap and hung himself on the line like a Christmas ornament on a branch. He felt safer after that.

They were waiting at forty feet when he noticed that the sea was darker than it had been a few minutes before. He blinked, suspecting some effect of depth, but it wasn't his eyes. As he hung there, looking up, the gloom deepened.

Half an hour later, they surfaced into a squall. Rain danced on lead gray waves, raising a mist so thick that he couldn't see the yacht, the barge, anything. The sky was black as dyed wool. He pulled off his mask and lifted his open mouth. The fresh water and real air, after so long below, made him feel like a marine Lazarus.

"Tiller!"

"Here, Shad."

The rain eased off to westward as he swam slowly toward the voice. The yacht appeared from behind it, like a stage setting as the curtain is drawn aside. She loomed over them like a polished iceberg, high and white and raked, then suddenly burst into a million flashing points of gemlike fire as the sun reappeared. He shifted his mask, slinging it rifle-fashion over his shoulder, and swam around to the stern.

A boat was made up alongside. Its diagonal blazon said BAHAMIAN CUSTOMS. Behind him, Shad muttered, "Uh-oh." But Galloway, exhausted as he was, had a moment of hope. Maybe Zeno had made his move. If the yacht was confiscated, Christian arrested, they could swim ashore and vanish.

He turned his head and muttered, "Let's get back out of sight—"

Gonzalo appeared at the rail. He called down, "Come on aboard, Tiller, Shad. It's all right."

When they'd handed up their gear, Galloway hung on the ladder for a long time, coughing. He hawked up phlegm and spat over the side. It was rust red. He paused for a moment, tasting blood, then pulled himself up the last rungs to the main deck.

The huge bald man lay like a sedimentary deposit in a lounge chair beside Christian. Galloway said, "Mr. Pepper."

"Hello, Mr. ah—"

"Galloway," said Christian, shading his eyes. "Well? How'd it go?"

"Well, uh—"

"Don't worry. You can talk in front of Telly. If it wasn't for him"—Christian patted the big man's arm—"we wouldn't be here."

"Oh . . . well, we got all the lift drums in. I've got the wires on the propeller shaft. We'll pick the stern up tomorrow with the barge, set the slings, and be ready to lift on the next tide, if you want to."

"You bet I do. As soon as goddamned possible."

"He looks worn," said the principal consultant to the Minister of Tourism. "Are you all right, Mr. Galloway?"

He didn't answer right away, though he was staring at the ginger-colored face. The last time he'd seen him, Lynne Parkinson had been on his arm. Should he mention it? Mention that he thought she'd set them up?

But the men who'd attacked them were black.

Like Pepper.

Bahamians, like Pepper.

While Parkinson was an American, though she lived here. . . .

It didn't add up. Finally, he decided he'd better just stay out of whatever shell game they had going, Pepper and Parkinson and Christian, Nuñez and Sears and Harleman. Just as he stayed out of other matters, things that didn't concern him and could only result in trouble. Beside, Pepper was right, he felt like shit.

He said, "Cold and tired. You lose heat to what you breathe, as much as to the water. Troy, okay if I . . . ?"

Christian waved languidly. As he trudged across the deck, he heard them talking behind him, lowered, confidential. The sun blazed down hot and welcome. But the only thing in his mind was, Could he get away?

And: Would Shad come with him?

Going down the ladder to the dining salon, his knees buckled suddenly and he only just caught himself before he fell. His legs felt numb and stiff. His hands were trembling like Christian's after a crash. What the hell was wrong? It hurt when he breathed deeply. His lungs felt full. He felt so weak, at times close to fainting. Some kind of toxicity, or edema . . . he didn't have any vertigo or visual disturbances, and there didn't seem to be any cyanosis, so he didn't think it was trapped air. But why was he bleeding?

Maybe food would help. And he did feel better after he got

seated, got some hot coffee down. He had Cuban-style black beans and rice and a plate of fried meat. He flexed the knee several times and the stiffness went off. The tremor eased off gradually, too, and he ate some cake without clattering his fork against the plate like a warning bell.

Roach pulled out a chair opposite him. The captain looked tired. Stubble made his chin look like gray cactus. He said, "I'll have a word with him, if you like."

"Who?"

"The *jefe*."

"About what?"

"About not diving tomorrow. I don't know what you're doing down there. But you're pushing it too hard, old man."

"He doesn't believe in days off. What's our weather tomorrow?"

"Partly cloudy. Light northeast winds. Chance of more squalls. Seas, two to three feet."

"If that wind picks up, the barge'll be bobbing up and down like a cork. Thanks, Pat, but we better finish rigging. We can rest while you're towing her in. Have you picked the spot?"

"There's a tongue south of Strangers Cay. It's sheltered, so we can finish the job from small boats. You still plan to yank her tail tomorrow?"

"Tomorrow early," he said, more confidently than he felt.

After another cup of coffee, he took the launch over to the barge with Roach. As they crossed, he saw the customs cutter in the distance, heading south.

Clatters, shouting, the roar of a winch engine came across the water as they neared. He scratched his back absently, examining the barge. It rode lower in the water, and the bare chests and arms of the men working on it were wet from squall and spray. They looked like bugs caught in a web of steel wire.

When they jumped down to the deck, one of them straightened and waved. As he made his way toward them, Galloway crossed to the side and looked down.

The hauling wires came up out of the sea and bent over orange-greased chafing gear at the turn of the deck. Then they ran through sets of threefold blocks rigged with chain stoppers, chain jacks, and turnbuckles, so that each wire could be slacked or hauled in individually with the winches. The purchase ends were

shackled to the samson posts opposite. It was a brute-force arrangement, but it looked like it would work. When he crossed to the
well and looked down, an uneasy mirror reflected the clouds.

"This is our chief rigger," said Roach. "His name's Phillip."

The chief rigger grinned at him without two front teeth. Galloway had a sense of near-recognition, but then it faded. Maybe it
was just the way the man smiled, as if he knew something his
bosses didn't.

"You ballasted down already," he told him.

"Dass right. We be ready, catch first smile of the sun
tomorrow."

"How fast can you pump it out?"

"Two three-inch pump, that be a thousand a minute."

"Cubic feet?"

"Gallons, mon."

His mind went back to the lift. "When's high tide?"

Roach said, "It's seven-twelve A.M. at Elbow Cay. It ought to
be close to that here."

"Range?"

"Two point seven, mean."

"You figured out how long it'll take you to pump her dry?" he
asked the rigger. Phillip said he had; it would take fourteen and a
half minutes to drop the water inside a foot.

"And the haul wires? What's breaking strain on those?"

"We rig 'e for six, d'ye see. I calc'ate each they good for twenty
ton. That's hundred and twenty tons."

"Should be plenty, with the buoyancy we got in her. Unless
that sand's got more suction than I think." He looked at the pump
spares, checked the winches, and asked about spare shackles.
Finally, he squatted over a row of lifting slings laid out on a clear
space of deck. An old, old man was securing the bitter ends
around thimbles. He grinned up, his worn yellow fingers weaving
wire with the skill of a basket maker.

At last, he nodded to Phillip and told him he'd done well. All
he had to do in the morning was be ready to move fast when the
stern came out of the mud. He stood around for a while watching
them work. They were ragged and scarred. He could hardly understand them, but they were watermen. Then, as evening came on,
he took the launch back.

He was lying in bed and his thoughts had just started to become disconnected, to become illogical as they did just before consciousness disappeared, when he winced at a sudden stab of pain, like an ice pick under his kneecap.

He'd been trying to deny it. Trying to ignore the symptoms: the itchy rash at his wrists and neck, the weakness and dizziness. Now he couldn't anymore. It was decompression sickness. In a commercial operation, he'd be in a chamber, repressurized, then coming back up slowly, breathing a special treatment gas.

But the long onset meant it wasn't as bad as it could have been. It should go away by itself, given time.

But it would come back again the next time he dived.

He stared up at the overhead, counting the little holes in the acoustic tile, feeling sweat run back into his hair. He bent the knee slightly and hissed through his teeth. The other one was stiff, too.

He turned his bunk light on and got up. He found aspirin in the bathroom and took four, chasing them with bourbon. Then he limped back to his bunk and turned the light off again.

He was lying there sweating, waiting for them to take effect, when he heard the doorknob make a quarter turn, then click open. Not all the way, just enough to let in a sliver of corridor light. Then it closed again softly.

He listened intently. Someone else was breathing in his room.

Galloway reached under his pillow. He slid out the dive knife, forgetting the pain as his wide-open eyes tried to see what was moving, barefoot-silent, toward him across the carpet. His other hand found the light switch.

When he pushed it, bringing the knife up at the same instant, the sudden brilliance showed him the haggard face, the dangling dirty hair, and the empty eyes of the woman from cabin number five.

14

"Conchita," he whispered. Then he remembered the knife. He lowered it but didn't let go. He was about to ask her what she was doing there, then remembered what Gonzalo had said. A gang of Peruvian bandits. She probably didn't speak English.

"My name is not Conchita," she said.

"Ah." He studied her in the light of the bedside lamp. She was wearing a rumpled, dirty dress of some soft fabric. No stockings. Dirty legs. She wasn't very big. But her eyes still frightened him.

He sat up suddenly, wincing at the pain in his knees. "What are you doing here?" he said a little harshly.

"Not so loud, please. I am here because your door was the only one that was not locked. Can I sit down, please?" Without waiting for an answer, she sagged into the chair. She let her head fall back, closed her eyes, and sighed. "You can put away your knife. I am not dangerous. Whatever they told you about me. Only sick. And very frightened. Can I have some water, please?"

"In the bathroom," he said.

When she came out, she said in a strange empty tone, "Thank you. I will leave now. Perhaps there are other unlocked doors—"

"Tell me what you came here for," said Galloway, swinging his feet to the carpet. "And who you are, if it isn't 'Conchita.'"

"That's what *they* call me. But my name is Anunciada Mariategui."

She paused, as if it might mean something to him. When he shook his head, she added, "The Mariateguis are a family well known in Peru. . . . You are an American, no?"

"Yes. My name's Galloway."

"You work for Don Juan Nuñez?"

"Not willingly, but I work for him, yeah. At least for a few days."

"What do you mean, 'not willingly'? What kind of work do you do, Señor Galloway?"

Galloway got up. He poured a finger of whiskey and set it beside her. He had a feeling this might be a long conversation. He poured himself two fingers and sat on the bed again. "I'm a diver."

"Oh. Now I understand . . . then you are saying he forces you to work for him. Threatens you."

"Right."

"Then our cases are much alike, no?"

"I don't know. Tell me about your . . . case."

"My father is a federal judge. *La Compañía* wanted him to cooperate when one of its men was caught. He decided not to. He had plenty of police protection. Unfortunately, he did not think of me. I was going to college in the United States, the University of Alabama. Three men showed up at my apartment one night. My roommate was there. They killed him and took me."

"My God," he said. "Is that true? They told me—"

"What did they tell you? That I was a *puta* brought aboard for the sailors?"

"Not exactly. But something like that."

"Believe what you like; but I am telling you now I must escape. Will you help me? I will do whatever you want of me if you will."

"I don't want that."

"Well, neither do I, but you see I am in so much trouble. They lock me in and make me the injections. Tonight, someone forgot. I will not go back. If you will not help me escape, let me go quietly. I will find my way out and jump into the water."

"I wouldn't try to swim ashore at night," he said. "It's three or four miles, and the cooks have been throwing their garbage over at night. The sharks will be right there—"

"Unfortunately, I cannot swim at all."

"Okay, I get what you mean." He thought about it for a little while. Till she said again, not desperately but with a hollow resignation, "Will you help me?"

"What do you want me to do?"

"I don't know." She looked at the drink in her hand. She hadn't touched it. Now she put it on the desk. Her eyes turned slowly to the door. Then she got up. "All right, I understand. You are a prisoner, too. But they have not done to you what they do to me.

I will go now. Will you please tell my parents what happened? Señor Georges Mariategui, Federal Court, Lima. That will get to him."

"Wait a minute. Sit down, damn it!"

She lowered her head. Her hair, black and tangled, fell forward to hide her face. Galloway was glad. It was easier when he couldn't see her eyes.

Finally he said, his voice harsh, "Take your dress off."

She rose without a word. Her head still down, she unbuttoned the soiled fabric. She had nothing on beneath but bruises, dried blood, and needle tracks.

He swallowed and looked away. Then he bent and picked it up from around her feet. With a savage jerk, he tore the cloth apart. "Go into the bathroom. Clean yourself up. See that terry robe—"

"Terry?" Her voice quivered, so low he could barely hear it.

"That white soft robe on the hook. Put it on after you finish washing. Stay in the bathroom and close the door."

"What will you do?"

"We'll discuss it when I come back." He limped to the door, cracked it, and slipped out.

Topside, the night was windy, warm, but starless. *Ceteris* rode to anchor without lights. The only sign of shore was a faraway aero beacon blinking red over Carter's Cay. He took a deep breath. He felt sick. Was she telling the truth, about college, her roommate? Or was she really some kind of criminal, or Communist?

Then he thought, Who cares? No one had earned treatment like that, no matter what her politics, no matter what she, or her friends, had done.

Okay, to work . . . he moved quietly along the deck, grateful for the overcast dark. He hadn't been topside at night before and he had no idea whether Christian posted guards. His deck shoes made no noise, and he opened his mouth to reduce the sound of his breath.

He was at the turn of the sun deck when someone called out in Spanish from above him. A faint voice from the dark answered the hail. He froze for long minutes, till the glowing butt of a cigarette sailed down in a fiery curve over him and hissed in the sea. Then footsteps moved away, and he exhaled, and slid another step aft.

The launch was still in the water, a patch of darkness in the darkness astern. He found its line, cleated off at the quarter. He bent beside it and stepped out of his shoes.

Moving quietly, he slipped off his T-shirt and trousers. Naked except for undershorts, he swung a leg over the rail. He winced as his knee bent, but the aspirin masked the pain.

He rolled over the rail and felt for the line with his feet. He dropped, caught it, and went down it silently hand over hand till he was in warm water. Just then, he caught the flare of a match or lighter from inside the cabin of the launch.

He didn't dare let go. He might lose the rope, lose the launch, lose the yacht, too, in the warm all-enveloping darkness.

He remembered the sharks then, and decided not to stay in very long.

He pulled himself along the line till it rose again and the pale sides of the launch loomed over him. Then he let go. The current carried him noiselessly along the smooth curved fiberglass. When he judged he was near the stern, he took a deep breath and slipped under.

Absolute dark, save for faint fiery flickers here and there below him. Without a mask, he couldn't make out what they were. He frog-kicked along beneath the boat, his back brushing the smoothness above him, a roof to the warm sea, till his outstretched arm hit the inboard/outboard unit.

Holding himself to it by one hand, he pulled the strip of cloth out of his shorts. He wrapped one end again and again around . the gap where the prop met the drive unit. Then let the rest of the rag trail out.

He let go and drifted downward, looking up at it, although of course he couldn't see anything.

Something slid past him. He didn't feel it, but he felt the current as it went by. The backwash rippled the hair on his back.

He swallowed. There was someone above him, on the launch. He couldn't go up there. But staying in the water didn't seem like a good idea, either.

He began swimming forward in the dark, the smoothness above and then beside him. He wanted to panic, churn the water in a crawl. Instead, he stared forward blindly, doing a smooth and rhythmic reach, pull, and kick.

Something greenish wavered off to his right, not far away in the black water.

Something hit the back of his legs; rough and rubbery at the same time. He swallowed his fear. Only a few more feet.

He came up at the bow, judged where the line ought to be, and lunged out of the water for it. He caught only air, and came down in a noisy splash, his hands empty.

"*Hay!*"

"*Que es ese sonido?*"

A light came on on the yacht and swept the black water, glittering off the smooth curved backs of the waves. He grabbed a breath and pulled his head under as it swung toward him.

Penetrating the sea, the beam glowed silently off a dozen blurry forms a few feet below him. They moved with a sinuous, excited rapidity, milling in and out and around in a silent, snakelike writhe.

Galloway reached up with his left hand and foot. He pulled himself up on the gunwale, as slowly as he could, but still the launch leaned to his weight. On the bow, between him and the light, was a man with a cap, who suddenly lifted his head, turning it from side to side, as if hearing someone behind him. The man pulled a cigarette from between his lips, flicked it into the water, and pulled the bolt back on a submachine gun.

Galloway's groping hand found the normal things on the gunwale of a powerboat: life-rail sockets, rod holders, handrail, a cleat. There was line around the cleat.

The smooth braided Dacron went silently around the guard's throat. The man's fingers came up by reflex, locking under the knotted rope. The gun clanked faintly as it slid across waxed fiberglass. His soft-soled shoes drummed on the deck for just a moment as Galloway, hissing through his teeth, hauled him bodily backward, then swung him around. His legs kicked up phosphorescence as he went down into the water.

"*Que esta pasado allí?*"

Galloway waited till the churning and splashing, the ripple of dorsals and the welter of corkscrewing black bodies had drifted astern, become flickering green whirlpools beneath the surface, become silence and shadows again.

He pitched his voice a little higher—it wasn't hard just

then—and called lazily, in one of the few words of their language he knew, "Nada."

• • •

The crew's dining room was empty except for one sailor. He glanced up without interest at the Yanqui diver with the coil of line under his arm, then returned his attention to what looked like a diesel-engine manual. Galloway got sliced meat, cheese, bread, and carrots. He carried them back to his room without meeting anyone else.

There was no one in his bathroom. He looked around; pulled the wet curtain back. The marble stall was empty, too. "Anunciada," he said, not very loudly.

The cabinet door under the sink clicked open. A hand came out and grasped his ankle.

"You're smaller than I thought," he said, bending to look in at her. Wrapped in the robe, crouched like a child not yet born, she blinked out and did not answer. "Are you all right? I brought food."

"It's so nice in here," she whispered. He saw that her hugged knees were shaking. Her eyes were huge and shadowed. "All dark and warm. I don't want to come out."

"You can go back if you want. But come on out for now. Eat," he said. He waved the bread in front of her nose.

"Your leg is bleeding."

"It's nothing. I fixed things so they won't search for you. And I brought you something to keep you company."

He took the parcel of rope from under his arm and unwound it. Bending down, he handed her the Uzi.

"That's nice," she whispered, and her voice held a childlike trust that made him feel like taking her in his arms. "But I don't want to kill anyone. I just want to get away. How am I going to do that?"

Galloway sighed. That answered one of his questions, at least. She was no guerrilla terrorist.

He said, reluctantly, "I'll have to do some thinking about that, Anunciada."

15

He came up from a dreamless dark, to find a sailor shaking him. He sat up quickly and glanced at his watch. Four. It would be an early morning, and a long day.

They dove as soon as the sun was high enough to slide light into the water. He was still sore, but his knees no longer hurt. The chest corruption, too, had eased during the night. But the lethargy had not, and now, dropping feetfirst into the blue, he felt a hundred years old and very tired.

Two sharks under the yacht eyed him, but the divers must not have resembled prey. Or perhaps, he thought with a chill, they weren't hungry this morning.

They had to pick up the slings from the barge. He let the current carry him aft. As he expected, Shad followed. As they passed under the arrowhead shadow of the Liberator, he heard Aydlett's voice in his earphone. "Hey, what's that?"

"What?"

"That there, on the launch—topside, you listenin'?"

Gonzalo answered, yawning. Aydlett told him there was something caught in the launch's prop, not to start the boat without checking it out. The Cuban thanked him and said he would tell the captain; it would be attended to.

Galloway didn't say anything.

On the bottom, without speaking, they connected themselves to the 244s. Not for the first time, he wondered what exactly he was breathing. It had helium and oxygen in it. But was it the proper mix? Properly filtered, clean gas? He wished he'd been able to supervise the fill.

Side by side, they swam aft, over the canted silent hatch covers. Not for the first time, he wondered what had possessed Nuñez to weld them shut.

He yawned into the regulator, trying to jump-start his mind. Today, the third day on the wreck, he wanted to finish rigging. If they worked like dogs, this could be the last dive.

Roach had anchored almost directly over the wreck, jockeying *Ceteris* carefully about while watching his fathometer printout. With the barge riding astern at short stay, Phillip's workmen had spent the last two days cutting and eye-splicing the elevator cable to Galloway's specifications, rigging and finally labeling the lengths in the proper sequence for installation. The first attached had been the three 630-foot lifting wires he'd made fast to *Guapi's* propeller shaft yesterday.

At midnight—low tide—they'd taken in the last of the slack, flooding the barge down, then grappling it down by six steel threads to the seemingly immovable weight far below.

Today, if all went well, the combination of internal buoyancy and the barge's lift would raise the wreck enough by the stern so they could get the slings laid out underneath her. He'd already calculated the proper intervals to distribute the strain on the hull. The rest of the day, they'd rig the last pontoon, then check everything over one last time.

He coughed weakly into the regulator, swimming aft. And that would be that. Then they could rest.

Wrong. Then he had to find a way to escape. And not just him and Shad now. Now he had to think about Anunciada, too.

Here was the bottom coming up, like the moon to an *Apollo* lander: twenty feet, ten, five, the *Eagle* has landed. How long ago that seemed. He remembered watching it on TV in a bar in Saigon. The slings and shackles thumped into the sand as he let go. His momentum took him right down to the bottom. His hand moved without his thought, venting a shot of gas into his BC.

A little murkier today. Fifty-foot visibility? For salvage work, that was almost unheard-of. He'd worked oil so deep there was no light at all; had worked hard hat on river bottoms in murk so thick that you couldn't see your fingers when you pressed them to the faceplate of your helmet. Braille diving, they called it. Not to mention the night missions, back in Vietnam . . .

Aydlett appeared ahead of him, also loaded with gear. Galloway's hands finished their job, cutting away the lashings on the slings. He bent his mask close and found the shackle with 2 painted on it. He hauled it free, inflated his vest some more, and began swimming for the stern, dragging the thirty-foot length of cable, eye-spliced and thimbled at both ends, behind him over the sand.

It wasn't easy. He was wheezing through his regulator before he got ten yards. Though he knew they had to work fast, he couldn't help looking up at the ship. It seemed huge underwater.

The wires for the shaft lift came down from a gray murk above them. Six black pencil lines, rigid and parallel under strain. Were they swaying? A grinding noise came through the water, and a puff of darkness rolled out from under the keel.

That was where they were going to be working. If a rogue wave dropped the barge, if she sprang a leak, if a cable broke . . .

No point in agonizing about it. They had to do it now. He couldn't take much more of this.

Aydlett approached from the dimness. Galloway passed him the eye and the attached shackle marked 1. He pointed to himself, then the port side. Shad nodded slowly, and positioned himself to starboard.

Between them, the stern lifted and fell, as if the wreck were breathing, or struggling slowly against their Lilliputian attempt to bind it. It was too murky to see any gap beneath it, or how wide it was.

He waved slowly and started forward, parallel to the hull and five feet away. The blocks he'd set along the starboard side had straightened it some. He yanked impatiently at the cable. It weighed six pounds a fathom; not bad as wire rope went, but awkward. He felt his partner's pull from the far side, heard it scrape as it slid along the keel.

Forward. The wreck groaned and cried out through the water. The cable dragged and scraped beneath it, vibrating in his gloved hands.

Then it stuck. "Hold on, Shad," he said. "She's hung up."

"Want to back up?"

"Yeah, try to jerk it loose."

It didn't move. It was stuck on something. Keel damage, or a fitting. He had a sudden fit of rage, like hot lead in his chest. Christ! They didn't have all day to get this done!

They sawed it back and forth, yanked at it, and it didn't move. Finally, he growled, "Keep it taut on your side. I'm goin' in there and see what it's caught on."

"Watch yourself, bo'."

He grunted something, and pulled himself hand over hand down the sling wire, under the suspended hull.

He crept in, feeling packed sand hard under his chest, the rough steel above him. Blackness seethed in front of his mask. It even had a taste, a strange pungent savor around the edges of his mouthpiece. He ignored it. His outstretched arm groped. He wiggled his fingers, lost the wire for a moment, found it again, then followed it. . . .

The hull rose an inch or two, vibrating with a tremendous iron groan, like ancient gates swinging open. His extended arm felt only smooth wire, running unimpeded over iron plate. Where the *hell* was the hang-up? He squirmed and burrowed in a few inches farther, turning his head sideways, and was immediately rewarded by a sharp edge biting into his palm: a tear or perforation, a protruding snag. It was curled under like an iron pencil shaving, and the wire was locked inside the spiral. No wonder it wouldn't come loose.

He got his fingers under it and unhooked it. It slipped off instantly with a low thud.

"Aw right, it just come loose, this side. You okay under there?"

"Yeah."

He was starting to back out when the hull lowered itself, slow and enormous and smooth, onto his head and chest. There was no time to squirm backward, no time to do anything more than think, *Uh oh.*

The pressure increased steadily. Three hundred-odd tons of deadweight, coming down flat on a steel keel plate. Images flickered through his mind as the air squeezed out of his chest: of a broken seacock on the barge, letting in the sea; of a cable slipping off a turnbuckle. He didn't know what was wrong. Whether it would keep coming down, or—

His right hand began raking at the sand, clawing out a hollow under his ear. The steel leaned down in darkness, ironing him down like a mouse under the treads of a tank.

"Tiller! You out yet?"

He tried to grunt, tried to scream, but only a wheeze came out of his compressing chest. Through the iron pressing his ear into the bottom, he heard, bone conduction now, the shuddering, scraping groan of settling steel, a cracking, banging cacophony drawn out for seconds as the settling keel flexed, transferring hundreds of tons of weight to the seabed ahead of him. The point of contact was moving aft. Toward him.

"Tiller! Goddamn it—*Till!*"

He squeezed his eyes shut and waited for the end.

The ship leaned on him for long minutes as he lay unable to move or breathe, watching white patterns chase across his eyes.

Then it complained again, long and low, and rose a millimeter. It hung there, trembling, then eased back another.

In a minute, he could breathe. In two, he was able to scrabble backward, sucking in air.

When he was free he floated aimlessly for a few seconds, hands clawing at his head.

The frenzied batter of his hands stopped. They went rigid, as if suddenly taken possession of. Then came slowly down. The claws relaxed into hands.

He forced his eyes open. Lowered his gaze to the white sand floor of the sea.

He found the wire loop again, lying on the bottom, and went grimly back to work.

• • •

Sawing it back and forth through the sand for the last few yards, they got the bow strop into place about fifteen feet back of the stem. He swam around to Aydlett's side to make sure the ends were even. Then, leaving the eye splices lying on the sand, they swam back for the next one.

This one went on smoothly. They kept it low as they approached the hang-up, and this time it slipped past. They placed the second sling thirty-five feet aft of the bow.

The third and fourth lifting slings went in aft of that, at twenty-foot intervals along the hull.

When they were all in place, Galloway called Roach topside and told him to have Phillip slack the lifting lines. Then he clung to the stern rail and rested, blowing out great clouds of bubbles.

He checked his watch. Only twenty minutes into the first tank, but it was already going dry. He was using air like a hurricane. He caught his partner's questioning glance through the acrylic window of the mask. Aydlett lifted his watch and tapped it; signaled; pointed toward the pontoon.

He thought a moment, then nodded.

They surfaced inside the black echoing well. A splash and thud was followed by yellow light. Aydlett set the lantern carefully back on the floating pallet.

Galloway unsnapped rubber. When he pulled his mask off, the cold helium atmosphere smelled of humidity and iron and something rotten, with a faint, faint aftersmell of gasoline. He felt his head carefully and examined his hand. No blood, but a mother of a headache.

It was almost impossible to understand him in the thin atmosphere, especially through chattering teeth, but Aydlett seemed to be saying he was goddamned cold. He agreed. They were both coughing and spitting. We can't keep this up much longer, he thought again. They rested for ten minutes, shivering and moaning in strange high pitches. Aydlett popped a plastic canteen and drank thirstily. Galloway took it next. Bourbon and fresh water put a little energy back in his legs, but he could feel himself failing.

He said, "Shad, you give any more thought to how we can get out of here?"

Aydlett looked at him levelly. He hawked into his glove, regarded it, and swished his hand in the water.

"I ain't going," he said.

"What do you mean? We got to get clear of these people. Once this thing's at the surface, that's our best chance."

"I ain't going. That's all. Nuñez, looks like he needs some good men working for him."

"And you mean to be one?" He didn't mean to sound sarcastic, but he was tired and had almost died, and he knew his friend was wrong.

"Up yours, Galloway. I'm tired of playin' second string in this partnership. You do what you want. I won't stop you leaving. But I'm not going back without my money."

"You're sure you know what you're saying, Shad? Know it—and mean it?"

Aydlett just looked at him.

Galloway felt a great sadness. He wanted to keep talking. He wanted to argue, curse, scream at his partner. But then he looked at his watch.

"We'll talk about it later," he said, and reached for his mask.

They slid out again and finned for the wreck. He turned his head this way and that, searching the gray dimness. Funny, the sharks didn't follow them down. He hadn't seen a single living thing on this wreck, except for the little jacks, or whatever they were, that had been eating the crewman's face.

He shuddered, and got his mind back on the job. Worrying about Shad and Anunciada just distracted him. He couldn't do anything about anything till this goddamn hulk was 250 feet nearer the sun.

Over the time they'd been resting, the riggers, topside, had slacked the cables. They dangled down now, no longer taking weight. *Guapi* lay immobile, still popping and creaking as she dug herself back into the sand. He wondered for a moment whether the hull would take the strain when they lifted it. The upper works looked solid, though.

Anyway, she sat straighter now; the stern lift had trimmed her up, as he'd hoped.

Now, to move the wires from the shaft to their proper points for the lift. Once more, he took the port side. The cables had come down with big shackles on them, the kind with pins that screwed out. The strain of hoisting the stern had bent them a little, but a screwdriver shaft from his tool bag got the one marked 2 loose. The cable swung free, a slight current dragging it out of his grasp. Three hundred feet of it was dangling down above him. He wrapped his glove around it and swam it forward, hauling himself on now and then along the trawler's rail. His breath wheezed in and out like a bath toy.

A hundred feet was a lot farther underwater than it was topside.

When he got to the bow at last, he let air out of his vest. The shackle, twenty pounds of forged steel, helped, too, and he dropped straight for the sand.

He reached the bottom where the eye splice marked 2 lay waiting. It was the work of five minutes to swim the bow bellyband around to Aydlett, arrange the one leading aft, slip the shackle through all four eyes, slide the pin back in, screw it down with his fingers and then the last four turns with the fid, and lash it with seizing wire.

One down, he thought.

He swam aft with the second bellyband slipping through his glove, noting absently that it was getting hard to breathe. He dropped the strap by the lift strop and continued swimming aft. He coughed cold mucus up and blew it through the regulator. Bubbles moved forward on the far side of the hull. At the stern again, he unshackled the wire marked 4, swam it forward, and shackled it to the strap eye marked 4 and the bellybands marked B and D.

Don't have to be no genius for this job, he thought. He just wished he wasn't so exhausted, and that it didn't hurt deep in his chest every time he coughed.

He was back at the stern again for the last wire when he ran out of air. Shit, he thought fuzzily. Lost track of the time. He reached up to his mask, turned the emergency valve, sucked in.

No air.

He turned the knurled plastic right and left. It moved, but nothing came through from the emergency tank on his back. He twisted, feeling back with his right hand along the supply hose. Where it met the bottle valve, it made a right-angle bend.

Broken, no doubt, when the ship had squatted on him.

He suppressed a feeling of unease and swam forward, grunted, using as little of the remaining breath in his lungs as possible, "Shad."

"Yeah."

"Need help. Out of air."

"Hold on. Where are you?"

"Pilothouse."

"Be right there."

The waterman came into view almost at once, but too far away. He needed air now, all the more desperately because he'd been working hard. He looked around quickly, then thrust his head through the shattered window. As he'd hoped, there was a bubble at the top of the pilothouse. He stuck his head up into it, pulled his mask away from his face, and took a deep breath—of air solid with the stink of rot, and fish, and death.

When he turned his head, he saw the skull smiling there, caught in the rusting framework of an electric fan, right next to his own.

• • •

After Shad got him back to the pontoon, they called topside. The spare band mask came sliding down the wire, weighted with a broken crescent wrench. He was back at work a few minutes later, attached to a fresh 244.

Only now he swam through cold lead, and his chest beat with a dull throbbing torment. His eyes burned, and his legs were numb heavy things he dragged. The world was going dark around the edges, and he heard from time to time a strange high song in his ears that did not come from the sea. He fought his way slowly to the stern, and with many fumblings and close peerings and feeble curses finished hooking up the last cable.

Then he drifted upward, looking down on the enwebbed hulk as his exhausted mind struggled to understand, remember, what it had thought through before in the comfort of his cabin.

Guapi lay almost upright on the slanting bottom. Six wires led down to her from above. The lift lines were attached to wire slings that cupped the hull beneath. They couldn't slip because the bellybands, horizontal wires run just below the gunwales, held them in place. So that was done. And what remained? . . . The other pontoon, and the final check. Yes.

When they had the last pontoon rigged and the compressor hose was bubbling inside it, he hung on the chains that held it to the stern, and thought back over his calculations. His mind felt over them like a blind man examining a loom that he once knew how to operate but now had forgotten.

Total weight of the ship, her total estimated displacement, loaded: 350 tons.

Minus the weight of the water her steel displaced: he'd figured that at 20 tons—330 tons.

Minus the weight of water her cargo displaced: And that was, he'd figured, around two hundred tons. The bonus was that cocaine, ether, and the other chemicals Gonzalo had named as the cargo were all either neutral or positively buoyant in saltwater.

That left 130 tons he had to lift.

Minus thirty-eight tons from the air in the fuel bunkers.

Minus fourteen times two, twenty-eight tons, from the two old fuel tanks that strained on rigid lengths of chain, like huge chained-down iron balloons.

And ten tons from the dozens of fifty-five-gallon drums they'd packed the ship with the first day down.

That gave him a total buoyant lift of seventy-four tons. He'd have to dead-lift the rest with the barge.

He remembered that figure and went back in his head and did it over again, this time using all the worst-case figures. It took him a long time because he was very tired. There was also one imponderable, the suction with which the bottom held the hull. But at the end, he came out needing ninety tons from the barge.

He had six wires coming down and each could pull twenty tons before it snapped. If Phillip evened them properly to spread the load, he ought to be able to get 120 tons clear of the bottom before they reached breaking strain.

So if the suction wasn't too great, he even had a little safety margin.

It wasn't the kind of job he'd want to have an insurance inspector inspect. It wasn't the kind of job the union would leave a diver on for half a second. It wasn't the kind he'd do if he had enough time, or the right equipment. But it should work—if nothing else went wrong.

"Shad?"

"Yo."

"We're done. Let's go up."

• • •

When they reached the surface four hours later, he floated prone on it like a dying fish. He couldn't get his arms to work anymore, or his legs, or anything else. So he just lay on the soft sea, breathing when the waves let him, gasping when they didn't. He felt like crying at the steadily growing torment in his legs and back.

Spanish crackled above him. Arms yanked him up bodily, like

a gaffed marlin. He shuddered and coughed as they carried him across the deck and laid him out. The harsh, bright reproaches of gulls fought in his ears. He felt hands stripping off his gear and then his clothes.

He lay naked to the noon sun, his limbs writhing slowly, like a blind worm hauled up from abyssal depths, destroyed by its translation to the regions of light.

A shadow between him and the warmth. And a high, impatient voice. "Galloway. You know anything about a missing guard?"

"No."

"Where's Mariategui? Have you seen her?"

He wasn't very clear what was going on, but someone inside him smiled bitterly; everybody was trying that one. He grunted, "Who?"

"Never mind. I think it's clear what happened to her. Are you finished down there?"

". . . Finished. Yeah."

"It's low tide now. Von Arx's niggers are over there getting things ready. Roach says they'll be ready to lift tonight. Is that right? Are you sure? I don't want any screwups, Galloway. I'm holding you responsible, remember."

"Tonight," he mumbled. He felt around in a mind murky as a chum bucket. "How about waiting . . . high tide tomorrow morning? Give us time to rest, case we have to—"

"We lift tonight. Understand? Get up when I'm talking to you, Galloway! Get on your feet!"

Get up? He could hardly keep his heart beating under the fullness that blocked his chest like a truck in a tunnel. So he didn't answer. He was done. Empty. Spent like a coin to fulfill the greedy will of a fat man in white linen. He waited with something like yearning for the words *Shoot him;* or maybe, *Throw him over the side.*

But Christian must have had other plans. Because after a moment, he realized the shadow had moved away.

Someone else was standing beside him. He turned his head but couldn't see a thing. "Shad?" he whispered. Then, again, "Shad."

The other man didn't answer, though. Instead, he said, in Aydlett's voice, "You need something done, Mr. Christian?"

"Not at the moment. You're looking fit. Better than Galloway. He looks like shit."

"I'm younger. And stronger."

"Is that right? If he plays out, you think you can finish things up down there?"

"He's got more experience than me, Mr. C. But if he can't dive, I think I can handle things for you."

Galloway stopped listening. He squeezed his eyes shut. But the sunlight still blazed through them, making the whole universe red as blood.

16

He wasn't really there while they took him down through ladders and passageways. But at the last moment, just as they reached his door, he suddenly remembered Anunciada. With a terrific effort, he sat up. "Hold on," he muttered. "Wait!"

But the sailors just pushed through the door, talking loudly among themselves in Spanish, and rolled him none too gently off the stretcher into his bunk. The part-time medic lingered a moment, looking uneasy. Then he smiled, turned his hands palm up, and gave a fatalistic, regretful shrug.

And he left.

Just like, Galloway thought hazily, the first of these thugs he'd seen, strolling into his shop in Buxton on a blazing afternoon. . . .

He lay twisted on top of the blanket, breathing shallowly. He could see a little now. The tunnel vision, that was oxygen toxicity. The stiffness and pain, the fullness in his chest, though—

At last, he rolled off and crawled on hands and knees into the head. When he was done vomiting, he caught himself in the mirror. Unshaven and gaunt. A blue bruise along the side of his face. The sutures in his cheek were buried in puffy red flesh. Infected. And he was shaking.

He drank water thirstily, took six aspirin, then turned on the shower. He crouched in the corner, his eyes closed.

Then he remembered again, and cursed himself and bent and unlatched the little cabinet under the sink.

It was empty. He stared, then bent farther. A drain pipe, a roach motel, a spare roll of toilet tissue.

Had he dreamed it? No, she'd been there, and now she wasn't. He hobbled back into the shower, too exhausted to think or wonder anymore.

He was lying on his bunk again, drifting off, when a voice whispered below him, "Señor?"

He rolled over and pulled the corner of the mattress up. "What are you doing there?"

"I became cramped under the sink. Here I can stretch out. . . . You do not look so very good."

"Don't feel so great, either."

"Have they missed me? Are they looking for me?"

He explained about her dress and the propeller and the sharks. She was quiet for a little while after he was done. "So they think I am dead," she said.

"I assume so. I haven't heard otherwise."

"That is good. So, are we going to leave?"

"I hope so. We lift the wreck tonight. Then we run north, to a shallow spot where we can beach it."

"We get off then?"

"On the way." He explained about going over the side and swimming for shore. She was quiet when he was done. Then the whisper came again. "I told you, I do not swim. But I am willing to try—if you will go with me."

• • •

"Señor Christian, he want you on deck."

It was the young sailor, the shy one, the *jefe*'s favorite. Galloway nodded, swung his legs down, and grunted.

The torture in his knees was back, and worse this time. His hands shook as he pulled on his clothes.

They'd finished the rigging just in time. The way he felt, if he dove again without being decompressed, he'd be dead. He might end up crippled as it was. Gas built up in the body over successive dives. Fatigue, lack of sleep, cold—they all contributed to decompression sickness. You couldn't predict how the bends worked. It wasn't the kind of thing people volunteered for research on.

He had to act as if he'd recovered, though. Otherwise, Troy Christian had no reason to keep him alive.

The late-afternoon sky was nearly cloudless; the squall line had passed off. The air was shimmering and the deck under his feet was cooking-hot. He hobbled toward a knot of men at the stern, keeping his face rigid against agony.

Gonzalo, Christian, and Aydlett were standing close together, laughing at something. As he came up, Christian glanced around. He reached out to clap him on the shoulder. "Tiller! You up and about?"

"We'll see."

"We'll see, all right. If this doesn't work, a little hangover won't be all you have to worry about. But Shad tells me it's solid work down there."

He nodded, not trusting himself to speak to the man who had been his partner. Aydlett met his eyes once, then looked away.

Nuñez's second was high again; that was obvious. He tapped his feet, his face was flushed, he couldn't stop talking even when he had to stop breathing to cough. His lips and nose were scorched. Galloway looked out over the sea while the *jefe* prattled on.

The barge rode low in the water fifty yards off. Roach had shortened the tow line. The launch rolled easily to port. The Indians stood in the cockpit. Beyond them was the low intermittency of islets, cays, then a huge cloud far to the west, over mainland Florida, perhaps; Palm Beach was only ninety miles away. He stared at it, forgetting his pain and danger for a moment in wonder at the livid neons, blending to soft, rose reds, of a Bahamas sunset.

"Galloway," said Christian, and his voice was no longer indulgent, but sharp.

He came back to the deck of *Ceteris*. "Yeah," he said. "Sorry, I was looking at the sunset."

"It looks like time to me. You agree?"

He glanced at his wrist. "Right. High tide's in an hour."

"Fabito, call the launch. Let's get over there and see what Pat's waiting on."

Gonzalo lifted a walkie-talkie. The launch lifted its nose and curved in toward them. One of the bodyguards went below, giving them room, but the other stayed in the cockpit. His dark scrutiny examined them with uninterested alertness.

The boat purred over the low blue waves, slowed, and bumped alongside the barge, leaving flecks of white gel coat on the rusty iron.

Roach must have been waiting for them. As Christian strode forward, stepping high over the maze of wires, come-alongs, and turnbuckles, a double clatter of diesels began. Water trickled, then strengthened into two glassy streams from the dewatering pumps. Galloway hung back. He caught Phillip's eye across the rusty deck, strewn with shiny bits of wire and tools, cigarette butts and beer cans.

The black man looked at him levelly, with the same knowing smile he'd worn when they met. After a moment he winked and held up his thumb.

Galloway nodded back. He crossed to the well and looked down. The black water reflected his face against the sky, reflected the glowing mass of cloud in scarlet dying brightness. The pumps droned steadily, tickling the soles of his feet. A popping came suddenly from the far side of the barge. He remembered that every minute the pumps ran meant three more tons of strain on the rigid wires around them. The thought made him uneasy.

He stepped over a bollard toward Phillip, and shouted into the rigger's ear over the roar. "Where's the rest of your men?"

"Only needing me 'ere, mon. Why put 'em in danger? Eh?"

Did Christian understand that, that this wasn't the safest place to be? He looked toward where the *jefe*, fascinated, was gazing into the sea. The number two wire emerged below him and bent around the coaming. It had already bit deep into the plating.

Phillip said, "No need for you to be 'ere, either."

"No, I'll stay."

He smiled, showing those missing teeth. "Then I will stay, too. Don't you be worrying about her. We rigged her sweet, she will all go fine."

Galloway said he hoped so.

The diesels droned on as the sun micrometered down toward the sea. He stood by the well, gnawing a tag of suture inside his cheek as he watched the water level drop. Though it was invisible, the sea around them was rising, too. The silent, slow, but immensely powerful combination of dewatering and tide was matched now in a silent struggle with the inert mass of steel and chemicals, cocaine and bones far below.

He felt uneasy. It seemed as if he should be doing something, checking something, but all there was to do was wait. The pumps hammered in his ears, spitting fire through their exhausts. He limped to the side and stared down at one of the wires. He kicked it, wincing as the shock stabbed up under his kneecap.

It didn't move, didn't twang. It was like kicking a solid bar of steel. He looked at his watch.

High tide in fifteen more minutes. If *Guapi* was coming up, it would have to be soon.

Once it began rising, the air inside the bunkers and drums and pontoons would expand. Lift would increase as it pushed out the water and in turn increased the force that drove it upward.

It still wouldn't be enough to raise the wreck, though. That was what the winches were for. Over several hours, Phillip's engines and tackle, geared down to a few inches a minute, would slowly hoist the broken-free hull toward the light.

Till the pontoons broke the surface. Then the trawler would stop, hanging fifty feet down, directly under the barge, with only the rusty tops of the old fuel tanks showing ahead and astern.

At that point, *Ceteris* would swing into position for the tow.

He thought next about Anunciada. The track north passed a few miles off Walker's Cay. There was a marina there and an airstrip. She couldn't swim? She didn't have any choice. Anyway, with an inflated vest on her, he could tow her. He didn't like the idea, but he couldn't think of a better one.

He had decided not to tell Aydlett about it at all. It was a hard and bitter thing to say, but he just didn't trust him anymore. Christian had won. The worm had entered his partner's heart, and he was lost.

He looked across the shimmering iron to where the three of them stood together.

They'd go tonight, in the dark. The important thing till then was to act like one of the team. You aren't much of an actor, Tiller, he told himself. But now is the time to use whatever talent you got.

The wire by his foot banged, springing flakes of rust off the plating, and skidded sideways an inch. He moved hastily out of its way, then walked forward, trying not to limp.

As he came up, Christian was saying, "Yes, I remember him. A damn good man. So you were his brother?"

"That's right," said Shad. "Meshach Aydlett. How long you know him?"

"Not that long, but he impressed me. He had ability and he

had ambition. Yes, ambition. That's something people of your
. . . race could use more of. I don't know that there's any real
difference in endowment"—Christian lifted his eyebrows, and
chuckled—"or maybe there is, in some areas. What I mean is,
we're always in the market for alert, capable men, whatever their
color, nationality, habits . . . sexual preferences."

"Girls is mine," said Aydlett.

Christian doubled in abrupt laughter. "Ah well . . . Here's Tiller. He's delicious, Galloway, where'd you ever find him? How's
the job progressing, Señor Salvage Engineer?"

"Seems to be going all right so far."

"How will you know when it's free of the bottom?"

"The wires will surge when the bottom suction breaks. Then
they'll go taut again as the winches take up the strain."

"There's no danger, is there?"

"There's always danger in a lift. Especially when it's rigged too
fast, with untested tackle."

"I have confidence in you, Tiller. You stood up to me when I
wanted you to dive with air. I respect that. I've learned a lot over
the last few days, watching you two. I might go down sometime,
just to see what it's like under there."

"I can give you a lesson, if you want," said Shad.

Roach straightened from the chafing gear. He said, "I'd stand
back from these wires if I were you. One of them lets go, it'll cut
a man in two. I've seen it happen."

Galloway glanced at his watch again. He felt cold and realized
he was sweating. It was 7:05.

The diesels clamored and the pumps roared, shooting their
curving jets, like wavering rainbows of ice, out to meet the sea.
Smoke drifted off. Evening was coming on, all right. No stars yet,
but he could make out the familiar beacon over Strangers Cay.

7:09.

7:12. Unconsciously, he'd expected something to happen at the
moment of high tide. They'd reached it, though, and the pumps
roared on. Minute after minute went by. The water in the well
was down nearly to . . . no. Looking down, he could see patches
of iron bottom, rusty and rough, between the sloshing sheets of
remaining sea.

With a sick feeling, he realized there was well over a hundred tons of lift on her now. *Guapi* should have left the bottom long ago.

"Galloway! Isn't it going to move?"

"It ought to," he said. He was puzzled. In fact, he couldn't explain it. Unless something was a *lot* heavier than he thought—

One of the wires bonged suddenly, plucked like a harp string. The note was damped by three hundred feet of water, but it came to his ears clear, a faint, deep, almost inaudible hum, as if the sun, dipping at that instant below the horizon, had snapped some celestial chord. At the same instant, the barge shivered, as if an earthquake were beginning under her.

The shudder ran up through the cables and shook the barge. The stretched wires hummed like a slammed piano. The steel deck trembled. "Here she comes," Roach shouted over the straining diesels.

He was looking at the samson posts, where the ends of the wires were made fast, when he saw something odd. One of the shackles had suddenly stretched, as if it were rubber. He took a half step forward. Then jumped back, scrambling over tackle and loose line.

The shackle parted with a crack like a rifle shot.

For a fraction of a second that he experienced as endless time, something deadly and invisible lived among them. It caught Roach across the back, knocking him into the air. He hung for a moment against the sky, his spine bent at a crazy angle, then disappeared into the water. He did not come back up.

Galloway found himself on his face between the other wires, and heard the deadly hiss pass just above his head.

The whip end flicked and clawed twice more about the deck, clanging on iron, biting with the random mindless malevolence of a frenzied, dying snake, before it disappeared over the side.

"Slack those wires!" he shouted, scrambling over the iron to the quick releases. Short lanyards led from steel pins in the doubled eye splices at each mooring post. Behind him, the chief rigger was shouting, too. He got to the number six wire and pulled the release. The wire bolted over the side, cutting a momentary gash down into the sea. Free them quick enough and the wreck would drop back to the bottom. If it got unbalanced, though—

"She jammed, Mist' G!"

"*Stop the pumps!*" Galloway shouted. No one moved. Christian seemed frozen in horror, staring at where Roach had disappeared.

He turned and ran across the deck, leaped a cable as it frayed, stretched, and suddenly parted. Wires were going off one after the other like firecrackers on a Chinese holiday. He reached the throttle and yanked it down. The pump stuttered to a stop. Into the sudden quiet, he shouted, "Phillip! Open the cocks! *Flood down!*"

But a warning rumble was growing underneath them. The forward wires groaned. To his horror, the barge swayed, then rode up abruptly under their feet as if rising on a tremendous wave. Only there was no such wave visible on the sea. It rolled in a kind of ponderous joy, free of the terrible weight beneath. The wires cracked and sang as they contracted again, as the terrible tension came off them.

He felt his skin creep in horror.

Fifty feet away, a small white patch appeared on the sea.

The tossing oval of froth widened. They all, the rigger, Aydlett, Christian, watched it silently. Galloway wanted to run. But there was no place to run to. Its seethe came clearly over the calm sea.

The sea began to boil. Black cylinders shot out of the churning, leaped high into the air, then fell back into the maelstrom, trailing snapped lengths of wire and chain. He saw with a frozen heart that they were fifty-five-gallon drums.

The bow pontoon came to the surface in a twenty-foot geyser of foaming water and depressurizing air. With a sullen roar, the bow came up after it.

Guapi rose into the lavender fire of evening like an enraged and dying whale, huge, dark, blasting water and compressed air from every port and hole with a hollow bellow like a rocket engine lifting off. It lifted into the view of man again like some new island appearing from the deep. Rope ends, lashings of cable, chain, and chicken wire gleamed black and rust red and green as verdigris. It rose and rose, suddenly and unnaturally resurrected, then hung poised, angled toward the darkening sky, like some massive beast never meant to see light, but that was now, tortured beyond endurance by terrible pain, straining to fly.

The trawler came some twenty feet out of the water at a steep up angle, venting air and water till she was almost hidden from sight in the mist. Then the roaring lessened, and as it ebbed, she slowed, hesitated, and then slid neatly and irrevocably and with great dignity backward, out of her bonds, back into the deep.

Through the tumult came a faint high keening. Christian was jumping about, waving his arms, his mouth wide like a screaming child. Galloway looked back at the sea, in time to see more drums pop to the surface, boil about like jet-propelled water bugs, then slow, sink, and disappear again.

The bubbling and hissing faded away, dwindling at last to a slow continuous eddy where the ship had shown herself. It looked, he thought vacantly, like one of the Jacuzzis in the fancy hotels in Virginia Beach.

The thin scream rose to audibility at last. It was shouting, "Galloway. *Galloway!*"

He sighed and looked about the deck. The wires hung slack— those that were still left. He felt as if he should be doing something. Searching for Roach? There didn't seem to be much point in that. He sighed again, and made his way toward Christian.

"What the hell does this mean. How could this happen! This is a disaster!"

"I told you—"

"Shut up. You, you're responsible for this." His hands shook. He seemed to be dancing on the air. "How am I going to explain this to Don Juan?"

Suddenly, for the first time, Galloway understood something.

Christian feared for his job.

And possibly his life.

Like everyone else aboard, the fearsome Christian was terrified of the quiet little man in the white linen suit.

He wasn't sane at the best of times. What he smoked saw to that. He'd said himself he wasn't responsible for what he did.

Now there was blood in the water. And that made Troy Christian as dangerous as a wounded shark.

But his instincts were ahead of his logic, as usual. Because even as he was thinking this, he was saying soothingly, "It's nobody's fault, Troy. Something snapped, that's all. It happens in salvage work. Our estimates were too light, or the gear was faulty."

"'Our estimates.' *Your* estimates, Galloway! You're the one who set this up. You're the salvage expert! I took your word!"

Christian's voice fell suddenly; he smiled like a wolf. "And now you've screwed it up. Don Juan's golden boy. Oh, I'm impressed. Are you impressed, Shadrach?"

Behind him, Aydlett stood impassively, his arms folded. He said nothing, neither to help nor hinder. Thanks, Shad, Galloway thought tiredly. Just stand back there. Maybe he'll give *you* the job next.

Phillip, looking scared, approached them with a hammer in his hand. Galloway turned to the chief rigger. "Let's check the gear," he said. "Which one went first?"

"Number two snap first, mon. Saw it go. It was t' shackle dat went. Must 'ave been cast wrong, a bubble in the metal."

"I don't think so. A one-inch shackle, that should be good for what, fifty thousand pounds?"

But when he and the Bahamian squatted over the twisted steel semicircle, he felt suddenly cold. Its surface was galvanized, dull gray zinc—except for where it had failed. That part was bright. He tilted it up and it glowed bloody in the final reflected radiance of the vanished sun.

Only part of it was the jagged, partially crystallized tear of metal failure. The rest was the smooth cut of a saw, halfway through its diameter.

He said, in a low voice, "What's that look like to you, Phillip?"

"Like somebody been sawin' on dis shackle."

"No shit. Was it you?"

"Mister, I got no reason to. Got to believe that of me. Nor any my men. I check them all—none of them looked cut—whoever did it must 'ave smeared grease on it after, so you can't see."

He stared into the Bahamian's eyes. He wanted to believe him. But if *he* hadn't, who *had* done it?

He couldn't think of anyone who'd want to dump the coke back into the sea. Not even himself. He wanted it up as much as anyone. Not only was it his only chance of getting home, it had become a challenge.

"Who else has been on the raft?"

"Don't know of nobody but you, and Mr. C, and the captain, and that Gonzalo. Oh, and dose guards. They been here every night. 'Side from that, nobody."

A sudden stutter of gunfire made them both jump. Christian

stood behind them, a smoking Uzi in his hand. A mist was settling down where the bullets had hit the sea.

"What about it, Galloway?"

He stood up casually, hefted the shackle, and tossed it into a wave. "It was the shackle," he said. "Probably a bad casting. Nobody could have told it was faulty without x-raying it. It was just bad luck."

"Is that what I'm going to tell Don Juan? That we had bad luck?"

He reached out his hand. Without direction or expression, the bodyguard slapped a fresh magazine in it. Christian dropped the empty, rammed in the full one, and jerked back the bolt. When it came up again, it was pointed at Galloway's chest.

He swallowed, looking down the barrel four feet away. It was still smoking. He heard a discreet scrape of leather as the rigger, behind him, edged out of the line of fire. "No. Just tell him . . . that I made a mistake, Troy. No big deal. We just go to plan B."

"I don't care about plans, Galloway. I want the coke!"

"I'll get it," he said. "You saw her. She's torn apart now. I'll go into the hold. Bring them up one by one, if I have to." He swallowed again.

"You have till tomorrow. Noon. I want to see the first drumful by then. You understand me, Galloway? That plain enough?"

"I'll try, Troy. But we can't dive right away. We've put in too much time below. I dive tomorrow, I'm dead. If I can—"

Gonzalo, behind Christian, put his hand on his arm. "Señor . . . he's right. The gas, it builds up. He can't—"

The next moment, the Cuban was staggering back, his mouth welling instantly with blood. When Christian brought the gun down, he was shouting, shouting at the bodyguards, who stood immobile for a moment.

Then they moved in on the little man.

In the soft wind, the sound of their fists on flesh was like ringside. But it went on. Galloway stared, trembling, as at last Gonzalo sagged to the iron, his head lolling.

When he raised his eyes, Christian was smiling, like a man who has just gained something expensive, something beautiful, something he's wanted for a long time.

"I know what you're planning. I know how you're plotting

against me! All of you! Trying to make me look bad in front of the Don! You think I don't see! Well, it's not going to work! You don't discuss my orders. None of you. You carry them out. *Compraste lo que te pedi?* I'll kill you all if I have to. Don't think I'll hesitate at all.

"You're on the bottom at first light, Galloway. Or you're dead. And Shadrach here takes over."

He lifted the gun again, and this time aimed, smiling, dead between Galloway's eyes.

"Now get to work."

17

But the next morning when he came topside they were underway, not at anchor; within the line of cays, not offshore. On the horizon behind them towered a high white silhouette, row upon row of windows flashing in the sun.

"What the hell's that? Looks like a cruise liner."

Gonzalo straightened from where he leaned against the rail. When he turned his head, Galloway saw his ruined face. "That's what it is," he said slowly, through swollen lips. "One of the Port Canaveral runs. They don't come through the Out Islands very often. It is unfortunate they had to show up now."

Galloway didn't say anything. As far as he was concerned, *unfortunate* wasn't the right word at all. He looked at the Cuban's mouth. "By the way. You got that standing up for me. Thanks."

The little man shrugged. "It will pass. But Señor Christian will pay for this one day."

He thought that was the end of it, but Gonzalo went on, forcing the words out. "Do you know why I was beaten?"

"*Why?* Because you pissed him off, I guess."

"Because I had no means of self-defense, Señor Galloway. That is why."

He couldn't disagree with that, though it was an odd way of putting it. So he just nodded. As the Cuban started to leave, Galloway said, "Wait. What about the barge? The crew? Where are we headed?"

"To Tanner, till we can be alone again out here." Gonzalo tilted his head toward the pilothouse. "Do not 'sweat it,' Tiller. Sorry, I have some work now."

"Yeah, see you later."

He took the Cuban's place against the rail, watching what he'd expected to be his last day on earth warm up.

At nine o'clock, the PA system said something in Spanish in Gonzalo's voice. He seemed to have taken Roach's place as captain. Galloway caught the word *helicoptero*. The crew ran about, dragging the panels over the pool and lowering the lifelines. He retreated inside as soon as he saw the incoming aircraft, a speck above the intense shallow blue that stretched farther than he could see.

It was the Baptist. Galloway caught sight of him just for a moment, walking across the deck with Christian. His head was down, and one hand clamped the Panama against the rotor blast. Christian was shouting into his ear. Nuñez was scowling. Then they passed out of his sight. Shortly thereafter, the *Agusta* lifted again in a drumming blast of sound and headed off to the west.

Ceteris swept slowly through the narrowing aisle of cays. Low bars lifted to starboard, and then the black dots of rocks, looking drab and lonely amid the wide-flung play of light. The line of cays to port went by like bus stops. He leaned on the rail and let the sun make him sweat and the wind make him cool and watched them pass.

It was enough, for a little while, to know that he had this day to live. By the whim of fate or luck.

It was such a goddamned beautiful world. Why did it have to hold people like Christian and Nuñez?

They anchored an hour later in the lee of Tanner Cay. Gonzalo did well enough, heading *Ceteris* into the wind, then backing as the anchor went down with a clatter. Galloway wandered up to the pilothouse. He found a sailor at the wheel and the Cuban with a copy of Knight's *Modern Seamanship* open in front of him. "That's what I call doing it by the book," he said.

"It's simpler than I thought."

"Till you got a four-knot ebb going one way, thirty-knot wind going the other, and your plow hits a rock bottom. Look, you run into questions, Shad or I can help you."

"Shad is a seaman?"

"Damn right, he's been running boats since he was twelve. His dad was Clifton Aydlett, first man to catch a blue marlin off Hatteras."

"Is that so."

"That's right. . . . I see Don Juan's back aboard."

"*Si.*"

"I was surprised he wasn't here for the lift."

"We do our work, Señor Galloway, and he does his. That everything goes well in higher circles." Gonzalo eyed him over the text. "As I think you know. How much rope should I put out?"

"We say, anchor line. How deep is it here?"

"Seventeen feet."

"A good rule of thumb is seven times the depth. How long are we staying?"

"Till the cruise ship goes away. No more than a day, I think."

He nodded, looking out over the shimmering water toward the soft green of Tanner Cay. Somewhere on the far side was Bayou Serene. And beyond it the coral head he and Shad had almost died on.

When they'd been fighting side by side.

Suddenly he was homesick. He wanted his partner back, like a lover who has been lost. But not every friend can come back. Not when they've left because of something too big to ignore or forgive.

Irreconcilable differences. Like my damn marriage, he thought. But he missed Shad more than he'd ever missed Ellie.

He yawned suddenly and his stomach rumbled. Now that he had a reprieve, if even for a day, he felt more hopeful about living through plan B. He looked at his watch. His appetite was back. It was time for lunch, and then, maybe, another few hours in his bunk.

He turned from the flower-laden wind, and went below.

• • •

He was awakened by Gonzalo on the phone. The Cuban wanted to know why they were swinging around on their mooring. Galloway advised him to look under the chapter on Tides and Currents.

He lay staring at the ceiling for a few minutes, then sat up. He looked at his watch and then out the little porthole. Getting to be evening. Boats were coming in, big tuna-towered charters back from billfishing, yachts and sailboats back from a day in paradise. Back into the sheltering stone arms of the quay, to the comforts of gin and dinner.

"Señor Galloway."

The murmur came from beneath him. He checked the door, then rolled over. "Yes."

"I need to use the WC. I need to walk around."

He'd almost forgotten her. He told her to wait, and got up. Opened the door, and checked the corridor. Empty. He closed it again and pulled the mattress up and then the springs.

She climbed out stiffly. He looked away as the robe fell open.

He stood by the door as water ran in the bathroom, ready to forestall anyone who showed up. When she came out, she looked wordlessly at him. Her fingers touched his cheek for a moment. Her once-empty eyes were filled with such trust and gratitude, he had to look away.

When he looked back, she was sliding into her hiding place again. He pushed the bunk pad back into place and smoothed the sheets.

This couldn't go on much longer. Sooner or later, someone would come in while she was up. Now, unexpectedly, land lay half a mile away, so close he could smell it. This could be his chance. But he'd need some way of getting her there—she didn't swim—and somewhere to leave her when they got ashore.

He pulled a shirt on and went out on deck. He leaned against the rail, not far from a group of smoking, joking sailors, and looked toward the cay.

The changing tide was swinging them slowly around. Most boats in Bahamian waters used two anchors, one laid toward the ebb, the other toward the flood. He wondered whether he ought to tell Gonzalo. Then he thought, Why should I? If *Ceteris* went aground, he'd have a few more days to recover.

He was still there when the Liberator came around the stern and made up alongside. Two sailors in jeans were sitting in the stern sheets. The men beside him threw their cigarettes into the water and ran down the ladder, laughing, tilting their caps forward.

Without taking time to think about it, he shoved away from the rail and followed them down.

In the launch, they glanced at him as he pushed through them and went below. He sat on the cushions in the V-cabin. No one shouted an alarm. No one seemed to have noticed.

The motor growled, and the yacht's side moved away. He saw *Ceteris* whole, framed by the window. Then he didn't see her at all.

They were close enough that whoever was at the wheel didn't bother putting the boat on a plane. They purred through the harbor entrance, past the beacon, and swung right for the landing. When the pier knocked on the hull next to his ear, he stayed put. The engine stopped and the cabin lights went out. He heard gay shouts, fading laughter.

After ten minutes, he put his head out. He was alone.

He stepped over onto the pier and followed the crewmen, letting them stay a hundred yards ahead. When they took the lit path uphill, he turned left instead, and strolled down the quay as evening took it. It rolled beneath his feet after a week under way.

Gradually, he put together a plan. Wait till full dark. Steal someone's boat. Get the girl aboard it somehow, then run her ashore. She could hide in the woods till *Ceteris* left again, then call Zeno from the hotel. If the DEA man wanted testimony, she could give him an earful. Probably she could call her father, the judge, from there, too.

But how could he get her out past Christian's guards? He'd managed it, but nobody had said he couldn't go. It wouldn't be that easy with a woman, especially someone they all thought was dead. The first sailor who saw her would scream his head off.

A lit alleyway opened to his right, off the quay. He rubbed his face, pondering, and turned absently down it.

It was a row of small duty-free shops. Swimwear, liquor, jewelry, art. He strolled down it, shoes whispering on the quarry tiles, looking absently at the window displays: gold, silks, expensive fashions. The art store had a curved stainless steel sculpture that made him think of a propeller blade. A woman was standing in the window, looking out. Their eyes met.

An instant later, she was reaching for the door. But his reactions, keyed up as he was, were a fraction of a second faster. He yanked it open and was inside as she changed her mind and backed away. Then she turned, and her mouth came open. He got his hand over it and dragged her back between the room dividers, into the watercolors of sailboats and island scenes.

They struggled for several seconds, knocking down a bronze

sculpture that clattered like a suit of armor. He kept his palm over her mouth, muffling a scream. She tried to kick him and missed. Then she tried to twist out of his bear hug. He kept moving her backward, a foot at a time. She was supple and fast, but this had nothing to do with agility or even strength; it was simple bulk. Her face was turning red. She bit his hand and he sucked air through his teeth, shifted his fingers, but didn't let go.

By the time they got to the back, she wasn't fighting anymore. Not being able to breathe did that fast. Now that they couldn't be seen from the front, he eased his fingers apart, giving her enough air to keep her from passing out, but ready to muffle her again. Her eyes rolled, close to his, dilated in fear or rage.

He said, "What are you doing here? You work here, is that it?"

"I own it," Lynne Parkinson said. "Now let me go. Let me go before I scream my head off."

"You're not going to do any screaming. You sent people to cut my throat. Now I want some answers."

"You're bruising me. I don't know what you're talking about."

"Don't try to con me again. It only works once. You're the only one who knew Shad and I would be on the reef that day. I even let you suggest the place, didn't I? The only thing I don't know is why." He eased his hand another inch. "There's somebody much rougher than I am who wants to know. But once I find out, I'm out of here. I'm not after revenge. Or you. But I want answers. Now."

She looked up at him sideways. Her eyes were a green blaze, like a fluoride compound held in a flame.

"You mean Mendieta Nuñez-Sebastiano," she said. "That's who you work for. But *he* already knows why. Why don't you ask him?"

"I'm not interested in sicking him on you, that's why. And I don't work for him. But I do get curious when people try to kill me."

"Are you serious? That's all you want?"

"That's all."

"How do I know that?"

"Because if I wanted something else, I'd have had it by now."

She thought about that for a minute. Then her eyes came up

again. "Come in back," she said. "Or, wait, let me lock up. Can
I lock up?"

"Yeah, but don't get any ideas."

He stood behind her as she turned the bolt in the door and
flipped the card from OPEN to CLOSED. Then she led him past a
display of porcelain fish and figurines.

Behind the sales floor was a sitting room, with easels and desk
and a microwave. The desk looked like his old one at the Buxton
shop, covered with catalogs and invoices. He slid the drawer open.
No hidden guns or knives. She was pouring herself something.
"Sure," he said, when she held up the bottle of Tia Maria.

When she handed him the paper cup, he saw that her hand
was steady. She wasn't frightened at all.

"Now, what are you talking about, not working for him? At
Bayou Serene, you said you were. If you aren't, who are you, and
what are you doing on his boat?"

"When they're around, I can't exactly speak my mind. I'm here
because he burned my boat, burned my store, and threatened my
friends. Am I 'working' for him? Or am I some kind of slave, or
hostage? You tell me."

She was sitting at the desk now, her legs crossed. She looked
completely at ease. "No, you tell me. All I know is that you get
drunk and attack people bigger than you are. Then you show up
on Tanner with the heaviest hood in the business. You act like a
thug; I see you with thugs. You look like a thug, too." The phone
buzzed softly; she didn't look at it. "What am I supposed to
think?"

"Okay, that justifies you thinking I'm a thug. But does it justify
trying to kill me? Who were those guys, anyway?"

"Friends of mine."

"They know their reef."

"That's because that's what it is. Their reef."

"And you? You've adopted them, or something?"

"Why not? Not every outsider has to exploit them."

"Hold it right there. Before we get into the class struggle, or
whatever it is, let's go back two spaces. You set me up for them."

"I told them there'd be two Ceteris men out on the reef. They
didn't care which two."

"And they're Bahamians. Now, enlighten me, please. I grant

you, the Baptist's crew aren't the kind of people I object too much
to wasting. But why do *they* want to kill them? I get the impression
he has the local palms well greased . . . including the fat shithead
you were with at the party."

"Pepper?"

"That's right. Belly, or whatever his name is."

"Telly. Yes. He's . . . sort of, leased the Out Islands to Nuñez's
organization. Unfortunately, those islands are not uninhabited.
And nobody asked the inhabitants how they felt about it."

"You mean nobody paid them off."

"You're a cynical man, Mr. Galloway. How did you get so cynical and still stay so innocent?"

"Call me Tiller. I didn't say I was innocent; I said I wasn't with
Nuñez. That's all."

"But you are. I saw you with him."

"I already explained that."

"Oh, right, he's forcing you to work for him. You're not involved in drugs. You're just his—what? His plumber? His
manicurist?"

"I'm— No. Listen. Here's the whole thing in ten words or less.
I used to work for him, years ago. I got busted, went to prison in
the States. I got out a year ago and I was trying to make a living
on my own. I wasn't doing real great, but I wasn't starving, either.
Then he decided he wanted me back."

"Running drugs again."

"Not this time. This time, he wants me to raise a wreck."

She sipped and pondered. He watched her ankle as it swung to
and fro. Her braided leather slip-on hung from a toe.

"Well, if that's true, then we owe you an apology. Wuckie
wasn't trying to kill you—"

"Like hell he wasn't."

"—or at least that's what he told me. If he was, then of course
I can't hold the . . . results against you.

"But that—Tiller?—is all I owe you, because as soon as we
found out what you were doing off Strangers Cay, they stopped
trying to interfere. In fact, they helped. You recognized Filly, of
course."

"Who?"

"Phillip Grahame. He works for Rolf Von Arx."

He stared at her. "Filly . . . It is, isn't it? At the Rooster. The one with the knife." Now he understood why the chief rigger had been grinning at him.

"And he helped you, didn't he?"

"Yeah, he's sharp." He paused. "Okay, so you stopped trying to interfere, coincidentally right after Shad and I sent your knuckle boys back tied in knots. So, why'd you change your mind?"

"*They* changed their minds. Because you were trying to get the poison up."

"Oh, the cocaine. Yeah—"

"No," she said. "Not the cocaine."

He sat rigid. Several lines of thought connected suddenly in his mind. He had a feeling he wasn't going to like the answer to the question he was about to ask. But it crouched there, like a spider, at the point where they intersected.

But she was still talking. "I mean, not entirely the drugs. Though hating them is what pulled the Dusky Damsels together in the first place. Filly—his son was a baser. He died in Freeport in a holdup. Wuckie used to work for Carlos Lehder on Norman's Cay. Your . . . employer's organization caught him and peeled the skin off his arms. Vernon Moor, one of the men you killed, had just kicked crack. He was three months out of Sandilands and he was so proud he hadn't gone back to what he called his 'horrors.'

"That's why they attacked you. Anybody off that yacht's the enemy. The Bahamas is caught between people like Don Juan and the number-one consuming country in the world. It's not just transshipment; the pusherman's here, too. The government sold out long ago. So they're taking it into their own hands now."

"What about the white guy?"

"Conchy Tarpum's not white. Almost, but not quite. His father was from Man-O-War Cay. Conchy had two daughters. They both went to Nassau, they both went to the pusherman. One of them's dying of AIDS. The other's still on the street."

Galloway felt sick. He felt the knife going in through the ribs again . . . into another man who'd fought the same fight he had. "I didn't know."

"Now you do."

"I'm sorry. But—you said it wasn't the drugs."

"Not this time. That's why they're helping you now. This time, I'm talking about the poison."

"What poison?"

"Whatever it is that's been killing their fish. They want it gone, and so do I."

"Maybe you better tell me what you think is down there," he said slowly. "And why. Because as far as anyone's told me, it's just a grunch of cocaine, mixed in with a few barrels of processing chemicals."

"*You* don't know what's down there?"

"All I know's what people tell me. I haven't been inside yet."

"I see. Well. We—I mean, the fishermen, the people who work off those cays—they saw the ship go down. It was on fire.

"But it's not how it went down that's important. These people know the sea. They make their living getting Nassau grouper and conch and snapper and lobster for the casinos and restaurants in Freeport and Lucaya.

"Mr. Galloway, the sea off these cays is dying. They don't know what's causing it and neither do I, but it's something on that ship. I've been trying to find out, tracing the registry, but you can imagine how far that gets me. All I could find out was the itinerary."

"What was it?"

"Colombia, Havana, New York, Colombia, Panama, Newark, and then cleared for Colombia again out of Charleston."

He thought about this for a while. She paced back and forth, her strong brown legs scissoring a few inches from his eyes. When he glanced at them, she said impatiently, "So you see why we backed off when we realized you were trying to raise it."

"I'm beginning to."

"What happened? Did you get it?"

"So you don't know everything. No. We didn't."

She stopped pacing. "Tell me."

"A shackle . . . snapped—on the barge. The trawler broke in two and went down again."

She stared. After a moment, she put her fist to her mouth and sat down. "It's still down there?"

"Yeah. But it wouldn't be if things went like I planned.

"Tell me again how committed everybody is to getting it up. Because the reason I failed was sabotage. That shackle, the rigging

I was lifting it up with, was sawed halfway through."

"Not by anybody from Gunwater or Pass Cay, it wasn't. I can guarantee you that."

"You act like you know them inside out. Maybe they don't tell their Great White Mother everything."

"They're not fools, Galloway. They don't destroy things for the fun of it, or because they don't know any better. They know if that wreck stays there, their fishing grounds are doomed. And they starve, or move away, or go to work for people like Pepper and Nuñez."

He sat irresolute. The thought was paralyzing. But the more he thought about it, the more sense it made.

There was something other than coke in the wreck, and something other than acetone and ether, too. Those were flammable, explosive under the right circumstances, but not what you'd call poisonous. In water, they'd dissolve and be carried off harmlessly, eventually to rise to the surface and evaporate.

But he'd noticed the strange taste, the murkiness, near the hold. Noticed it, he suddenly remembered, even *under* the wreck.

And there were never any fish around. Plenty near the surface, above it. None on it.

His skin prickled.

And it made sense that if that were so, then no Bahamian, none of the riggers, would have sabotaged the lift. Whatever was in it, they wanted it gone.

But someone had.

So there was someone else among them, someone working against them, against Nuñez, too; someone who did not want *Guapi* to see the light of day.

Who?

And why?

She was looking at him, waiting. He shook himself and said hoarsely, "I guess—we're not on opposite sides, after all."

"Then maybe we should work together."

"What you got in mind?"

"A deal. Sit down."

This time, they sat side by side on the couch. She half-turned toward him, and he watched her breasts move under the soft cotton. The light came over her shoulder and it was just like, he suddenly thought, the very first time he'd seen her; golden light, shining through the down on her cheek, and her eyes in shadow. And come to think of it, her half smile was the same, too. What did it mean, that faint curve of her lips?

But she was talking, and he blinked and listened.

"Something like this. You try to get all the poison up. Whatever it is. We don't care where it goes, but we don't want it here.

"In return, Filly and the guys watch out for you. I act as a link to the locals, and I have some pull with Pepper and Sears if we need it. We help you survive and maybe even hurt Nuñez, if you want to, that is."

"It's the only way I'm ever going to be free. But hurting him—that's not a good idea."

"To get the law on him? U.S. law, I mean?"

He said slowly, realizing this for the first time even as he said it, "That wouldn't work, either. I'd never be safe. 'He who strikes at the King must strike to kill'—I heard that in a play once. That's my only choice. Do what he wants, and hope he lets me go, or else kill him."

"And neither of those may be possible for you, working alone."

He nodded grimly.

"There you are. It's a natural partnership."

"I suppose. What if there's trouble?"

"Then like I said, we'll take care of you."

"How?"

"We'll figure that out when it comes. But it's better than being on your own, isn't it?"

"True." Even having someone who would hide and feed him in a pinch would put him ahead of where he was.

She smiled. "So—deal?"

"Sounds vague, but I'm game."

"Good."

He remembered then what he'd come ashore for in the first place. "Look, talking about cooperation, I need some now. Tonight. There's a woman aboard that yacht who needs help."

He explained. She tensed when he told her what had been done to Anunciada Mariategui. "And you're hiding her?" she said.

"Well, that's what I was getting to. But I've got to get her ashore. If I can, do you know anyone who can take care of her

till we leave again? She has family in Peru. I'm sure they can wire
money—"

"I wouldn't take money for that."

"I meant for plane tickets, expenses."

"Of course I'll help. We'll get her tonight." She touched the
back of his neck lightly. "And it was—you did right, taking her
in. Maybe I owe you an apology, too. That's not the kind of thing
a—thug would do."

He wanted to say, there wasn't much of a choice; but the way
she was looking at him, then leaning forward, didn't leave him
room or time for words.

He had a moment of holding back. Fighting it, as one fought
narcosis. Then he forgot why he was fighting. He just wanted her.

Her hand came up and curled around his neck, bending him
down.

And outside on the hill, the fireflies burned white, mocking the
stars, and the sailors rolled through the winding paths, shouting
and laughing with the maids from the hotels, waiting for their turn
for love and intoxication, the love of women, and the intoxication
of dream.

• • •

He was floating, falling away into black depths, when she said
into his ear, "Why did you hesitate?"

"What?"

"I saw it in your eyes. For a moment. What was going on
there?"

"Do you have to know?"

"Curiosity is the first requirement of an artist."

He said unwillingly, "I was thinking of a woman. Back home."

"In the States?"

"That's right."

"Your wife?"

"No."

"A live-in."

"Not exactly. A lover."

"Which means what? That she loves you? That you love her?"

He didn't answer her.

"But it didn't stop you from doing everything that needed doing. And doing it very thoroughly."

"Story of my life." He half-smiled in the semidark. Her finger traced his cheek and he flinched back.

"What's that? Did I hurt you?"

"It's where your friend stabbed me, out on the reef."

"I told you it wasn't meant to be that way. How were we to know? To the Damsels, you were just two more hoods."

"To the what?"

"That's what they call themselves. The Dusky Damsels. I asked them what it meant once. They just smiled."

He smiled too. "It's a fish. Only a couple inches long, but it guards its territory. It'll nip whatever comes close, no matter what it is. A bigger fish. A diver. A shark."

"Oh . . . anyway, I'm sorry it happened."

"Okay. You already apologized." He looked around the room. "Which of these are yours?"

She smiled slowly, then reached up her hand. Directly over the sofa. He looked up, and his eyes widened.

For a moment, he thought it was Pass Cay. There were the same little houses, the same trees, the same people. Only these houses were vibrant, vivid, almost radioactive, and the rabbit-tails and jacarandas glared with blood red and indigo and vibrating saturated green. The people were solid, more than three-dimensional, more alive than the living life. The rumps of bending women echoed the shapes of the golden peach mangoes they lifted. A man's spine slumped under a load of fish on a pole, and Galloway felt the solid weight of flesh, the fatigue of a long day fighting nets, and the tired triumph of the man who brings home food. In the middle distance, the path wound to a boat yard where tiny figures labored in the incandescent glare of all-pervading color. But somehow the painter had made them sing, too, with the pride of work under the island sun.

"Where is it?" he said. "I think I've been there."

"It's a cay . . . kind of idealized. The way I think it looks to the people who live there, to people who love it."

"It's beautiful," he said, and felt how weak the word was. "I mean it. You have talent."

She smiled and patted him. She didn't speak for a while. Finally, she got up and went for a washcloth. He looked at her back as she bent. The heavy curve of her breast was just visible. Her hair hung down as she brushed it. Her buttocks and thighs were strong and square. Not like Bernice's; attractive in a different way.

Now that it was too late, he felt rather sad. He hadn't intended to do this. It had happened without warning. Driven by lust, he'd done something he was sorry for.

But sorry only now, after the fact. . . .

But hadn't that always been his trouble? He knew right from wrong. Growing up on Hatteras Island, you didn't get out the door without learning that. Especially when the lessons were backed up by Lyle Galloway II's leather belt.

He knew what he shouldn't do, but still he did it. Where did he get off high-hatting Shad? He was just like him.

It looked like his lessons weren't over yet.

She came back dressed, in jeans and boat shoes without socks and a dark long-sleeved turtleneck. "You ready?" she said.

"Oh. Yeah." He swung bare legs out and pulled on shorts and shirt. She took a waterproof flashlight from the desk. "You got a boat, right? Or access to one?"

"Yes. What do you want me to do? Do you want me to come aboard with you?"

"Christ, no. Don't even think about setting foot on *Ceteris*. Just drop me at the boarding ladder. What I want you to do is run half a mile downcurrent, turn off your running lights, and anchor. Is there an anchor light on your boat?"

"A white light, on a sort of little pole?"

"That's it. Leave it on. I'll get her into the water somehow. Once we're near you, I'll show a light and you pick us up. Oh, and one last thing—have you got some clothes for her? A T-shirt and sweatpants, or jeans, something dark."

"I have some rags I wear for painting. But wait. What if I miss you?"

"Then we'll come ashore somewhere on Little Abaco, I guess. But I should be able to find you. Just keep that light on, and stay alert." He paused. "If there's trouble—shots, or shouting—don't come in. It's too damn dangerous. Too many armed, crazy people who don't even speak English. Just come back here and I'll get in touch somehow later."

"If you say so."

The boat was an open runabout, not very big. It rocked as they stepped aboard, and water slanted to and fro in the bottom. Parkinson groped under the dash for a few seconds. A black Mercury whined, then burst suddenly into noisy, smoky life. He peered into the back. She had one half-full six-gallon tank and another one that felt full. "You're okay on gas," he said. "Whose is this, anyway?"

"Mine. Undo that rear-end rope, will you?"

"Uh, sure."

She might not be so hot on the nautical terminology, he thought, but she knew to the inch how much clearance she had astern. She turned end for end in the narrow space between piers and then straightened, aiming the red and green bow lights for the basin entrance. Beyond it was full darkness now, darkness and the circus glitter of riding lights from the anchorage.

He stood up in his seat and found *Ceteris*. Parkinson hit the gas and the little boat hammered down the waves. As they neared, he saw that the ladder was still down and the launch wasn't back yet. "Come in slow; don't scare them."

"Gotcha."

He didn't put a line over, just stepped across the two feet that separated him from the boarding ladder when she drifted by. "Thanks," he called loudly, and waved. She waved back and hit the throttle again. He didn't look after her.

One of the bodyguards was frowning down from the top of the ladder. Galloway staggered upward, steadying himself on the lifelines, and tossed him a jaunty half salute. The Indian hesitated, fingering his Uzi, then grunted something and stepped back.

He went straight to his cabin. The light was off. He turned it on. He bent to the bunk and whispered, "Anunciada. It's me."

"*Sí.*"

"Come on out. We're leaving."

"Now?"

"Right now. Got a boat standing by. Hurry. Don't catch your hair on that spring."

She swayed when she stood up and he had to steady her. Could she make it? Hell, she had to. He explained what was going on as he handed her the bundle. "All we have to do is drift. Don't even have to swim, just float. I've got a life vest I'll put on you. Understand?"

"But how will you get back?"

He hadn't thought about that. "That's not important. Maybe I can come back with the sailors. Get lost in the group. Let me worry about that. There, you look good. Ready?"

"I guess so," she said. She looked very small in Parkinson's clothes. Like a dressed-up child.

"Okay, let's—"

The door tapped twice. Before he could move, it came open. Shad Aydlett said, "Hi, Till."

For a moment, he couldn't figure out why the waterman wasn't surprised to see her. Then he felt her warmth and realized she had stepped behind him, was directly behind him, pressed to his back like a shadow at noon. She thought fast, this one.

Standing carefully motionless, he said, "Hi. What you need? I was just turning in."

"Where were you? I called you on the phone. No answer. Didn't see you at supper, either."

"I went ashore for a beer."

"Without me?"

"Yeah, without you."

Aydlett looked around the room, then back at Galloway. He said slowly, "I get a real unfriendly feeling here, Tiller. Like I been getting for a couple days now. I wanted to say that we are still partners, as far as I am concerned."

"That's not true for me, Shad. Not since our talk down below."

"About not running out when we almost got our hands on some real money? I didn't say anything about breaking us up, Till. I only said, I wasn't leavin' till I got paid." He took a step forward, lowering his voice. "Being partners don't mean we always got to agree. Means neither one of us orders the other around. Right? The way you are acting, if I want to stay and work a while for Nuñez, catch up some on my debts, you make that out to be some kind of betrayal. Well, it ain't, it's looking out for myself, and that is exactly what I plan to do."

"Uh-huh. Let's talk about this tomorrow, okay? I want to get caught up on—"

Aydlett frowned. He took another step, looking at the carpet. Then his eyes widened. "Holy—"

Galloway said in a hoarse whisper, "Keep it down. Don't say anything! I've been hiding her here."

She stepped back, and he felt her warmth recede. Aydlett nodded twice slowly, staring at her. He whistled soundlessly. "Everybody thinks she dead," he whispered.

"Let's keep it that way. We're going over the side."

"*Now?*"

"I'll be back, but she won't. That's all you need to know."

"Uh-huh. Well—you need help?"

"No. Thanks, but I've got it all arranged. Just leave quietly. You know what happens if they catch her again."

"I can guess. Okay." He moved toward the door, but stopped for a moment with one hand on it. "But we got to talk some more about this."

"Tomorrow, Shad!"

Aydlett eyed him. Then nodded once, sharp, and went out.

"Okay, let's go. I'll check it out topside, then come back. Stretch those kinks out. Be ready to hold your breath. We'll go right over the side and we won't come up till we're clear."

"Okay," she said. She looked scared but game, standing by the telephone. He patted her shoulder.

Outside, the corridor was empty except for a sailor standing at an open panel on the bulkhead. Galloway glanced over his shoulder as he went by; the man was testing contact points on a breaker panel.

Topside, the deck was still brightly lighted. But the electrician had given him an idea. He went up two decks and forward to the bridge. A short search of the pilothouse located the lighting switchboard. He patted his pocket, making sure of the flashlight, then ran the edge of his hand down a row of switches. As he left, sliding out onto a suddenly darker night, he locked the door behind him.

When he got back down to the cabin deck, the sailor was gone. Someone was shouting back by the boarding ladder. He reached in, hissed "Come on," and pulled her after him out onto the port side.

He was crouching there, snapping on her life vest, when a light hit them. He looked up, blinking, shielding his eyes against an electric dawn.

It was Troy Christian, with his two Colombian robothugs. He was holding the light and smiling. "Why, Tiller," he said, "I had no idea. So she wasn't dead, after all?"

Galloway didn't say anything, just slowly clicked the last D ring into the snap. Gonzalo came out of a side door, ran a few paces forward, keys jingling, and disappeared into the pilothouse. A moment later, the deck lights came back on, and the Cuban, breathing hard, joined Christian. He stared at Anunciada with dismay.

"It does look like we happened by just in time. I have to say, though, I'm disappointed, Tiller. I've been more and more disappointed in you lately. Don Juan will be disappointed, too. Now we'll have to do all sorts of tiresome, unpleasant things."

He half-straightened. Was it worth begging? Probably not. But it wasn't for himself.

"You can do what you want with me," he said. "But why not let her go?"

"Let her *go*? That's a dangerous woman, Galloway. I told you that once."

"Horseshit. How can a twenty-year-old college student threaten you? Don't give me that bandit story again, Troy."

"Why not? It's true. My orders were to dispose of her. I've built my reputation on that, you understand . . . on carrying out orders. So . . . now that I find she is still alive . . . and almost escaped, I really can't keep her in the land of the living. That was Fabito's idea. I see now I was wrong in agreeing, but I wanted to indulge the crew."

Beside him, the Cuban said something. Christian turned his head slightly to listen. Then said, "Well, *I* thought she was shark meat by now. Yes? . . . Perhaps you're right. Perhaps that is still the best solution." He looked down at Galloway again and pursed his lips. "Do we have a butcher aboard?"

"A cook, but he can butcher," the Cuban said.

"You see we have everything on this wonderful vessel, Galloway. Fabito, refresh my memory. The sanitary system, the garbage disposal and macerator—it was giving us problems last week."

"It is fixed now, Señor."

"Good. Chain him up in a safe place. Kill her, turn her into garbage, put her in the sea."

Galloway didn't waste time shouting. Never telegraph an attack. He came to his feet in one motion, pushing her through the life-lines with his left arm, going for Christian's throat with his right.

But he never got there. He caught a peripheral glimpse of the gun butt, then the night sky came crashing down. The last thing he wondered as his face smashed into the deck was, How had they known?

He could only come up with one answer.

Damn you, Shad Aydlett.

Damn you to hell.

18

When he came to, he was doubled like a sheet bend between V-cornered walls. No light met his eyes even when he got them open. He tried to turn his head, heard plastic crackle by his ear, and froze.

He lay still, trying to make sense out of it by slight movements, hearing, and smell.

There was a plastic bag over his head, and a foul-tasting rubber tube was jammed into his mouth. He was getting air through this, but he didn't know where the other end was. His hands were tied behind him with what felt like duct tape. There was tape on his ankles, too, and they were doubled under him and tied to his chest with rough rope—sisal, or manila. The deck he lay on was checkerboard sharp: steel grating, most likely. He smelled vomit, and by the way the blackness was swooping up and down, accompanied by a swishing gurgle, he was going to add more to it soon.

By the feel of all this, he didn't think he was going to get free. But he tried anyway, straightening his legs. Immediately, his air stopped. He pulled them back up and sucked frantically. The tube stayed bent. He pulled at it till he saw red flashes, then got hold of himself. He blew out, putting every molecule of air he could muster back into the hose.

It gave a faint pop and unkinked, and he could breathe again, as long as he didn't demand too much.

From the motion, and the shape of the walls, he was in the forepeak, down in the bilges.

He hoped they came back for him. Otherwise, he was going to die down here.

He lay there for what seemed like days. He didn't struggle anymore, though from time to time he couldn't help groaning as

cramps harrowed his back and legs. There was no point in struggling. All he could do was endure.

And think. He had plenty of time for that.

Interminable eons later, the hollow clang of footsteps brought
him back to the red-shot blackness. Suddenly light crushed his
eyes. Hands like cargo hooks closed on his feet. The hose crimped
and he convulsed, choking and strangling, till someone pulled the
bag off. The tape that held it on took skin with it. Air hit his wet
face and hair like ice.

He blinked, blinded by the weight of light. In it shapes swam,
dimly seen, as if he was underwater without a mask. Two men
were holding him up. Another head bobbed in front of him.

A knife gleamed, and he could move his legs. A hand yanked
his head back, pulled out the tube, and thrust something smooth
and hard into his mouth, chipping a tooth. He drank by reflex
before his throat closed and he coughed out whiskey. When he
caught his breath at last, the hard, brilliant face of Troy Christian
hung before him pale and eroded as a newly risen moon.

"We're here, Galloway. Get your gear on. You better do things
right this time."

He cleared his throat. It felt raw. The liquor made his eyes
water. On the second try, he said, "No."

He was still unsteady and the slap almost knocked him down.
It came out of nowhere and rocked his head back in a flashbulb
burst. "I said, we're here. Listen hard, Galloway! No more ex-
cuses. No more delay! Your partner's getting ready. Get to work!"

He said hoarsely, through a throat that felt as if it had been
bastard-filed to bare metal, "I said no. I'm not diving for you anymore. You can throw me back in your hole. Or throw me overboard. You bought Shad. But not me. I'm on strike."

He grinned bitterly. He'd waited a long time to say that.

"Beat him—no, wait."

The Indians, the men holding him up, hesitated, their fists
raised. The slim man took a step back. Galloway saw that they
were in some kind of gear locker. The overhead was low and the
steel bins and shelves were filled with heavy-looking shapes
wrapped in waxy brown paper. It smelled of grease and paint and
bilge water. And vomit, but he was to blame for that.

Christian took out his handkerchief, coughed into it, then wiped his lips slowly. He squinted at Galloway, and for the first time there seemed to be doubt in his eyes, faint, like a single drop of dye dissolved in the sea.

"Is it worth beating you, Galloway?"

"Cripples can't dive."

"So it's Catch-22. If I beat you, you can't dive, and if I don't, you won't."

"Life's full of tough choices, Troy."

Part of him was wondering how far he'd have to go to make Christian shoot him.

"You still got a wise mouth. What if I just pitch you back in there till you change your mind?" He nodded toward the forepeak.

"Then you lose three, four days—at least. And after that, I won't even be able to stand up, much less go to three hundred feet."

"I'll give you cocaine. As much as you want, soon as you come up."

"Don't want it," he lied.

"Whiskey, then. Money. How much?"

Galloway said slowly, "I don't want it." He added an obscenity that had been in use among Hatteras watermen long before it became obligatory in the movies.

"Okay, so what *do* you want?"

"I want Anunciada Mariategui."

One of the Indians must have understood some English, because he snickered. Christian smiled. "She's no longer available."

"Meaning, you murdered her?"

"Processed her. The finest modern disposal equipment. No incriminating traces. Fabito tells me even the bones are gone."

Galloway closed his eyes. She'd trusted him to save her. He opened them again to fluorescent light and Christian's steady mad gaze, bluer and more penetrating than ultraviolet.

"Everybody wants something, Tiller. Even you. You can't have her. What else do you want?"

And he sucked a breath, feeling the trembling in his legs, and said, "I want to talk to Don Juan."

• • •

They checked the tape on his wrists and took him up to the main salon and shoved him into a seat at the table. It was set with fruit and a silver wine cooler. He stared at Poseidon rising from the sea. How long had it taken *him* to decompress? Beyond it, through the windows, was the by-now-familiar broken line of Strangers Cay.

"From Pella," said an urbane voice. A heavy round body in white came into his peripheral vision.

The Baptist paused for a moment as one of the guards held his chair, then sat down opposite Galloway. He put the Leica down carefully beside the fruit bowl.

"Do you know where that is, Tiller? It was the capital of Macedon when Alexander the Great conquered the world. Odds are he walked on those little tesserae of marble as a boy, before his great adventure. The sword and the spear are from the same dig. I can't guarantee they were his, but it's possible."

"That's nice."

"It's not cheap, getting a three-thousand-year-old mosaic floor out of Yugoslavia these days. That's where Macedon is now. Yugoslavia."

Galloway took a deep breath. "Don Juan."

Nuñez said, not unkindly, "Tiller, we are wasting time. Why aren't you working? Why are you being stubborn? Troy says he's talked to you, without success. I understand you insisted on speaking with me. And, you see? I am listening. But I don't have infinite patience. I would like to get this thing done, get *Guapi*'s cargo aboard, and leave." He reached for wine and poured a glass. "But, let it not be said that I am unwilling to hear you out. You have something to say? Please go ahead."

"I'm not working because your dirty-jobs man killed a woman he had no reason to kill. Also, I've been lied to. You put us on the bottom without giving us the information we needed to do the job. There's something else down there. It almost killed me. That makes me mad. That's why I'm not working."

Nuñez sighed. He reached into his jacket and took out a pair of half-moon glasses. It was the first time Galloway had seen him with them. They made him look more like a professor than ever.

"So that's why you're—on strike, was that how Troy put it?"

"That's about it. Since there's no way to resign."

"That's fairly serious, Tiller. It compounds the fact that you didn't do very well, I understand, on trying to get *Guapi* up."

"I had it free of the bottom. One of the shackles broke." He thought again of the hacksaw marks. But it was too late now; he'd thrown away the evidence. "It was an accident. I was being rushed. We had to use jackleg gear, hasty rigging, wire we picked up at Von Arx's junkyard. It's a wonder more people weren't killed."

"Ah, yes, I missed Captain Roach. But the yacht agency's sending us out a replacement . . . however. What you're saying is, you don't like the terms of our bargain."

"That isn't all. Killing people who can't harm you—"

Nuñez rode over him smoothly and imperturbably, still speaking to the mural. "Pardon me for interrupting. . . . Troy."

"Yes, Don Juan."

"Bring Fabio here, please."

"Yes, Don Juan."

Nuñez lifted the Leica. He peered through it, focusing on Galloway, then put it down. "But she *could* have harmed us, Tiller. Mariategui was captured operating against our organization along the Colombia-Peru border. She wasn't one of the hangers-on. She was Sendero Luminoso cadre, a convinced Communist and a determined guerrilla. I had her sent here for interrogation; leaving her alive after that was more than she deserved. If she had escaped, she could have caused the Compañía a great deal of trouble.

"Those are all normative considerations. But the terms of your employment, your working conditions, pay . . . that's a different matter. I admit it, I imposed a one-sided contract on you. But you have countervailing power in this situation—an indispensable skill for which we have no direct substitute except Aydlett, who doesn't have your experience.

"So my only recourse is to accede to your demand, and increase what I am paying you."

Galloway didn't say anything. He hadn't said anything about money, but apparently that was what the Baptist had heard. Well, if Nuñez had to lie again about the dead girl, if he had to go through some kind of economic analysis before he made a decision, that was all right with him.

He preferred to think of it in terms of poker.

Christian came back, with Gonzalo a few steps behind. The hatred between them was palpable. The Cuban said, bowing his head slightly, "Don Juan, you asked for me?"

"Yes. Mr. Galloway wants to know exactly what we have down there in *Guapi*. Tell him the facts, please. All of them, exactly as you told them to me."

"Ah," said the Cuban, blinking. For a moment, he looked even more like a bird. Then his glittering eyes swung to Galloway's.

"*Guapi* was not originally Don Juan's ship. In fact, it belonged to what might be called his competitors. Some of them are Cubans, the exile community. Others have been trafficking in narcotics for much longer. It was a loose cartel, but well financed. I was in charge; not as the captain, but as the representative of the organization. The crew was sound; in fact, they had just done another run north to the States."

"What happened to it?" said Galloway.

"Well, let me continue. We were detected somehow by the Coast Guard north of Matanilla Reef. The captain and I decided not to stop for them. Instead, we headed for Bahamian waters, where they could not pursue. They chased us in the fog, and fired at us.

"Well, we . . . escaped from them, but we were hit. My men tried to save the ship, but it was not possible. And so we sank. Not far from shore. But unfortunately my men were not good swimmers.

"I was the only survivor. I came ashore on Pass Cay. The people there saw fit to turn me over to the authorities."

"Who, fortunately, happened to be Telly Pepper," said Nuñez, smiling faintly.

"Yes. Consequently, Don Juan was kind enough to express an interest in me, and in the course of our conversation he pointed out that this might be a profit opportunity, if handled properly, for both of us."

"You mean, you decided to sell out your old boss, in return for a share of the cargo."

"You might put it that way, Señor Galloway, though I would

not. I've been . . . very impressed with Don Juan, his wisdom, the logic and strength of his arrangements. I believe this is the future of the trade, one *corporación*, one large *organización*, with him as leader. I want to be part of that future. But you are right, my former employers would be very angry if they found out what I had done. And in view of this, I hope that Don Juan will look on me with favor in years to come."

Galloway caught, from behind him, Christian's tensed fury. He switched his attention back to Gonzalo. The Cuban looked relaxed, eager to help.

Nuñez was smiling. "Do you understand all that, Tiller? The Coast Guard chased it, it sank, and took down with it all the men aboard except one. This was Señor Gonzalo. It was he who told us what the cargo was. He is a man who understands reason; he wished to work with me in recovering it, in return for a generous share.

"Well, I did not plan to recover it immediately, for reasons which I will explain in a moment, but he impressed me, and I took him into my service. Where he has done well, as you can see.

"Now. I was tempted to recover this cargo when news of it first came into my hands. But frankly, having it stay where it was, that was not at all bad for me. In the first place, it had not been mine, and the original owners did not know where it was or what had happened to it. Nor would they, as long as I kept him in my bosom, so to speak."

Nuñez paused to refill his wineglass, and in the silence Galloway heard shouts from on deck. Through the window, he glimpsed the black bulk of the barge, two or three miles ahead.

"In the second, all this took place in a period when *coca* was relatively plentiful. It is a simple matter to reason that if there is less of it on the market, my own holdings are rendered that much more valuable. In fact, once the price elasticity of cocaine is known, and total production is estimated, it became possible to calculate exactly how much it was worth to leave it on the bottom. I did this, and found that it added approximately fifteen dollars per kilo to my selling price. This may not sound like much, but since my organization moved a hundred and twenty metric tons last year, it adds up."

He shifted in his seat, and his eyes came down from the curling beard of Poseidon to pin Galloway. "Since then the situation has changed. The backlash in Colombia has made it harder to obtain product for export. Second, the U.S. naval interdiction has created a bottleneck in transport. The combination has tripled the price in New York. So the market signals me that now is the time to raise *Guapi* and sell its cargo. As I said—all very reasonable."

"I see that. But my question wasn't about economics. What's in there? I don't care who tells me, but I need the truth."

"As we all have told you, Tiller, cocaine."

"Yes, but what about the other drums? What's in them?"

Gonzalo said, "Troy, I mean Señor Christian, told you that, Señor Galloway. They're petrochemicals. Raw materials used for extracting and purifying the *coca*. And those raw materials fetch a good price. It's much more efficient to use a bottom both ways." Nuñez nodded silently. "Surely you can understand that."

Lying bound hand and foot, he'd been able to reason through a lot of things that till then, driven by the press of events, he'd taken just on faith. This was one. "No," he said, "That *doesn't* explain why there were chemicals aboard. If the main cargo was coke, then it would be going north. If the cargo was chemicals, then *Guapi* would be going south. Am I right? So why would both cargos be aboard at the same time? And which way *was* she going?"

Behind Gonzalo, Christian frowned. Nuñez cleared his throat and looked grave. After the shortest possible pause, the Cuban said firmly, "*Guapi* was going north, of course."

"Then why would there be production chemicals aboard? Unless somebody's planning to start growing coca bushes in New Jersey, and purifying it there."

Neither Nuñez nor Christian nor Gonzalo smiled. Finally the Cuban shrugged. "To that, I was not a party. I had my orders, and I followed them. Ballast, perhaps. Or to confuse drug sniffers, if the Coast Guard boarded."

Galloway sat up in his chair. He wished his hands weren't taped. He was sweating despite the air conditioning. He had to do this without making them suspect anyone else. He had no illusions about what would happen to Parkinson, Wuckie, Filly, and the other islanders if the Baptist found out how much they knew.

"You want to know what I think? I don't think those are production chemicals. Or maybe there're *some*; the best cover story's always partly the truth.

"But I've noticed things, down there on the wreck. There are no resident fish. You get 'cudas and silversides on a wreck the same day it goes down. Cobia take a couple weeks. But that ship's been there a while, and there aren't even any morays. No minnows, no baitfish schools. The water has a funny taste. And it gives you a rash where the wet suit lets it in.

"So, what is it?"

Nuñez smiled regretfully. "All right. You've all but guessed it. Perhaps you might as well know. Tell him, Troy."

"Excuse me, Don Juan. We are approaching the site. I should be on the bridge."

"Go on, Fabio. Oh, and will you send the other man up, the black man? Aydlett? Thank you."

Christian stared angrily after him as he left, then swung to face the table again.

"Tell him," said Nuñez again. "As I said, Señor; do not make me repeat myself."

Christian said, "There's another line the industry has gotten into in the last few years, Galloway. Something new since you were with us before.

"It's efficiency, like the Don says. The big organizations realized they were running cargo north but coming back empty. They did production chemicals, occasionally arms, but there wasn't always enough to make it pay.

"They made it known through their contacts in the United States that they had cargo space. Finally, some other people, in a related line of business, figured out how they could make money without even delivering."

"How's that?"

"Load a few drums, carry them offshore, and dump them, one at a time, at night. That's what *Guapi* was doing off Abaco. Our ships do it, too. There's also a bonus. The waste serves as cover; no dog's going to smell coke when that stuff's around."

"Waste. What kind of waste?"

"Chemicals," said Nuñez. "By-products. The sort of thing a plastics plant, a pesticide plant, can keep around only so long."

Galloway said, "You mean *toxic* wastes? Exactly what have I been diving in?"

"Don't get excited," said Nuñez. He sounded faintly contemptuous. "I thought you were a brave man."

He leaned trembling against the edge of the table. Skin eruptions, headaches, vertigo . . . "If I had known that," he said, controlling his voice with difficulty, "we could have worn dry suits. We could have worn gloves, covered our skin with petroleum jelly. I was working for you, Don Juan. Didn't you feel you owed me the truth?"

He didn't know what he expected. But all he got was a raised eyebrow. Finally, the Baptist said, "Perhaps. Shall I make it up to you now? How about this: a hundred thousand dollars U.S. in apology and bonus. Does that appeal?"

A deep voice said behind Galloway, "I been down there just as much as him. How about me?"

"Mr. Aydlett, please join us. And another . . . fifty thousand for your hardworking partner.

"There, so now you have the whole story and a valid offer." Nuñez stood, dusting his trousers. "We are almost there. Now, will you cease this silliness and get to work?"

"No."

Nuñez tossed his head back. His gaze hardened. He looked at Christian, and nodded.

Christian said something in rapid Spanish to the larger bodyguard. The two men turned to leave. They smiled at Shad, turning their bodies to slip by.

Then they took him, from both sides. Aydlett had no time to defend himself before he was on the deck, looking up. The muzzles of two submachine guns were pressed to the top of his head.

"It seems we disposed of the woman too quickly." Nuñez stood by the door. His voice was soft. "We could have used her now. Mr. Aydlett, though, should work in her place.

"You can retrieve our cargo alone, Galloway. It will be slower than with two divers, but I feel sure you can manage. That means that though we can't touch you, your friend is expendable. We can do without him. But can he do without his hands?"

Aydlett struggled, then seemed to realize it was useless. The wire twisted till it disappeared into his flesh.

His fingers turned dark with trapped blood.

"In half an hour, they will be dead. Then we will bind his feet. Et cetera. Till your little fit of pique is over. Understand?"

"Troy," Aydlett said hoarsely. "Troy! Help me out, man. Don't let him do this to me."

"Shut up," said Christian, not looking at him.

"You got to help. You said, you and me, we's going to work together."

"Shut up, nigger! Whine to your goddamned partner!"

Galloway took a step forward. His boyhood friend knelt on the expensive carpet. He felt a great sadness. The sadness of a man who is proven right too late for it to do any good.

He said, "You see how it really works, Shad? You see how much you mean to them?"

Aydlett didn't answer. His head hung down. Finally, in a muffled whisper, he said, "I didn't understand."

"It's what's going to happen to both of us."

"I didn't know."

"Well, now you do. And now you know how Anunciada felt."

"For God's sake, Tiller!"

"Why did you do it, Shad? It didn't gain you anything, to have her die."

"I don't know what you're talkin' about, before God I don't."

"Did you help them do it? Did you help them butcher her? And what did they give you in return? Just tell me, Shad. Be honest."

"I never told them!"

"Nobody else knew she was there."

"I never told them!"

One of the bodyguards bent down. An animal howl filled the room, echoing from the ancient mosaic, from the expensive paneled walls.

Galloway shuddered. He tried to steel himself by thinking of Mariategui. Other eyes that had trusted him. Eyes that this man had betrayed and destroyed, for a handful of white powder.

But his mind, treacherous and cunning, gave him another image instead.

It gave him the terrified eyes of Meshach Aydlett, looking up at him from the water as he aimed a pistol—and pulled the trigger.

Who was Tiller Galloway, to act in the name of justice? Who was he, to reproach another man?

A man whose brother he'd killed?

So his boyhood friend had done wrong. But Lyle Galloway III had done wrong, too. And come, in time, to know it, and regret it.

Maybe someday the same thing would happen to Shad Aydlett. He had the right to sacrifice his own life. But not another's.

Through a great silence, a great weariness, he heard himself say, "Okay, you win. I'll get your cargo for you. Let him go."

Christian spat Spanish. The guards bent. A moment later, wire clattered softly on the carpet. Aydlett knelt there still, silently massaging his wrists.

But Galloway couldn't miss the gleam of hatred when Shad lifted his head at last.

19

He carried the sense of doom out into the sunlight. He heard Aydlett's boots following him. But he didn't look back, and neither of them spoke.

Gonzalo was at the stern, directing several crewmen as they rigged the gas tanks for lowering. Galloway asked him to make up two reels of light line, three hundred feet long. The Cuban said they'd be ready in a few minutes. He added that their gear was waiting. He'd replaced the batteries in the lights and tested the regulators himself.

He cleared his throat. "Fabio takes good care of us."

"Uh-huh," said Shad.

They dressed out rapidly and in silence. He glanced up once, to find Christian gazing down from the pool deck, the wind flickering his hair like red flame.

Sweating in the sunlight, carrying their coiled umbilicals, they shuffled down the ramp. A line led over the side, angled downward. Gonzalo explained that their helium/oxygen mix was waiting at the bottom.

He nodded, looking around the horizon. A calm sea, light breeze, hot. There'd be more wind later, but the weather should hold. He looked back at the Cuban, who stood straight, as if waiting for orders. "How about lifting lines? If we can get to the drums?"

"I didn't want to tangle you on the way down. We'll drop them once you are on the bottom. All you have to do is put them around the proper ones, and we'll pull them up."

"The 'proper' ones?"

For some reason, Gonzalo's voice dropped. "Look on the side, about two inches below the lip. There will be a small X scratched there, on the ones we want. Do you understand?"

"Small X," said Aydlett.

"Yeah, we got it," grunted Galloway. "Ready, Shad? Let's get this over with."

He waddled the last few steps and sealed the band mask. Flat glass excluded the sun, the breeze, the anxious birdlike face that peered down at them. He twisted the valve, inhaled, and stepped off.

• • •

The sea was the same. So much had happened in the world he lived in that for a shutter flick he was surprised. Then it was only natural. The sea changed less in a million years than the land in a century. Compared to him, to human things, it was eternal.

He sank through the shimmering play of light, out of a pale blue sky.

A silvery missile shape drifted in. He put his hand over his regulator to mask its gleam. But the barracuda kept coming, its black silver-rimmed eye fascinated, its undershot old man's jaw slowly opening and closing. He could see every tooth with perfect clarity. He flicked his left hand. The fish didn't blink, as if it was all part of the show. It was easily six feet long.

Not for the first time, he thought how lucky it was that, though barracuda were fascinated by divers, they almost never attacked. There'd be no way to work in warm waters if they did. He knew only one man who'd had an unfortunate experience. It was in the Gulf of Mexico; they'd been raising a platform wrecked by a hurricane. 'Cuda had been hanging around for days, feeding around the divers as they worked. His buddy had been wearing a spare regulator, dangling by his side. Then, out of the blue, one had struck, darting in so fast that no one could move. Its teeth had punctured the thin steel casing of the regulator. It hadn't bitten the diver, but the impact had ruptured his spleen; he'd died that night, on the helicopter to New Orleans.

At forty feet this one lost interest. Without moving a fin, it vanished, reappearing ten feet above him. It studied his bubbles, then disappeared again. When he squinted up, he could make out fifty or sixty of them, patrolling about slowly in random directions between him and the light.

He looked down again, wondering what they'd find on the bottom.

He'd worked out by now what had happened when *Guapi* had broken loose. The barge lift had hoisted her on an even keel at first. But then the snapping of the shackle had dropped her stern. The air in her voids had surged, putting more weight on the remaining lines, snapping them one after the other.

But something had occurred then he still didn't understand. The higher the bow tilted, the more the air in it would expand, and the more lift it would generate. Still, it shouldn't have brought her to the surface. That was the part he didn't get.

Now she was back on the bottom, though, somewhere in the sapphire fog below, and they'd have to get inside her and get her cargo up. No matter what.

Yeah, Nuñez and Christian had made that plain: that this was their last chance.

He turned his head, sinking on his side like a sleeping child, and caught a flash of sun off Aydlett's faceplate as his partner looked back. Their bubbles converged into a silvery stream, expanding as they rose toward the golden light.

He lifted his hand. Aydlett hesitated, then waved back.

God, it was clear today. Such a beautiful world . . . he was glad, no matter what happened, he'd lived in it. In two worlds, really: the world of man, and the separate, timeless world of the sea. Oh, there were things he regretted. Tad . . . he'd spent far too little time with his son. Bernie . . . he'd wanted to resolve that. He knew now, had finally understood during those dark hours in the forepeak, that she had been arguing not for herself but for him.

And other things. Things he wished he hadn't done. People he should have apologized to long ago. People he should have told he loved them.

A hundred and eighty. The edges of his mind blurred. Something dark seemed to move in the gray mist below.

His mistake had been in thinking he could cooperate. He should have run. Hirsch had been right. He'd been a fool to think it could end in anything but this.

But she'd been wrong, too. You didn't expiate evil with punishment, and return clean. It was like nitrogen under pressure. You breathed it and it became part of you. Deny that, and it killed you. Only gradually, only over years, would it bleed away.

Two hundred and fifty feet. He sucked compressed air thick as ten-weight oil through his regulator. He'd forgotten how cold it was down here, how dim. He shuddered inside his wet suit.

And there it was, emerging suddenly from the violet gray, snapping into reality.

He valved air into his vest, and a little more, and drifted to a stop twenty feet above the shattered wreck of a ship dumped twice to the bottom, sawed apart by steel cables and blown open by expanding air.

His slow mind followed his eyes over what was left of *Guapi*.

She no longer looked like a sunken ship. She looked like Von Arx's junkyard. She'd disintegrated, tumbling down in sections, each one bursting like a seedpod as it hit. Her remains lay in a rough line, some drums scattered across the sand, others half-visible inside wreckage. Cables twisted in and out. Pontoons lay half-buried at the edge of his sight. The forward mast had broken free; falling, it had thrust itself into the sand like a huge bent spear.

He saw a section of bottom plating, split like a torn tent seam, and suddenly he understood how the wreck had grown suddenly lighter. Her bottom had torn out. No wonder she'd darted upward, fighting for the surface like a hooked mako.

The water shimmered, like air on a hot day, and he knew the wreck was leaking. *What* it was leaking, he didn't want to think.

Just do it, he thought dully. Hi ho, hi ho, it's off to work we go. Only can't whistle underwater.

Getting silly early this time, Galloway. Not a good sign.

Motioning Shad forward with a sweep of his arm, he headed for the green cylinders. They lay on their sides not far from what looked like the trawler's bow.

His mind cleared with the first breath of heliox, and his lungs relaxed. The thin gas swirled into his brain, blowing away the drunkenness. He blinked. A butcher's shop like this was dangerous, but it also exposed much of *Guapi*'s cargo. By the looks of it, at least half the drums were already in the open.

A colorless flutter above their heads, and a snaky blackness fell toward them: the lifting ropes, not loose, but bundled so they could attach them without swimming back and forth. Nice job, Gonzalo, he thought. The little Cuban was always thinking. He'd go far in the Combine.

It was pretty evident that Troy Christian was past his peak and headed down.

They hadn't bothered with a phone line to the surface this time. But there were mikes in their masks, and their umbilicals were connected. So now he cleared his throat and said, hearing his voice high and comical, "Let's start gettin' this shit up. You get the ones in the open. I'll work inside. Then we'll swap off. Okay?"

And a familiar voice, distorted but still familiar, said, "Sure, Tiller. But, one thing—"

"If it ain't about recovering coke, Shad, it's got to wait."

He grabbed the bundle and towed it toward the largest section of wreck. It lay on its starboard side, a torn-open cave, night-black against the dim gray of the bottom. He pulled out the penetration spool and tied the end to a bent stanchion. Then felt around for his light.

The darkness fell back before a burst of brilliance. The gray of the abyss gave way to rust red, flaking black paint, the silver threads of freshly torn steel.

Holding the flash with one hand, spinning line off the penetration spool with the other, he moved forward, into the dark.

20

Galloway pursued the brilliance down a twisted, canted corridor that receded endlessly before him into darkness. A few yards in, the bulkhead buckled. He brushed the steel with his glove. It had been torn apart like cardboard run over by a truck.

He pulled in his legs and did a slow forward somersault over the edge, holding his umbilical clear. Wouldn't be good to tear it. He had maybe three minutes left in the emergency tank. Enough to get out, if he didn't get lost. Well, follow the line and he'd have no trouble. It was bad, but it wasn't as bad as it might be.

As he thought this, the wreck groaned above him. Something cracked, and flakes of rust drifted down like russet snow. Putting out a glove, he braked himself, floating, on a handrail below him.

It was dark here, inside the smashed carcass of a ship. But not too dark to see the strange tide that flowed slowly past him, welling upward, like the Florida springs he had dived in once. Only those springs were clear as liquid light, and so pure you could take out your regulator and drink, accepting it in a kind of sacrament.

This current was a slow brown, roiling with immiscible oils that oozed upward like the fluid in a lava lamp. An all but tangible smell seeped into his mask. It was bitter and nauseating, oily and pungent. It was a dangerous, strangely attractive reek, like a drug, or a strange perfume. A taste like the temptation of incest.

The skin of his face, his wrists, his ankles began to prickle.

A hoarse choking made him start. His throat had closed and he was trying to breathe. Christ, he thought. Do I have to go into this?

For a moment he thought of giving up. Just taking off his mask. No, he didn't relish drowning. Switch to air, that would be better. His fear would dissolve in a toxic euphoria. He'd live his last seconds in a nitrogen high, and snicker at death.

He hesitated, his hand tightening on the rail. Why not? Christian would kill them when their work was done. Why do the work at all?

Then he remembered how life had a way of surprising you. It was something he'd noticed as a boy, when he'd broken windows or failed geography, and feared his father's anger. Life never happened the way you expected. They might surface to find there'd been a coup, and the Bahamian Defense Forces had taken over *Ceteris*. Christian might go mad and shoot Nuñez. They might have simultaneous heart attacks. It was unlikely, but possible. He'd been in tight situations before—in Vietnam, off Hatteras, in oil-field work. And made it back.

You couldn't give up till the game was over. And that meant double zero on the seconds to play.

He took a trembling breath. He commanded himself to let go the rail. And finned slowly forward, into the eddying fog.

At least there wasn't any silt. Raising and then dropping her had shaken her clean. Aside from the murk, the water inside the wreck was clear.

He didn't even have to watch out for morays.

He squirmed up a ladderway that had once led down, and stopped, hanging motionless, playing a brown beam of light over a wilderness of steel.

In the canted hold, the drums had rolled, crushing some, penetrating others, as the slow chemical welling showed. A few floated above his head, trapped inside the curve of hull by their own buoyancy. They were all colors, rust-stained, with ragged waterlogged shreds of paper and plastic trailing from them. Which of them held what the Colombian wanted? He had no idea.

That was the whole point of the poisonous, mixed, deceptive cargo of M/V *Guapi*.

A faint click, and his beam died. A fainter, bluer light glimmered somewhere above him. Excellent; he could hoist the drums through a tear in the plates instead of wrestling them back through the corridor. He switched his light on again and focused it on one of the floaters. Shoved it, setting it swaying, and ran the beam around its edge, its bottom.

He didn't see anything resembling an X.

He hesitated. A slow smile curved his lips under the plastic oral-nasal cup.

He fumbled for a moment and came up with his diving tool. Steel scraped as he drew its point across the drum, once up, once across.

• • •

Somebody up there, probably Gonzalo, was thinking hard and rigging fast. Most of the ropes came down with slings, short wire straps with hooks at either end. For heavy drums, he set a hook over the lip at each end, tugged twice, and let go. Occasionally they dropped him a bare line. He put the lighter barrels on these with timber hitches.

He worked steadily and it went fast. He had the first compartment cleared by the time he needed to change tanks. He swam back, to find Aydlett tapping on the fitting with the butt of his knife. It came free in a burst of lead-colored bubbles.

"Tiller."

"Yeah." He turned his emergency valve on, hating to go back to air; took two breaths; disconnected from the old, and switched to the new tank. Water shot into his mask, but only a cup or two. Getting good at this, he thought. Then helium and oxygen again, light and clear after the narcotic syrup that air became under ten atmospheres of pressure.

"You puttin' X's on all yours?"

"Yeah. You?"

"Uh-huh."

"Good. Let them figure it out, I can't."

"Right." And it got all the toxics off the bottom, too—at least the ones that hadn't leaked yet. He grinned to himself. He'd keep his promise to Parkinson, anyway.

Aydlett caught a line out of the blue and moved toward another drum. Galloway heard him pant as he bent to it. Then he heard, "Uh, Till . . . thanks."

"Forget it."

"But, something you got wrong."

"What?"

"I didn't tell them about you and the girl."

Forgetting his plan to swap jobs, Galloway swam for a second piece of wreckage. It loomed slowly over him, like the carcass of a dinosaur. He was the little mammal, worrying out the sweetbreads. . . . "What?" he said, not paying much attention. He wished they still had the pontoon to rest in. Instead, they'd just have to work till they were done. "Come on, Shad, it's over. Let's not talk about it anymore, okay?"

"No. It makes me too freakin' . . . mad. Look, I'd tell you if I did, you know? I ain't . . . saying Shad Aydlett's the preacher's boy, but he admits when he does wrong."

Heavy drum, scarred white paint, marked dimly ATSB 109-34-3487, DO NOT STORE IN PROXIMITY TO WATER. Was that a cross scratched on it? Too rusty to tell. He added one of his own and sent it up. "You didn't?" he panted, heading for another. Green drum, heavy, dents on one side but looked tight; marked in Japanese. "Then who did?"

"I don't know." Aydlett was raising clouds of sand and bubbles at the dim edge of his sight, but his breathing sawed and rasped in the earphone. "Who else knew she was there?"

"Nobody. Just you, me, and her."

"Maybe Christian guessed. He's crazy but he's no dummy."

Red drum, Exxon trademark . . . no, it was ruptured, full of water. He leapfrogged it to the next. "Well, damn it, I didn't tell him."

"I didn't, either. Say, Till, how about just takin' that on my word? You used to take me at my good word."

"That was before you got around these people, Shad, around all that shit and money."

"I ain't no worse than you was. My pop warned me about you. You know that? Just 'fore he died. 'Shad, you watch out for that Galloway boy,' he said. 'Good family, but he's gone to the bad, anymore he's crooked as they come.' For a long time, I thought he was right."

"I loved old Cliff," Tiller said absently. "Remember that trick he used to do with the Johnson, hold it out with one arm? Jesus."

Meanwhile, he was examining a white drum, rather crudely

stenciled MOLASSES. Was that a cross? Yes, definitely a marked drum. His arms were burning under the wrist cuffs, where they met his gloves. He scratched them, attached the hooks, sent it up.

"Okay, Shad. If you say so. Maybe somebody else saw us I didn't see."

"Thanks, Till. Means a lot."

Then for a long time, there was no sound on the line but their wheezing, their mumbled curses, the dry clicks as they tried to bring moisture to mouths parched by anhydrous gas.

"Now lemme ask you something," Aydlett muttered. "About that cable on the barge, the one that busted. That was you—right? D'you do that?"

"I didn't saw that shackle," said Galloway, before he remembered Aydlett didn't know.

"Oh ho! You say *sawed*?"

"That's what I said."

"You sly son of a bitch. I figured it was you."

"Goddamn it, I just told you—"

"I got you, Till. You didn't do it? Oh yeah, I'm glad I got the straight on that."

"For Christ's sake, why would I do it?"

"You never wanted to be here in the first place," said Aydlett reasonably. "Shit, this damn—there. No, you never wanted to do nothing these people wanted. You figured if it went to shit, they'd say to hell with it, or if it took too long, the Coast Guard might stroll by and take an interest."

He didn't bother to argue. It was hard enough just to breathe. Working hard, you pulled three or four times resting demand, and the regulator could only handle so much this deep. He glanced involuntarily at the green cylinders. Once they were empty, that was it.

The only trouble was that he didn't want to die. . . .

But you could only think on dying so long before it bored you, too. His mind moved on. To what Gonzalo had said.

Interesting . . . that everything they'd been told on this job had turned out to be a lie. It wasn't Nuñez's trawler, and it hadn't been sunk in a collision. It wasn't coke and production chemicals, but something considerably nastier.

This whole business about Gonzalo was puzzling. Something about it didn't feel right. Like a stone in the pocket of your fin. He said he was from Miami. Great, but who had he been working for? "Competitors," he'd said.

As he worked, Galloway fitted this slowly together with what Parkinson had told him about *Guapi*'s itinerary, what he knew about the smuggling business, and what little he knew about toxic waste.

He came up with Mafia.

Itinerary . . . the itinerary. Something about that, too. But it was getting harder to think—

He was watching a black drum rise like a balloon, spinning slowly at the end of a line that curved up into the hazy blue, when he remembered the last name on the list of ports of call: Charleston.

But when Nuñez had asked Gonzalo about that, he'd lied. The Cuban had said *Guapi* was headed *north* when she sank.

And carrying waste, *too*. A "few" drums, Christian had said. To hell with that! There was a full cargo of the shit here! Why would a ship full of toxic waste be going *north*?

Somebody was still lying. Was it Gonzalo? Why should he? Nuñez seemed to trust him. So much so that Christian had his knife out for him. He couldn't see replacing Troy with Fabio as a good move from the Baptist's point of view, though. Don Juan needed a loose cannon, someone to intimidate or eliminate people he couldn't buy or outmaneuver. Gonzalo was efficient, but he wasn't the kind of mad dog you needed in an enforcer's billet.

Boxes inside boxes. Speaking of boxes, he didn't want to go back in that forepeak. Shit, no, he thought. Before they pull that again, I'll—

Suddenly, he remembered the Uzi. The nine-millimeter submachine gun, fully loaded, that he'd taken off the guard on the launch. He'd given it to Anunciada. But she hadn't had it when they left his room. Ergo, it was still there.

If he could get his hands on it . . . the odds would still be against them. By twenty to two. But it would be better than going into the face-off with no weapon but his knife.

Assuming, of course, that they let him and Shad out of the water at all.

He came back from his pondering and realized it was getting hard to breathe again. He looked around. Wreckage blocked his path; he couldn't see the tanks. No problem, he'd just follow his umbilical. He pulled himself along it hand over hand, came out into the open. Shad's line stretched northward, toward the bow section.

He switched tanks, panting, then held his breath, waiting for water. None came. He sucked; no air, either. Then he noticed the position of the valve. He'd connected to an empty tank. Shit, Galloway, he told himself, You are getting stupid. And it's getting cold.

At the second try, his shaking hands connected to a full tank. He inhaled deeply, expanding his chest, like a smoker taking the first long lungful after trying to quit. His face burned. He tried to scratch it clumsily at the edge of the mask.

Drums to the right, lying on the sand in random directions. As he made for them, his thoughts went back to *Guapi*'s cargo like parrotfish back to a tasty piece of reef.

So what they were talking about was two separate organizations, one of which, probably Sicilian, had owned the coke. The other, Nuñez's, was retrieving it. Funny the original owners hadn't interfered. That meant they didn't know what had happened to their ship, or where it lay. If Gonzalo had told the truth about being the sole survivor, that made sense. As far as its owners knew, it had just vanished at sea.

And the third complication: the Bahamians. The officials were honest, in their way. Like Lax, they stayed bought. The island folk weren't. Not when you were spoiling their fishing and killing their children. In a way, they reminded him of Hatteras people.

But no matter what Lynne said, that son of a bitch Wuckie had been trying to kill him. His heart speeded up remembering it: trapped in the coral, no air but the breath in his lungs, and the big body hovering above him, waiting for him to come out like a teased langouste. . . .

Then he thought about her for a while, about how stocky blondes look against smoky light.

He smiled under his mask as he worked.

• • •

At the end of two hours, they'd sent up all the drums they could reach. There were more under the wreckage, but most of them had been crushed or pierced; there'd be no salvageable drugs left in those. He looked at his watch and then at his gauge. He had half a 244 left. Would there be air waiting at the decomp stops? Would there be enough?

He called Aydlett in and explained the situation in short sentences, economical of breath. The waterman nodded, his eyes worried behind the mask.

They agreed that it was time to go up.

They swam to the wreckage and tied the ends of their reels to it. Then lashed their BCs to the last tank. Gas hissed and they began to rise, unreeling line hand over hand. Galloway kept a close eye on their ascent rate. His body wanted to shoot to the surface. His mind knew this was the most dangerous part of the dive.

He knew now, after thinking it all out, that they'd probably not live much longer. As the sea grew lighter, he wondered how it would happen. If he knew Christian, it would be as they bobbed up. An arched eyebrow and a sneering word of farewell. Then a nod; expressionless eyes behind leveled barrels; a burst of spray on the water. Then two bodies spiraling downward, trailing a red smoke that became green, then blue, then black as the sea stole energy from light itself.

But if they did get back aboard . . . he thought again of the gun. Visualized it, dark and compact beneath the bunk springs. Nuñez and Christian had ruined too many lives. His . . . Shad's . . . the Bahamians' . . . Anunciada's, and thousands of anonymous victims, on the streets of America and Colombia, too.

Nuñez liked to talk about "goods." But what he sold was death. Every shipload, every kilo, every gram generated it like barracuda slashing through a school of blues.

Then he thought, Enough moralizing. Kill him if you can, Galloway. But remember, you were part of it, too.

They reached the first decomp stop and halted. He squinted upward into the bright. He couldn't see any tanks up there. Nor the black spearhead of *Ceteris*'s hull. Surely they hadn't left? He hadn't heard engines. But if they had, they were both dead.

He looked at his partner. Aydlett hung writhing at the end of his line. Behind the tempered glass, his eyes were closed. Galloway was racked by continuous shudders. He wished he could talk to Shad. Reassure him. Maybe even say goodbye. But he couldn't speak through the chattering of his teeth, the icy mass of phlegm in his throat.

He hung shivering, bitting his lips, blinking up from time to time into the mystery of light.

21

He was more than surprised when he made out the tanks hanging below the yacht. He was suspicious. It wasn't as if he had a choice, but he took the first mouthful like a Parisian tasting a California wine.

It was good air as far as he could tell. Aydlett pointed at the other one. He nodded vigorously.

They hung there together like nursing twins, shuddering with the cold they'd brought up with them. His skin itched and flamed. He looked yearningly toward the surface. From time to time, he caught the blurred, distorted reflection of two mortally tired men waiting to see whether they would live or die.

Finally it was time. He checked his watch twice to be sure. All right, he thought. If this is it, I'm ready.

He pointed up, and a moment later their heads broke the surface.

"Hey! Galloway!"

The dense rich air was like breathing cake. It was so wonderful, he couldn't understand how anyone could be unhappy who had enough of it. He sucked it in, and heard Aydlett whooping it in, too, groaning in delight.

"Look out!"

Gonzalo's voice. He squinted up in time to see the bowline drop out of the sun. A few seconds later, they were alongside, looking up into a ravaged, rage-filled face.

Christian said, his voice like a file dressing steel, "Is that all? Did you get them all?"

"Yeah, Troy. Except the ones that were crushed."

"How many of those? How many'd you leave down there?"

"Twenty or thirty. But there won't be anything in them." For a moment, he was afraid Christian would make them go down again. Then he didn't care. He couldn't, that was all. If that meant they'd shoot him, so be it.

No sailors on the platform this time. Just the sheer side of the yacht. Its white reflective smoothness was marred now with grooves and smears of scum and grease. Above it, looking down, were Christian, Gonzalo, and behind them, like a Creator high above his angels, Nuñez.

And, beside Christian, both bodyguards, with their Uzis pointed down.

He was too tired to care. Just let him breathe a little more air and he'd be ready to die. Beside him lead thudded into the platform. Aydlett was slowly taking off his gear. He found his own weight belt in his hand and realized he was doing the same thing. He tripped the backpack and slipped out of it.

"Hey, how about a hand?" said Aydlett. His voice was loud in the silence.

Christian snapped Spanish and a sailor scurried down the ladder. He looked apprehensive. Galloway grabbed the extended hand, got a knee up, and rolled onto the platform on his belly. He lay motionless for a few seconds, feeling limp as a jellyfish, then got to his knees. How warm the sun was! He pulled his fins off and stood, clinging to the sailor's shoulder.

"Come on, get up here," snapped Christian, above them, and the sailor bent, hurrying him up the ladder.

The oiled teak was scarred and dirty now, and the spacious sweep of *Ceteris*'s afterdeck was crammed solid as a pistol magazine with drums. What he'd known as a taste below was a smell here, bitter and choking. It brought tears to his eyes. Pry bars, wet line, and rags lay among the rusty metal barrels.

He looked at the men above him. They gazed steadily down, either expressionless, like the guards, or furious, like Christian. Don Juan's face was one of the impassive ones.

Galloway cleared his throat and took a tentative step aft.

"Hold it. Where you think you're going?"

"Back to my cabin. I'll grab a quick shower, pull on some—"

"This won't take long. You stay here."

Defeat hit him like a boot in an empty stomach. He had a brief melancholy vision of the gun. Why hadn't he used it when he had it? "Well," he said. "We got them up, Troy. Just like you told us to. Did you get what you wanted?"

"Take a look, Galloway. Feast your eyes."

When he took his hand off the sailor's shoulder, the man scuttled away instantly. He limped to the nearest drum. The lid was loose, already pried off, just sitting on the top.

Here it is, he thought. The white powder so many had died for. But its journey was only half-complete. Now it would reap a new harvest, in crime, disease, poverty, hate. It wasn't a drug. Drugs healed. This was a poison.

To his horror, something in him still wanted it.

He fingered the steel lid, already sun-hot to the touch, and then jerked it up.

Inside was a purplish, semiliquid pudding, flecked with red and bronze. A heavy, sweetish, almost visible odor welled out.

The lid rang as he dropped it. He limped to the next and opened it. The same. The third . . . a verdigris sludge, nearly solid.

He jerked the lids off a dozen more. He glanced up at the silent faces above.

He ran staggering along a row of drums, and the covers clashed and rolled, cutting toothlike scars in the smooth wood. Two held a clear liquid with the volatile reek of acetone. The rest held more waste.

None of them held cocaine.

In the silent heat, he felt sweat break under the black rubber of his suit.

"Now, Mr. Galloway. Explain why what we want isn't here."

He unzipped his top and stripped it off. Across from him, Aydlett was peering into another barrel. He was frowning, lost in thought.

"Me? I don't know anything about this, Troy. We just followed orders. Bring up all the drums with X's."

Above him, Christian leaned forward. His face was the color of refined cocaine hydrochloride. He was shaking; Galloway could see that even from below. "Don't shit me, Galloway! Those marks are fresh. You put them on!"

Suddenly, he lost patience. Anger ignited where he'd thought only resignation was left. "All right. Yeah! I did. Because I

couldn't see. For Christ's sake! You don't know what it's like down
there. It's not like pulling stock out of a warehouse!"

"You could tell the marked drums from the unmarked ones,
Galloway. And you left the marked ones down there!"

"That's crazy, Christian! That's crack talking now. Don Juan!
Are you listening? I want to get out of here alive. Why would I
pull something like that? I know suicide when I see it!"

"What about it, Aydlett?" said Christian. He was almost whispering now. His eyes burned down like matched ultramarines set
in ivory, fixed, beyond rage into madness. His hands clenched and
released the varnished rail.

And behind and above him, leaning back in a deck chair, the
man in the white Panama looked silently down on them all.

Shad said, "We sent 'em all up, Troy. We couldn't tell sometimes, so cross or no cross, we sent it up, less'n it was stove in.
Just like the man says." He stopped, then pointed suddenly up at
the *jefe*. No; at the man beside him, at Gonzalo.

"He's the one told you there was coke aboard, right? He's the
one swam ashore? Ask *him* where it is. Ask him if there ever was
any."

Christian's head came around slowly. His face took on a look
of discovery, then pleasure. "Yes. Yes! How about that, my clever
little friend? *Where's the coke you said was here?*"

The Cuban had had his head lowered, examining his shoes,
apparently. Now he looked up. "The *coca*? It's in the drums. The
ones with crosses, just as I said."

"That's funny," murmured Christian. He was smiling now.
"Because I don't see any. Why don't you show us?"

Above them all, his face in shadow, the Baptist spoke for the
first time, quietly, like God backing up his Son. They all looked
up. "Yes, Fabio," he said. "Show us."

The little man stood immobile for a moment, looking out over
the sea. His chin was lifted, his shoulders set with the same disci-
plined pride Galloway had noticed the first time they'd met.

Then he turned. He marched quickly to the ladder, disappeared, his head bobbing, and came out a moment later on the
main deck. As he crossed toward Galloway, he called up, "I told
you the truth, Don Juan. The goods are in the marked drums."

Behind them Aydlett said, "Here's one."

Galloway turned. Shad was standing by one of the barrels. He recognized it. The white one labeled MOLASSES. Aydlett tapped two rusty scratches in the steel.

"We already looked in that one," said Christian.

A low voice from above them said, "Look again."

"You heard the *patrón*! Look again!" Christian's shout had gone high, and he leaned forward, shaking. His bodyguards leaned with him, as if they were attached by glass wires. "*Look again!*"

But Aydlett had the lid off already. It clanged to the deck and rolled around him, rolled in ever smaller circles, till finally it collapsed in a clatter. But then they were all staring at the slick, bubbly surface it had revealed.

Gonzalo, beside them now, said nothing. Close up, Galloway saw his face was coated with a liquid gleam, as if it had just been dipped in varnish. He was good, though. Unless you were that close, he didn't look worried at all.

No one said anything for a long time. *Ceteris* rode in the focus of a vast bright bowl of dazzle. Galloway blinked. He couldn't see well. Something fuzzy about his sight—

He cleared his throat. It was his turn now. But it had to be done right. Or Christian would just kill them all.

"He's sandbagged us, Troy. There's nothing here but this chemical shit. I don't know why, but he took us all for one hell of a ride.

"So, we did our best. So did you. No reflection on either of us. Right? No way Don Juan can hold you responsible; no way you can blame me. Isn't that right? We're all done. So how about letting us go?"

"I guess you're right," said Christian, and his lips moved on after he was done speaking. "At least, that you're done."

One of the Indians laughed, then stopped, and everything was silent again. Somewhere in the salon, behind Christian and his men, a clock began to strike. The faint clear sounds reverberated in Galloway's memory. The interval between each stroke was so long that many things passed through his mind while he waited in soundless suspension for the next. It sounded like the old Ingraham in his father's study. "Five bells, that's five half hours past the watch change, Lyle," said a voice in his memory. "So what time would that be? Answer me, boy! Your brother knows!"

"Ten-thirty," he whispered, but only with his lips. The rest of his body, frozen, waited for the words of the Baptist's executioner.

Shad Aydlett broke the silence. "Yeah. We're done. So how about our money? Don Juan, he promised to pay us. He don't strike me as the kind of man who goes back on his word."

Above them, the Panama dipped; the pudgy hand came up, flashing fire from a massive diamond. Juan Alberto Mendieta Nuñez-Sebastiano was drinking chilled champagne. For perhaps a minute after that, nothing happened. Then he leaned forward, and the fire disappeared into his jacket.

A white envelope slipped over the rail. One of the bodyguards caught it and handed it to Christian. Who hefted it, then smiled. "Oh, you're right," he said. "Don Juan keeps his word."

The envelope arched through the sunlit air. It was too heavy to flutter. It thudded into the deck at their feet.

"Go ahead. Pick it up."

Galloway said, "Don't move, Shad."

"Cash in there, Till."

"Don't move."

"Pick it up," said Christian again. His smile spread.

Galloway glanced back. Aydlett and Gonzalo stood behind him, the black man easily, resting one hand on the rim of the marked drum; the Cuban stiffly, as if at attention. Aydlett squinted at him, puzzled. Tiller shook his head, very, very slightly.

Aydlett's eyes widened suddenly.

Yes, Galloway thought. His partner understood now.

As soon as they were paid, the deal was complete.

He turned back to their silent jury, the judge above them all. Pitching his voice upward, he said, "The deal was not just to pay us, Don Juan. You know that. The deal was to let us go.

"Look, forget the money. Just put us ashore. We'll find our way back. Okay?"

He didn't hear what Nuñez murmured in reply. He cupped his ear. "I'm sorry. I didn't catch that."

"I said, that's true, Tiller. I promised that. But understand my position. This is an unsuccessful enterprise. I have to liquidate it and transfer my operating capital elsewhere. Now, this is nothing new. Every entrepreneur has failures. But it's inadvisable to let your competitors know about them. A wise director makes sure his mistakes never come to light."

"We'll keep quiet."

"I'm sure you will." The white hat dipped. "I'm sure you will. The foundation of a healthy market is sanctity of contract. So, I'll do what I contracted to do, Tiller. I'll return you to the States . . . both of you. To Miami Beach, how will that be?"

"That'll be fine," he said, feeling his breath shallow and quick in his throat. "That'll be fine, Don Juan. Thank you."

"But nothing was said, when we discussed all this, about returning you—alive."

Behind him, Galloway heard Aydlett mutter, under his breath, "Hey."

His whole body tensed, waiting for Christian to give the order to fire.

"Hey," said Aydlett again.

When he turned his head, his partner was bent over the drum, frowning. Suddenly, he cocked his head, looking around the deck.

Aydlett took two steps to the scuppers. He came back with one of the wire braces. He held it up for a moment, displaying it to the men above, like a sweating and desperate magician, before he thrust it in.

Galloway caught a movement out of the corner of his eye. Above him, on the salon deck, but forward of where Christian and his men waited. But when he looked, there was no one there.

Gonzalo recalled his attention by pulling at his arm. "What is he doing?" he said. "Your friend? There is nothing there."

"You got some explaining to do, if there ain't," said Aydlett. He bent forward, his tongue visible as he probed to the very bottom. "They're kind of teed off at you, seems like."

"They're fools," said Gonzalo, and for just a moment his dark eyes twinkled at them.

"There's something down there," said Aydlett then.

"What? Speak up," said Christian sharply.

"Said, feels like there's something down there. Not very big. May be just a solid chunk of this crud—"

"Get it out."

"I can't quite—"

The *jefe* shouted, "Reach in and get it! Damn you!"

Aydlett grimaced, his eyes coming up in mute appeal.

"Stand back," said Tiller. He put his rubber-booted foot, squishing with seawater and sweat, against the metal.

The drum went over with a hollow boom, and the viscid mass inside gulped slowly out over the deck. Pasty liquid crept for the scuppers, smoking as it hit air, and the fumes came up so strong they all stepped back.

Something solid lay in the jellied slime. Galloway looked at the Cuban. He was staring at it, his lips parted, his eyes fascinated as a barracuda's.

He pulled his wet-suit glove back on. It felt clammy. He worked his fingers into it, then bent.

His fingers closed over a rounded smoothness, but when he tried to lift it, they slipped off. He squatted, frowning, and tried to get his nails—no, impossible with the thick gloves.

"Here," said Shad. He glanced up, nodded, and took the knife. Carefully, not touching the slime, he worked the tip under it and got it up.

It was the size and shape of a quartered peach, with the stone missing. Its weight surprised him. Heavier than lead. Much heavier. He held it to the light. Smoking-hot drops ran off thick transparent plastic. There had been lettering on it once, but the acid had eaten the ink. Through the coating he caught a silvery glint, like the scales of a tarpon.

Suddenly he realized that the heat was coming from the metal itself.

"What the hell *is* this?" he said. He lifted it a little higher. The eyes above him followed it; and for a moment, in the silent suspension, the guns sagged, forgotten.

Beside him, Gonzalo dropped, and shouted as he rolled behind a drum, *"Dispare a ellos!"*

Galloway jerked his head around and saw gun flashes above him. His reflexes took him down, but not before he saw dark faces turn, transformed in an instant from immobility into astonishment. Christian's hands flew up. Galloway caught a freeze-frame of his face, eyes wide, mouth still bowed in a forgotten smile as three bullets stitched across his chest. They cracked into fiberglass and wood. Beside him, one of the Indians dropped his gun, staggered back against and over the rail, and fell ten feet to the main deck. The other got his Uzi halfway around before his face exploded in a cloud of red mist.

The clatter stopped. Blue smoke blew away in the clear bright sunlight. Nuñez had jumped to his feet behind the dismountable lifeline of the pool deck.

"Excuse me, Señor Galloway," said Gonzalo, behind him.

He walked forward, his back straight. The small figure on the salon deck, holding the Uzi still pointed at the others, glanced down with remote dark eyes. She raised her other arm in a clenched-fist salute.

Galloway stood up slowly. He looked up at her.

Behind him, Aydlett muttered, "Explains a lot, don't it?"

"Yeah," he said. He understood it all now.

She was still wearing the black jeans and the paint-stained sweatshirt. But she didn't look like a child anymore.

He said, hearing the words hoarse and strange in his ears, "Hello, Anunciada."

22

From where he stood, the takeover looked professional. Within seconds of the last shot, Gonzalo's voice was shouting orders over *Ceteris*'s announcing system. As her crew came up, puzzled and apprehensive, Mariategui waved them back to the stern with her submachine gun.

Except for two. A small sailor and a large one. They joined her before the full-length windows of the salon, then bent. The small one wiped blood off a weapon with his cap, then tossed the hat overboard. He joined her at the rail, covering the growing group below.

The large one looked where she pointed, nodded, and ran heavily down and aft, threading among the drums to the boarding platform. Propping his gun between his boots, he began hauling in the launch hand over hand.

Galloway became conscious that he was still holding the chunk of metal. Its curved density felt comfortable, warm, even through the thick rubber of the diving glove. It wasn't an unpleasant sensation. Still, he didn't like it. He didn't like it at all.

Holding it behind his back, he drifted toward the side of the yacht.

But Gonzalo saw him. He called down, his voice sharp, no longer self-effacing. "Señor Galloway! Bring it up here. Quickly!"

"Better stay down here, Shad," he muttered. "If they start shooting again, take your chances in the water."

"Be careful, Till."

On the salon deck, white fiberglass was spattered with red. Blood ran sluggishly along the scuppers, clotting around the drain holes. The three bodies lay tossed atop each other like sacks of soybeans. Across from them, leaning tensely against the rail, stood Nuñez, facing Mariategui's Uzi. As Galloway pulled himself up the ladder, the Baptist's eyes flicked to him. His face was set, lips compressed to a downcurved line under pasty, flaccid cheeks.

He looked away, seeking the gaze of the woman he'd befriended. But she wasn't looking at him. Or at Nuñez. Instead she was looking down, at empty eyes that blinked up at the bright sky beyond them all.

"Christian!"

The rain-blue irises came down slowly from whatever they had been contemplating. He coughed, and a bright stream ran down into red-gold hair.

"*Venceremos!* The cause of the workers and peasants triumphs. Despite your cruelty. Despite what you have done to me."

The *jefe* stared up at her. He glanced at Galloway, and his eyes crinkled. He was conscious, then. There was recognition there, and also hatred so intense, Galloway felt the hair rise on his back.

Suddenly he understood who had sabotaged the lift. Only one man could have thought, in his drugged paranoia, that he had anything to gain from it. From a failure that would make Tiller Galloway look bad.

The eyes slid from his, leaving him feeling as if a snake had crawled over his face. They went next to the woman. He understood that. She was the one with the gun.

"You thought you penetrated our organization. You thought the Shining Path was like another criminal-capitalist combine. But instead, we penetrated you."

Christian's lips worked. A hand twitched, then tried to crawl, like a dying spider. Galloway couldn't understand what was keeping him alive. There wasn't much left of his chest. Then he saw what Troy Christian wanted. What his bloody fingers were creeping toward.

A package had fallen out of his slacks.

Mariategui saw it, too. She spoke to the little sailor, and laughed. He chuckled, too, as he knelt.

He picked up the transparent envelope. Opened it—it was ziplocked—and tilted it over the open, panting mouth.

The whiteness streamed out steadily, ounce after ounce. The dying man closed his eyes at first. Then, as it continued to pour down, they snapped open again. He rolled his head, trying to turn away.

The sailor adjusted his knees, one to either side of Christian's head, and kept pouring.

The thin body began to writhe. His legs kicked.

When the packet was empty, the sailor tamped the last of the powder carefully into the full choked-open mouth, the packed nostrils.

Galloway felt ice coat his spine as he realized the blue eyes were fixed on his. He saw the fear in them. Saw the lips move around a word that had no breath at birth.

He looked steadily back, knowing this was how it ought to be. He only wished he could have pulled the trigger himself. He couldn't hate Christian now, facing the curtain every man had to step through at the end. But he wouldn't lift a finger to save him.

No one on earth cared enough for Troy Christian to ask for his life.

The blue eyes rolled backward. Beneath the spreading blood, his body wrestled an invisible enemy. The pure whiteness that filled his mouth and nose seeped red. Then he shuddered, and the fine, emaciated body went hard as chiseled marble.

When it was over, the corpse lay with one hand extended, as if in a final plea for deliverance, or mercy after death, toward a pair of white suede shoes.

Troy Christian no longer needed anything at all.

When Nuñez looked up, his face was bleached pale as old conch and the muscles around one eye twitched. His fingers rubbed the machined metal of the Leica.

"*Muy bien*," he said. "You have destroyed him. My most effective *jefe*. Well, I understand. After what he did to you.

"But now let's talk about where we are going from here."

"We are going south, Nuñez." No Dons, no Señors for her, Galloway thought.

The Baptist must have noticed it, too. His voice dropped. "I mean, what will happen wherever you are going. *Compraste?* I am the master of hundreds of men. Thousands more obey my associates. You are alone. You wished for revenge on this man? You have it. Now let us make peace. Give me the gun, and I will let you live."

"I do not like your idea of peace." She smiled at the little sailor. "And we are not *alone*. Are we, Luis?"

"Fabio," said Nuñez. He raised his voice. "Fabio!"

Gonzalo slid forward, turning to pass between Galloway and the rail. He carried a bucket of what smelled like diesel fuel. He touched Tiller's elbow.

Galloway started. Watching Christian die, and then the face-off between Nuñez and Mariategui, he'd forgotten what he held. "Place it in the bucket, please," said the Cuban. "Thank you."

The funny thing was that even after he let go of it, his hand still felt warm. He stripped off the glove. His palm had a red spot on it the size of a quarter, slightly swollen, as if he had burned himself.

Gonzalo set the bucket down. He cocked his head, and his bright black eyes gleamed. "You asked for me, Don Juan?"

"Yes. *Que esta pasando aqui?* What is this material, from the drums? It's not cocaine."

"I'm sorry to have misled you, Señor. Unfortunately, I must now tell you that there is no cocaine aboard *Guapi*. Though at one time there was; oh, yes, there was. Fifty-two drums, just as I said."

He shrugged. "But I am afraid it is all delivered. We have already traded it for the material that Señors Galloway and Aydlett have so bravely retrieved for us from the depths of the sea."

"I see there's no *cocaína*. But what's that in the drums? It is valuable?"

Tiller said slowly, staring at his palm, "It's uranium. Or some other kind of radioactive metal."

Gonzalo clapped him on the back. "Very good, Señor! To be exact, it is plutonium. From old American bombs."

Galloway cleared his throat hoarsely. Something about the warm metal frightened him more than anything he'd seen three hundred feet down. "What's it doing here?"

"It is here because we need it. Can you understand that? Or do you feel only your own country has the right of self-defense? It is easy to see that soon we will no longer have the backing of the Soviet Union. Then we will have to face the Yankee alone. Our leader has decided. We will provide our own deterrent."

He said, "You're Cuban. But you're not from Coconut Grove."

Gonzalo wheeled away abruptly, as if the conversation had gone in a direction he didn't like, and confronted Nuñez. "Don Juan, you are under arrest in the name of the Republica de Cuba. You are in the hands of the DGCI, the Directorate for General Counterintelligence, Narcotics Division; you will address me now as Commandante, which is my military rank. We will soon be on our way to Puerto de Gibara, where tomorrow you will be given a trial, found guilty, and shot, thus disproving American propaganda that socialist Cuba protects drug shipments through its territory. Do you have anything to say?"

Nuñez gave him a flat glance. He shook his head silently.

They were interrupted by a hail. The Liberator was coming alongside. Its bimini was just visible over the break of *Ceteris*'s quarter. Galloway couldn't follow the exchange, but at the end of it, Gonzalo shouted what sounded like an order combined with a threat to the crew and engineers assembled on the afterdeck.

But they didn't look resentful. They looked relieved. They began pushing their way toward the launch.

Except for one small face, shining with tears. The boy stared up to where a body lay, an arm dangling over the break of the deck.

Galloway thought, I was wrong. There's one person who'll mourn Troy Christian. Damned if I know why. But there he is.

Beside the boy, he caught Aydlett's questioning glance. He frowned and motioned him back, hiding it with his body. Somehow he felt it would be safer to stay aboard. At least till he understood more clearly what was going on.

More orders from Mariategui, and the little seaman darted down to the afterdeck, where he began examining the remaining drums. Galloway heard him say something to Aydlett. The black man pointed at a violet barrel with black lettering. The seaman nodded, then stepped back as Shad kicked it over. A few seconds later, he called up in excited Spanish, and held up another nugget of heavy metal.

"Shad," Gonzalo called, "Do not open the plastic. Put some clean fuel in a bucket. Keep them submerged in the oil. And don't put more than two segments close together. Do you understand? This is important. It could cause an accident."

"Till? That right?"

Well, well; Shad Aydlett was asking for advice. "Do what he says," he called.

When Galloway stepped back, his toes squished inside the booties. He felt like he was melting. Hell, he was still half dressed out.

He stripped off the Farmer John bottoms. The air felt cold as it hit his soaked trousers. He worked his fingers, examining the burn again. Then he looked at the plastic bucket, and moved a few more feet away.

Nuñez began to speak, or rather, to make a speech. His Spanish was rapid and impassioned. It sounded like a combination of promise and warning. Galloway couldn't follow it, though he heard words he recognized: *Cuba*; *Colombia*; *dinero*, money; and *dollars* were mentioned, too.

When he was done, Mariategui shrugged. *"Dónde está?"*

"En el cuartoseguro. Detrás de nosotros."

"Did you know of a vault aboard *Ceteris*, Tiller?" Gonzalo asked him.

He remembered a conversation in a tossing raft. He said slowly, "I heard of one."

"Don Juan's offering us money. Says it's aboard here."

"Why not? He's got to keep his operating funds somewhere."

Mariategui asked Gonzalo a question. They talked rapidly together for a time. She listened with her head cocked and her eyes locked on Nuñez's. Galloway noticed that the white linen suit was wilting.

It was the first time he'd ever seen the Baptist sweating.

At last, she said, switching back to English, "Very good. We will go there, and you will get it for us, yes."

"No." Nuñez smiled faintly. "Not now. Later, when we make port—either the Bahamas or Florida.

"But think of it. A million dollars, cash, and many kilos of valuable goods. You can walk into Miami with it. Or Freeport. And disappear. Go wherever you like. None of my people will bother you."

"Do not haggle with me! You offer a million. So how much more do you have aboard? Twice as much? Three times? We will find out. You will open your vault to us now."

When Nuñez shook his head, she didn't argue. She didn't threaten. Instead, she looked around. Galloway did, too.

The launch still rode against *Ceteris*'s starboard side. The big sailor waved to her from its bow. None of the crew was visible. Locked below, into the cabin, he thought. It would be cramped, but tolerable for the run to shore.

When she called "Jorge!" the large sailor cupped a hand to his ear. When she stopped, he answered respectfully but with a note of objection.

She shouted again, her voice a cutting edge, and he stiffened. Galloway tensed, too, leaning forward.

Jorge swung himself down to the boarding platform. He cast off the launch's lines, aft first, then forward. It was so quiet, Tiller heard them splash into the water. The sea appeared between the two hulls. Engine off, with no one at the wheel, the boat drifted slowly away.

Then Jorge looked up again. Mariategui lifted her chin slightly. The sailor unslung the Uzi, knelt, and aimed.

The first short burst hit the launch just above the waterline. He paused, sucked a tooth thoughtfully, then aimed again.

The second burst tore a ragged hole between wind and water. The third stitched a row of black perforations across the engine compartment.

A faint, wild clamor became audible when the firing stopped. The launch began to lean, dipping the holes beneath the surface as it listed.

"Tiller," said Shad from below him.

He couldn't respond. He stared in horror as the launch leaned, going down by the head. As the bow dipped under the wails, the screams and hammering of the trapped men rose to a faint thunder.

Then it faded. A frothy vomit of air and gasoline bubbled up from where the top of the cabin shimmered sky blue, then turquoise, falling away beneath the pale translucent Bahamas blue.

Someone near him was muttering under his breath. It was Nuñez, his round face taut. As he leaned against the rail his fists clenched and unclenched, the blood darkening in the backs of his hands.

"I have no difficulty watching enemies of the people die." Mariategui brushed her hair back with a delicate hand. "Your men have killed many of the Sendero Luminoso. I will have no difficulty killing you."

"So, now let us go and see this money you talk of."

The big sailor, Jorge, came up the ladder, prodding Aydlett ahead with his gun. The waterman was carrying two bright yellow plastic buckets; the sailor had another in his free hand. "How many did you find, Shad?" asked Gonzalo.

"Twelve."

"Well, we started with eighteen. I think that will be an acceptable rate of loss. Considering all that's happened. It should be enough for three devices. One for demonstration, and two for use."

"Those are . . . nuclear weapons parts, you said?" asked Galloway. He looked at his hand again.

"Yes, from the triggers of Air Force hydrogen bombs. They are segments of the plutonium implosion sphere. They were being reworked into cruise missile warheads. The metal was all we needed. Everything else is ready."

"How did you get them? You stole them?"

"Nothing so crude, Señor! Some members of our consortium have gambling interests in Nevada. There were certain weapons engineers, from Los Alamos, who gambled . . . and lost. They could not repay their debts. My friends thought of a way things could be worked out."

"The Mafia, you mean?"

"Impossible," said Nuñez. "I've dealt with them. They'd never sell such things to Communists."

Gonzalo shrugged comically. His bird's eyes twinkled at Galloway. "Perhaps not. But I admit, I misled them a bit. They thought it was going to Brazil."

"And you traded cocaine for it? Is that the idea?"

"Well, we are short of hard currency." The Cuban smiled again, then looked more serious. "You are an enemy of Nuñez's, too, no? Have you thought of working for the future of mankind, instead of the past?"

"For the Bearded One, you mean?"

"For the only remaining inheritor of true socialism. The last bearer of the banner of Marx and Lenin. For *El Supremo*: His Excellency Fidel Castro."

"I get a lot of offers, Fabio. You understand. I can't take them all."

Mariategui spoke rapidly. Galloway got the message: They were going below. Urged by pointing barrels, they went through sliding doors into the salon. The air was icy, and the carpet soft under his bare feet. Poseidon looked down coldly as they filed by. When they reached the stairway, she spoke again, sharply, to Nuñez. "*Dónde está eso?*"

And the Baptist said grimly, "Follow me."

• • •

The vault was painted steel masked by a polished mahogany door. They were deep in the ship, on the lowest deck, the whine of machinery and pulse of pumps steady around them.

Nuñez touched the lock, pursing his lips. He said, "How much of this will you be able to keep for yourself?"

"Why do you speak English? *En español, por favor.*"

The Baptist looked at the sailors, then back at her. "Because we should discuss this privately, you and I."

"Do not insult me," said Mariategui sharply. "Comrade Stalin robbed banks to finance his revolution. I rob you."

"But it doesn't make sense. What do you get out of it?"

"I fight for the people."

"And then what? You'll be dictator, lead them?"

"It is more likely that I will die. If not in the struggle, afterward. Revolutions devour their makers."

Nuñez seemed to be thinking about this. He spun the dial idly.

"Do not delay! Open it!"

The Colombian straightened. He shook out his jacket, passed his hands over his thinning hair. Suddenly, Galloway respected the man that up to now he had only feared. Alone, threatened, forced to conduct his enemies to the heart of his power, he seemed to have regained his confidence.

"Listen to me. You're missing an opportunity. Let me point it out.

"I admire your dedication. Both of you. I compliment you on it. But is your idol worthy of you? Communism has failed.

"Let us speak realistically. Who is to know what happens between us? Let us eliminate these pawns. They are traitors to me; who can tell when they'll betray you also? We can do without Galloway and Aydlett, as well.

"Let us say that you also vanish. Whoever your superiors are, they will know only that you have disappeared. I can reward you, *personally*, with . . . *ten* million dollars. Each! You can live in luxury in Europe. Or, even better, you can become my partners."

He was speaking to Mariategui, but she only sighed. So he wheeled on Gonzalo. "*Commandante.* What about you? What does the secret police pay you a year?"

"Not much. But we can shop at a special store." Gonzalo cut his eyes at Galloway.

Hell, he thought, at least the Cuban had a sense of humor. But this Mariategui made him feel icy around the heart. He understood revenge, after what Christian had done to her. But to kill a boatload of men—

"Well?" Nuñez said. He adjusted his tie, fidgeted with the camera.

"Again, do not insult me. Open it."

The pouchy eyes narrowed. Reluctantly, the fat man bent.

A few seconds later, the lock clicked, and the jamb parted, showing a strip of darkness. Nuñez stepped back. He made an elaborate gesture of presentation. "*Entre, por favor.*"

"You will go in first."

The Colombian hesitated, then nodded. But Galloway saw him press a switch before he crossed the threshold.

The lights flickered on. It was hard, bright light, the kind installed in machinery spaces. He didn't follow the others inside. Still, he could see the built-in shelves and trays. Stacks of plastic sacks, reinforced with wooden dunnage to keep them from shifting. And stacks of wooden boxes, as high as a man, roped securely to tie-downs.

When the first one came open, he saw that it was full of cash.

He stood sweating in the corridor, listening to the murmur of voices inside. Just counting the boxes seemed to take forever. The big sailor, Jorge, stared steadily at him. He looked at the submachine gun, thought about trying to take it. The seaman waited, lips slightly parted, eyelids drooping. Galloway didn't like the way his finger tapped the trigger. Forget it, he was primed.

When they came out, Don Juan stopped in the passageway. He sagged against the bulkhead, hand shading his eyes. "Seventy-five million," he muttered. "*Maldito sea!* My entire cash reserve.

They're destroying me, Tiller. They might as well shoot me now."

"*Bueno*," Mariategui was saying. "This will buy many arms for our fighters. But what is wrong? Suddenly you do not look well."

"You've ruined me, that's why. This is what a bankrupt capitalist looks like."

"*Coraje*; we are almost done. Now there is the matter of your overseas accounts. Switzerland. Panama. You will give us the numbers now, the institutions, and the approximate amounts in each account."

Nuñez straightened. His face flushed suddenly. "That was not mentioned. Then you will have no reason to keep me alive at all."

Gonzalo said, "Then you can discuss it with the Counterintelligence Directorate, Don Juan. I hope you enjoy the accommodations at Villa Marista."

Nuñez looked shaken. He cast a glance at Galloway and Aydlett.

"Into the vault, then," she said. "Until we are there. Back inside!"

"Wait. No! Don't put me there! There's no air in there—"

The Baptist screamed shrilly as they shoved him in. The heavy door boomed shut. The patter of his fists on steel lived in the corridor. It was all but lost in the thrum of pumps.

She looked at Galloway, and yawned, suddenly, putting a small fist to her mouth. For a moment she looked like a sleepy child. "Such dramatics. A bullet in the back of the head is better. Do we have any further use for the *Yanquis*?"

"Wait a minute," said Galloway. He searched her eyes for the woman whose softness he had held. "I saved your life. Don't you remember? You came to me and asked for help, to be hidden—"

"You didn't do that for me. You did that for a bourgeois student, a judge's daughter. Would you have done that for a Communist? A revolutionary fighter?"

He thought about it. Then said, "Yes."

"I don't believe you. And even if I did, such emotion has no place with us. No. You will—"

Gonzalo interrupted her, speaking Spanish. She listened unwillingly, glancing at Aydlett and then at Tiller. She shook her head once and he spoke again, at more length. Finally, she shrugged and rolled her eyes.

"All right. *Basta!* But I think it would be simpler if they only disappeared."

Gonzalo said, "You heard her, Tiller, Shad. I suggest you come with me."

• • •

The door clicked. Aydlett whipped around, jerking at the knob, but it was solid. Locked, from the outside.

At the same moment, a thrill ran through the deck. The room seemed to leap forward. Galloway staggered, and caught himself against the desk. Outside the porthole, the sea began to move, slowly at first, then faster, until the waves nearest them melted into a blue blur.

"How far you figure it is to Cuba, Shad?"

"Why you askin' me? Hell, this the first time I been out of the country. Don't you know?"

"As a matter of fact, I do."

"How far?"

He looked again at the burn on his palm. Something about it fascinated him, as if he could read his fate in it.

"At this speed? About eight hours."

23

He could visualize their route on the mind's-eye chart his runs in these waters had left him. *Ceteris* was headed southeast. Gonzalo would stay well offshore; a man who had to look up anchoring in a book would avoid shoal crossings. That would take them along Eleuthera and Cat Island. He'd head for the deep water between Rum Cay and San Salvador, then turn south through the West Channel to the north coast of Cuba. Eight hours? Yes, that would be about right.

They had that long to decide what to do—or whether to do anything at all.

"What're you thinking?" asked Aydlett, sitting across from him on the bunk. "You look like the dog that lost the fight."

"What?"

"Nothing. What is the plan, Tiller? We going to Cuba, like the man says?"

"That might be the smart thing to do. I don't think Gonzalo means to hurt us, as long as we cooperate. Mariategui—she's a different story."

"Then what?"

"I don't know. They don't need us anymore. The only thing I can think is, he plans to use us. But I don't know how."

"I don't like it. I told Latricia I wanted to travel, but not there."

He nodded soberly. He felt the same way. No matter what Gonzalo had in mind, once they were in the custody of the Cuban secret police it would be all too easy for somebody senior to him to decide they were inconvenient witnesses. "Well, we got no say in the matter, unless we can get out of here somehow."

"Wish I had me my ten-gauge back."

"So do I, Shad."

They sat with their thoughts for a few minutes. His eyes strayed back to his hand. The blister seemed larger. He touched his tongue to the inside of his cheek. Sore as hell. Infected, all right.

Then he remembered Christian, half his chest shot away, strangling on pure coke. If he'd been standing beside him, he'd be dead now, too.

"Is that right, what he was saying? About that stuff being atomic bomb parts?"

"Yeah."

"How you know that? You ever seen one?"

"Yeah. On carriers on Yankee Station. And we trained on mock-ups, in case we ever had to retrieve one. Those quarter spheres—that's plutonium, all right." He opened his palm. "Look at that. Radiation burn."

Aydlett almost touched it, then jerked his finger back. "Jesus! How you figure they got hold of it?"

"Like he said, I imagine. Somebody owed a lot of money. Their family got threatened. And they broke."

His partner whistled. Galloway glanced at him. Then he got up and undogged the porthole.

Spray lashed his face. *Ceteris* was on a plane, cutting through the water with a smooth high howl. He pulled his head back in and examined the frame: glassed in, and not much wider than his head.

The door? Locked, and occasionally they heard Jorge as he strolled back and forth, or sang in a husky bass. The tunes were marches. Revolutionary songs? Some of them sounded familiar. Ought to learn some Spanish, he thought. No, to hell with that. If he got out of this, he wasn't even going to Taco Bell anymore.

The overhead? He stood on the bunk and lifted panels of soundproofing as Shad watched. Cables, pipes, but steel four inches above them. The ventilation ducts were too small, too. He let the waffled squares drop back into place.

The bathroom? He went into it and tapped on the bulkheads, the marble of the shower, bent to the sink. . . .

The sink. One thing he knew about ship design was that after the hull was faired in and the machinery located, the hotel spaces, salons and staterooms and galleys, were laid out around the soil drains. Otherwise, they'd have too many bends, or the runs would get too long, and they'd clog. Which was even more inconvenient aboard ship than it was in a house.

To keep that piping simple, adjacent spaces usually shared drains.

He opened the washstand door and bent. A faint scent lingered. He remembered her huddled here, shunning the light like a wounded animal as she went through a cold turkey withdrawal. Her eyes had seemed like portholes to a whole dark Latin world he knew next to nothing about. A universe of poverty, oppression, death squads, slums, and juntas. Che Guevara and Daniel Ortega, Castro, Noriega, the land seemed to breed revolutionaries who in their turn became dictators and bred revolution anew.

He'd seen her as a victim. And she was. But she wasn't a passive one.

He knew next to nothing about Anunciada Mariategui, and he didn't like Communists. But suddenly, he found himself admiring her.

He blew out, and pushed at the back of the cubby. Solid. "Crap," he whispered.

He closed it, turned, and saw the bolted panel behind the toilet. "Shad," he said softly, "we been ordered around long enough. How do you vote? Want to check out a Cuban prison? Or do we shut this operation down?"

There was no hesitation at all in his partner's reply.

• • •

Half an hour later, with Aydlett running the shower and singing Hatteras High fight songs, he had their panel free and was working on the one on the far side. They opened into a common crawl space between the staterooms. The screws wouldn't turn from the inside. Finally, with Aydlett bellowing at the top of his lungs, he had to hammer them through.

The panel popped free, and he slid his feet in. The soil pipe, heavy black plastic, divided the space and he had to squeeze past it.

He emerged into an empty stateroom with dirty uniforms on the bunks and Puerto Rican skin magazines on the floor.

Wet feet slapped, and Aydlett's face appeared upside down in the opening. Water dripped from his hair. He whispered hoarsely,

"I don't think I can get through there. Can we move this pipe?"

"We could saw it, if we had a saw. Can you bend it? I can't."

Shad tried, his face darkening as he applied leverage in the cramped space. It didn't budge. "Forget it," Galloway muttered. "I'll have to take the guard out."

"How? Soon as you come out that door, he's going to start shooting."

Shad was right. There really wasn't any way of taking him by surprise. He thought of having his partner sucker him into the room somehow, then slipping around and coldcocking him from behind. Then he thought he'd just check. He moved silently to the door, cracked it, very slowly, and peeped through.

The corridor was empty.

His bare feet made rapid kissing noises on the parquet. He jerked the door of number twelve open, to Aydlett's astonished look. "Lucky at last. He's gone. Takin' a leak or something. Hurry up. Lock it behind you!"

The safest course was downward. They didn't stop running till they were in the crew's quarters. Here the overhead was lower and the deck was painted steel. The machinery noise was louder here. He pitched his voice above it. "*Bueno*, like the lady says. Okay, first thing, we got to stop her. Or if we can't do that, run her ashore. You go for the bridge, I'll take the engines."

"I want the engines."

He sighed. "All right, Shad. But be careful, okay?"

Aydlett winked, and a moment later was gone.

Galloway turned forward and jogged toward the stairwell. He slowed as he reached it, ready to duck back, but he saw no one.

He came out three decks above, in the pilothouse. He hesitated, looking around at windows, instruments, charts, and an unattended wheel that hummed quietly to itself.

Ceteris bounded across the gently heaving sapphire with a soft roar, like a powerful, expensive car over undulating asphalt. Another beautiful day in the Bahamas. There was nothing in sight but the sea, the clouds, and the horizon prick of a small boat, many miles astern. It was eerie to see her running all out with no one at the helm, no one up here at all. Like a ghost ship.

The chart lay on its table. NOAA 11013. *Straits of Florida and*

Approaches. From Vero Beach to the west edge of Haiti. When he smoothed it out, he saw the pencil line that ended at Cuba's northern coast. Red digits flickered on the loran. The wheel crept left, then right, singing to itself as the autopilot kept them on course.

He bent over the compass: 130. The nearest land would be Eleuthera, then. But when he shaded his eyes to starboard, he saw only sea. They were well offshore. He looked at the fathometer: 2,500 fathoms. Yeah, well offshore.

Time seemed suspended. In the midst of the sea void, the bridge was animate, mysteriously inspirited, a humming intelligence. He remembered Pat Roach. It was as if he were here somehow, invisible, but still in charge of his beloved ship. *Ceteris* moved of herself, like the old tales of ships manned by the damned, doomed to everlasting voyage.

Thinking of the old man, he slid open the drawer beneath the chart table. A fifth of Bushmills, and a single rather crusty glass. He lifted the bottle for a moment in salute, and took a short one. It burned the inside of his mouth, but it helped.

Holding the bottle, he leaned a hip against the console, studying the keypads and readouts on the integrated autopilot/navigation panel. Run for land? That went against all a seaman's instincts, running for a harborless shore. He could imagine the old captain's response: a red-faced roar of outrage. But a 175-foot yacht on the rocks would be hard to keep quiet. Especially once he got on the radio, and told the U.S. Coast Guard what she was carrying.

He took another nip, capped the bottle, and slid the drawer closed. Suddenly, it was settled, clear, and he knew what he had to do. Stop *Ceteris*, stop Gonzalo and Mariategui, whatever the risk. A nuclear-armed Cuba, ninety miles off Key West . . . the inevitable pressure for a preemptive strike . . . he didn't want that on his conscience.

And what had Gonzalo meant by a "demonstration"?

The trouble was that as soon as she heeled into a new course, somebody with a gun would be on the bridge asking why. He decided the radio came first. He reached up and pulled the mike down.

He was punching up channel sixteen when someone said gently, "What are you doing, Tiller?"

He turned. The little Cuban was sitting in Pat Roach's big leather captain's chair, Uzi propped in his lap.

"Señor Galloway, I am disappointed. You couldn't stay where I wanted you. You couldn't . . . cooperate."

"I never rated high in that, Fabio. It's been a problem since kindergarten."

"Yes, Christian was right. You also have the smart mouth. Poor Troy . . . turn the set off! Now replace the mike. Move away from that console, please. Move, Señor!"

He froze instead, staring into the little tunnel of the gun barrel. Looking into the two black tunnels of the Cuban's eyes. Like three holes in the world through which death would flood in. He knew that as soon as he moved, Gonzalo would fire. The only thing keeping him alive was the electronics behind him. If those went bye-bye, the Cuban was lost; he wouldn't know where he was, or which way to steer.

Behind him, his hand slid down to the panel.

"Move, Galloway! Is your partner still in your cabin? Where is he? Galloway, *move!*"

Gonzalo was sliding out of the chair. He was coming toward him. In a moment, he'd be able to fire upward, missing the console.

He slammed the heel of his hand into the panel, driving in buttons and switches, and made a running dive-and-roll for the door.

The *commandante* cursed in Spanish, and fired. A three-round burst slammed through the opening. By then, Galloway was on all fours, scrambling for the ladder down.

But he didn't make it. Beneath his feet and hands, the deck was tilting, leaning, in an accelerating topple that pushed him to his knees again, clutching the rail as 175 feet of megayacht snapped left and began chasing her own tail at thirty-five knots.

"Galloway!"

He glanced back, to see the Cuban flung out of the bridge. He tried to aim, but lost his footing instead, sliding feetfirst into the lifelines. Above them, the turbine exhausts howled, winding up to maximum revolutions. Brown smoke unrolled across the blue sky, forming an arc, then a circle as *Ceteris* thundered around, slamming and pounding as she cut her own wake.

Weaponless, he had no choice but to flee. The back of his neck itched for cover. He snatched open the door to the salon deck. Bullets cracked into it, raying the smoked glass with silver webwork. By then he was inside, running down the passageway toward the main salon.

He felt naked, as he had the night he'd frog-kicked above the silent writhe of sharks. He had to find a weapon, or somewhere to hide.

The whole length and expanse of *Ceteris* was too small for a hunted man.

"Galloway! *Pare!*" Gonzalo's voice echoed behind him. "Stop!"

Too late, he remembered how long the salon was. He put his head down and sprinted for the far end. His bare heels thudded like a rabbit's heart. He wasn't going to make it. He saw that with sudden despair.

He dropped, diving for the carpet, skidding on the labyrinthine pattern that burned his bare palms.

A long burst ripped through the closed space. Mirrors burst over the bar. A slug skidded along teak, plowing up a spray of splinters like a Cigarette boat on a calm bay.

Velcroed behind the sofa, Galloway hugged the deck till the firing stopped.

He heard Gonzalo chuckle. *"Dónde está, mi pequeño zorro?"* he called.

When he heard Gonzalo jerk open the liquor cabinet, he sprang up, panting hoarsely, and zagged left.

Crystal exploded on the table, sending fruits and coke into the air. The glass case below the mosaic blew apart, scything space with glittering shards. A silver wine server rang like a gamelan. He zigged right, and slammed to a stop against the wall. The ancient stone was cool under his hands.

His arm lay across the display case, across the mounted spear.

He reached in, grabbed it, and pulled with all his strength. The mountings resisted, then broke with a double snap. It came away in his hands, and the bronze brackets bounced on the carpet.

Bullets bolted through the crazily slanting air and exploded where he'd stood. Poseidon's beard and face burst apart, three-thousand-year-old squares of stone whirring like mortar fragments. When they hit carpet, they bounced, leaving dents. Where they hit metal, they exploded in their turn, staining the air with chalky smoke. Where they hit him, sprawled beneath the expanse of patterned stone, they left bloody marks. Craters exploded across the mosaic. The chandelier shivered, and glass rained to the floor with a brittle, glittering laughter.

Three feet lower and he'd be dead. If the Cuban had been used to the gun—if the deck had been level, instead of tilted at this crazy angle, slamming across the waves—

The moment he heard the snap of a trigger pulled on an open bolt, he was up again. He heard metal clatter, then the click of a new magazine going in.

Meanwhile, he was running as he'd never run before. He was five strides from the door; he was at it.

An ax-blow slammed down on his shoulder, paralyzing his entire side.

The deck came up and belted him in the face, but he didn't stop. His body knew that meant death. Through starry pain, he scrabbled on hands and knees down the ladder. At *Ceteris's* power-driven list, he was crawling almost horizontally. He half-descended, half-fell, rolling like a trained bear. To his surprise, he found the spear still locked in his left hand. He couldn't feel anything from that locality, the shock of the nine-millimeter slug was still too great, but it was closed tight. Jammed, like a shackle under too much strain.

Gonzalo's voice floated down. "Tiller! A deal. Stop and I'll stop shooting. *Galloway!*"

He didn't answer. On the main deck, some of the drums had spilled. Most of them, though, had slid still upright across the slick, stinking deck, and huddled now against the downside as the yacht commenced another howling circle. He ran past them, slipping, cursing as his fingers found the bloody tear in his shoulder. Where was Shad? Where was Mariategui and her two bully boys?

And what was he carrying this damned spear for? Bronze wasn't much good against a submachine gun. Even if it did have a nice new shaft fitted to it. Some heavy, smooth, strong wood. But, Christ!

Like a hunted animal, he flinched as a shot clanged off a fire-extinguishing reel. He ducked away, inside again. Single shots now, he thought. So that's his last magazine.

The lower lounge was empty. He scuttled the length of it, bent into the lean of the deck. The Cuban wasn't used to running on a reeling deck. He was. But he couldn't run for much longer.

He reached the stairwell and flung himself down its sweeping curve, cursing as he stumbled, then caught himself, using the ash shaft as a crutch.

The ship felt empty as a church at night. He didn't understand what was going on. He felt dizzy. Ought to catch his breath, fix some kind of bandage—

Hell with that, Tiller-me-boy. You got to stop this bozo behind you. Or you're fish food.

On the second deck down, he left the ladder for the maze of galley and storerooms forward. As he entered them, he suddenly became aware of a chemical smell. It wasn't strong, but it was sharp. It smelled like Hirsch's nail-polish remover.

Bernie. Was he ever going to—

Think about that some other time, damn it.

He scrambled down the corridor, apelike, crablike, panting. Hearing the footsteps behind him on the stair, coming down, not fast, not hasty, but deliberately. Like a man with all the time in the world.

Then he saw the fire extinguisher.

It wasn't a weapon. But it was what held it to its bulkhead mounting that caught his eye.

The thick rubber shock cord, with steel hooks at both ends.

He tore it free, cursing in a desperate whisper. Sweat ran down his face as he threaded the hooks through the haft. His hands shook. But at the same time, he felt like he was in a dream. He felt detached, weird, fuzzy. It was like breathing air at three hundred feet. . . .

"Galloway!"

He swung to face the doorway. But the Cuban wasn't there. He blinked.

"Over here, my friend."

He jerked around, to see Gonzalo's hawk eyes glittering at him from a sliding window. From the pantry. Over the sights of the submachine gun.

"*Lo siento*, Tiller. I am sorry. You and your friend are brave men. I had hoped to arrange your release. Use you as messengers, to prove we had what we said we had. But I see now that my comrade had the more realistic view of things."

He shrugged, and the dark eyes twinkled. "It has been enjoyable. But even the best of friends, it seems, must one day say— *adiós*."

Galloway stood motionless, helpless, spear drooping toward the deck, the unhooked sling loose in his hands. So this was the end. It filled him with bitterness. He'd tried. But he'd made too many mistakes.

Now, at last, it was time to die.

Suddenly a soundless grip crushed his chest. Weight like the sea pressed his eardrums. A lightless warm fist knocked him back full length into the stainless door of the refrigerator. He saw Gonzalo blown off his feet, staggering back, his free hand windmilling.

Then the Cuban regained his footing, and brought the gun up again, his mouth opening in a shout or scream as he saw Galloway, still upright, slip the sling into place, twist his hand into it, and bring the point up.

The ancient bronze flashed in a shallow arc between them and vanished through the window. The gun went off in a stuttering clatter, climbing forgotten in Gonzalo's right hand as his left clawed at his throat. Then he went over backward, and fell through the open door into the freezer.

Galloway stood crouched, waggling his head like a fighter who takes a hard punch just before the bell. Through the haze behind his eyes, he slowly became conscious that something had changed. Deceleration was pulling at him. Heat was growing behind him, and a low roar. He hesitated, staring at Gonzalo's boy-sized shoes. They kicked a few times, then relaxed.

He limped around the pantry wall and checked the body, staggering a little as he bent; the deck was coming level once again. Then he picked up the gun. There were two rounds left, one in the breech, one in the magazine. He put the safety lever on and went back into the galley.

A surge of nausea hit him there. He leaned against a soup vat for a few minutes, gagging, but nothing came up. Then he crossed to the door leading aft.

When he jerked it open hot air gushed out, freighted with smoke and heat. He remembered that the turbines lay just below. The engine spaces—

"Shad!" he shouted. His shoulder smarted suddenly and he clenched his teeth. It would get worse. The numbness of a new wound was wearing off.

"Tiller?" A faint cry from the smoke.

"Shad!" He bent as another wave of weakness seized him. He clutched the side of the hatchway. He ought to go down after him. But if he did, he might never come out.

But Bernie had gone after him, on the *Marcon*.

And Shad had saved him, too, down on the wreck of the *Guapi*. . . .

Pulling in a great breath, he lurched forward, feeling with his bare feet for the rungs.

Aydlett crashed into him before he had taken three steps. "Shit! That you?"

"Yeah."

"Gotta breathe. . . ."

"Top of the ladder."

They pulled each other up. He screamed as Aydlett tugged the wrong arm. Then they were back in the galley, and the waterman was coughing black slime out onto the polished floor. Galloway waited, breathing raggedly, the Uzi aimed at the door. There were still three hostiles unaccounted for.

"You okay, Shad? What happened?"

"I set a fire."

"Is that what I smelled?"

"If you smell ether. I took that drum of it and dumped it down into the engine room. And the acetone, or whatever that other shit was. Figured it'd find a spark somewhere down there. Who's that in the fridge?"

"Gonzalo."

"Dead?"

He nodded. Ether was more flammable than gasoline. And it also accounted for the drugged feeling. The way his arm felt now, he wished he had more.

"That his gun?"

"Yeah."

"Uh-huh, good job. Now what?"

"I don't know."

"That arm hurt? Pull your sleeve up. There're some clean towels here. Jesus, it just missed the bone. Where're the others?"

"Don't know. I haven't seen them."

"They're not down below, either. Funny . . . you got another gun?"

"No, but you can have this one. It's hard to shoot with one hand. Only two rounds left, though. Uh . . . Shad."

"What, Till?"

"Did you give any thought, when you set this fire, as to where we were going to go?"

Aydlett looked surprised, then sheepish.

"Never mind. You know how to shoot that? This is the safety. You got a grip safety, too. Aim low, it jumps."

When they came out on deck, he saw that *Ceteris* had coasted to a dead stop. She was back on an even keel, but rolling slowly, picking up the period of the swells. Smoke was streaming out of the ventilators and uptakes, rolling out downwind over the sea. The flames shook the deck. He bent and put his palm flat on it. It was warm.

Interesting, he thought. Trapped aboard a ship on fire. Crammed with toxic waste and plutonium. Along with 75 million bucks and God knew how much coke. Where was Mariategui? Where were Luis and Jorge?

Then he remembered Nuñez. Locked below with his cash and his drugs, and the secret numbers he'd chosen to die for.

The deck he was standing on was going to get a lot hotter. Turbine fuel was kerosene, not as touchy as gas, but it would burn like hell once it caught. When the fire got to that, they'd be dancing.

The trouble was that Mariategui had sunk the launch. Even the little painting dink was gone; he and Shad had lost it on the reef.

It would be life rafts, then. *Ceteris* had two of the encapsulated type aft of the pilothouse. If they could get one of those into the water, they'd have a fighting chance.

He looked around the horizon again, hoping for land. There

still wasn't any. He looked for the boat he'd seen before, but didn't see it, or any other evidence of life.

The ventilators stopped running. He could hear the fans slowing, dropping in pitch, then ticking to a stop.

The smoke came up faster now, in eddying brown streams. He had to make a decision.

The money?

The plutonium?

Or the rafts, before it was too late?

"What we ought to do, Tiller?"

"I'm going below," he muttered reluctantly. He touched the towel Aydlett had knotted around his arm. "Shit . . . I'm going to see if I can get into that vault."

"Get that cash, huh? Thought you was above that kind of thing."

He said slowly, "I ain't above nothing, Shad. But I don't like the idea of leavin' a man to burn."

• • •

Two decks down, groping through the haze with a wet T-shirt over his mouth, he wondered how true that was. Was it the Baptist he cared about? If only because they'd been enemies for so long? Or did he still want the money, some reward for everything he'd been through since a pockmarked man in a windbreaker had walked into Blitz Brothers' Diving, Buxton, North Carolina?

For everything he'd been through since that long-ago day on the Golfo Triste . . .

The truth was that he just didn't know.

On the lowest deck, the smoke flowed along the overhead like a gray river. Near the deck, the air was clearer, and he bent as he ran, coughing through the damp cotton. He looked at the bottoms of the doorways. Wood, wood, wood—steel.

The vault.

Fire roared above him, and the ship quivered. She could explode at any moment; rupture her hull, and fill with the sea. He'd never get topside before she capsized.

He gagged on hot smoke, thinking of Christian. He hadn't seemed sorry to die. To get it over with. As long as he had what he needed.

His fist boomed on unyielding metal. "Nuñez!" he shouted, then coughed till he couldn't breathe.

If there was an answer, he couldn't hear it over the hollow flute note of the flames. A smoky amber light began to glare through the eddying haze. The fire crackled and spat, and a warning tremor ran beneath his feet.

He pounded on the door, shouting. His fist felt like a child's, and pain shivered to his elbow.

There was no answer. Maybe Nuñez was overcome already. Maybe the ventilators had sucked smoke into the vault. He twisted at the dial, yanked the handle. It had all the give of a battleship anchor.

A sizzling spatter came from behind him. He jerked round, to see glowing metal dripping from the overhead. A growing wind blew past his cheek, feeding the flames.

Ceteris didn't have long to live.

He kicked the door petulantly. Hesitated for one more second; then spun and ran for the stairwell.

Despite his terror, he ran with something like joy in his heart. Something like the lightning rush of coke.

He'd never see the Baptist again. He'd never see Troy Christian. It was over.

As he climbed the marbled stairwell, it began to slant again. Beneath his staggering legs, *Ceteris* was lying down, like a great beast going reluctantly to sleep.

He didn't care. He was blinking rapidly, laughing and weeping at the same time.

He was free.

• • •

They were all waiting for him by the pool. The water lay slanted against the blue tiles, gnawing at the edge. Shad. Luis. Jorge. And Anunciada. The smoke streamed up behind them, rolling away downwind in great billows.

The life raft, unlashed and unrolled, lay at their feet. It was still inflating, popping as the reinforced rubber sprang into tumescence.

"Come forward," said Mariategui. Her voice was rough and exhausted. Her face was sweaty, smoke-stained, like those of the sailors. He thought, That's where they were, fighting the fire. "You are wounded."

"Fabio shot me."

"And he?"

He said, feeling tired, too, "Dead."

A pile of canvas sacks in bright colors lay beside the raft. They looked like laundry bags. They bulged full. He already knew what was in the yellow buckets. Aydlett squatted on the deck, looking glum. "They surprised me, Till," he said, spreading empty hands. "I laid it down to unroll the raft, and there they were."

Galloway shrugged. The smoke streamed up like a rising curtain, making it hard to see astern. The sun shone through it with the same bloody light they'd walked beneath on Treasure Cay, on their way into this.

"Forget it. If they jumped you, they'd have jumped me. There're two rafts, Anunciada. Can we have the other one?"

"No. You have wrecked our venture; you must suffer punishment. Also, we need them both. We have much to take."

"Cash, and coke, and . . . that. I see." He squatted abruptly beside Aydlett. Together, they watched Luis begin inflating the other raft beside the first.

"I will have to shoot you," she said, tossing back her hair. "You understand that. To be certain. It will take us a while to get ashore. We will have to bury everything, then make contact with our friends. But I will say—*gracias*. For trying to save me. But the revolution . . . it is larger than any of us."

Galloway shrugged. He got up and moved a few inches, sat down on one of the poolside recliners. The same one Nuñez had lounged in.

She snapped to the little man, "*Tenemós agua? Alimento? Tela, por hacerse a la vela?*"

"*Si, camarada.*"

The yacht was sagging off. Now the water from the pool overlapped its coping, pouring across the deck in a transparent tide. The fire roared sullenly from aft. "She will turn over soon," Mariategui said, standing up. She pushed down the selector on her weapon. "You would not live much longer in any case. So it is not too bad for you. Stand up!"

"Tiller," said Aydlett.

Galloway stood up. He looked just past her, into the sky.

She said to Luis, *"Ey!"* They both lifted their guns.

With a strange screaming cry, five black men came up the ladder, swinging cargo hooks, rusty cutlasses, double-bladed axes. A huge man with scarred arms and a bandaged thigh wielded a gleaming machete. An old man, his hair lint white with age, aimed a pump shotgun. Mariategui froze, then swiveled, swinging toward them.

The lounge chair was light metal and fabric. He brought it around with all the strength in his right arm. It knocked the gun from her hands, sent it flying into the pool. Aydlett hit Jorge at the same moment with a savage flying tackle that sent them both crashing into the wet tile.

The little sailor, Luis, stared at the brass bead of the shotgun, then opened his hands. His Uzi clattered on the deck.

Galloway slapped a broad back as it lumbered by. "Wuckie, you fat son of a bitch, I never thought I'd be glad to see you."

He patted Mariategui down quickly, then held up his hand to Aydlett. Shad threw him a lashing from the raft.

When her hands were fast behind her, he straightened and looked over the side. Masked by the side of the listing ship, the little fishing boat bobbed, battered, colorful, toylike. Lynne Parkinson stood at the wheel, shading her eyes, looking up.

She was in deck shoes again, and the shorts and the polo shirt. And now that she saw him, she was smiling, that teasing smile he'd seen for the first time across a smoky goombay barroom.

"You keep your promises," he shouted down.

"You got that shit out of our fishing grounds, didn't you? We almost lost you, though. This thing goes a lot faster than Filly's trawler."

"But how did you—"

"We've been following you since Tanner. Hung around inside the cays while you were bringing up the stuff. Pretended to fish. Didn't you see us? When you took off, we headed after you. Then when you stopped, we came in from downwind, out of the smoke."

Galloway remembered where he'd been when they left Tanner Cay. Hog-tied in the forepeak, and since then, either underwater or locked below. "I haven't had a lot of time to look around. But I'm glad you're here."

She glanced aft. Then shouted up, "Tell the guys to get off. I can see the propeller thing, on the back."

"What we got to do here, mon?" said Phillip, moving busily about the deck. "We need to be taking all this? Let's get going along."

"The bags, and these three. They can walk. Just push them."

"These buckets, what is they?"

"We don't want those. Leave them here."

"Tiller—"

"It stays, Shad. This is where it belongs."

"It's valuable, isn't it?"

"We got seventy-five million in those sacks, Shad. Ain't that enough for you?"

Aydlett raised his eyebrows. He looked after the islanders, who were sliding down the ladder, canvas bags over their shoulders like stuffed sausages. "*Seventy-five million?*"

"That's what Nuñez said. It's his operating reserve. That make you happy?" He grinned.

His partner grinned back slowly. "I guess it'll go far to. Yeah."

Galloway walked uphill to the buckets. Six of them, each with two little peach segments nestled in the down side, beneath their blankets of diesel fuel.

One by one, he picked them up, swung them by the bails, and got rid of them. He tossed two underhand into the gape of the starboard turbine exhaust. He heard them rattling on their way down, fainter and fainter. Then, silence. Two more went down the port side. The last two went down separate ventilator intakes. That would keep them far enough apart for safety.

Gritting his teeth, he slid down the ladder after the others.

Getting down to Filly's boat looked tough. A knotted rope led down from a grapnel hooked on the main-deck lifeline. That seemed to have been how the Damsels got aboard. But he couldn't make it with only one arm working, and the others were too burdened. At last he shouted to Parkinson to bring it around to the bow. It was low to the sea now. They climbed over the rail and jumped down.

"All aboard?"

"Pull away, Lynne! She's going!"

The yacht put her flank into the sea like a great animal resigned to death. He heard the rumble as machinery tore from its footings and slid through the interior. From aft, a slow, smoky blossom of orange fire sprang into bloom above them. "Faster!" he shouted to Filly, who had taken the wheel.

"This all the faster we go, mon! She is no Cigarette boat, you know!"

Ceteris Paribus was as beautiful as ever in the last moments of her life. Her underwater curves were lovely as a woman's, smooth and sweet to the eye. The shark fins of her stabilizers rose dripping into the air. He looked the length of her bottom, black and graceful and fine.

Then she was gone. Another rumble came through the ocean, another long peal of muffled thunder, like a submarine earthquake. The blue boiled where she had disappeared, smoking and foaming as the trawler's worn old engine clattered and her wake slowly stretched out behind her.

He sighed, still staring aft. Poseidon had returned to the sea.

Suddenly his legs gave way. He collapsed onto a thwart beside Wuckie. He felt wrung out and tossed away. He hurt all over, and his shoulder fired pain into his brain with every beat of his pulse.

It was over. Christian was gone and Nuñez. The waste and the plutonium were on their way down, two miles down, where no one would ever think of bringing them up again. They'd have years to dissolve, protected by *Ceteris*'s hull.

It wasn't perfect disposal, but it was a hell of a lot better than off Pass Cay.

Filly came back from the wheel and squatted beside him. They looked back for a while in silence. Then the rigger cleared his throat. "Cap'n, what we going to do with these druggies?"

He looked dully around the scruffy paint-smeared deck of the trawler. Mariategui and the sailors squatted sullenly, their hands bound. The Bahamians had stacked the bags around them. That would be the next step, he thought. To split it up.

"They're not druggies, Phillip. Why not just let them go?"

"Let dem go, you say?"

"Yeah."

"Why you say that, eh?"

"They were fighting Nuñez, too. You didn't know that, but I'm telling you now. Plus, think about this. Those sacks are full of cash. They know that. How are we going to keep it, if you turn them in to the government?"

"Cash, eh? That is worth thinking about."

"Damn right it is. Put 'em ashore. There's enough people died over this."

Filly rubbed his face, then unfolded himself. He went to the stern and stood pissing into the wake.

Galloway became conscious of Aydlett next. His partner was standing beside him. He said, "Uh, Till—is you figuring to split with *them?*"

"With who?"

"These uh, these natives."

"I think that'd be fair. Don't you?"

"It's too much for 'em. What'll they do with that much money?"

"They could hire a real salvage company. Finish cleaning up their fishing grounds. Then build themselves some decent houses, for starters."

"It'll spoil them, Till. It'll just make 'em unhappy."

"Maybe." He stretched, wincing. "But better them than us, right?"

"Wait a minute—"

"Just joking. Anyway, *they* rescued *us,* remember? So the only fair way's an equal split. There's six of them, plus Parkinson, and two of us. That's nine million apiece, give or take a few hundred thou."

He smiled suddenly, fiercely, despite the increasing pain. The long nightmare was over—smuggling, prison, parole, struggling to survive as a penniless ex-con—and he was rich. God damn it, he'd scored at last! "We can do things with that kind of money. What do you say . . . partner?"

Aydlett chewed it over, then smiled, too. He took Galloway's extended hand.

They sat together, looking aft. The last turbulence was gone now. The only sign a ship had ever existed was a dissipating haze of smoke over the western sea.

He said, "Only one thing I wish had turned out different."

"What's that, Till?"

"I wish I could have had it out with Nuñez, face-to-face." He shook his head. "But maybe this way—"

A smooth, cultivated voice interrupted them. It said, "Turn around, Galloway. Tell your friends to put down their weapons. And maybe I won't have to kill you all."

24

The Baptist stood at the companionway with one arm around Parkinson and the other behind her. His hat was gone and his cheek was scraped bloody. The sleeve of his linen jacket was torn, and he was smeared with oil and black paint. He was smiling, but it wasn't pleasant to see.

Galloway said, "I thought you were trapped below. I went back for you."

"Really? That was thoughtful of you. But I wasn't there, was I?" Nuñez spat over the side. "*She's* not in the business, the Communist, she's not a business person at all. Of course I had a way out of my own vault, in a ship I custom-designed."

"I wondered. You sounded a little dramatic when she was shoving you in."

Nuñez showed his teeth. "I hope I didn't overact."

"Well, it worked." He looked back at the dissipating smoke. "And then you came down the rope."

"That's right. I came down the rope."

He looked around. The others on deck were looking from the Colombian to him. He stood up, though his legs were too weary to hold him for long.

"Let her go, Don Juan. There's no point anymore. It's over."

"Has someone put you in charge, Galloway? I don't remember you being so commanding the last few days."

"Have you got a gun there? Let's see it. Or else let her go." He took a step toward them. His shoulder flamed, but he didn't care now. All the old ghosts had risen at the sight of the man in white. "Let her go, or by God, I'll kill you!"

The Baptist took his hand out from behind her. Metal glinted, and Galloway blinked. It was the Leica.

Two of the islanders laughed, but uneasily. None of them made a move, though several had their hands on weapons.

He sounded stupid even to himself as he said, "You're holding her hostage with a camera?"

"Not with a camera, Galloway." The fat man tilted it. His finger rested lightly on the shutter button. Inches away, Parkinson's eyes showed white. "With a grenade. A steel camera body with four ounces of plastic explosive and a two-second fuze.

"Now, back to the stern, all of you. Right now!"

From the deck, someone spat four slow words of Spanish. Galloway caught only the last word: *madre*. Mariategui was staring up, her lips twisted.

The Baptist stared down at them contemptuously. He said, "As for them, throw them into the water. As they are."

Galloway stood undecided. He wanted to go for Nuñez's throat like a rabid dog. Only uncertainty held him back. The Baptist had always carried the Leica, though he never seemed to take pictures with it. Galloway had thought of it as an idiosyncrasy, part of his mania for expensive antiques. Now that he thought about it, though, it made perfect sense.

"Get back," he said. "Everybody."

"Good. That is the right decision. Now, take those three, and—"

But Galloway had already bent, and had his good hand under Mariategui's arm. She slid across the boards, flinching as splinters tore her skin. Wuckie and Shad got the sailors.

When they had the suddenly empty deck between them, he called, "No, Don Juan. It's a standoff."

Nuñez pursed his lips. His eyes searched their faces. Finally he shrugged. He transferred the camera to his other hand, keeping it close to Parkinson, and reached inside the trawler's little pilothouse. When it came out, it held a microphone.

He spoke into it in Spanish, waited a few seconds, then called again. This time, a voice answered. He gave orders, then stopped. Looked at Galloway. "Where are we?"

"I figure about thirty miles off Eleuthera."

"That's right, mon," said Phillip. "Right off the elbow."

The Baptist nodded. He looked them over warily, then finished his message.

When he replaced the mike, he said, "Now, throw me a knife. And that piece of rope."

• • •

The helicopter found them an hour later. An hour of rolling lazily in the baking sun. They were all sitting by then, exhausted, but still wary of one another. Nuñez had climbed to the top of the deckhouse, shoving Parkinson up ahead of him. He stood and waved as it grew larger and the beat of its circling wings came to them.

Then it was above them, and a hoist was whining down. Nuñez lifted a loop of line, and settled it around the hook. He stepped back and lifted his thumb.

The hook began to rise, and the rope gathered in the sacks from the deck. They shifted, then soared up together, dark against the sky, and a few seconds later swung into the cabin of the helicopter. Only one remained behind, the smallest, limp and shrunken on the oily deck.

The Baptist shouted, "Well, goodbye, Tiller. I'm sorry this job wasn't profitable for you. I lost, too, you know."

Galloway shielded his eyes, looking up at the man who swayed atop the cabin, torn coat fluttering in the rotor blast, reaching up as the line came down again.

"But you tried. I treat my workers fairly. And you, you Bahamians—" He made a grand gesture. "I know that you are friends of friends of mine. That last bag, it's for you. Divide it equally, and *vaya con Dios.*"

The horse collar met his hands. Still clinging to Parkinson, he stepped into it. He arranged it under his arms, then looked up.

The beat of the rotors increased, and the line came taut.

Twisting away abruptly, the fat man kicked himself suddenly backward into space. The line caught him up six feet off the waves as the helicopter tilted forward, and he moved off, legs dangling as he rose.

Beside Tiller, Aydlett grunted wordlessly. He pulled out an Uzi from beneath the thwart.

Galloway put his hand on his arm. He said quietly, "No."

"I can hit him from here."

"Maybe. But if you miss, he'll send somebody back with a machine gun. When you strike at the king, you got to be sure you'll kill him.

"He's outsmarted us, Shad. Just like he outsmarted everybody, all along. Except Gonzalo. Let him go."

They couldn't see him anymore; he was inside the chopper now. It banked delicately for the horizon, for the land that lay over the silver curve of the sea.

Parkinson crept down from the cabintop, came back to Wuckie, and leaned into his scarred arms. Galloway saw that she was shaking. He was a little sad she'd gone to the Bahamian instead of him. But also, a little relieved.

Aydlett was squatting over the bag, pulling out flat packs of bills. The Bahamians bent over him, quieting, then bursting into shouts and ecstatic dancing as he shoved money into their hands.

Shad came back and handed Galloway his share. He flipped through the ten-dollar bills. There were thirty of them. He looked up. "That's all?"

"Wasn't much to start with, and it's less, divided up. That cheap son of a bitch." Shad shook a fist to westward.

Galloway stared at the money. His hand came up, came back, about to toss it overboard.

Then he sighed. He folded it and put it away. His partner was right. It wasn't much. But it might get them home, if they didn't eat on the way.

The sun was hot and the wind was fresh. He balanced in the sternsheets, lifting his face to the yellow heat that came through his closed eyes.

So they'd end up with nothing. Which was what we started with, he thought. Nothing but our lives. And we still got those. Yeah, still got those.

Still got Hatteras to go back to. And Bernie? Maybe. He'd just have to see.

Filly went forward and started the engine again. The trawler gathered way, rolling to the swell as she came around, then steadying as she faced it. She plunged to the blue rollers, her blunt nose sawing up and down as she headed back to the islands, headed home.